Advance Praise

"*Another Heaven* made me painfully aware of the enslavement associated with terrorism which is contrary to the popular belief that terrorists are always willing participants. Subramanian has created a fascinating story with a suspenseful plot and rich with characters you care about and root for until the end."

– Holly Mckenna, Professional Media Lecturer, University at Albany

"*Another Heaven* is compellingly and artfully written, and it takes the reader into places most of us cannot even conceive of. Subramanian has a grasp of the complexity and depth of issues related to human trafficking and terrorism."

– Dr. Rudy Nydegger, Ph. D., Chief, Division of Psychology, Ellis Hospital

"The author takes the reader inside the world of religious fanaticism in this novel about manipulation and human trafficking in India. The results are suspenseful, haunting, and extremely enlightening. I found it hard to put *Another Heaven* down!"

– Janet Hutchisen, Open Door Bookstore

"*Another Heaven* is an affecting read which delves into the intricacies of a terrorist's mind. A novel which addresses both human trafficking and terrorism, it showcases the detrimental aspects of the system and the society."

– Nikhil Sharda, Managing Editor – *eFiction India*

"I was hooked to the novel right from the prologue! This spellbinding page turner has it all...intrigue, innuendo, religion, greed, fanaticism, suspense, relevance and a surprise ending."

– Inez Bracy, Inez Bracy International, Living Smart and Well-Online Radio

"A vital book for our time. The pages of the novel almost turn themselves, and the reader really cares about the characters in *Another Heaven*."

– Joan Mary Hartigan, CSJ; Professor, Maria College

Another Heaven

A Novel

Annu Subramanian

Dear Terry
Best wishes
Annu Subramanian

Apprentice House
Loyola University Maryland
Baltimore, Maryland

First Edition Printed in the United States of America

ISBN: 978-1-934074-87-9

This is a work of fiction. All the characters, names, incidents, organizations, and dialogue in this novel are either products of the author's imagination, or they are used fictitiously.

Cover design by: John Dievendorf
Internal design by: Estefanie Zurita
Back cover by: Jeff Goronkin

Published by Apprentice House

Apprentice House
Loyola University Maryland
4501 N. Charles Street
Baltimore, MD 21210
Ph: 410-617-5265 •F ax: 410-617-2198
www.ApprenticeHouse.com
info@ApprenticeHouse.com

Dedication

The Diameter of the Bomb
By Yehuda Amichai
Translated by Chana Bloch and Stephen Mitchell

The diameter of the bomb was thirty centimeters
and the diameter of its effective range about seven meters,
with four dead and eleven wounded.
And around these, in a larger circle
of pain and time, two hospitals are scattered
and one graveyard. But the young woman
who was buried in the city she came from,
at a distance of more than a hundred kilometers,
enlarges the circle considerably,
and the solitary man mourning her death
at the distant shores of a country far across the sea
includes the entire world in the circle.
And I won't even mention the crying of orphans
that reaches up to the throne of God and beyond,
making a circle with no end and no God.

This book is dedicated to mothers and fathers, sons and daughters,
brothers and sisters, husbands and wives—all the souls who have been
unwittingly snared by human trafficking and cruelly victimized
by terrorism.
You will always be in my thoughts...
Annu Subramanian

Preface

Another Heaven, a thought-provoking novel by Annu Subramanian, addresses the horrors of human trafficking and terrorism. Focusing primarily on three factors—human rights abuse, fanatical religious beliefs, and the psychological fraud of terrorism—the narrative objectively speaks to a universal audience.

The novel begins in Pennsylvania, USA, where a young doctoral student of psychology is doing research to understand the insanity of a terrorist's mind. Her search for counterterrorism efforts takes her to an internship in India. Here, she encounters a victim of human trafficking who has been abducted to play a vital role in one of the missions. Consequently, readers discover an organization, orchestrated by a terrorist, that is recruiting and training missionaries for mass destruction and gradual degradation of humanity. While not a typical terrorist story, *Another Heaven* exposes a terrorist's mind, with psychological fraud as the core of the narrative.

Another Heaven takes its readers to various vignettes—missions that involve human trafficking, missionaries who are subjected to lifelong servitude or terminal missions, and ordinary humans who are extraordinarily affected by one man's destructive decisions. The novel, while portraying the collapse of mankind that is triggered by fanatics and violence, tries to stress that global discord is everybody's concern.

Another Heaven aims to call for a bold campaign against a system that systematically demolishes humanity.

Prologue
Circle of a Mission

Kuyil Extension, Seloor District, South India
October 15, 2009 • 2:45 p.m...

A young woman walked gently down the dirt road along the railway tracks facing the perimeter of the railway colony. Gathering a dirty cloth bag to her breast and covering her head with a scarf from the light drizzle, she quickly went past a couple of scrawny dogs and sat under the overpass. Her nervous glance reached up to the palm trees, to the branches swaying gracefully in the October breeze. Then her furtive glance ran to the railway schedule in the bag and jumped to the coded instructions scribbled on a crinkled note. In spite of the gentle breeze, she began to sweat profusely and wiped her clammy face with the fringe of her frayed, bright-green, cotton sari. Looking to her right and left, she picked up a cell phone from the cloth bag. When her other hand touched her padded blouse, she gasped in pain as the craftily assembled wires crushed her young breasts, and she let her hand slide to the dirt with a new abandonment.

2:53

The slouched figure of the young woman straightened with a strange determination as her ears picked up the sound of an approaching train. Her eyes absentmindedly scanned the surroundings—an emaciated cow was listlessly chewing a tuft of dry grass, a young man whizzed by pedaling his bicycle, a couple of children walked on the other side of the dirt road towards the railway colony, their little heads tucked under an umbrella. The cyclist paused, turned and looked at the woman with significant interest, and left the dirt road when he lost hope of snaring her attention. When the train rushed towards the overpass, unbridled and furious, the young woman tried to hold the cell phone steadily with her unsteady hand.

2:55

She began to chant... *In the name of Allah, the most beneficent, the most merciful...* As the wheels touched the tracks above the overpass, the train exploded into fragments and left a canopy of hazy smoke over the expanse of crowded little houses making up the railway colony. And the young woman's nineteen-year-old, mutilated body scattered along the dirt road while the flying flames hungrily licked the glass windows of various compartments.

- 1 -

Ashville, Pennsylvania • October 22, 2009

The end of all means is the beginning.

What the hell does that mean? Tina wondered broodingly, running her nervous fingers through her long brown-black hair. She read the anonymous declaration, *the end of all means is the beginning,* again and again and again, but she still got stuck in a dead end. What did the terrorist mean by that? Feeling weary and frustrated, she returned to the unsavory task of reading another report on the most recent explosion.

> *. . . The number of casualties from the recent explosion in South India is increasing rapidly as more bodies are uncovered. The Express, about to arrive at Seloor, a small train station in Tamilnadu, India, did not deliver passengers where welcoming arms were eagerly waiting on the platform. It s uffered a miscarriage, triggered by a suicide bomber. According to a statement submitted by the police, the militants, in an attempt to create fear and panic just minutes before the bomb exploded, called the Town Police Station with an intriguing message: The end of all means is the beginning. The authorities suspect there might be a connection between Al Qaeda militants and the recent explosion. "Islamic Jihad is not just a catalyst for territorial*

> *destructions. It is also a global vehicle for anarchy and terrorism," points out Dr. Augustine, a leading analyst who is periodically consulted by the officials.*

Tina picked up a cup of cappuccino on the way to Professor Katz's office. When she knocked on his door before entering his room, *the end of all means is the beginning* still followed her like a heavy, nauseating hangover, and she could not shrug it off.

"Hi, Tina, you brought your own coffee, I see. You don't trust my brand?" asked Dr. Alan Katz, filling his mug with the freshly steaming brew from the small machine on the shelf. As he walked back to his desk, a strong whiff of peppermint pipe tobacco walked with him.

"It's just that I wanted cappuccino today, Alan." Tina's eyes rested on her advisor as he wearily sat behind his desk, and she took the usual armchair. "You look tired."

"Tired? Yes, I am. Might be the weather. Just look at that rain," he sighed, staring at the foggy window. "It has been pouring with a vengeance. Another month and this would all be snow. I should probably listen to my wife and move to Florida, but it won't be easy after spending most of my life in Pennsylvania."

Tina's affectionate glance settled on the man who had mentored her since the first day of her doctorate program. How old was he? Sixty-five? Seventy? His silver goatee and heavy-rimmed spectacles added a few extra years to his smiling countenance. *And he could use a haircut*, she thought, glancing at his Einstein-ish, frizzy, gray hair. But his broad smile that unvaryingly reached his eyes made him look like anybody but the mad scientist.

"And I'm sure you're looking forward to your trip to India. At least, you'll be away from the nasty cold weather for a while, Tina," he continued. "I must begin to clean this mess if I need to retire in six months. It's so cramped."

"How long have you been here, Alan?" asked Tina, her glance flitting from the loaded bookshelves to the dusty desk.

"Close to forty years, my dear. I came here straight from Harvard, and I've been stuck here ever since. Now let's get to business," he suggested, switching to her forthcoming trip. "I know you've been looking forward to this internship. Dr. Augustine would be a great mentor, Tina. He is an excellent analyst, a very reliable researcher in the field of counter-terrorism, although I'm surprised that he is still plodding along with his work. He was in the hospital a couple of times last year. Cancer! But he is quite resilient. So, Tina, any last-minute concerns before you go to Chennai?"

"Nothing much. But I've been reading some old files on Lashkar, actually where we left off after our discussion last time."

"And?" asked Dr. Katz, catching Tina's anxious tone.

"The rebellion confuses me a little, Alan."

"Still?"

"You see, when radical activity in Kashmir was at its peak in northern India, I think around 1987, most Kashmiri militants were considered nationalists who spoke on behalf of an independent Kashmir, not a submissive partner of Pakistan. The religiously motivated militant groups also advocated the same sentiment. I can understand territorial unrest, but the headlong collision to terrorism boggles my mind."

"Which part of the activity confuses you?"

"That there are individuals who would pawn their lives to take Kashmir away from India. I understand the mindset, I understand the hatred, but I cannot understand the absolute abandonment."

"That's not easy to understand, and you know what motivates them. My dear, you've got to train your mind to look beyond religion, anti-religious sentiments, and territorial entitlement when you want to continue to study a terrorist's motive. Remember, Tina, there's a psychological motivation behind every terrorist's decision. That has been the pivotal part of your thesis. Tina, THAT IS your thesis."

"I know. I know," she sighed, a little frustrated. Otherwise, why would she be sitting in his office, week after week, seeking his advice? "I understand the psychology behind such actions or whatever I can understand fundamentally, but…"

"Yes? What is it, my dear?" asked Dr. Katz, noticing her quivering lips. Her olive complexion was steadily turning pale, and her brown eyes furtively traveled from one corner of the room to the other.

"I'm afraid I'm not going to be good at this. I don't think I'm prepared to meet Dr. Augustine in Chennai and work with him…" Tina's voice faded, zigzagging through an unfamiliar territory.

Dr. Katz got up instantly and sat on the chair next to Tina's, taking her hand in a fatherly manner. "Not prepared? My dear, you're one of the best students I've mentored during my long career as a Professor of Psychology. Why this doubt, suddenly?"

"It's not a doubt, Alan, it's…" Tina fumbled for words, tired of wiggling in and out of a winding, disturbing topic. "It's the recent explosion that took hundreds of lives in South India."

"I know. It's news today, was yesterday, and will be tomorrow. The incident occurred near a railway junction, about three, four hundred kilometers from Chennai. Is that what's worrying you, that the disaster happened somewhere in the same state you would be visiting?"

"No, I'm not afraid of that, Alan. You know me. I want to go there now more than I did before, but can I make a difference? Whatever I've been slogging to accomplish, my research...would it even make a dent in the...what am I saying?" asked Tina, making an effort not to burst into tears. And there were some unshed, unknown tears waiting to spill. She knew what was dragging her down—not her lack of confidence, not her apprehension of internship, and not the insane search for understanding the insanity of a radical's twisted mind. Those eight maddening words, *the end of all means is the beginning*, were obstinately crawling back into her mind like a colony of ants.

"We can only hope that it would make a difference, Tina. Listen to me. Shrug off those doubts. You have to do whatever you can, and you must move on. You can't stop, not until you're tired of research. You'll know when you come to the end of the road. Tina, you're the best. I've told you that before, and I'm telling you again."

"Thanks, Alan," Tina smiled gratefully. "It's that baffling statement made by the unknown leader of the terrorist group that destroyed hundreds of lives a few days ago: *the end of all means is the beginning.* I can't get it out of my mind. I guess that suggestion of an endless cycle, a never-ending chain of terror, threatens my confidence, my sense of security."

"That damned statement is what feeds the venomous fear, and," continued Dr. Katz, grinding his teeth, "it's exactly what causes terror in innocent minds and even courageous minds—yours, mine, and everybody's. When you think about it, that terrorist's declaration works. The fanatic feels victorious when minds tremble over that unceasing element of horror. That radical's aim is to make our future dangle precariously on a thread of insecurity and lies. Lies, Tina, just lies. Where is the truth in violence?"

"Yes, yes, exactly!" smiled Tina, breathing deeply. "Where is the truth in violence? Only lies—lies and violence. That takes my mind to Solzhenitsyn and our discussion last week."

"Ah, Alexander Solzhenitsyn. You somehow manage to come back to him. I didn't realize his words have made such an impression in your mind."

"They have. It's your fault. You introduced me to his books. And his words are timeless, Alan. Didn't he try to convince the world that violence thrives when it's intertwined with lies? And we don't need much convincing. That's what we see everyday when we turn on the news. You know, it makes sense to me. *The end of all means is the beginning*. Nothing but the sum of all lies." Tina took another deep breath. "It's all lies. I'm not going to let it bother me. I guess I needed this discussion."

"We all need such discussions occasionally, my dear. Where would we be without a dose of reassurance?" Dr. Katz patted Tina's hand affectionately. "Now, when you return from this internship, you better take me to dinner and tell me all about it. And I'll probably be looking at a different Tina Matthew when you return."

"I promise you a dinner, and I'm sure I'll have so much to tell you,

Alan, but I don't think I'll change much in six weeks. I do hope I learn a lot from Dr. Augustine."

"You're leaving on October 25th from Pittsburgh?"

"Yes. I'm going home day after tomorrow, and I'll leave right away."

"Good luck, dear. Have a safe trip," wished Dr. Katz, taking Tina's hand warmly. "And stay out of trouble."

Tina stuffed her laptop into her backpack and picked up her raincoat before locking the door. She took the stairs two at a time and stopped at the vending machine on the first floor for a cappuccino. The rain had ceased, but there was no sign of sun at all. It was a typical autumn day—chilly, bleak, and on the brink of turning very cold. She gathered the shawl around her shoulders and quickly got into her car. She thought the campus looked beautiful, despite the cloudy day, with the leaves turning yellow, orange, and red. She looked at the stately crest of the tall pine trees skirting the roads and felt, not for the first time, how lucky she was to be there.

When Tina reached her studio-apartment in the corner of Elm Avenue and State Street, *the end of all means is the beginning* continued to follow her like a lurking shadow. Unable to shrug it off, she warmed the canned chicken-noodle soup, took a handful of oyster crackers, and went to the couch to eat her supper. Her hand automatically reached for the remote and she turned on CNN. There it was again in the news, the horrific explosion in a small city in South India. Explosions of that caliber usually occurred in major cities, where militant activities sprouted like wild mushrooms. How did a small town in South India become a victim?

"Hi, Dad," said Tina, answering her cell phone.

"Tina, how are you, my dear?" greeted Dr. Peter Matthew, with absolutely no anxiety in his voice. Years of conversations with his daughter, some most unpleasant, had taught him how to approach a problem where his daughter was concerned—at least how not to approach a problem. So he patiently waited for a good opening.

Tina, meanwhile, wondered if she had overestimated his paranoia. Her eyes fell on her father's photograph, and she wondered how much older he looked—with a shock of grey hair, enough creases on his forehead to make a bracelet, and that undiluted smile. Tina often heard that she had inherited her father's smile, and she was thankful.

"Are you busy at the moment? I should've called a little later. I'm sorry," apologized her father.

"No, I'm not busy. I came to my apartment a little early. I needed an evening of rest."

"Good. May be you should have a healthy dinner today for a change, Tina."

"Dad, I just ate some rice, chicken, and vegetables," Tina lied, feeling a little guilty, but there was no other way to bypass his constant anxiety. "Did you have a good day?"

"A couple of patients cancelled their appointments. I was glad to have a short work day after a few hectic weeks."

He was silent for a few moments, and Tina waited anxiously. She knew why he called. And then Peter Matthew's paranoia burst like an inflated balloon suffering under the pressure of a sharp needle. "Tina, I'm scared to send you there. You've to put yourself in my place. Won't you please listen to me?"

"Dad, that disaster happened in a small city, several hundred kilometers from Chennai. Do you think I don't know that? Why won't you trust me?" asked Tina, frustrated from many years of haggling. A new exasperation rushed into her stubborn veins, and she desperately held on to her temper. "Don't people visit New York after 9/11? Don't you go to Mumbai after the disaster in 2008, although the memory of losing your friend in that explosion is still painful? We've got to be strong and move on, Dad. I'm going to stay in Chennai with Aunt Rita, who is your SISTER, and her husband, Uncle Theo. Where is the problem with safety? Besides, Dr. Augustine, my mentor in India, is Uncle Theo's family friend. What could go wrong?"

"You promise me you'll be safe?"

"Yes. I'm twenty-six, Dad. I won't do anything impulsive," Tina sighed wearily. "Are you calling from home? Where is Mom?"

"Yes, I'm home. Gia is teaching this evening. She'll call you soon. Good night, my dear."

Gia Matthew opened the trunk to help Tina with her suitcases. "Tina, your dad would have liked to be here. Too bad he has hospital duty today," said her mother, pulling the roll-on suitcase along the sidewalk.

"Mom, I know he would have liked to be here to send me off, but he would be nervous and miserable."

"He's so proud of you, Tina. He loves you more than God loves his children," laughed Gia, walking towards the terminal.

Tina entered the crowded terminal through the swivel doors after Gia.

"You've at least half hour to check in. Would you like a cup of tea?" asked Gia.

"Sure!" Tina followed her mother into Arnie's Café, not far from Gate B.

While Gia went to the counter to place their order, Tina turned towards the television screen mounted on the wall. A reporter at CNN was recapping the recent explosion that was already haunting Tina.

> *...The number of casualties from the explosion in South India is still on the rise. Officials are intrigued by the statement made by the leader of the militants; the end of all means is the beginning. The authorities suspect a connection between Al Qaeda militants and the recent explosion, although reasons for such a speculation are yet unknown. Analysts have cautioned that Taliban and Al Qaeda cells may be extending their roots for a unified jihad.*

The district police also added that the hands of the security forces were tied due to a carefully planned suicide mission that left no suspicious trails...

Same old news and same old coverage, thought Tina, shutting her eyes as the camera focused on burnt, mutilated bodies at the scene of the blast. But the pain that dug into her heart was not the same old pain. A different agony possessed her, leaving her helpless.

Gia placed a small tray on the table in front of Tina. "Here, honey, I got you a chocolate scone." The mother's attention was briefly on the television. "You know, it's a good thing that your father is not here right now, watching this gruesome report at the moment. He would have dragged you to the car and taken you home," smiled Gia, a tiny crease crinkling that smile.

"Mom," began Tina, a strange sentiment anxiously clinging to her, "I know you're worried, probably as much as Dad is. I want to thank you for trusting me, for being brave, brave enough for yourself and Dad." Tina observed her mother as though she were new to her. Gia's sandy eyes twinkled when she smiled and they matched her cinnamon-brown hair perfectly. She was the Little Italian Woman, but there was nothing little about her warmth, elegance, and quiet beauty. To Tina, she was the perfect woman.

Gia took her daughter's hand tightly into hers. "Tina, we women have a certain strength that men don't have. That's the way life is. But your father has other burdens, and he carries them like a champion. The problem is...when he loves, he loves with a passion, and when he doubts, he loses faith in the world. I've not come across an intensely sentimental man like him. You know, he loves you very much."

"And he loves you, Mom!"

"I know. I scold that poor man at times because he's like a child. The thing is he is such a child—insecure, anxious, and a little stubborn! But I can count on his affection, no matter what. And you know, Tina, that's the most comforting part of our marriage? I hope one day you can find a wonderful man like him."

"Paranoid and sheltering?" asked Tina, wide-eyed. "But I know what you mean. And I hope I find a kind man like you did."

"Well, you'll know him when you see him." Gia's eyes fretfully settled on the scattered crowd. "Tina, when you return from India, we must go somewhere for a vacation."

"I'd love that, Mom. What time is it?" Tina quickly looked at her watch.

"I guess it's time to go," replied Gia, with the slightest quiver touching her voice. "Give me a hug, darling. Promise me you'll be safe, and take care of yourself. And here is a special kiss from Dad. He wants you to stay out of trouble."

"Bye, Mom. Now go home. Don't wait in the parking lot until my flight departs, like Dad does."

"I won't," laughed Gia, her firm hand still clinging to her child's. "But please call me when you're ready to board."

- 2 -

Railway Depot 24, Pennoor Junction, South India
November 10, 2009 • 6:05 p.m.

An old green van slowed down by the cluster of flower stalls about two kilometers from Pennoor junction, puffing exhaust fumes and making tire marks on the rain-soaked avenue. When the van came to a complete stop in front of a crowded corner store, the owner looked at the bright red *R and J Construction* printed on the side of the vehicle and smiled at the passengers.

"Is this a good spot, Imran?" asked the driver, throwing hasty glances to his left and right. When he opened the window to toss his cigarette butt on the dirty pavement, a medley of smells—from the snacks on the vendors' trays to the strands of jasmine and roses suspended from the rickety roofs of the flower stalls—descended in the air like a wave of uncontainable soap bubbles.

"Yes," replied Imran, who was sitting in the back. A few urchins looked up at the dust-covered vehicle and began to stare at him as he gingerly got out of the van. "Get out of my way, you bastards," he shouted, pushing his greasy, raven hair away from his tanned forehead. When the children scattered across the heavily trafficked avenue in search of other prospects, Imran walked closer to the man sitting next to the driver and whispered, "No need to wait, Yusuf. I'll be fine."

"No, I'm not going to wait here. I'll pick you up on the other side of the depot." Yusuf's innocent smile made his childish face appear angelic. "Imran, remember to keep it low key with minimum noise. Sahib is expecting only mild rubble." Yusuf took his colleague's mind to their master's specific instructions, while his eyes quickly moved to Imran's sagging cloth bag.

"Yes, I'll remember. I'll see you soon. Inshallah," whispered Imran, raising his eyes to the sky in praise of his god.

"Inshallah," repeated his friend, and signaled to the driver to move on.

Imran avoided making eye contact with the pedestrians and took quick strides towards the depot on the other side of the avenue. He crossed the railway tracks slowly and steadily while taking stock of the busy linemen and the barefooted sweeper who was dawdling with a broom in his hand. When the contents in his cloth bag clattered, he gently gathered the bag to his chest. He reached the depot and let his trained eyes roam over the entrance, the sliding door, the low-roofed, tile-topped shed, and the few bicycles leaning on the walls displaying obscene graffiti and streaks of stale urine. He knocked on the door, and a middle-aged man with a scanty beard and scantier hair opened the door slightly and gaped at the visitor.

"You're a little early, aren't you?" whispered the bearded man, glancing furtively at Imran's bag.

"A few minutes early. What's the problem?" asked Imran, fixing his eyes steadily and menacingly on the clerk's face. "Aren't you in charge at this hour? Who else is inside?"

"Nobody," responded the clerk, letting Imran in and closing the door. "This is my shift, but I haven't made the phone call...the call to keep my manager away."

"Call right now," ordered Imran, and took a quick stock of the supplies lined along the walls. It was a disorganized arrangement of parts and paraphernalia which did not speak for the employees' efficiency. He walked into the manager's room and emptied the contents of his bag on the dirty desk. "Make sure you lock the depot from the inside and close all the windows. Give me five minutes. Now go make that phone call to delay your manager, in case he has suddenly turned conscientious about his work."

The clerk threw a frightened glance at the items on the desk and quickly shut the door. He began to recite *I am a son of Allah...I am a servant of Allah...*repeatedly in his mind, trying to justify the impending activity. But the assortment of wires which were keeping the visitor busy at the moment churned his stomach. He never developed the nerve for such a sight, and he believed he never would. When he returned to the manager's room shortly after making his phone call, the visitor was done with his work.

"Get out of here as soon as I leave," cautioned Imran, avoiding the man's eyes altogether. "Sahib appreciates your assistance in this mission," he added, reinforcing his master's omnipotent role in the daily scheme of things. "Collect your payment tomorrow from Zakir."

"I will. Thank you. The damage?" asked the clerk, alternating his glance between the wall of supplies and his visitor's face.

"Very little," assured Imran, folding the now nearly empty bag and shoving it into his pocket. "The depot will be gone, these supplies will be gone, but it will be a mild blast. Very small scale. There will be some delays and commotion at the junction. Of course, the ripple effect will reach the bus stand and the streets, and the incident will result in the normal nuisance, but nothing beyond that. Sahib has arranged for some kind of commotion at Tirupur to add to the chaos from this incident," paused Imran, summing up his master's organizational skills. "Now if you get out of the depot as soon as I leave, there will be no loss of lives either."

"I do whatever it takes to serve Allah," hissed the clerk, defending his ardent faith and unwavering resolution, in spite of the intimidating visitor and his sardonic smile. "I always do."

"I'm sure. Otherwise you wouldn't be aware of what's about to occur. If we had any doubt about your resolution or faith, I would've blown this place without your knowledge while you were lounging inside. There is no need to be defensive. It's just that I know you don't have the stomach for weapons and sorts. Some of us do. Some of us don't." Imran quickly glanced at his watch and ordered, "Let's get out of here."

When the clerk gingerly opened the door, anticipating unexpected visitors, there was not a single soul outside. Imran began to walk towards the other side of the depot without even a cursory glance at the clerk. As he had promised, Yusuf was waiting across the avenue in the green van, his childish expression changing to a smile at the sight of his friend.

The clerk closed the exterior door and walked steadily towards the railway tracks, remembering not to look at the green van even once.

- 3 -

Pennoor Junction • November 10, 2009 • 6:25 p.m.

The train wheezed to a halt by platform # 3 on that weepy evening. Tina looked at the throng of people—porters in red, passengers crisscrossing towards exits, and vendors screaming through their lungs to tout their products. The window looked foggy, sadly glazed in mucky water and grime. She pressed her nose against the milky glass and noticed the small *Nilgiris* café next to the Deltanet telephone store where her contact from *The Express* was supposed to wait for her. Then it started to rain again. Tired and annoyed at the end of the three-hour delay, she reached for her small suitcase when the earsplitting announcement threw her off balance.

"Attention, please. All passengers who are about to leave any train that has just arrived will remain inside the train. All passengers waiting to board one will assemble in the nearest shelter on the platform," the announcer cleared her throat and continued. "We are facing an emergency. Please remain calm and follow these instructions in an orderly manner."

The announcement was repeated in the same monotonous tone in Tamil, Hindi, and English. After a lapse of a few silent minutes, the station was caught in a wave of hustle and bustle as the crowd tried to find an exit. The train began its slow departure in the middle of whistles and noises, and an assortment of anxious men and women quickly got into the moving train, frantically piling on any flat surface.

"What's going on?" asked a middle-aged passenger.

"Those politicians, naturally," another passenger disgustedly spluttered the name of the ruling party, "they're trying to stall the opposition's meeting."

The train picked up speed. While a few passengers reached for their cell phones, Tina tried her aunt's number.

"Aunt Rita?" Tina desperately hoped to get hold of her relative, but all she heard was a buzz. Next, she tried to send a message via e-mail, but she could not connect to the Internet. Her voice, unfortunately, attracted the attention of the rest of the passengers, and they stared at her curiously.

Tina tried to retreat into the corner as far as she could, pushing her long, wavy, brown-black hair away from her forehead. She was used to being stared at—her light brown eyes and olive complexion announced to the public that she was not a local. Especially in that closed atmosphere, during an uncertain journey, she wished more than anything to be home.

Tina swallowed nervously and wondered where the train was going. As she took stock of the newly boarded passengers, she noticed that some of the men were overtly staring at her. While she nervously wiped her sticky palm on her faded jeans, the train slowed down and stopped at a small station. Most passengers rushed to the door to get out, and Tina was glad. That would leave fewer eyes to stare at her. She didn't mind the company of the men who had occupied the compartment since her departure from Chennai. One, an elderly gentleman, had introduced himself as a Professor of Biology who was ready to retire in a year or two. The other was a psychologist.

Tina's anxious eyes went to the milling crowd on the platform. She read the name of the town on the large yellow slab of stone; Seloor. Why did that name sound familiar? When she turned her nervous glance at the newly boarded passengers, the psychologist smiled at her.

"Excuse me, are you going to get down here or…?" he asked.

"Do you know where the train is going?" Tina asked him.

"At this point, all I know is that it is taking a detour," he replied, curiously looking at her.

The first whistle blew. A couple of passengers who had just boarded looked absolutely unsavory. Tina made up her mind. She grabbed her suitcase and gingerly stepped down. Then she took out the small address book from her backpack to see if her aunt had written down any other useful information beside the phone numbers.

Sylvia Joseph
236 First Cross Street
Seloor...
Sylvia Joseph... Aunt Rita's friend...

Seloor! No wonder, the name of the town sounded familiar. Tina's thankful glance went back to the inscription on the large yellow slab of stone. Her aunt's friend would be glad to help her. Then, she read the note she had scribbled below the address: Sylvia will be out of town from November 8th until December 12th.

That was the end of Sylvia Joseph. Tina's disappointed eyes moved rapidly through the next few contact numbers. Hadn't her aunt written down a list of small hotels? Seloor had some kind of bed-and-breakfast facility annexed to a YWCA building. It shouldn't be difficult to get accommodation in one of those establishments. Feeling a little relieved, she dropped the address book into her backpack and followed the psychologist out of the platform.

Tina's hopeless glance flew to the few taxis and private cars parked in the tiny parking lot, and there was already a long line clamoring for the remaining taxis. She stared inquisitively at the dense throng of people—a woman selling flower garlands in a rickety stall, a young man scurrying about with a stack of regional newspaper in his arms, the mixed aroma of coffee, tea, and grilled savories—a strange harmony in a whirl of chaos. The soothing breeze, laced by the willowing *neem* branches, licked her tired face. Pushing her dancing hair away from her eyes, she let her uneasy glance settle on the name of the station, fighting for attention in the dust-coated, white piece of stone. Seloor. Kuyil Extension. *Kuyil*

Extension. With a painful gasp, she realized that she was in the district where the horrific October blast had occurred. Once again wondering why she took the train alone, Tina stole a glance at her companion.

"Hello, yes, it is Shaker here," said the gentleman, answering his cell phone. "I can hardly hear you. The connection is very fuzzy. I don't know what happened at Pennoor Junction. I was forced to sit in the train and then got down at Seloor. Can you send a car to the station? Oh, you already sent one? Thanks. I wasn't sure if you had received my earlier message. I'll just have to stay somewhere and catch a bus or train to Pennoor tomorrow morning."

He switched off the phone and turned towards Tina. Only then she noticed how he effortlessly towered over her slim, five-foot-six-inches frame. An arrant tuft of wavy hair persistently fell on one side of his broad forehead. She tried to guess his age, slyly glancing at his smiling eyes, broad shoulders, and sharp features. He could be anywhere between late-twenties and mid-thirties. *Shaker. A psychologist.* Of course, she had come across his name in journals.

"May I give you a lift to…wherever you wish to stay tonight?" he asked, smiling.

"Stay tonight?" asked Tina, desperately searching for the right words.

"Most probably, every bus that could take us to Pennoor would be booked to the hilt. There won't even be standing room. People panic, naturally, and they must be trying to get away after what happened at the junction. I heard the trains are all cancelled, and I don't think one will leave until tomorrow morning. All taxis here must be taken, but my friend has arranged for a hired car to take us out of here."

"Your friend? Does he live here?"

"No. If he did, I wouldn't be looking for a place to stay right now. He has some business connections here, and he contacted a friend to get us out of this mess, at least temporarily. A private taxi should arrive soon."

"Oh, that's a relief. Could this driver take us directly to Pennoor instead of a hotel or some other place? It couldn't be far?"

"Unfortunately, they can't spare the taxi tonight. The driver can't take us farther than twenty, thirty minutes. Anyway, my friend cautioned me that the access to the city is blocked and it may not be cleared for several hours. The buses, even if we can get into one, would probably take a long detour. I'm not sure."

A small car, rather old and dented, stopped by the bend near the exit.

"Dr. Shaker, it is good to see you again," smiled the driver. He opened the passenger door for the psychologist while inquisitively staring at Tina.

As Tina was shuffling her feet in embarrassment, Shaker opened the back door for her. She absentmindedly stepped inside, and he took the seat next to the driver's.

"To the guest house, Dr. Shaker?" asked the driver.

"Not yet. Let's find out where the lady wants to go."

The driver looked sharply at Shaker. "Oh, sorry. I thought she was going with you," he whispered and turned to Tina, trying not to gawk at her perfectly shaped lips and beautiful brown eyes. "Where do you want me to take you, Madam?"

Where did she want to go? She didn't want to admit that she had nowhere to go.

"Can you please take me to the YWCA hostel?" asked Tina, taking a quick look at the list of phone numbers and addresses. "It's on Temple Street." Then, she tried the number of her aunt's home again. "I don't know why my phone isn't working. I charged it only this morning."

"Why don't you try mine?" asked Shaker.

She gladly took his phone and tried her aunt's number again. "No, it's not working. I don't think it's the phone. It must be the connection to my aunt's," sighed Tina, returning his phone to him.

"You can understand why the driver can't take us directly to Pennoor. It would probably take several hours at this pace," said Shaker, impatiently observing the plodding, bumper-to-bumper traffic.

"Yes." Tina smiled nervously, not really wanting to understand. Frustrated and tired, she let her weary eyes rest on the beautiful countryside, and her weary eyes saw a sea of green as far as they could reach. The route got gritty and uncomfortable, especially with the crawling traffic and puffing exhaust fumes, but her eyes were busy absorbing the thickening greenery, the slinking streams, and the birds' noisy journey to the welcoming branches. Then they saw something that took her breath away—a tall dilapidated building behind a thin, short curtain of trees. It looked like a ruined temple, a crumbling structure with graceful columns, the kind that inevitably appears in tour books and vacation brochures.

The taxi reached the hostel in the next ten minutes at a snail's pace, and there was nothing surrounding the building except wide green fields.

An elderly guard opened the rusty gate and demanded, "What do you want?"

When the driver began to speak to the guard in speedy Tamil through the window, Tina's anxiety increased.

"Let me ask the manager," grumbled the elderly man, and walked towards the main building.

"If they have a room available, would you like to spend the night here?" asked Shaker.

Tina looked at the stately structure again as the amber sun threw meager light on the ancient building. It appeared to be a big home that had received no favors from its residents. The guard soon returned with a lanky man, who brought with him an unpleasant odor of sweat and stale coffee. He nervously looked at the visitors through heavy spectacles, combing his unkempt hair with his fingers. Tina took another look at the manager in the fading light and wondered if she should simply return to the station and wait there till help arrived.

The manager spoke briefly to Shaker and turned to Tina and asked, "I've a room available, if you wish to stay here tonight?"

"Sir, are there quite a few guests…women staying here right now?" asked Tina, moving her eyes from the manager to the expansive building.

"Yes, Madam, we have some guests today, some women and children," the manager took a quick breath and blurted awkwardly, "and we're renovating."

Renovation. Tina glanced at the building again. She could not make much of it in the rapidly increasing darkness. A couple of windows let out a dim light, and for the most part, the brick and mortar looked weary and spent.

"But," continued the manager, looking directly and a little awkwardly at Shaker, "Sir, the warden of the facility won't allow men to stay overnight. It's regulation. Sorry."

"I understand," responded Shaker, glancing up at the tall building.

"Should we take your bag inside, Madam?" The manager's voice brought Tina back to her precarious situation.

"Yes, please," she replied, stepping out of the car.

The driver retrieved her small suitcase from the trunk and followed the manager towards the entrance. Tina was surprised and relieved to have the psychologist walk with her.

"Dr. Shaker, thank you for all you have done. I can't tell you how..." Tina's voice stumbled, a little overwhelmed by his share on that strange and unfathomable evening.

"I'm glad to be of some help. I'll return tomorrow morning, and let's see if we can catch a bus or get a taxi to Pennoor, that is, if you still wish for some assistance."

"Yes, I still do need your help, and thank you," Tina spoke sincerely before stepping into the dingy foyer that was tightly enveloped in musty smells. An indistinct and nauseating odor was bursting from the interior, despite a strong suggestion of disinfectant.

"I wish I could find a better place for you to stay," said Dr. Shaker, giving the room a disapproving look, and moved a step closer to her. His spontaneous concern softened his sharp features.

An unconscious thought knocked on her senses from somewhere in the back of her mind. The stranger owed her nothing. Still, there he was—kind, thoughtful. "Where are you staying?" she asked, feeling compelled to say something.

"I was thinking of a guesthouse. It is shared by a publishing company and another business. I've stayed at the facility a couple of times. When I called earlier, they said they didn't have a vacant room, but I can spend the night in the foyer until morning since I know the manager." He hesitated before adding, "That's why I can't offer to take you with me. I mean it's all right for me, but for you to stay all night in such an area without a room..."

"Don't worry," interrupted Tina. "You've done enough already, but…" she lingered, holding on to one more possibility before he disappeared through the night, "if you must spend the night in a foyer, why not here, if it's all the same to you?"

"I'd like to, but remember, the manager was reluctant to let me stay. He said that the warden wouldn't allow male guests here due to regulations, probably because this place is allotted for women at the moment. Again, if I knew for sure that I could get you a decent accommodation elsewhere…"

"That's quite all right. I should be fine here for a night. I probably should've waited at the station until I found another train to Pennoor or one back to Chennai."

"No. That wouldn't be safe," he whispered, taking a long look at her anxious expression. "But if you really insist on waiting at the station, I'll wait there with you."

"No, that's silly. I'll spend the night here."

"Well, in that case, here is my card. This is my cell number. Please don't hesitate to call me any time tonight. May I have your number?" he asked, quickly registering the information in his phone. "I'll be back in the morning. Good night." He held out his hand.

Tina reluctantly extricated her shaky hand from his firm grip and turned towards the front desk. A stocky woman was standing now behind the manager's desk, wearing a crisp, starched cotton sari in pale blue. Her black hair, with specks of gray, was pulled into a tight bun. "Should I pay for the room now or in the morning?" asked Tina.

The stocky woman's cold glance first rested on Tina and then traveled to Shaker. "You can pay now. That's the regulation," she replied flatly, smoothing the sari across her ample bosom. "I'm the warden of this facility," she continued, as though like an afterthought. "Currently, we're operating as an interim shelter for homeless women and children. I mean, a part of the building is reserved for that purpose."

Homeless women and children? Tina sadly observed the dusty shelves and cracked walls. When she reached for her wallet inside her backpack, Shaker stopped her effortlessly.

"Please let me," he whispered, shoving some money into the woman's hand. "Take care of the young lady," he said to the warden. "I'll be back in the morning."

His gesture, however kind and thoughtful, made Tina feel like a child. She took a last look at Shaker, who was still standing by the desk, and followed the warden up the stairs. Tina placed the suitcase on a rickety table inside a small, musty room. Under the table was a dented metal stool. The only other item left in the room was a camp cot with a pillow and a crumpled white sheet.

"There's some water on the table. Don't forget to lock your door, and don't wander about the building. That's prohibited!" The warden's rigid words matched her severe personality as she made her smile-less exit.

Tina sat down thankfully on the cot, but she wouldn't dare rest her head on the pillow. The pillowcase was dirty; it couldn't have seen soap and water in weeks. Disgusted, she got up and surveyed the small room. She noticed a door at the other end. Initially, she thought it was a closet. But when she peered through the narrow glass panel, she saw a set of descending stairs, and the door was locked. On the other side of the room was a small bathroom, with a stained toilet and a grimy shower stall.

She walked back to the bed and sat gingerly on the edge. Again, like a forlorn knell, the terrorist's declaration sat in the silent room with her. The end of all means is the beginning. How she wished to bury that maddening statement! Perhaps, if she could fall asleep. She opened her suitcase and pulled out a towel. She placed it on the pillow, set the alarm on her phone for 5 a.m., and closed her eyes to find asleep.

- 4 -

November 10, 2009 • 6:45 p.m.

The green van carrying Imran and Yusuf from Railway Depot 24 near Pennoor Junction went past Government Hospital and turned right on JP Road towards Seloor. Although the evening traffic was not yet insane, it would be soon—an anticipated result of Imran's recent artistry at the railway depot. Imran stepped out of the green van outside Flower Market, combing his straight hair away from his tired eyes.

"Come back to headquarters as soon as the job is done," instructed Yusuf, squinting his eyes to see the man sitting inside the flower stall. "The master wants to see all of us tonight after supper."

"I will reach there on time, even if I have to borrow his cycle," responded Imran, looking at the man on the bench, whose short frame was partially concealed behind strands of flowers suspended from the roof of the stall.

"You're sure I don't have to wait here for you?" asked Yusuf, glancing at the row of stalls displaying varied garlands of flowers for all occasions—from christening to cremation—before turning his glance to the noisy traffic.

"No. I know the master wants to see you immediately before he meets all of us tonight. I will finish the next two errands and catch up. I don't want you to be delayed."

Before the vehicle moved on, the vendor inside the stall tried to read the sign painted on the side of the van. He thought he saw *R and J Construction* in the dim light offered by the kerosene lamp. Dropping the basket of flowers on the floor, he got up and moved forward to receive his guest.

"Imran Sahib, I am so happy to see you," the vendor greeted his guest with the highest degree of respect, although he was old enough to be the visitor's father. His right hand imperceptibly dimmed the already dull light on the lamp while his left hand wiped his sweaty forehead.

Imran took a good look at his host's much-used trousers, his off-white cotton shirt with many brown rings around the collar, and his bare feet. He went farther into the tea stall, as far as he could go to lean against the flower-filled platform, and waited for the vendor to recite his information.

"Sahib," began the vendor, carefully gathering the words before they splattered out of his dry mouth. "They are keeping him in a secure room in Medur police station. They might move him closer to Chennai to keep him safe from...from..." the vendor struggled to finish his thought. How was he supposed to say *from the wrath of your organization*?

"Hush. You are absolutely sure?" asked Imran, dropping his voice to a whisper, reminding the vendor to speak very softly.

"Yes, Sahib. His stall is right across the street. His cousin is taking care of it while he is away. We were not on speaking terms because he got out of our union." The vendor was eager to inform the guest that no regard subsisted between him and the man who was being sheltered by the police, the same man who was hunted by Imran and his associates. "He was bragging that he saw the girl at Kuyil Extension while she was waiting by the overpass for the train to arrive. In fact, he swore he saw the explosion from a distance. The problem is, Sahib, he might remember seeing her in this neighborhood before the incident and..."

"Yes," Imran cut short the vendor's narrative, worried that his guttural voice might be overheard. He took a small wad of currency from his pocket and shoved it under a thick bunch of marigold. "I need to borrow your cycle. I will bring it back tomorrow. You've done well," he continued, walking out of the stall without glancing at anybody in sight. He pushed the cycle which was leaning on the bench and started to pedal towards Cross Town Road.

As expected, the traffic started to thicken along the main road, particularly near Seloor train station. Imran parked the cycle outside Naim Tailoring on the edge of Cross Town Road and walked straight into a small room in the back of the shop. The tailor, a young man in a loose shirt and scruffy pajamas, followed Imran into the room and shut the door.

"Call your contact in Medur," began Imran, repeating the information he had just received from the vendor in Flower Market.

The tailor promptly followed the visitor's instructions.

Satisfied that the transaction was successfully completed, Imran exchanged a few words with the tailor and started to ride his bicycle towards Market Street in Seloor.

Medur Police Station • November 10, 2009 • 8:30 p.m.

Exactly an hour after the young tailor called his contact, one of the guards at Medur Police Station looked up at the clock. It was his turn to carry the dinner tray to the man resting in the room upstairs. He started to climb the stairs when his eyes saw something they usually did not notice on the mosaic floor; a patch of red stain, and another, and another. His trained eyes did not need clarification. He triggered the alarm, and his suspicion made the headline next morning in *The Express* and in other news bulletins.

> *The flower vendor, who was safely guarded at Medur Police Station, was found dead when one of the guards went to his room with his dinner. Following the vendor's statement, based on what he had witnessed on that fateful afternoon near Kuyil Extension when the tragic explosion occurred on October 15th, the police had kept a tight watch on the gentleman to offer him protection while conducting*

their investigations. How did this breach occur? Who is responsible for this atrocity? Police protection is becoming a joke and…

- 5 -

19 Temple Street, Seloor

Tina woke up, alerted by a soft voice, a woman's voice, and it was right outside her door. She sat gingerly on the edge of the cot, and the consistent tapping on the door accelerated her heartbeat. The knocking again was accompanied by a frenzied whisper for help.

"Please help me quickly. Please, now," begged the desperate voice.

Tina stood by the door, wondering if she should open it. The next instant, she unlatched the bolt and tremblingly stared at a stranger's face. A woman was leaning over the threshold, dressed in a tattered sari, clutching something against her chest with both hands. So tight was her hold that her knuckles seemed to burst through her fragile, bruised skin.

"Yes? Who are you? What happened?" Although her curiosity had prompted her to open the door, the stranger's appearance made Tina extremely nervous. The woman's furtive glance and something strange that twitched along her temples—everything spoke of unusual behavior.

Panting for breath, the young woman continued. "I…I came running from that room," she pointed at the other end of the corridor, "I must get out of here. Please don't ask me for details. Hide me. They torture me. Please hide me."

At Tina's apparent hesitation, the stranger began to cry.

"Please, I beg you. I need your help. I came to your room and knocked on your door because I knew you were the only visitor in this building. I overheard the warden telling someone about you, and I know this room is usually allotted for visitors. Please believe me, and this room is the only one upstairs that has a direct exit to the grounds outside," the young woman begged desperately, throwing rapid glances at the door inside the room leading to a set of stairs.

But the stranger had no chance to complete her plea. Hearing hurried footsteps on the stairs from the other side of the hallway, she turned immediately and had her back towards Tina. In an instant, she transferred whatever she was clutching to her right hand, which she held against her back. Tina noticed that it was a crumpled paper. As the people on the stairs neared Tina's room, the bizarre visitor tossed the paper on the floor and started to run, but the men surrounded her in no time.

Tina was not sure what kind of intuition prompted her action at that moment. She pushed the paper with her foot and saw it safely sliding under the cot. As she instinctively tried to shut the door while her heart seemed to thud out of its shell, a couple of men walked to her door. One of them was the manager. The other man had a thick mustache and a nasty scar on his right cheek.

"I haven't seen you before. Have I, Madam?" the man with the scar asked her. He seemed a little stunned as he gaped at Tina, assessing her frightened brown eyes, questioning her foreign appearance.

"No," stammered Tina, trying to steady her quivering lips. "I… I was stranded at Seloor station, and I thought this was a YWCA facility."

"Yes, yes," he continued, exchanging a glance with the manager. "Madam, did that girl bother you? Did she say anything?" His voice held more anger than concern.

"No." Tina swallowed anxiously before asking, "Who is she? What's wrong with her?"

"She is mentally disabled. She's been trying to run away. Are you sure she didn't say anything?"

"No, she did not," Tina replied firmly. "She was just crying and knocking on the door."

"She must be crying because we're taking her to an asylum."

"But she looks..."

"Madam, shut the door, bolt it, and stay inside." His formidable tone, unbendingly set on steel, discouraged her from asking more questions.

As Tina was about to shut the door, she saw the warden in the group that was crowding the hallway. She secured the latch and retreated into the room, trying to calm her pulsing heart. *Mentally disabled!* Could that girl really be insane? Who were those men? Her relatives? Employees of the asylum?

Tina sat on the cot and turned off the alarm on the phone. Sleep was impossible at a time like that. Anyway, she had intended to wake up in the next half hour. Those men... Men! And that warden would not let Dr. Shaker stay in the foyer overnight because the place was filled with women and women only. Why did she lie? What were those men doing there? Obviously, they must be staying there if they had come to transport the poor woman to an asylum. But why was she staying in a shelter? Was her group stranded at Seloor station as well?

Tina took a few deep breaths. The recent panic made her feel parched, and she reached for the water bottle in her backpack. Her mind jumped to each frame of the incident while meandering through various, unfamiliar faces. The young woman's pathetic face was etched in her memory. She could never forget that face. And those men's severe expressions—intimidating, daunting. And Tina was sure she saw the warden among the men who were chasing the unfortunate woman. What was her role in that group? Was she assisting those men to capture the fugitive?

Tina wandered to the window and stared at the grounds steeped in darkness. Except for a stray cyclist in the distant lane, there was no activity. When her glance fell on the edge of the paper under the cot, she picked it up curiously. It was nothing but a scrap cut out from a newspaper. Why did the fugitive leave it behind? Was she trying to convey a message? Disappointed that it was nothing important, she decided to ignore it. She retrieved her laptop from her backpack and tried to send a message to her aunt, but there was no wireless connection. Having nothing else to do, she decided to take a quick shower. When she entered the bathroom, the same nauseating and revolting odor that had invited the visitors the previous evening permeated the atmosphere. She undressed and turned on the tap while looking for a shower fixture. There was none. All she saw were a dented metal pail and a plastic, quart-size mug into which a cockroach was contemplating a sly journey. A skimpy flow of cold water trickled into the beat-up pail. She poured a few mugs of water on her unwilling limbs while working up a good lather with her fragrant soap. When she returned to the room, there was a knock on the door.

"Who is it?" asked Tina, considerably nervous.

"It's me, the warden. The gentleman is here for you."

"I'll be downstairs in a few minutes. Thank you for the message." Tina picked up her belongings and bolted out of the room. As she began to walk towards the staircase, she noticed another set of stairs at the other end of the corridor. Again, the size of the building impressed her—rundown but roomy. She quietly and quickly walked to the foyer.

"Good morning. I managed to hire a car to get us to Pennoor. Did you rest well?" asked Shaker, taking the suitcase from her hand.

"Yes. I'm so glad to see you."

Tina briefly looked at the warden, trying to trace some kind of acknowledgment of what had happened with the fugitive, but her rigid face expressed nothing. Her hair was still restrained in a tight bun, and Tina vaguely thought that everything about the woman was a little tight—her generous breasts seemed to be stuffed inside a one-size-too-small blouse, and her cotton sari was clinging to her solid frame like a wet newspaper on a chunky pillar. The manager appeared at the front desk, looking even more haggard than he had seemed the previous night, his furtive glance traveling from Tina to the warden. When he opened the front door, Tina followed Shaker to the small courtyard that was already draped in amber streaks of dawn. Her eyes wandered to the number plate nailed on the lintel—19 Temple Street. *A strange name for a street that had no temple in sight*, she thought. She glanced at the rusty number plate again and at the shabby wall that badly needed a coat of paint and followed Shaker to the waiting car. He deposited the suitcase in the trunk and opened the door for her. Tina settled in, dropped her backpack by her feet, and turned her head to look at the receding structure with an immense sense of relief.

"Where to? Pennoor?" asked Shaker. "I'm sure you've eaten nothing since yesterday. May we stop on the highway for breakfast in half hour or so, or would you like to stop somewhere right now?"

"May we stop on the highway? I can't wait to get out of here."

He laughed and drove through the rusty iron gates.

"This is a beautiful countryside. It's just that the building looks quite bizarre in the middle of this lush greenery. These are paddy fields?" asked Tina.

"Yes. They grow a lot of rice here. And yes, that building could use some attention. It must've been a gorgeous structure at one time."

"What do they do with the money they collect?" asked Tina, looking again at the receding hostel.

"The money goes into some pockets, certainly not the right ones."

Tina's attention was caught again by the decaying building behind a line of trees in the middle of the paddy fields, and she thought how much she had to tell her aunt and uncle when she returned to Chennai. Reminded of her hosts, she tried her aunt's number again and was delighted to hear her voice.

"Tina, where have you been? That reporter, Mark Stevens called yesterday. He said he wouldn't be able to pick you up at Pennoor junction. What's happening? And where are you? Theo and I have been so worried."

"Oh, Aunt Rita, I'm fine. Please tell Uncle Theo that I'm all right. I've been trying to reach you since yesterday. I was stuck in a small town called Seloor, an hour or so from Pennoor and," Tina narrated all about her misadventure—all but the incident involving the fugitive. She did not wish to add to her aunt's existing worries. "By the way, Aunt Rita, I did reach Mark Stevens this morning. He is going to meet me at Palace hotel, which is where I'll be staying."

"Good. I'm glad you got hold of him. Theo and I tried to contact you so many times last night, but the only message we got was that the number was not in service. We thought that you lost your phone. Well, what matters is that you're okay. You know, Sylvia would have gladly helped you last night. She lives in Seloor. Remember, you have her information? Too bad she is out of town right now. She would've taken care of you."

"I know. I almost called her number and then realized that she wouldn't be home."

"When are you returning? Next week?"

"Yes. I'll call you tonight."

"Tina," Rita said hurriedly, "you're calling Peter and Gia everyday, I hope? Sorry to be nagging, dear. But your parents worry about you, your father more than your mother."

"Yes, of course. Don't worry. Please give Uncle Theo my love." Tina replaced the phone inside her backpack and stole a glance at the man sitting next to her.

"It must've been quite an experience. You'll have something to talk about when you return home." He was silent for a moment. "Tina..." his voice lingered. "Is it short for?"

"Christina. But it's always been Tina."

"And I've always been Shaker. No Dr. Shaker, please. I'm glad last night is over."

"Last night might be over, but it'll never be over for me."

"Why?" asked Shaker, concerned at the concern in her voice.

"Actually it was very early this morning. It was around four when I heard a woman's voice outside my room. She was knocking on the door, trying to wake me up. I opened the door. I shouldn't have, probably, I don't know. Anyway, I saw a young woman, perhaps twenty-something, begging me to let her into my room. She said that she was being abused. Shaker, she looked horribly thin. She was running away from a group of people. Before I could say anything, a few men ran towards my room.

That was the end of it. They took her away."

"Did the men ask you anything? Did they say something? This is so strange."

"Yes. One of the men seemed to be angry that she had come to my door. I felt so bad for her. I told him that she said nothing. He said that the woman was mentally disabled, and they were taking her to an asylum." Tina took a deep breath, as though glad to get the strange incident off her chest.

By then, they reached a railway crossing and were forced to stop at the red light.

"This can take a while," sighed Shaker, noticing the long line of compartments linked to the slowly moving train. "A mentally disabled woman knocked on your door? Did she tell you her name?"

"I don't know her name. There was no time to find out."

"Did she say anything about who she was?"

"No. Yes. Yes, she did. She left a crumpled piece of paper with me. I'm sure she did that on purpose. I mean, it seems as though she expected someone to read it."

Tina bent down to retrieve the paper from her backpack. As she raised her head, she looked behind the car at the approaching sounds and noticed a blue van slowing down to a stop just a few feet behind their hired car. A burly, bald man got out of the van and walked to Shaker's side.

"What do you want?" Shaker's voice barely concealed his irritation.

"Sir, sorry to bother you. I just wanted to know if you've seen anybody suspicious in this area—a young woman?" He took out a photograph from his shirt pocket and brandished it in front of their faces. "This was taken, well, maybe a year ago." As Shaker and Tina stared at the photo, he continued, "Take a good look. She's dangerous."

Tina recognized the face in the photograph; the fugitive from that morning.

"Dangerous? Why?" she asked the stranger, wondering if he would repeat what she had heard earlier.

"Because, Madam, she is mentally disabled. She escaped from an asylum. We found her, but…"

"If you already found her, why are you talking about her now? What do you want?" asked Shaker.

"She stole some valuables from the asylum before she escaped, the asylum where she was placed until last week," he replied, rather monotonously, wiping the sweat off his flabby cheeks with a crumpled handkerchief. "We don't know if she had an accomplice. We're wondering if she contacted anybody or left anything behind."

"No, we've never heard of this woman until now," Tina replied while keeping her eyes focused on the rearview mirror. She saw another man getting out of the blue van. She recognized him. He was the man who had ordered her to stay inside her room earlier that morning while a group of people surrounded the fugitive. Tina promptly pushed the paper into her backpack and looked again at the mirror. The mustached man was walking towards their car, tentatively touching his scar.

"I've seen him before, at the hostel, just this morning," Tina whispered.

"Madam," continued the bald man.

"We're in a hurry. We've to go," said Shaker.

The man with the scar came to the car and looked alternately at Shaker and Tina. "Oh, I remember seeing you earlier at the…shelter, Madam," the man said politely.

"Is the young lady all right?" asked Tina, swallowing nervously.

"Of course, she is in a safe place. We were stranded at Seloor junction, and we decided to stay overnight at the facility where you stayed because there are no hotels in this town. We are on our way home now. You see, we are worried that she tried to escape. One of the most painful aspects of her ailment is...she is very good at inflicting wounds on her body. You might have noticed it. This can be very harmful. We want to be sure that such things don't happen in the future. That's why she needs to be placed in the hands of good doctors in a proper hospital." The man looked intently at Tina for a couple of moments and asked, "Madam, did she leave anything with you? We believe she stole something earlier from the other asylum, and we would like to do the right thing, of course, and return it to the right place. Did she?"

"She left nothing," replied Tina, avoiding his eyes.

The light switched to green and the gate opened slowly. By now a few cars had lined up behind the blue van. When the drivers started to honk impatiently, the bald man shouted obscenities while showing an angry fist at the annoyed drivers.

"Madam, we're her family, and we want to make sure she is safe in the future. When I asked you earlier at the shelter, you told me that she said nothing to you. Are you sure she didn't say anything?" asked the man, absentmindedly touching his scar.

Tina looked at his intense expression. Had he overheard what the fugitive had told her, at least part of it? "I was shocked and naturally confused when you asked me the same question earlier at the shelter. I'm sorry. I think she said that she was being abused by someone and she was trying to escape. That's all."

The man smiled. "Typical. That's her standard line, unfortunately. It scares people, you know. Thanks for taking the time to talk to us."

"What's her name?" asked Tina, a little surprised at her own question.

He stared at her. "We're sorry, but that's confidential, Madam," he replied, moving away, and the bald man followed him to the blue, dusty van that had *R and J Construction* printed on the side.

- 6 -

From Seloor to Pennoor

Shaker turned on the ignition and steered the car towards the main road where the traffic was steadily getting heavier as the city got closer.

"Tina, did you tell anybody in the hostel that you were going to Pennoor?"

"I didn't. The only person I spoke to was the warden. And I can count the words we exchanged. And with that girl, of course. But that was hardly anything, perhaps a couple of minutes." Tina thought for a moment. "But did you tell the manager where I was going? I mean, last night when I was looking for a place to stay?"

"You know, I might have. I'm not sure. Where are you staying in Pennoor?"

"Palace Hotel, but I haven't checked in yet. I did call them this morning. I hope they're still holding my reservation."

"I'm sure they would, especially considering what happened at the station and the chaos that followed afterwards. May I see the paper she left with you?"

"Of course, here. But what's this?" asked Tina, holding the piece of paper.

"It looks like an advertisement for a cultural program, and she left it with you."

"Yes, she quickly tossed it into my room before they took her away.

But why did she leave this paper with me?"

"I'm not sure. But if she is insane, would she rationally think about what she must do? Her family members who intercepted us just now looked really worried about the girl, and I'm glad she is not on the run anymore." Shaker parked the car on a quiet road. "Come. Let me get you a cup of coffee and some breakfast. I don't know about you, but I'm starving. I know a decent restaurant at the end of this street."

"Where are you from, Tina?" asked Shaker, taking a sip of the flavorful coffee.

"I'm from Pittsburgh. My father is from South India, a small town in Kerala, and my mother grew up in Italy, until she was five, and then moved to New York City with my Italian grandparents. So," smiled Tina, "now you know why I look this way."

"Well, there's nothing wrong with the way you look," smiled Shaker, glancing quickly at her twinkling brown eyes and the beautifully shaped lips which were shyly twitching at the moment. "But I know what you mean. You must get some curious glances, especially when you travel around small towns here. What brought you to India, Tina? Vacation?" He stared doubtfully at the hazy window as the rain fiercely began a torrential beat.

"No, but a vacation sounds like a good idea. I'm on the last stretch of my doctorate program. A short-term internship in psychology brought me here."

"An internship? And you're working with?"

"Dr. Augustine, in Chennai. It's my bad luck. I started working with him for a week and now he is back in the hospital. His cancer has..."

"Dr. Augustine!" interrupted Shaker. "So you're the student he was talking about, the one from Pittsburgh. Don't you work with Dr. Katz?"

"Yes. He's my advisor."

"Dr. Augustine and I frequently work together. He was my mentor a long time ago. Actually, he was discussing your research with me the last time I was having dinner with him. Isn't this a convenient coincidence? He won't believe we're sitting here, talking about him. What a small world!"

"My internship might be suspended now because Dr. Augustine's cancer has taken a bad turn," said Tina, her frustration over the wasted time occupying her troubling thoughts more than the coincidence and the small world. "I've to come back when he's feeling better."

"That's too bad, a wasted trip. Dr. Augustine had asked me if I could help you with your research while you were working with him. I was actually looking forward to it," Shaker added disappointedly.

Tina smiled, somehow relieved to discover mutual grounds. She opened her book and studied the piece of paper, searching for the reason it was left behind by the fugitive.

"What's that book?" asked Shaker, picking it up curiously. "*One Day in the life of Ivan Denisovich*?"

"Yes, by Solzhenitsyn. Haven't you read it?"

"No, I haven't. Somehow Solzhenitsyn missed me, or I missed him. You look disappointed. Should I feel embarrassed?"

"Embarrassed? Of course, not. But he's more than a writer to me. Dr. Katz gave me this book as a gift at the end of my first year in the program. Initially, I read this one out of curiosity. Solzhenitsyn soon became a part of my daily life, and I began to read all of his works, one by one."

"All of his works?" laughed Shaker, his stern features relaxing, as he pushed a stray strand of hair away from his wide forehead. "Now I really feel embarrassed."

"No need to be. But Solzhenitsyn's words get to me, gnawing at my conscience. His convictions, how violence lives on lies, have become my convictions, my sacred mantra. My family teases me that I'm obsessed with him because I take him with me wherever I go. But," hesitated Tina, watching the misty window, "his words remind me of my search, especially as a psychologist who is trying to understand the violent world we live in, why terrorism swallows the heart of humanity, and how we allow it to defile the core of human nature." Tina returned her glance to Shaker, smiling a little shyly. "See? I am obsessed."

"Wow! I didn't realize what I've been missing. Perhaps I shouldn't read Solzhenitsyn because he seems to be an all-consuming habit," he smiled, noticing the disappointment that was still lingering in her telltale eyes. "Your trip doesn't have to be a waste. Tina, would you like to work with me?"

"You mean you would be my mentor? I can call Dr. Katz to get his approval. I'm sure he wouldn't object. I think your name has come up during our discussions."

"I'm not surprised. I've a couple of papers with Dr. Katz. I know," laughed Shaker, amused by Tina's raised eyebrows. "Which psychologist doesn't have a paper with Dr. Katz? Well, let's get back to finding a mentor for you. Tina, how long is your internship here?"

"Six weeks, but we can make it shorter, if you want," she added hurriedly, worried that he might withdraw his generous offer.

"Not necessary. Any associate of Dr. Augustine is welcome into my office. What brought you to Pennoor from Chennai?" he asked, taking another sip of his coffee.

"I stumbled on a few articles on terrorism by a journalist called Mark Stevens during my research. I wanted to interview him, get his opinion on some of the recent incidents. He's working in the Pennoor branch of *The Express* for a few weeks, and he invited me here for a few days. This is actually Dr. Augustine's suggestion. Especially since he is indisposed, he asked me to spend a week here with Stevens."

"Yes, that would be a nice change of scene, plus you'll gain some material for your research. Unfortunately, you didn't anticipate the incident at the station and what happened thereafter," smiled Shaker.

"No, I didn't. No wonder my aunt told me 'I told you so' a little earlier when I called her to let her know where I was."

"Your host in Chennai?"

"Yes. Aunt Rita is my dad's sister. Her husband is Theo Edwin, who recommended me to Dr. Augustine."

"The *Theo Edwin* who knows Augustine? Then I know your uncle. It's inevitable with my line of research, naturally. Mr. Edwin is an indispensable figure in counter-terrorism."

"Looks like now I've no secrets from you!" Tina laughed, sheepishly but happily. "Aunt Rita and Uncle Theo wanted me to take a flight to Pennoor instead of taking the train alone. I probably should've listened to them."

"Why did you take the train?" asked Shaker, directly looking at her.

"I wanted to see the countryside, observe the locals, and get a flavor of the small towns," she replied, not relishing his blunt question. Despite his gentlemanly demeanor, she found him a little carelessly direct. "That's why I purposely took a day train instead of traveling by night."

"I usually take the overnight train, but this time I made an unscheduled visit and the Express was full."

"What brings you here from Chennai?" asked Tina, trying to understand the routine of her new mentor.

"They are setting up a trauma center near the airport and I'm one of the consultants. Are you ready to go to your hotel?"

"Yes, thanks. But you know, I can probably take a taxi from here. Wouldn't you like to return to your work?"

"No. I won't let you go alone in a taxi after what you went through last night and this morning."

Shaker led Tina towards the front door. The rain had subsided significantly, and she still was not used to the desperate downpour and the urgent retreat. The drive was ironically smooth, considering the emotions sloshing in her restless mind. The highway soon picked up various noises as they neared the city, and Tina saw the crowd thickening along the bus stops and in the street corners. Her alien eyes curiously jumped from rattling auto-rickshaws to crowded buses and settled on the unfamiliar faces.

"I'll drop you at the entrance," suggested Shaker. "I'll park the car and follow you."

"Oh, you don't have to come in. I can take care of it from here," she smiled, a little tired of following his lead.

"No, I must come in. I've to make sure that your room is still unoccupied. Besides, until your contact meets you, how can I be sure that you're safe? Remember, Tina, now I'm your mentor?" he smiled genially, when she was still hesitating. "No arguments."

She could not return his smile while she was considerably annoyed. The last thing she wanted was her father's paranoid shadow, but she quietly followed him out of the car.

An old blue van was waiting in the last row of the parking lot, not far from the main road. A man with a scar on his cheek, sitting on the driver's seat, exchanged glances with the bald man sitting next to him when he saw Tina and Shaker walking towards the entrance to the hotel.

- 7 -

19 Temple Street, Seloor • November 11, 2009

A tall, gaunt, elderly man—with a startlingly white beard and a white tagiyah covering his head—stared at the paddy fields surrounding 19 Temple Street from his window.

"Kumar, you're sure her name is Tina Matthew?" he asked, looking at the bald man standing in front of him.

"Yes, Usman Sahib," Kumar replied respectfully. "That's how she registered at the front desk when she arrived at Palace Hotel, when Manohar and I followed her."

"Yes," confirmed the man with the scar, who was standing by the door. "Dr. Shaker is here on work. I got that checked out. It's Tina Matthew who is still nagging me."

"I've been reading about Dr. Shaker and the psychological gibberish he writes. He should return to the United States soon, I think. Nuisance! I can't afford any wrinkle in my next mission. Call Abdullah, Kumar," commanded Usman, his worried mind darkening his angular face. "Ask him to come here today for a meeting. We need to transfer Maya to a different location right away. And ask Yusuf to see me when he returns from his errand."

"Yes, Sahib." Kumar hurried out of the room.

"Manohar, ask our man at *The Express* to make a report, especially in the city edition which Dr. Shaker and Tina Matthew might read," said

Usman, turning to the other man, and began to dictate exactly what he wanted to see in the paper and exactly what Shaker and Tina would read later in the day.

A grey Mercedes Benz pulled by the front door of 19 Temple Street in the next hour. A tall, grotesquely obese man got out of the car when the driver opened the door.

"Sahib, he is waiting upstairs." Kumar respectfully greeted Abdullah in the foyer.

As the visitor breathed heavily and dragged his feet laboriously up the stairs, his chest moaned in misery. Usman was sitting on his usual chair behind the usual desk, but he did not have his usual smile when his friend shut the door upon entering the room.

Kumar lingered for a few seconds, hoping that Usman would invite him to join the discussion, but he walked away disappointedly.

"Is Abdullah Sahib here already?" asked Manohar, stepping out of the room across the hallway. He tentatively touched his scar and glanced at the closed door.

"Yes." Kumar, after another longing look at his master's closed door, walked towards the other end of the hallway.

"And we're not included?"

"No. This must be a very private meeting. Usman Sahib doesn't invite us to all the discussions, but one day he would. After all, we're becoming quite indispensable. Aren't we, Manohar?"

"You think so? But he pays well, Kumar," whispered Manohar. He pulled out a couple of cigarettes from his shirt pocket and offered one to his friend. "Come, let's go check on Zakir."

Kumar and Manohar went up a set of staircase at the end of the corridor and began to walk towards the opposite side of the building where a room in the corner was reserved for interrogation.

"Does Usman Sahib frighten you sometimes?" asked Manohar.

Kumar looked puzzled by the direct question. "He can be a little intimidating. I know what you mean. There's always a space between him and me, no matter how much I do, no matter what I accomplish. After all we've gone through, I still feel he doesn't trust me. I don't mean *trust me* like it sounds," Kumar added hurriedly, "but I'll never mean to him what Yusuf means to him."

"Well, Yusuf is his kind, just as Abdullah Sahib is. Usman Sahib will never consider us in the same vein. My friend, they're different breed."

"Because they are Muslims and you and I are not?"

Manohar nodded his head. "Well, Usman Sahib favors Yusuf and there's nothing we can do about it. Yusuf has a cold focus that's similar to our master's. Perhaps that's why he's special in his eyes."

"But we're loyal to our master. What difference can it make...what breed we are?"

"We're here for the money. They're not, and that makes all the difference."

"So the inner circle is out of the question?" asked Kumar, smiling wryly.

"Yes, and we better remember that." Manohar stopped outside a room from where suffocated groans were seeping through a small opening under the door.

"Your project is still alive." Kumar stepped into a small, dark, grimy room.

A man was tied to a metal chair, his bare body gleaming in streaks of blood and sweat. A couple of men were standing on each side of the chair with blunt instruments and vicious expressions. As one of the men raised his instrument towards the victim's head, Manohar raised his hand to stop him.

"I want to talk to the manager. Wait outside for my orders." Manohar shut the door as the other two men left the room.

The victim stopped groaning and began to breathe arduously. His face, almost unrecognizable through raw bruises, contorted in pain as he struggled to breathe.

"Usman Sahib is furious because you disobeyed orders. Why did you let a visitor stay here last night, Zakir?" Manohar asked softly.

Zakir did not answer for a few seconds. He tried to move his jaw slowly in an attempt to open his mouth.

"WHY DID YOU?" shouted Manohar, throwing the cigarette butt on the dirty floor.

Zakir tried to speak. Kumar looked at Manohar in confusion.

"I don't understand a word he is saying," whispered Kumar.

"Go close to his mouth and try to listen," suggested Manohar. "You are the manager, Zakir. Why did you disobey?" Manohar asked again.

"He is saying that he felt sorry for the woman who was stranded," Kumar explained, moving away from the victim's face.

"Did anybody ask you to let in a visitor?" asked Manohar, lighting another cigarette.

"No." Zakir shook his head.

"Did anybody pay you to let in a visitor?" asked Manohar, blowing rings of smoke towards the ceiling.

"No," whispered Zakir, crying like a baby. He hissed in pain as the salty tears cascaded down his fresh wounds.

"LIAR!" shouted Manohar, and pressed the glowing end of the cigarette on Zakir's cheek, close to his left eye.

Zakir gathered strength from somewhere within his retching body and let out a bone-chilling scream.

"You've to stop now if you want Zakir to live tonight, and he must live until we can find what we need to find. How can you let him die of pain if you expect to get information from him?" whispered Kumar.

"Let's get out for now." Manohar walked towards the door, his cold glance estimating the victim's degree of pain. He stopped by the two men waiting outside the room and said, "Give Zakir food and let him rest. I'll continue tomorrow."

- 8 -

From Palace Hotel to *The Express*, Pennoor

The spacious foyer of Palace Hotel was nearly empty. Tina looked at the marble floor, the crystal chandelier, and the mix of artwork on the walls. How different it was from 19 Temple Street! She saw the friendly smile of the clerk at the front desk and promptly went to him.

"Yes, Madam, we have your room ready for you and," the clerk turned towards a cluster of chairs where a few guests were lounging, "a gentleman is waiting for you."

A young man approached Tina with an extended hand and said, "Miss Matthew?"

"Yes. Mr. Stevens?" Tina looked at her contact's face again. He was not at all what she had expected to see. He was supposed to be an upcoming reporter, possibly in his late-twenties, but he had the appearance of a college student, with a shock of wavy hair and spectacles.

"Yes, I'm Stevens, but please call me Mark. I'm so happy to meet you at last, and I'm glad you're okay."

"Thank you. Mark, this is Dr. Neil Shaker. He is the one who has been helping me since yesterday." Tina awkwardly introduced one gentleman to the other when she barely knew the psychologist and had just met the journalist.

"Shall we have a drink? Hope you had a chance to eat some breakfast." Mark led the other two towards the large restaurant.

"We've eaten. Thank you. I could use a cup of tea, though," Shaker replied absentmindedly, leading Tina to a comfortable chair.

As the waiter left with their order, Tina looked at Shaker again. A part of her, defiant and assertive, wondered why he was still there. The other ridiculous part, hanging on a tremulous and unknown vein, wished him to stay. Somehow, for a mysterious reason, he held the key to her peace of mind after the previous night. He was, after all, the only sane link during the recent, peculiar turn of events.

"I'm sorry about the confusion at the train station yesterday, Miss Matthew. I'm so glad you're okay." Mark tried to break the silence.

"Oh, please call me Tina. What happened at the train station?"

"There was a minor explosion, just a few minutes before your train arrived at the junction. Incidentally, there was a political rally near Tirupur, which is where I was stuck. In fact, I didn't reach Pennoor until 5:00 this morning. The newspaper says that the blast occurred at one of the depots close to the station, not far from that platform."

"A major explosion happened there only last month, not right there, but not very far from that station. A repetition so soon?" asked Shaker. "Any party claimed responsibility for it yet?"

Tina remembered the previous bombing incident very well, and *the end of all means is the beginning* momentarily visited her lingering fear. And she noticed an extraordinary agony touching the reporter's expression. But it passed as quickly as it appeared.

"I'm not sure who is responsible. No deaths or injuries were reported. I guess it was a scare tactic. Anyway, that announcement must have been unnerving while you were about to get off the train. And I'm sorry you had to find accommodation in a strange place."

"It was strange, but what is more unnerving is my adventure this morning," said Tina, somewhat glad to recount the incident with the fugitive. "But I'm glad her family followed her promptly and took her to safety."

"That can scare anybody. Again, I'm so sorry you had to go through what you did. Well, you'll never forget this visit," smiled Mark, refilling her teacup. "Are you ready to visit my office?"

Tina did not expect to see such a lush landscape surrounding *The Express*. The grounds looked like an amusement park, with clusters of graceful palm trees, meticulously cultivated hibiscus bushes, colorful borders of pansies and balsams, and gushing water fountains. She followed Mark into an air-conditioned foyer and noticed that the place was tightly guarded.

"Looks very serious, Tina, doesn't it?" asked Mark, looking at the armed guards. "We've had a series of hate mail and some unpleasant incidents and threats from anonymous groups."

"Islamic militants? I read about it recently."

"Yes, mostly. They don't approve of what we print in the paper, and we occasionally hear from some angry Hindu activists. We've got to be careful. Tina, I thought we could go to my room and prepare a bit before we join my team for lunch?" asked Mark, walking towards the elevator.

It was very crowded inside the elevator. Tina moved towards the back wall, or she was made to move by the milling crowd. Was Mark inside? She couldn't see him. A couple of passengers smiled at her. Had she seen them before? She had seen so many new faces in the last two days. She was glad when the elevator finally reached the fifth floor.

"I'm sorry. I didn't realize you got pushed to the back," apologized Mark, right outside the door.

"Thought you were already tired of me," Tina replied jokingly, trying to conceal her anxiety.

One of the men in the elevator walked towards the window and called Naim Tailoring. In a couple of minutes, a call reached his phone from19 Temple Street. "That woman is in *The Express* office," he informed his contact, and carefully listened to the flood of instructions.

After introducing Tina to a couple of his colleagues outside the elevator, Mark asked her to follow him to the end of the corridor and into a messy room. "Since you're going to be here only for a few days, I've made a small workspace for you in my office. Is that enough?" he asked.

"Whatever you've arranged is fine," replied Tina, hesitantly looking at the cramped office. The single four-drawer filing cabinet, bulging like a pregnant woman's belly, added to the general claustrophobia.

"I'm sorry about the mess," he smiled, guiltily resting his eyes on the clutter. "What do you want to do first? I'm sure you want to have a meeting with Varma?"

"Sure, I'd love to have a talk with your manager," Tina replied eagerly. Varma could lead her to a very fruitful assignment in the future. "How long will you be in Pennoor?"

"A few weeks. I'm vacating my office in Hyderabad. I've been offered a position in Chennai, and I'm going to move there in a few weeks. So, Tina, what would you like to discuss first?"

"How about the October 15th explosion near Seloor station? I've read the news articles on it. I want to know what you think of it."

"Oh, that!" His face twisted in pain.

"Mark, are you all right?" asked Tina, worried about his alarming expression.

"I lost someone very dear in that explosion."

"I'm so sorry," babbled Tina, acutely embarrassed and extremely sorry. "Let's move on to something else. We don't have to talk about that incident, Mark."

He was silent for a few moments, absentmindedly smoothing his wavy hair with his nervous hands. "Yes. We must. As painful as it is to me, I must remember that it's very painful for many—all those lives lost in the rubble!"

He began to explain the disaster, much similar to what she had heard and read earlier, but his narrative terrified her and took her erratically to *the end of all means is the beginning*. She wondered about the 'someone very dear' lost in that explosion, but she didn't have the nerve to ask him.

"Tina, would you like to visit the scene of the disaster? I'm going there tomorrow."

"Thank you. Yes," Tina replied gratefully, eager to gather what she could by visiting the unfortunate location, deeply conscious of what her father might say at that very moment.

The taxi dropped off Tina by the circular drive in front of Palace Hotel just after 5:00 in the afternoon. The beautiful air-conditioned foyer was a balm to her tired eyes. She admiringly looked at the vast bronze bowl filled to the brim with water, a sprinkle of rose petals and jasmine swimming in it.

"I'd like to have a cup of tea. Should I call for room service?" Tina asked the manager standing behind the front desk.

"I'll be glad to send a tray to your room, Ma'm, with some biscuits," replied the young man politely, discreetly letting his eyes travel from her brown-black hair to her beautiful hazel eyes which were assuming a tinge of green in the fluorescent light. "Would you like anything else?"

"Nothing else, thank you. I'll take a copy of the newspaper, if I may?"

While Tina was going through her wardrobe to choose an outfit for the evening, the doorbell rang. Room service was fast. After locking the door, she picked up her robe. Having more than two hours to kill, she decided to soak in the tub and turned on the faucet. Leaving the tea tray on the small table by the tub, she got into the scented water. As she blissfully breathed in the heavenly fragrance, her thoughts flew to the derelict bathroom in the hostel at 19 Temple Street. That address had a ring to it, and it tiptoed into the room and stole her peace of mind. Was it because it was the last thing she noticed as she left the dreadful building? She cursed the explosion by the railway station which somewhat forced her to stay at that strange hostel. When she was still trying to scrub away *the end of all means is the beginning*, the desolate hostel and the ghostly woman began to gnaw at her peace of mind. Was her visit to India jinxed?

Tina went to the wardrobe and chose a pair of off-white linen pants and a blue cotton kurti with white embroidery. She had become a fan of the comfortable tunics. When she got dressed and began to brush her hair, her cell phone rang.

"Tina, it's Shaker. Would you like to have dinner with me?"

"Oh," she hesitated, happy and surprised, "I'd love to, but Mark is picking me up soon. Actually, a couple of members from his team are joining us for dinner."

"That's quite all right. I should've made plans to meet you for dinner when I dropped you off at the hotel this morning. Tina," he lingered, "did you get a chance to see the paper today?"

"No. I just picked up a copy of *The Express*. Why?"

"Look at Section A 5, about a missing young woman who has a mental illness. It's on the left column."

Tina read anxiously. "Is she the same woman I saw early this morning?"

"Very likely. It says she was rescued around Seloor."

"Then she's all right?" asked Tina, hopefully.

"Looks like it. How long are you planning to be in Pennoor?"

"I was planning to stay here only for a week, while working with Mark, but if I must begin my internship with you…"

"I'm going to work here for another two weeks at the trauma unit. If it doesn't make any difference to you, why don't you work here with me instead of returning to Chennai? Once it is time for me to leave, we can go to Chennai together and continue to work on the pending projects."

"That's fine. And thanks for calling."

Tina looked at the clock. It would be 5:30 in the morning in Pittsburgh, and her parents would be asleep. She had to call them later. Yes, much later. She smiled in relief and looked at her reflection again before going to the foyer to wait for Mark.

- 9 -

19 Temple Street, Seloor

While Zakir was being questioned by Manohar inside the dark and filthy room at 19 Temple Street, Abdullah sat on the chair facing Usman's desk.

"You wanted to see me, Usman Bhai?" Abdullah's rugged face softened in affection. Usman held the status of his big brother, and there was nothing Abdullah would not do for his bhai.

Usman looked at his friend's tired and puffy eyes from hectic days, parched leathery lips from incessant smoking, and a rotund body from excessive alcohol and reckless eating. "Abdul, I need a new location for Maya."

"What happened?" Abdullah was disturbed by the urgency in Usman's tone.

"There was an episode last night," Usman hissed, recounting the fugitive's accidental encounter with Tina Matthew.

"I've always been nervous about letting a guest into the building, even if it is on rare occasions, and I've expressed my concern before."

"But you see, it was a nagging necessity, or at least earlier we thought it was. We couldn't have an organization here without the occasional interference."

"But this is supposed to be an interim shelter for women and children. That has worked for several months. Hasn't it?" asked Abdullah, upset that a breach occurred in spite of meticulous planning.

"Yes, but when we first set up this establishment, we let in an occasional guest out of necessity. Remember, we bought the property which was functioning as part of a YWCA facility. I had issued orders to stop using the spare room for a guest, but Zakir..." Usman ground his teeth.

Even Abdullah, who had seen the worst, was intimidated by the red rage in Usman's eyes. "What should we do with Zakir?"

"He is already in the corner room in the other wing. Zakir is devoted to our cause, and there is no better assistant, Abdul. But he is soft. I don't see how he can ever develop the strength of mind he needs to be a vital member of our organization. After all, we have sheltered him under our wings for more than ten years. I decided to give him a desk job and made him the manager here. Looks like he can't do a good job even behind a desk. We can patiently train minds, but Zakir is not ruthless. It's just not in his nature. Sometimes it's foolish to wait indefinitely for that strength of mind to sprout."

"Yes, Zakir is not ruthless, and he'll never be. How often have we discussed that? He hasn't improved at all," agreed Abdullah, thinking about the corner room where punishment was generously dispensed. "And Zakir's mild nature can ruin our missions. Who is working on him?"

"Manohar. I decided to make it his project."

"Good. It's important to make him and his kind feel rather important once in a while," smiled Abdullah, appreciating Usman's strategic decision. "Usman Bhai, you look very tired. In fact, you look ill. Do you think you need a short rest from all this?"

"Rest? I probably do. But I can't afford to lose time. As you know, there are two projects coming up—minor but important. And my rest can wait. It'll come on a glorious day, Abdul. After all, we're doing Allah's work. Aren't we certain that there is a distinguished place reserved for us in heaven? Here, now, we must struggle on this arduous road to heaven..."

"By making life hell for some. Well, such is our chosen path!" exclaimed Abdullah.

"Yes, our chosen path is what keeps me going, especially during the times I'm tired, tired of what I do day after day—constant recruitment, continuous missions, unvarying loss of lives." Usman's deep-set eyes, steeped in frustration, made him appear like an evil sorcerer. "Yet, such is my calling, our calling."

"How are the recent recruitments coming along?" asked Abdullah, eager to see a glimpse of something positive during the bleak review of their cursed lot.

"Salman is coming along very well. He would be ideal for a domestic mission."

"Not a terminal mission?" asked Abdullah, who had high hopes for the boy who was a unique candidate.

"No, of course not. As I said, this boy is very promising. I want to groom him for the long-term benefit of our mission. He has perfect qualifications—he is homeless, angry, disillusioned, vulnerable, and he is very disjointed. Most importantly, he hates the police. I want to be cautious because of his young age. But based on my last assessment, I believe he is one of our best recruits. And there is that young girl, Saira. She is about fifteen, I think."

"Fifteen? What circumstances?"

"Similar to that boy's, but she is not homeless. You know that case already."

"Oh, you mean the recruitment in which Sayeed assisted?"

"Exactly. Salman is priceless, Abdul. His innocence is already shattered, and he's ready to attack the world. I'm going to leave him in my Yusuf's hands. And I'll work very carefully with Saira, now that she's been with us for some time."

"And how long are you going to let Kumar and Manohar linger?" asked Abdullah, lighting another cigar.

Usman smiled at the thought of his two minor assistants. "They're aimless, brainless idiots, with no sense of religion. Abdul, what good is a man, what is he worth, unless he has strong roots in a superior faith?"

"Absolutely nothing, Usman Bhai!"

"I know that Kumar and Manohar could be dangerous to our long-term security. Those two, with no belief in any religion, with no connection whatsoever to Islamic faith, work for my mission for only one reason; money. Money is a good incentive. It would remain a great incentive as long as the pipeline from the northern borders is not severed."

"But tangible money is not reliable, Usman Bhai. All it takes is another source that's willing to offer a better price. Money, unfortunately, cannot buy loyalty. A strong faith in religion and its cause, on the other hand, would buy lifetime loyalty." Abdullah's voice resonated passionately. "But I don't need to tell you that."

"True, Abdul," agreed Usman. "Extremists are our backbone. Sadly, I've lost quite a few of my devoted followers during previous missions. Not that all of them have been wiped out." Usman's mind rapidly assessed the number of men and women strategically stationed in the market, bus depots, railway stations, and school campuses. His gaunt face grew dark in resentment. "But my list of disciples is a little lean at the moment. No wonder, I've to resort to idiots like Kumar and Manohar."

"Do you think Maya talked?" Abdullah asked, trying to divert his friend's mind to the current mess.

"It seems she was crying and knocking on the guest room door. Remember, that's the only room in the building that opens to a set of staircase directly leading to the grounds. We need to move her out of here."

"What about my warehouse? I'll make sure she is secure there, and there are a couple of spare rooms where she can be kept isolated."

"Eastern Exports? Why not?" Usman sighed gratefully. "I know she'll be in good hands when she's in your care. Can we move her there soon?"

"Let's move her this afternoon, in case there is a police report. What about the woman Maya talked to? What do we do about her?"

"She is an outsider, and she should return to her country in a few weeks. I'm going to keep an eye on her and see if any police report sprouts from her concern. She must be curious. I'm sure she has spoken to that man, Dr. Shaker, about the incident with Maya. But I've sent a story to our man at *The Express* to be printed right away—that a missing young lady from a nearby village, delirious due to psychological issues, was taken to safety yesterday by a team of family members and the police. A human-interest story, Abdul, is quite appealing. I made sure no description of the lady or the location was necessary because the lady's family would much prefer to keep it that way. I also made sure the news was top priority, especially in the city edition, which Tina Matthew and Shaker are likely to read."

"Shaker...is he Indian? His name is very Indian!"

"His father's Indian name, Shekar, was converted to Shaker, I think. He has Indian heritage, grew up in Chennai for a while, but he is not an Indian citizen. I've always been interested in him, even before this incident with Maya. I'm curious about anyone who is curious about terrorism."

"But you think he's all right?" Abdullah asked doubtfully.

"I'm sure he is. Bookish and very focused on psychology and all that nonsense. Has a keen interest in terrorism from a psychological point of view, and he writes about it. Very suitable for publications, Abdul, and that's where it stops. But you see, my friend, every element in life has a psychological point of view."

"True." Abdullah readily acknowledged his friend's statement, admiring his meticulous study of human nature that made him a remarkable leader—a dangerous man, but a leader in his own right. "So you've decided to leave Tina Matthew and Dr. Shaker untouched?" asked Abdullah, admiring his friend's temperance when it came to eliminating potential enemies.

"For now, yes. They're both temporary residents here. I'm not at all worried about them. Besides, Abdul, if I decide to get rid of Tina Matthew, it has to be a perfect accident. There can't be any complication. She is from the States, and so is Dr. Shaker. The media would analyze her death and his till the end of time."

"And Dr. Shaker has a license to practice? How does that work?" asked Abdullah, trying to see what Usman saw clearly.

"Dr. Shaker is here on an extended project. He comes and goes. He frequently works with Dr. Augustine, another crazy psychologist, who is passionate about terrorism."

"They're more passionate about terrorism than we are, Usman Bhai," laughed Abdullah, his flabby cheeks jiggling like jello. "They analyze terrorism and tear terrorists to pieces, if caught. Champions of counter-terrorism! Anyway, if you think Dr. Shaker is not an obstacle, then I'm not going to worry about it."

"I don't think I would worry about him. I sent Kumar and Manohar on the road early this morning to intercept Dr. Shaker and Tina Matthew to reinforce the *mentally disabled* theory regarding Maya."

"I'm glad you did that. I wonder who else Tina saw or spoke to, besides Zakir, while she stayed here overnight?" asked Abdullah, eager to clear all angles.

"Maria, of course, but she had no choice but to follow Zakir's decision. She did not know that I had issued a new order that no overnight guest is permitted."

"Maria? The woman who is employed as the warden of this shelter? Is she absolutely dependable?"

"Yes. She is almost mechanical when it comes to following my instructions. She is very useful, especially because of her training as a nurse. And I know Tina spoke with no one else. She wouldn't even have seen anybody besides Zakir and Maria. The foyer is situated on this side of the building, far away from the residents. And the guest quarters where she stayed is right above the foyer. Maria told me that she took Tina to her room last night and brought her downstairs this morning. Tina didn't have a chance to even glance at the other wing. And remember, Abdul, that room has an attached bathroom. So where was the need for our guest to go anywhere from there, especially when she was cautioned not to roam around?"

"Then I'll make arrangements to get Maya to my warehouse this afternoon. But what about the rest of the residents, Usman Bhai? After this morning's incident with Maya, do you think this place is safe for preparing future missions?"

"No, it's not. You read my mind very well. Do you think I should transfer quarters closer to your warehouse?"

"Yes. I'm thinking of the building behind my warehouse. It needs a little work because the place has been left empty after I closed that section of my sweatshop."

"That's a great choice, Abdul. That house…" Usman reflected for a moment, smiling happily. "That'll be The Jannah…"

"Jannah? A heavenly place! I like that. The house behind my warehouse shall be The Jannah. I'll get at least one of the rooms there prepared for Maya right away. We can move her there this afternoon, and we can move the other residents in a few days. And don't worry, Usman Bhai. According to your judicious statement, *the end of all means is the beginning*. So you see, they'll never get us."

- 10 -

19 Temple Street • November 11, 2009

Usman observed the young boy sitting in front of him and smiled affectionately, the wrinkles gathering ripples on his bony face. "How have you been, Salman?" he asked, noticing his healthy cheeks and hesitant smile. "How are your lessons going?"

"I am fine, Sahib. I think I've been a very good student. I'm waiting to start my next assignment. When can I?" asked Salman, a little worried about questioning his master.

"Soon, Salman, soon. First, we're moving to a new home. I'm going to send you as an assistant on a small mission after we move. You'll be very proud to do God's work, helping Jamil. Be patient," smiled Usman, admiring the young ward's passion, still unable to believe the transformation in the boy since the day he had arrived at his organization. He had been a very different child then, very different. How long ago it seemed!

A Boy Named Salman • Seloor • January 5, 2009

The market in the heart of Seloor was bursting with life. It was the busiest hour in the morning, and it stayed hectic from sunrise till the tired vendors vacated the booths. Manohar, standing under the awnings of the tea stall, glanced at the activities in the market square. His hawk eyes concealed behind sunglasses and his morose expression hidden behind a bushy mustache, he made it his business to observe a boy, perhaps about twelve or thirteen, scuttling from one end of the market to the other. The boy was always there, but what was he doing in the market, away from school, day after day? Manohar's experienced eyes picked up obvious signals of poverty—the boy's tattered clothes, bare feet, shock of unruly hair, and his grubby face. There was nothing new about poverty, but was this boy an orphan? Was he homeless, or did he come from an impoverished family that simply didn't care about his fate? Manohar decided to launch his research and ran to his master for approval.

The master was finishing his tea when Manohar entered his room.

"What is it?" asked Usman, without taking his eyes off the document he was reading.

"I came to consult you about a potential catch," responded Manohar, hoping for undivided attention. *Where would Usman be*, thought Manohar, *without his employees' dirty, hard work?*

"Go on." Usman's eyes were still fixed on the file.

"I've been observing a boy in the market. Seems to be a good candidate for one of your...our future missions. Would you like me to pursue?"

Usman's cold eyes measured his underling for a few moments, as though the switch from *your* to *our future missions* did not escape his attention. "What about one of MY future missions?"

Manohar, despite his bruised ego, made an effort to speak impassively and described the status of the young boy in the market.

"Can you guess the boy's religion?" asked Usman.

Manohar, attempting to defend his initiative, blurted, "Not yet. I thought his poor circumstances might matter more at this time."

Usman's glance went up to meet his employee's expectant eyes and slid down to his bushy mustache and the deep scar on his cheek. "Manohar, poverty is not a direct ticket to destruction. Haven't you understood that from various assignments?"

"What I mean is...the boy seems to be homeless and extremely poor. Two characteristics that are important, as you told me once?" Manohar insisted defensively.

"I also told you that disillusionment is the primary characteristic, a dominant trait necessary for a candidate. When a human hates mankind, order, and peace, you've spotted a good candidate. When that human's bitter experiences thirst for anarchy, then you've selected a perfect candidate. When that human's blood boils for more blood at the expense of his own bloodshed, then you've bred the ultimate candidate."

"I understand." Manohar stood in front of his stern master, awestruck and wide-eyed. He had always admired his employer's primal, unwavering focus, and he knew that no man was a better hunter.

"Go see if that boy is pliable and if your assessment is correct. I'll send Yusuf for the final evaluation. Now go on." Usman returned his attention to the file.

Yusuf! Manohar concealed his surly expression until he left the room and sighed in frustration after shutting the door. He decided to ignore his own inferiority and marched out of 19 Temple Street, determined to look good in his master's eyes.

When Manohar returned to the tea stall the next day to start the groundwork, he was not alone.

"The time is ripe to initiate the hook. Don't you think, Imran?" Kumar asked his associate, who looked very working class in a crinkled pair of khaki pants and a wrinkled, short-sleeved green shirt. His raven, straight, greasy hair was combed carelessly away from his tawny forehead.

"Yes." Imran's trained eyes followed the boy's every move.

It was very early in the morning. The boy went gingerly to the public water fountain in the middle of a mossy slab of cement, throwing furtive glances to his right and left, and hurriedly got a drink of water. Imran walked towards the boy and smiled kindly.

"It's not the same, is it?" Imran asked the boy. "Water can never replace a cup of tea."

The scraggy child, about to move away quickly, was arrested by the kindness in the man's voice.

"Come, let's have a cup of tea," invited Imran, waiting for the boy.

"I can't. Not yet." The boy avoided Imran's eyes.

"Why not?"

"I don't have any money, not yet...for today," replied the boy, a little shamefaced.

"Don't worry. I can get you a cup of tea," Imran insisted, when the child stood rooted to the mossy platform. "We working-class people must take care of each other. Come on. Don't be shy," he continued, trying to tap on the communal bonding among lesser children of God.

The boy took a long look at the man, at the strand of raven hair touching his smiling eyes, and quietly followed him into the tea stall. This was new to him, very new. No eye stared at the boy. And the eyes belonged to the usual customers—a few bus conductors, lorry drivers, a pimp, and a couple of vegetable vendors. The man got the boy a steaming cup of tea and a big piece of bun, and the bun was an unexpected bonus! The boy sat on the edge of an old bench and ate hurriedly while taking quick gulps of the tea. Although nobody intimidated him, he felt strange sitting inside the stall. He was not used to this luxury. Even when he could buy a scrap of bread and half a cup of tea, he usually sat on the bench outside the stall. He just didn't belong inside.

"Thank you." The boy's shy eyes would not meet the man's.

"That's all right." Imran followed the boy out of the tea stall. "So what did you mean when you said you didn't have money for tea today? Did you forget the money at home?"

"No. I haven't made any money today."

"Oh? Do you have a job?"

"No, I'd like to have one, but..." the boy opened a shabby, yellow cloth bag that was home to a small tub of shoe polish, a piece of dirty rag, and a sponge. The bag also contained a puny slab of soap, a greasy comb, a pair of threadbare khaki pants, and a frayed shirt that was several sizes bigger for the boy's lean frame. "But I just polish shoes."

"Oh," sighed Imran. "That can't get you much."

"It doesn't. Polishing a couple of pairs of shoes gets me a cup of tea. Polishing a few can get me a cup of tea and a piece of bun. Sometimes I carry heavy parcels to rich people's cars. Then, I can really get a meal."

"When do you go home?" asked Imran, smiling warmly at the destitute child.

And the child liked the smile that held something he had not felt in a while—a long-forgotten caress, a touch of affection—and he cherished it for a few moments. "I don't go home," the boy responded softly, looking away. He wouldn't look at the man's face because he didn't want to cry. And there were unshed tears sloshing within his small frame, trying to break loose. "I don't have a home."

"Oh...then where do you sleep?"

"I sleep just about anywhere—under that shade when it rains a lot," he said, pointing at the awnings of Sri pharmacy, "under that big tree when it doesn't rain, and in dark alleys and on a bench in the railway station to avoid policemen."

"Do you get into trouble with the police?" asked Imran, smiling indulgently.

"No, but a policeman beat me because I was taking a leak in the corner of that street. Where else am I supposed to take a leak when I don't have a home?" asked the boy, an unknown anger creeping into his young, sore mind.

"It must have hurt so much. You're just a child. How can that policeman treat you like that?"

"He was cruel," hissed Salman, his dormant frustration and helplessness gathering to the surface like an unexpected, rapid storm. He lifted his shirt a few inches to exhibit the purple bruise on his ribs.

"Look, look how the policeman beat me."

"This society stinks, I tell you. And the policemen are heartless monsters. Who is there to protect you?" asked Imran, defending the boy's human rights. "Who is there to question that horrible policeman?" continued Imran, looking equally frustrated.

"There is nobody."

"What's your name?"

"Salman. I've to go," said the boy, still lingering. "Soon the customers will arrive. It rained last night, and the roads will be dirty. I think more men will want their shoes polished today."

Imran walked away, but he continued to observe the boy through the window of a corner store.

"Looks like your first meeting went well, Imran?" asked Manohar, standing by him.

"Yes. His name is Salman, and..." Imran told his associate whatever he needed to know.

"Let's meet here at the same time tomorrow. See you soon." Manohar began to walk towards a waiting taxi.

"But don't let him notice you, Manohar. I'll buy him tea a couple more times. I want him to get very familiar with me, but you stay out of his sight."

Manohar and Imran observed Salman for over a week. The boy had a quick wash by the public water fountain before sunrise. It had to be an early wash because women started lining up with their pails for water to cook and to bathe. On the seventh day, Manohar waited with Imran to observe the young boy, but he was nowhere to be seen. Salman finally appeared after the sun was up, squeezing his eyes and smoothing his disheveled hair.

"Salman must have overslept," hissed Manohar, impatiently pulling smoke from his cigarette.

"What are you doing, you rat?" one of the women shouted, throwing her pail at Salman when he reached for some water. "Do you know you've to pay money to stand in line here? I'll call the police if you touch the tap again with your filthy hands."

Manohar watched the child's humiliation and helplessness from the tea stall. "A poor boy. A helpless child. It's time to organize the hook, Imran," he whispered, exchanging a very satisfactory smile with his associate.

A week later, Imran spotted Salman under the awnings of the pharmacy. It had rained a lot during the previous night.

"How have you been, Salman?" asked Imran, approaching the boy. "Come, let's have some tea and nashta."

Salman smiled when he recognized the kind man. "Nashta?" he asked, trying not to drool. He had not eaten a proper breakfast since his mother died.

"Come on, Salman, don't be shy. You know me quite well by now."

Imran ordered an omelet and bread for Salman and settled him at one of the tables in the back. Salman started to eat ravenously when he realized that he had not thanked the generous man properly. He looked for him, but he was not there. Where was he? Wasn't he hungry? Didn't he need some nashta?

Manohar, standing across the tea stall, waved and nodded his head. Promptly at the cue, a couple of uniformed policemen walked into the tea stall. As Salman was about to leave, one of them took hold of his collar.

"Hey, what are you doing here?" asked the policeman.

Salman looked at the officer who was towering over his puny frame. What was he supposed to say? And why shouldn't he be there?

"Answer me. What are you doing here?" roared the policeman's voice.

"Having a cup of tea," Salman trembled. He didn't like this. He didn't like this at all.

"What's your name?"

"My name is S… Salman."

The other policeman's red-shot eyes rested on Salman's frightened expression. "Empty your pockets, and what do you have in that bag?" he screamed.

Salman gathered his dirty, yellow bag to his chest and froze.

"I asked you to empty your pockets," barked the policeman.

Salman's terrified eyes flew from one end of the stall to the other end, frantically searching for the kind man who had bought him tea and bread and omelet. Where did he go? Why did he disappear?

While the first policeman took the bag away from the wailing boy's clutch, the other emptied his pockets. The left was empty. The right had half a beedi and a small plastic bag containing a whitish powder.

"Who gave you this?" asked the second policeman, dangling the plastic bag of white powder in front of Salman's face, while the other held the boy by his crumpled collar. "And already smoking beedi at your young age?"

"I don't know what you are talking about," replied Salman, fear invading his usually vacant eyes. "I've never seen that before, and I've never smoked."

"Really? Then how did this plastic bag get inside your pocket?"

"I don't know. I really don't know. Please let me go," cried Salman.

The first policeman struck Salman violently across his cheek. When he reeled to the floor, a few heads turned in his direction.

"This is the last thing I need for my business, especially first thing in the morning," muttered the owner of the tea stall. "I hope the policemen haul the boy out of here quickly."

And the policemen did haul the boy away, first out of the crowded stall, then into a jeep. Manohar, watching the human indignity from a distance, smiled contentedly at Imran. He knew Salman would be finally hauled into an airless, bleak room at the police station.

"Looks like the hook is secure," whispered Imran, his eyes away from

Manohar. "Now make plans to seize the prey."

Town Prison, Seloor • January 14, 2009

Salman looked at the four walls—dirty, smelly, faded walls. He had not eaten in two days; his shorts were damp from urine, which he couldn't control when one of the policemen mercilessly punched him in his stomach. A long time ago, his mother had told him about hell; a place that pulled in liars, thieves, and sinners. That jail must be a pitiless, violent hell. He never told a lie, never stole, never hurt a fly. Why was he sent to hell?

A bulky policeman came into the room after whispering something to the guards outside the door. "Salman, you look terrible. You'll starve to death if you don't tell me where you got that drug. Who gave it to you?"

Salman, while suspended from the ceiling like a butchered goat, tried to breathe. What could he say? His muscles were numb, and he felt a different pain stabbing at his heart. He didn't know how that drug came into his pocket. What tale could he spin? What would the police believe?

"I don't know," Salman whispered in a feeble voice, his innocent, bleeding humanity gaping at an impassive world. "I don't know. Please believe me."

"You must be thirsty. Here, have a drink of water." The policeman picked up a dented metal pitcher and stared at the boy's gaunt face. The young prisoner's empty eyes and jaundiced skin stared back at him. "You parasite, you would like some water, won't you?" he asked, tossing the pitcher at Salman. "I'll make you drink from the toilet again. You, mother f…" More obscenities catapulted from his foul mouth.

Salman tasted the blood trickling down his nose from his forehead. The heavy pitcher had made a wicked gash on his already bruised skin, but he didn't feel much pain. His semiconscious state wouldn't allow him to feel the raw pain.

The policeman's attention shifted from Salman's face to the creaking door as it opened.

"So, this is how you treat a young prisoner?" asked a man's voice. "He is just a child. Your superiors and mine will hear about this."

Salman's eyes tried to focus through the streaks of blood and water dripping from his face. A man was standing at the open door, but he was not in a khaki uniform. When Salman closed his eyes and opened them again, he noticed that the visitor was dressed in a suit and a tie. He had a briefcase in one hand and a piece of paper in the other, and his eyes were flitting back and forth from Salman to the policeman.

"Who the hell are you?" shouted the policeman. He turned to the guards outside the room. "And what the hell are you idiots doing? Who gave you permission to let this man inside this room?"

"Sir, he has a pass," replied one of the guards, nervously glancing at the piece of paper the visitor was brandishing.

"Let me see it." The policeman snatched the paper from the visitor and glanced at it irritably. "Come here," he shouted at one of the guards. "Unhook the boy and get him to rest on the cot. Give him some food, but not too much. Start with just a little gruel." The policeman soon walked out of the cell.

The visitor, after a long look at the boy, followed him.

Salman closed his eyes in relief as the guard shut the door.

"Hey, Manohar, new suit and tie? You look like a bloody executive. Not bad," laughed the policeman, once he reached his office. He sat on the chair behind his desk and asked the visitor to take a seat.

"Well, is it convincing, Ravi?" asked Manohar, sitting on the chair opposite to the policeman.

"Oh, it's very convincing," laughed Inspector Ravi, his eyes traveling from the visitor's scar on his right cheek to his thick mustache that effortlessly concealed his smile.

"I see you've worked well on the boy. Is he ready to be rescued from your grip?"

"Of course. I scared the shit out of him. Now he needs some tender love and care. I'm sure your organization will take care of that."

"Yes, we will." Manohar pushed a packet across the desk, and Inspector Ravi grabbed it with greedy eyes and eager hands.

"Your boss is generous, whoever he is," lingered Ravi, hoping to discover the identity of the individual who paid him generously during various hunts.

Manohar stared at the man, at his meticulously groomed mustache and chubby cheeks. "Yes, my boss is generous."

"He must be a rich man." Ravi hopefully looked at Manohar for that one name.

"Ravi, no amount of money and no incentive on earth would encourage me to reveal my employer's name," hissed Manohar, a menacing smile lacing his tone. Whichever part of the world he went to, Usman would have him killed. "See you soon, Ravi, when we need you for another assignment. I'll return in a few hours to take Salman away from here."

"I'll look forward to hearing from you." Ravi smiled courteously, although he did not relish his visitor's haughty tone. *Manohar ought to realize that he was speaking to an officer of law*, thought Ravi, bitterly regretting his own lack of authority in front of the mercenary. But he relished the money Manohar brought to him from time to time. He needed all the help to tackle his mortgage payment.

19 Temple Street, Seloor

When Salman woke up, he was no longer suspended from the ceiling. He was on a cot in a strange room, surrounded by a few men. A large woman applied some ointment on his bruises and smiled compassionately. Was he in a hospital? He wanted to get up and run, but his body felt so heavy, and every inch of him hurt. When he was again debating if he should stay or run, his glance fell on the kind man who had authoritatively questioned the policeman's cruelty.

"I see you're all right, Salman," smiled the man. "You're safe now. Don't worry."

"Who are you, and…where am I?" whispered Salman, still quite afraid. He could not open his mouth wide enough to speak clearly.

"I am Manohar. This is our leader, Usman Sahib," he explained, smiling at his master who was standing a few feet away from the cot.

Salman's wary glance alternated between Manohar and the old man, who was wearing a white tagiyah on his head.

"This is an organization that fights for human justice. You're young, and you're very tired," smiled Manohar. "You won't understand much in your condition, but we're here to help helpless children like you. That's why I rescued you from that villain, that policeman."

"How did you find me?" asked Salman, a different fear stirring his senses. He could not believe that he was out of that hell. His face contorted in pain when his swollen lips and distended jaw reminded him of the recent horror.

"Oh, remember that kind man, Imran, who bought you tea and nashta? Those policemen wanted to get him for some other incident. They made you pay for Imran's mistake. Isn't he such a kind man?" asked Manohar. "He feels bad for your suffering."

"Where is Imran Bhai?" asked Salman, gratefully thinking about the kind man who had touched his heart with the affection of a brother.

"He's all right. We saved him, and he is resting in his house. Don't worry," assured Manohar, glancing at Maria. "This lady is a nurse, and she is going to give you an injection to relieve you from pain."

"Here, child, have some milk," Usman smiled, gently bringing a glass of milk to the boy's lips.

Milk! Salman had forgotten the taste of milk. He savored it very slowly. He had to take a mere sip very leisurely because his bruised lips wouldn't allow him to drink the milk fast. As Salman drifted into sleep, he thought of heaven, his father's heaven. This must be heaven, where kind people lived, where there was no malice, no deceit, and no hunger.

Manohar whistled softly as he walked out of the room and waited respectfully for his master to follow him soon.

"That boy, I think, is a good catch," said Usman.

"Salman was an easy prey," acknowledged Manohar, proud about scoring a winning point.

"He might have been an easy prey, but I want to assess the boy's reaction to his new surroundings in a week."

"So soon?" asked Manohar, feeling his glow of victory fading a little.

"Yes, soon. It is essential to gauge a victim's durability as much as the same victim's initial potential." Usman's tone did not conceal his derision as he tried to review the fundamentals of human trafficking with his irritating employee. "Remember that."

Usman went past the kitchen and saw a group of people scattered in the small dining area. He picked up a tray by the grimy sink and walked into a musty room. When he shut the door, the thin frame of a boy, sitting on a metal chair, didn't stir. Either the boy didn't hear his soft steps, or he didn't care.

"How are you, Salman?" asked Usman. "I can't believe it's been a week since you came here."

Salman, still staring at the window, didn't respond.

"You do remember me, don't you? We met last week when you arrived here after Manohar rescued you from those horrible policemen."

Salman was still silent.

Usman smiled patiently. "We're here to help, you know. But we can't help unless you want to be helped." He placed the tray on a dented stool and walked to the other window. He studied the boy's face—an ordinary face that displayed a tuft of unruly hair, almost fleshless cheeks, and grubby skin. But those eyes were hunting for something, someone, with the glint of a wild animal's. Those eyes disturbed him, and he was not a man who was easily disturbed.

"I've brought some food for you. You'll never go hungry here. Come on, eat something," encouraged Usman, pulling the stool closer to Salman.

Salman's glance jumped from the tray—with a mound of steamed rice, lentils, and potato—to Usman, and returned to the tray.

"Son, no need to be shy. We're all a big family here. Come on, eat."

Salman's glance moved to his host's bony face, gray beard, thin frame, the white tagiyah covering his head, and settled on his soft eyes and gentle smile. He tentatively took a bite, suspiciously staring at the tray. But when Usman turned his face away, pretending to look at the paddy fields beyond the window, he wiped the tray to the last morsel.

"Salman…you have a good, solid, Islamic name. Get some rest. We'll have a talk in the evening. All right?" asked Usman, moving towards the door. He didn't bother to draw the latch like he did with some other new arrivals. The old man was sure that the young boy would stay. The child's eyes and his appetite said it all. Besides, why would the boy wish to return to the market square, with no roof over his head, when he was protected and cared for at 19 Temple Street?

When Usman knocked and entered the room, Salman was staring at the star-filled skies through the window. The boy looked a lot better than he did a week ago, although his jaw still appeared a little swollen. And his bruises looked less wicked, shifting from a deep purplish hue to a dull brownish tinge. But his smile-less face was still vacant of any emotion.

"Salman, why don't you walk with me to the balcony and get some fresh air?" asked Usman, when the boy turned his attention away from the window. When Salman offered no response and merely stared at the old man's white cloth cap and silver beard, Usman extended his hand, smiling kindly. "Son, let's go."

Salman followed Usman, but he did not hold the old man's hand. And the master retracted his hand imperceptibly, although a little disappointedly, and threw open the door to the balcony. It was a pleasant night, with just a hint of humidity hanging from the passing clouds. As the wide branches of the coconut trees swayed gracefully, the wind tunelessly sighed over the cascading hills. The meager frame of the boy stood unsurely next to the wiry, tall figure of the elderly man, and a discordant, unknown beat began to stir the boy's consciousness.

"Have you been resting well, Salman?" asked Usman, leaning on the iron railing, looking at the distant hills.

"Yes, Sahib." Salman stared nervously at the now colorless paddy fields.

"Son, we want you to be healthy," sighed Usman, still searching for something through the distant hills.

"Yes," muttered Salman, grateful, bashful, and conscious of his stroke of good luck. "Thank you for saving me. I mean..."

"I know, I know. You were fortunate. Manohar spotted you from a distance when the police started to harass you near the tea stall. I've trained my men to help helpless young souls like you. Somebody must, you know. What's the point in praying to Allah if we cannot do a good deed whenever we can?"

"That policeman... All policemen are villains. Aren't they?"

"Most of them are! And they hate our kind. That's the sad part."

"Why?" asked Salman, looking up at his benefactor's face. He noticed a trace of gentleness in the wrinkled face that he thought was dead in mankind.

"Because of our religion and what we struggle to uphold," sighed Usman, a strong tinge of sadness covering his face.

"But that's not right."

"Here, have a seat." Usman invited the boy to sit on the bench.

Salman sat nervously on the edge and respectfully made room for his elderly friend to sit by him.

"What were you saying?" asked Usman, thoroughly conscious of what Salman said a minute ago. But he was anxious about having the boy's anxiety pulsing towards the impending danger to Islam.

"What's wrong with our religion? Why should that policeman care?" asked Salman.

"What's wrong with our religion?" repeated Usman, a resolute nerve twitching on his temple. "What's wrong with Islam? Nothing. Nothing. They do not want us to do well and be successful." Usman looked directly at Salman. "They wouldn't let people like you—unprotected, vulnerable, and helpless—survive in this rotten world."

"I hate that policeman!" Salman barked, his young eyes shining in anger. "I hate all of them."

"I understand. That policeman, his society, all of them…they're nasty scoundrels. What harm did you do? You were just trying to live. LIVE! And they wouldn't let you. That's what makes me angry, so ANGRY!" Usman shouted, grinding his teeth.

"Then what should I do about it?"

"Indeed! What can YOU do about it?" Usman asked, the thrill of the kill clinging to his breath.

"I want to do something. I must. Somebody has to."

"I'm trying to establish our rights with the help of a few loyal assistants. Our basic rights are at risk, Salman." Usman turned his face away from the boy, quite pleased with the way the wind was blowing. He had a feeling that Salman was attached to his tempting leash.

"Thank you, Sahib, for helping poor people like me," Salman whispered gratefully, smoothing his disheveled hair with his unkempt fingers. "Who are your assistants?"

Usman did not respond instantly. Although Salman was a puppet in his hands, he wished to tread gently, carefully. "Manohar is one. You know, he is the man who spotted you while you were in distress. Kumar is another. But they're just employees. Imran... he is devoted to our cause. And so are Salim, Amjad. You'll meet all the devotees soon. They'll be your brothers, sisters, uncles, and aunts. But my best, my most devoted assistant is Yusuf. I must add...my affectionate assistant." Usman paused before placing his most valuable card on the table. "You remind me of Yusuf, Salman. He came to me when he was your age. He was almost dead." Usman shuddered at the thought.

"Dead!" Salman shouted in horror. "Then some of the victims simply die in their hands!"

"That's a sad truth. It's unbelievable but happens all the time."

"I want to be like Yusuf Bhai!" Salman exclaimed passionately. "I want to help. I want to kill that policeman."

Usman gasped in disbelief and held the boy's hand kindly. And the boy did not cringe at the touch.

"Slow down, slow down, my child." Usman laughed gently. "I do see Yusuf in you. From the moment I saw you, I knew Allah sent you to me. But I cannot endanger your life, you know. Just because my organization saved you, it doesn't mean that you owe us anything in return."

"If you believe Allah sent me to you, why can't you accept me as your assistant?"

"I can. I want to. But I need to be convinced that it is the right path for you. The point is I want to serve Allah, and I want all of my assistants to serve Allah. We can talk more about it later," suggested Usman, looking at Salman's eyes in the moonlight. He was struck by the ardor and commitment in those intense eyes. The boy was so young. Yet he was so passionate. Yes, he was another Yusuf.

"What can I do to make you believe me?" asked Salman. "I want to serve Allah, with you and your other assistants. Please accept me, Sahib, please. I'll give my life for you. I'll give my life for your cause."

"Our cause. Son, it is our cause!" Usman pronounced every syllable delightedly. "Now I truly believe Allah sent you in my path. You have to first recover from the way you were treated by the police, so shockingly, so cruelly. Shall we talk soon when you're healthy again?"

"Are you going to ask me to leave your home?" asked Salman, a new fear occupying his twelve-year-old, telltale eyes.

"Ask you to leave this home?" Usman asked incredulously, kindly pressing the boy's hand. "No, no, I don't work like that. I opened my doors to let you in, and you're in until YOU decide to leave. And this is your home as long as you want to treat it that way. All right? Son, you can trust me."

"I trust you, Sahib. I trust you like I would trust my ammi and abba." Salman spoke passionately, happily clinging to his new family, his new life.

I trust you like I would trust my ammi and abba. The boy's mother, father—he must tap on that information soon and seek a permanent place in Salman's trusting heart. "I'm so grateful you feel this way," Usman smiled, glancing at the quickly gathering clouds covering the charcoal canvas of twinkling stars. "Looks like it's going to rain again. Come, let's go inside."

Salman readily took Usman's extended hand, and the pair quietly exited the balcony.

- 11-

19 Temple Street, Seloor • November 17, 2009

When Manohar knocked on Usman's door, Yusuf stepped out of the room. Sayeed followed him in the next second.

"Usman Sahib doesn't want to be disturbed," cautioned Yusuf, shutting the door.

"But I've to see him," insisted Manohar, considerably affronted. "He would like to know that I have news about a candidate. He asked me to see him today."

"Stop nagging. He is expecting you, but don't go in yet. He is in a meeting with Abdullah Sahib and Zakir. He'll call for you soon. Wait here."

Manohar obeyed Yusuf's order and began to wait patiently outside his master's door.

Inside the room, Abdullah was seated on an easy chair close to the window, with a cigar in his hand, his bulky form occupying the corner like a giant statue. Usman was sitting behind his vast desk, his gnarled hand thoughtfully stroking his silver beard. Zakir stood in front of his master, his matted, unkempt hair skirting his blotched, perspiring face. His heavy spectacles were beginning to turn foggy with his rapidly increasing perspiration.

"Sit down, Zakir," said Usman, with his eyes on a document in front of him.

Zakir sat down promptly, his hands trembling, his mouth turning dry, his eyes locked on the paper in front of his master.

"The plan is complete, Zakir. Yusuf and Sayeed will go with you. Are you ready?" asked Usman, closing the file.

"Yes, Sahib, I'm ready," responded the young man, steadying his voice. His eyes traveled to Abdullah who was still sitting in the corner like a giant statue. The only sign of life from that end was the smoke steadily emitting from his lungs. Zakir nervously transferred his gaze to Usman, wondering how long he must sit there.

"You've been a good servant of Allah, Zakir," Usman continued. "You've tried to serve well as the manager here. You made some mistakes in the past for which I've forgiven you. Unfortunately, you made a tremendous mistake when you let a stranger stay here overnight, but you can remedy that by serving like only a few can."

"Yes, Sahib. I'm glad…I'm glad to serve." Zakir did not know where to look. He knew that his tremendous mistake had turned into an unforgivable mistake because the stranger had accidentally seen Maya.

"Glad?" asked Usman.

Zakir's heart thudded in fright. Did he mention something he shouldn't have?

"Glad?" Usman asked again. "You mean...privileged?"

"Yes, yes, Sahib. That's exactly what I mean."

Usman smiled, and Zakir's pulse eased a bit.

"Do you have a last wish, Zakir? Is there anything we can do for you?" asked Usman. His glance momentarily traveled to Abdullah before settling on his employee.

"No, Sahib," muttered Zakir, taking a deep breath. "Actually, there is…"

"What is it?" asked Usman, sitting straight. His deep-set eyes compellingly locked with the young man's.

Zakir could hardly breathe. How in the world was he supposed to speak? But a few random words clawed their way out of his frightened mind. "Sahib, I'm thinking of my mother, my sister. I'm so worried about them."

"And?"

Zakir could tell nothing from Usman's tone. It held no anger, no threat, nothing. "I want to…to be sure they're taken care of…that they'll be safe." Zakir's speech came in spurts, but his hands surprisingly did not tremble anymore. In fact, his body was incapable of feeling anything.

"But you know they'll be taken care of, Zakir." Usman leaned back on his chair, his hawk eyes resting on his employee's anxious face. "Didn't we already discuss that? You doubt my words?"

"Oh, of course not, Sahib. No, no." Zakir stumbled on his thoughts.

"We don't need every family member for our crucial missions, if that's what you're worrying about. You've, well, you're going to do your ultimate duty, and I'll make sure your mother and sister are provided for. No job gets accomplished without a payment, and you're going to earn your payment tomorrow."

"Shukriya, Sahib." Zakir brought his hands together and thanked his master.

"Your sister's nikah will not be forgotten. She'll get married just like your mother wishes. Rest assured."

"I am so thankful, Sahib." Zakir took a deep breath. Actually, he had no reasons to doubt his master's words. There had been other crucial missions in the past. And invariably, the missionary's family was looked after. At this comforting thought, he tried to breathe normally.

"You look relieved, even relaxed. Ready?" asked Usman, with a slight smile touching his thin, parched lips.

"Yes, Sahib." Zakir tried to smile.

"Inshallah," praised Usman, standing up, his hands and his face facing heaven.

Zakir stood up and repeated, "Inshallah."

The door opened in the next minute, and Zakir walked out of the room.

"Let's go, brother," said Yusuf, at the head of the stairs.

Manohar watched as Zakir walked down the stairs with Sayeed and Yusuf and breathlessly realized that he was seeing him, his knotted hair, and his glazed spectacles for the last time. He went to the window on the landing and continued to watch as the group got into a green van.

Chennai • November 18, 2009

The van rolled noisily on the highway and reached Chennai within the next seven hours after just a couple of interruptions. When the designated site was checked for clearance, the driver moved to the flyover off Mount Avenue through mid-morning traffic and went past the Consulate General's office and skipped the first six side streets. Then he turned right on Breams Road and parked the van in front of Divan pharmacy.

"You're ready, Zakir?" asked Yusuf, keeping his eyes on the pedestrians and the sprinkle of tiny corner stores along the road. The humid heart of the city perspired miserably. "Remember, you're here to fulfill your ultimate duty."

"Yes," murmured Zakir, sandwiched in the back between Yusuf and Sayeed, the two cardinal gatekeepers of crucial missions. His hands did not tremble as he pulled down his thick shirt that cleverly concealed the vest strapped to his chest. Then, with the slightest tremor of anxiety, he checked the time on his watch. It was 10:22. Eight more minutes.

"Zakir," began Sayeed, looking deeply into his eyes. "I know we can count on your loyalty. But...in case you have second thoughts, let us know now. I hope you don't lose heart when the time is right."

"I won't lose heart," promised Zakir. How could his heart lean on an erroneous decision? Sayeed and Yusuf knew where his mother and sister lived and under what indigent conditions they lived. And what would happen to them, especially his young sister, if he lost heart at the last minute? And entertain second thoughts? He could not afford second thoughts. If he did, he would be back in Usman's room as soon as Sayeed and Yusuf transported him to Seloor. And Zakir knew that would be a fate worse than executing his ultimate duty. "I'm ready." He shoved his cell phone into his shirt pocket.

"And don't worry, Zakir. Somebody will keep an eye on you to make sure you don't stumble on an unforeseen obstacle," assured Yusuf.

Zakir knew what unforeseen obstacle Yusuf was thinking of. Where could he run now? His listless eyes went up and down the dusty road. And even if he could run somewhere, what plight would await his mother and sister? No. No. He could not run. He would not run.

The driver turned on the ignition and drove slowly down Breams Road. At the corner of Breams and R.H. Road, he stopped briefly near Amir's Sweets, and the driver exchanged a glance with Amir who was standing under the dust-coated awnings. Zakir quickly got down with a pounding heart. Soon, the van went past R.H. Road and merged into traffic going towards Mason Colony.

10:26. Zakir waited on the sidewalk and looked at the pedestrians scampering up and down the wide avenue. He saw a small boutique with shimmering fabrics—the dainty garments he would never buy for his sister. When he saw a middle-aged woman walking speedily on the other side of the avenue with her head covered in a black hijab, thoughts of his mother touched his aching heart like a forlorn funeral song.

10:28. Zakir began to cross the street and went up another few yards. An assortment of shops and boutiques and men and women floated in front of his limited vision. Then sporadic memories of his dead father, his smiling mother, and his dear sister painfully invaded his thirty-year-old, hollow mind.

10:30. Zakir silently recited *In the name of Allah, the most beneficent, the most merciful* and picked up his cell phone. With a shaking hand and a quivering pulse, he pressed the switch. Then his world disappeared behind a curtain of acrid smoke and leaping flames.

- 12 -

Chennai • November 25, 2009

Tina followed Dr. Shaker out of Kamaraj Terminal in Chennai, staring at the quickly gathering crowd outside the airport, and thought the city never took a break. Although adventurous, she still could not get used to the mere volume of heads moving about at any hour of the day. And the stark anxiety the gathering crowd caused in her foreign mind was still fresh. While she waited on the sidewalk, staring at a stray dog that was running in hot pursuit of a leftover meal in the hands of a beggar, another wiry dog decided to join the chase, and Tina moved away quickly to avoid its path. With a childish curiosity, she tried to absorb everything in that smorgasbord land, where modern technologies imperceptibly seeped in while grounded traditions stubbornly lingered. When Shaker went to the Airport Taxi Service, she skeptically looked at the crowd exiting the airport, but the taxi was promptly waiting at the exit. Despite the crowd and general hubbub, some routines went on like well-oiled machines.

"Sir, where do you want to go?" asked the driver, curiously gawking at Tina's slightly foreign appearance, her creamy complexion, her hazel brown eyes.

Shaker asked the driver to go to Narula Estate in Mason Colony and opened the door for Tina. A flabby man, who was standing right behind Shaker, stepped into a jaded taxi and asked the driver to go in the direction of Narula Estate in Mason Colony.

Tina picked up her screaming cell phone. "Yes, Aunt Rita? We just arrived. Oh, I'll tell him that. Thanks." She turned towards Shaker. "Aunt Rita and Uncle Theo want you to have lunch with us. They insist. You're free, I hope?"

"Yes, thanks. I'm always free for a free lunch," he laughed. "In fact, I wanted to talk to Mr. Edwin about a case I've been working on."

"Talk to my uncle? About which case, if I may ask?"

"Of course, you may. Most segments of the case are classified, which I'm not aware of. But I've been allowed to visit the inmate in prison. He was captured after the last explosion near Hyderabad."

The taxi struggled to get out of the perimeters of the terminal and ambled towards Rajaji Extension.

"Is Chennai always so hot?" asked Tina, wishing she insisted on having an air-conditioned taxi.

"Sorry, Madam, I forgot," apologized the driver, switching on the small fan clamped to the side panel.

"Yes, Chennai is always hot. You're lucky this is the end of November. Try coming here from March through June. You could get slow-cooked," smiled her companion.

"Well, that's probably why Uncle Theo and Aunt Rita asked me to work here in November and December." Tina looked wonderingly at the tiny fan whistling a thin strand of cool air. "Shaker, do you think the authorities would let you take me with you when you go to the prison to question the inmate?"

"I don't see why not. You're working with me now. I'll be glad to take you."

"Thanks. I've never visited a prison before. The steps we gradually take…"

"True. We need to seek whatever means it takes to find an end to this mindless violence!"

"Whatever means it takes? But what still worries me is that *the end of all means is the beginning*."

"Is that still bothering you? I know it can be a mind-boggling declaration, if you let it get to you. Don't let it."

"I know. I've to somehow bury that. I remind myself many times that the maddening statement has sprouted from lies." Tina's insecure mind made a swift visit to Dr. Katz's office, securely hiding behind tall pine trees in Pennsylvania, and she was glad to remember his comforting words. "Where is the truth in violence?"

"What are you doing?" Shaker asked the driver, when he bypassed the shorter route and took an unusual detour.

"Sir, Breams Road is closed at this stretch. I've to go through Rajaji Road," replied the driver, maneuvering his vehicle around narrow lanes.

"Is that where it happened?" asked Tina, looking at the roadwork and at the mountain of debris in the distance.

"Yes, that's where there was an explosion last week," confirmed Shaker, looking intensely at her worried expression. "This has been just too much for you, Tina. Hasn't it?" he asked, gently taking her hand in his.

Tina wiped her forehead with her other shaking hand. "Yes," she stammered. "I seem to be chasing explosions—first in October, and now, just a few weeks later. Sometimes I can't sleep at night wondering how dark a radical's mind is—the corrupt nature that can effortlessly destroy lives."

"Yes. How dark is such a mind? Something that we can only try to understand, if at all we can. By the way, I started to read Solzhenitsyn."

"Really?" asked Tina, happy that he had taken her obsession to heart.

"Well, I first read his essay on Nobel Lecture. 'One word of truth outweighs the world!' Quite compelling, actually." He turned the fan towards Tina's face and asked, "When are you returning to Pittsburgh?"

"End of December."

The traffic thinned to make room for a vista of tall palm trees and cultivated gardens. As the salt-coated air seeped into the car through the open windows, Tina looked at the distant waves and the bleached shores, getting closer and closer, as the taxi wound its way down the newly paved, wide avenue.

"So soon?" Shaker asked, looking directly at her.

"Sir, what's the door number?" interrupted the driver.

Shaker turned to Tina and she said, "45 Villa Circle. It should be coming soon, on the left." She looked searchingly at her mentor, at his sharp features, at the creases on his wide forehead. He had a bad habit of asking a direct question when she least expected it. "I want to be with my parents for New Year. Why? Do you think my work would be incomplete?"

"Incomplete? No, no. I thought…I thought you might want to hang around a little longer, Tina. See a bit of the country. You told me you've seen so little of it!"

"Well, I'm going to come again next year for a vacation. At least, I hope so. When are you going back?"

"I'm not."

"You're not? Don't you want to go back to Boston?"

"No. Why?"

Why? She didn't know why. "How long have you been in India?"

"I've been here off and on, but this time I've stayed for almost three months. It's the longest I've spent here."

"Really? Why?" she asked. Direct question was not just his prerogative.

"I don't know. I would like to think *why not* rather than *why*. I've been reevaluating the priorities in my life, and something is lacking, something that slips away as I grope for it. And I'm determined to find it."

She was dying to know what was lacking in his life. "And you can't find that in Boston?" asked Tina, trying not to sound curious.

"Why shouldn't I find it here?"

"What about your home, your family?"

"My parents don't live in one place, now that they've retired. Remember, they were both professors? They're living in Crete for a few months."

"Really?" Tina was surprised at the unexpected response. "That's what I would like to do when I retire. See the world. But what about your job back home?"

"I need to get a license to work here on a long-term basis. And I'll have my writing done from anywhere. You see, I'm primarily a consultant, and I travel frequently. I'm not going to quit Boston altogether. I just want to spend some extended time here. Anyway, home is what you make of it, Tina. To me, it's a state of mind."

"To you, everything is a state of mind." Tina laughed. "Aren't you a lucky world traveler?" She thought, with gratitude, how lucky she was to get his professional advice. "I'm glad you took me in when Dr. Augustine had to back off due to his illness."

"It's Dr. Augustine's loss, and I think he would've made a better mentor. So you think I'm lucky?" he asked, again locking his eyes with hers. "Oh, you're probably jealous of the miles I collect for a free ticket?" he continued, when Tina looked slightly embarrassed.

The driver turned the taxi towards Villa Circle and stopped in front of a bougainvillea-covered gate. Rita looked out of the window from the drawing room and waved. She was at the gate in the next few minutes.

"Dr. Shaker, how nice to see you!" Rita extended her hand to him after embracing her niece affectionately.

"I brought your niece back to you safely," smiled Shaker, shaking hands with Tina's slim, middle-aged aunt, and the niece rolled her eyes exasperatedly as she took her backpack from the driver.

"Come inside and have lunch with us," invited Rita, short of dragging Shaker through the gate, while the driver brought the suitcases to the verandah.

As the group went into the house, the jaded taxi that had been following the other vehicle from the airport rattled to a stop a few feet away from the bougainvillea-covered gate. The flabby man, sitting inside the taxi, called Naim's Tailoring, and the message was relayed instantly to Usman at his new headquarters behind Eastern Exports near Seloor.

"Please have a seat, Dr. Shaker. My husband is in the study, buried in phone calls as usual. What can I get you to drink? Beer? Juice?" asked Rita.

"Cold beer sounds good. Thanks." Shaker sat down on the easy chair.

Edwin soon came out of his study, pushing his spectacles up his hawk-like nose. He looked much older than his fifty-five years, with thinning salt-and-pepper hair and a graying goatee. He promptly took his niece and the guest to the dining room.

"Hasn't this been an adventurous trip for our niece?" asked Rita, fussing over the arrangement on the table. "Sounds more like a soap opera. An insane fugitive? Scary."

"Oh, you mean the stranger visiting her room when she was at the hostel in Seloor?" asked Shaker, taken back by Rita's sudden reference to that sore incident.

"Yes, that was quite an adventure," agreed Tina, in the process of loading her plate with a generous helping of *naan*, her favorite flat bread, and the potato-peas curry floating in tomato sauce. Despite the sight of the delicious food, she did not feel hungry anymore. The memory of her strange adventure always had an eerie effect, crushing her appetite, sucking away a moment of happiness.

"We're glad you were there in the same train, Dr. Shaker," smiled Rita, passing the yogurt-cucumber raita.

"Yes," agreed Edwin, reaching for the basmati rice. "And we're glad Tina has a mentor now. Have you worked out a schedule?"

"Tina and I decided that we would work together in the afternoons." Shaker took the raita from Tina's aunt and observed her face as though studying it for the first time. It was not a particularly beautiful face. Her ponytailed hair bounced with her animated talk while the creases on her forehead deepened as she smiled. And Rita had a dazzling smile that brightened the room like a ray of sunshine. There was a determined geniality oozing from her nature that made her chubby nose, small insignificant eyes, and characterless cheeks attractive.

"Dr. Shaker, we are meeting next week, I hope?" asked Edwin. "Dr. Augustine frequently tells me how indispensable your research is."

"Thanks. I'm very thankful for his long-term mentoring." Shaker reminisced gratefully. "He took me in nine years ago when I expressed an interest in counter-terrorism profiles."

"And ever since then you've made many visits. When are you returning to Boston?" asked Rita, signaling to the servants to make room for dessert.

"I'm not. I just want to linger a bit longer and see what happens. I'll basically step in where Dr. Augustine left off."

"Well, well, I'm glad to hear that. And Sharif knows about this, I'm sure?" asked Edwin, easily slipping into shoptalk. "Your name came up yesterday while we were in a meeting."

"Of course. He seems to know everything, everybody," laughed Shaker. "Sometimes I think Mr. Sharif is more of a psychic than a formidable officer in the counter-terrorism unit."

"You're right, but don't tell him that," cautioned Edwin, smiling at the group. "We're supposed to have a sixth sense. Sharif is endowed with a seventh, eighth, and perhaps a ninth."

"Yes," continued Shaker. "Mr. Sharif is keen on looking into the core of every explosion instigated by terrorism, and the core contains many facets. The primary facet, he believes, is the effect of psychology."

"That man's life is his work, and his work is his life!" exclaimed Rita, criticizing her husband's friend of many years. "Does he think of anything else?"

"Probably not," agreed Edwin, turning towards Shaker. "But your theory of psychology is interesting. And that's precisely why our Tina is working with you now."

"During the first year of my internship with Dr. Augustine, my homework was learning the psychological perspectives of terrorism. We know that every element in life manifests a psychosomatic aspect. It makes sense, naturally."

"It makes sense, naturally, to you and your kind, Dr. Shaker," laughed Edwin. "Anyway, I'm glad you're gradually stepping into Dr. Augustine's shoes, considering your careful training for so many years."

- 13 -

The Jannah, 248 Park Road, Seloor • December 2009

Usman studied the schedule on his desk and looked meditatively at the young man sitting in front of him. And the young man, with lanky arms, unbridled hair, and an impending mustache, nervously looked at the stray objects in the room.

"Salim, what did you learn at Dandiar?" asked Usman, while the young man restlessly transferred his glance from his master to the window. "Some discipline, I hope?"

Salim squirmed in embarrassment, but he felt he deserved this reprimand. He knew he would be paying dearly, for a long time, for impulsively pulling the trigger on the man inside that rickety shed. "Yes, Sahib," replied Salim, sorely recollecting the grueling lessons he had received in a small, deserted village tucked in the northern border of India.

And Usman's mind was not far from the episode, the incident-at-the-paddy-fields, which forced his organization to move from 19 Temple Street to 248 Park Road. "Good. I know you're tough. The key is to keep your thoughts at check all the time. All the time, do you hear? Allah did not give you your brain to act without thinking thoroughly. Your father did remarkable service to our cause," sighed Usman, his thoughts fondly running to his friend. "You remember Saira? A fine girl. She has been receiving considerable training here, and she has already assisted in a couple of minor assignments. Now I have a job for the two of you. I've already gone over the plan with her. You'll travel as brother and sister to Mumbai..." Usman continued to explain one of the forthcoming missions to the nineteen-year-old missionary.

After dismissing Salim from his office, Usman went downstairs to have a talk with Saira. Every time he rested his eyes on her beautiful face, he noticed a degree of change. She had aged drastically, but that was an inevitable, routine outcome of the intense training. But Saira's mature acceptance of her fate and her resolution to do God's work, any way her master deemed right, were singularly unique.

"Saira, how are you, my child?" asked Usman, remembering the day she was sighted for his organization, several months ago.

Saira

Seloor • March 2009

Kumar took the cold soda from the vendor's hand and continued to observe the steadily increasing crowd at the carnival as the gathering gray clouds briskly drew batik motifs on the stainless blue sky. But the humidity didn't stop the spectators. While he was wiping his sweaty forehead with his handkerchief, he saw her again with her children. She was a very attractive woman—not young, not old. Unfortunately, the sides of her beautiful face were concealed by the folds of a beige hijab which was loosely covering her head. Her indigence shamelessly clamored for attention through her repeatedly used, faded cotton sari, her worn out flip-flops, and her sun-ripened skin.

"Is she the one you were talking about?" asked Kumar's associate.

"Yes, Imran." Kumar carefully observed the target again.

"She is a good-looking woman."

But what really snared their predatory eyes was the girl standing next to her. They already knew that the young girl was that woman's daughter, but they were eager to know more. Imran exchanged a very speaking glance with Kumar before walking to the other side of the avenue.

"I'm looking for change," the woman said to the snack vendor, looking embarrassed. The little boy, standing next to her, had already taken a bite of the hot-pink cotton candy. The girl was steadily staring at the ground.

The vendor rolled his eyes and started to twiddle his thumb. A small line was forming behind the woman by now.

"I'm sorry. I don't have enough change," the woman apologized, unable to look at the vendor.

"You should've made sure you had enough money before buying something," shouted the vendor.

Imran walked closer to the woman. He took out a handful of change from his pocket and threw them on the counter. "Don't you have any compassion?" he asked the vendor, and the line of men and women mumbled in pity.

"Thank you," the woman appeared more relieved than grateful before walking away with her children. "Sir, thank you so much," the woman repeated, smiling at her benefactor. "My children were hungry. I…I," she paused, unable to continue.

"Cotton candy for hunger?" asked Imran, sympathy and concern oozing from his eyes.

The boy smiled. The girl still kept studying the ground, a slight tinge of pink spreading on her cheeks.

"You look tired, Madam. Have a seat, please." Imran led the family to a bench in the shade of a huge peepul tree.

The boy sat down promptly. The girl stood by the little boy.

"You're so kind," smiled the woman, taking the fringe of her sari and wiping the boy's sticky face.

"Please stay here," requested Imran, before walking away from the group. He returned in a few minutes with a couple of packets of savory snacks and a bottle of soda and deposited the whole lot in the woman's hands.

"Oh, no. Sir, I'll never be able to pay for all this," she stammered, confused and embarrassed.

"No need to pay me. You see," continued Imran, encouraging her to sit on the bench by her son, "what's money? It feels good to help each other," he smiled, glancing compassionately at the family.

"Thank you. If you tell me where I can find you, I'll return the money, that is, as soon as I find work."

"No. No, that won't be necessary. I'll tell you where you can find me—not to return my money, but to find work. You see that building, the one behind the merry-go-round? That's one of the places where one can usually find me, but," he said rather hurriedly, "don't come there."

"Then where can I find you?" asked the woman, a little bewildered.

"Why not here, somewhere near the market? The reason I don't want you to come to the office is because," Imran looked to his right and left, "it's because some make fun of me. They say that I'm quick to offer jobs to everybody who needs help. By the way, what do you do? What's your skill?"

"I was a tailor's assistant, but the shop where I used to work is closed now. The owner moved to the city to get better business. The other tailor who has a store in the market already has enough assistants."

"What do you do now?" Imran asked, his eyes glued to the young girl standing by the woman. She still had not looked at him, and he was desperately trying to make eye contact.

"I'm a maid at a lawyer's house, but it's barely enough to feed the children. Actually, I came here today looking for work."

"Let me see what I can do. How many children do you have?"

"Two. This is my daughter, Saira, and my son, Kabir. And I'm Abida. Their school is closed today."

"And," Imran's voice lingered. "Your husband? What does he do?"

"He died last year."

"I'm sorry. It can't be easy to raise a family on your own." Imran transferred his glance from the woman to the girl. "And you can help your mother when you're ready for a job."

"Yes, I would like to get a job, but my mother wants me to finish school." The girl finally looked at him.

A strikingly beautiful face, thought Imran.

"Yes, I want her to finish school," Abida began with a sudden note of determination, her overworked, chapped fingers nervously smoothing her son's hair. "The government schools have been good to us. My children get a decent education, and they are fed during lunch time. What more can I ask for? Saira helps me whenever I get an odd job here and there. I keep telling her that she might be able to find something better with a high school certificate."

"Of course, but the school closes for summer in a couple of weeks. I can get her a temporary job through my organization. That'll give her some experience, and she'll have the satisfaction of helping you," Imran suggested, looking alternately at the mother and the daughter.

"You can find a job for Saira?" asked Abida, half in surprise and half in doubt. A thin strand of hair escaped from the confines of her hijab and began to tap on her parched, quivering lips.

"Let's do this. I'll talk to a couple of my colleagues and see if I can first get a job for you. Perhaps I can get Saira a job at the same place. Can you come here on Thursday, around five?" asked Imran, effortlessly hiding the eagerness in his voice.

"Yes, I can. And thank you again." Abida turned to her children. "Thank this nice gentleman."

The boy whispered a shy "thank you" while the girl thanked the man with a trace of a smile. When the family walked away, Imran began to cross the road.

"Ammi, why is this man so nice to us?" Saira asked her mother, following her to the other end of the market square.

"I don't know, Saira. It's a great stroke of luck that we met him today. What a generous man he is!"

"Well, Imran?" asked Kumar, puffing rings of smoke in the air.

"I think it'll work," Imran replied satisfactorily. "She is a good catch. Isn't she, Kumar?"

The young girl was indeed a good catch, with a striking pair of furtive eyes, soft cheeks where a stubborn strand of hair danced in the wind, raven hair kept in two braids, and beautiful lips that looked like pink shells.

"Yes, she is a good catch," agreed Kumar. "A diamond in the dirt. It's a shame we've to recruit her for Usman Sahib's organization. This girl is more like a box-office hit. She should be spotted by a movie scout. Then again, she's more likely to be spotted by a pimp."

"I know," laughed Imran. "I bet she's a virgin. She must be worth something in the market. I'll keep you posted."

"Good." Kumar threw the cigarette butt on the ground and walked away.

The 6:10 Cheran Express from Chennai Central to Seloor Junction was sauntering on the tracks due to inclement weather. *It's already 7:15, and there's no sign of the station,* cursed Abdullah, tired and impatient. He stepped gingerly into the toilet stall and quickly shaved using a cordless shaver. After splashing cold water on his face and slapping aftershave on his leathery cheeks, he returned to the corridor and opened the shutter. He badly wanted to smoke and reached into his pocket for a cigar, but he picked up his ringing cell phone instead.

"Hello?" greeted Abdullah, without enthusiasm. He had not slept well, although the sleeper compartment was comfortable. "What is it, Imran?"

"Need a quick job, Sahib." Imran replied respectfully. "I couldn't get Sayeed Bhai on the phone. That's why I'm directly calling you."

"That's all right. Who will be the candidate? And what skills?"

"It's for a woman, may be late-thirties. Seamstress."

"How soon would you need the job and how long will she stay?" asked Abdullah. "Would she be part of a mission?"

"We'll need a job for her right away, Sahib. She wouldn't be part of a mission, but her daughter would be. She is about fourteen or fifteen, I think."

"I'll call you with something concrete this afternoon. I've to check the job status at the warehouse." Abdullah disconnected the call.

When the train reached the station, Abdullah got a hot cup of tea and stepped into a taxi. He decided to go straight to his warehouse instead of going home and asked the driver to go to Eastern Exports on Park Road.

"What's going on?" Abdullah asked the driver, looking at the pile of vehicles. His heavyset body occupied almost three-fourths of the back seat.

"There was a big riot yesterday. It left quite a mess."

Abdullah turned to the window to hide his smile. Usman's men must have been busy. While the taxi took the long-winding detour, he worriedly thought about the condition of his warehouse that manufactured delicate, ethnic garments, which were exported to fine boutiques and department stores abroad. The cheaper outfits went to Canal Street and Jackson Heights in New York City. The more expensive cuts went to the air-conditioned malls and elegant boutiques. He never saw the buyers or his representatives in the sales department. He couldn't care less. The real money was not in garments, or boutiques, or air-conditioned department stores. But he must do something about the working conditions at his sweatshops before it was time for another inspection. He knew he could buy any inspector, but some were a little hard to please.

The taxi driver saluted gratefully for the generous tip and drove out of the gates. It was an excruciatingly hot morning, and Abdullah's obesity heaved in agony. He took the stone steps very slowly and entered his air-conditioned office upstairs. It was still early. The employees had not showed up for work, but they would arrive soon. Most of them had a twelve-hour schedule, an agenda which Abdullah's foreman had cleverly crafted using a modern technology.

"Come in," Abdullah said impatiently, wondering who had come to pester him so early. But he was happy to see his foreman. "Oh, it's you, Sayeed!"

"I thought I heard a sound in your office, Sahib. I didn't know you were here already. I didn't see your car in the shed." Sayeed was confused.

"I left Chennai a day early. I didn't even call for my car. I took a taxi from the station."

"Can I get you some coffee, Sahib?" asked Sayeed, looking worriedly at his employer's exhausted face. "And some nashta?"

"I already had tea at the station. And I'm not hungry yet for nashta. Do we have a slot for a seamstress?" asked Abdullah, directly coming to the problem at hand.

"I don't think so. Is there someone who needs a job?" asked Sayeed, trying to assess the necessity.

"Yes. I don't know the duration. Create one. It's for Usman Bhai's project. Make it quick and make it Level 3."

"Man or a woman, Sahib?" Sayeed wondered about the plight of the future employee.

"A middle-aged woman. Younger than middle-aged, I think. Her young daughter of about 15 would be involved!" Abdullah finished Sayeed's thought, staring at the young man, whom he had nurtured meticulously with affection and dedication. Sayeed looked more like a well-dressed employee of the corporate wing, with his pressed shirt, well-groomed hair, and polished shoes. His very fair complexion, angelic expression, sultry eyes, and the dark lashes curtaining those sultry eyes belonged to a woman, and his innocent smile belonged to a child. But everything else about him belonged to him and to him only. His preying instinct and fanatic passion for Islamic fundamentalism made him the most loyal follower of Abdullah and, subsequently, a favorite of Usman. *No money could buy Sayeed*, Abdullah thought happily, proudly. "Go, get to it, my boy."

Sayeed promptly left the room.

Abida was almost done mopping the marble floor when her employer stood a few feet from her exhausted, bent form.

"Abida," came her sonorous voice. "Your mind is not at all in your work these days, I see. My daughter's in-laws are coming here for dinner, and you still haven't finished your work in the kitchen."

"I'm sorry, Madam. I'll get to it soon," apologized Abida, wiping her sweaty face with the fringe of her sari. "And, Madam," she lingered. It was now or never.

"Yes, Abida? What is it?" The sonorous voice bounced off the wall again.

"May I please have a little advance from…from my next month's wages? It's my son's birthday tomorrow," begged Abida, reluctantly trying to appeal to her employer's good side.

"An advance, Abida? Have you forgotten that you've already withdrawn half of your next month's wages? How are you planning to manage a home if you keep using the money before you earn it? What're you going to use to buy provisions next month to cook for your children? Are you using your brain at all?" asked the employer, with one muscular arm resting on her roomy hip.

Abida looked timidly at the fierce woman who was her only source of income. She wanted to tell her formidable employer to go to hell, but she could not—not when Kabir and Saira needed to fill the void in the stomach by sunset, not when it was her little boy's birthday next day. Perhaps if that nice man could really fetch her a decent job, as he promised in the market, then she wouldn't have to grovel like a beggar in front of that heartless, arrogant woman.

"I'm sorry I'm so much trouble, Madam. I'm going to try and use my brain. But could you please give me an advance just one more time?" asked Abida, burying her pride. *Pride?* She could not afford it.

Abida's employer rolled her eyes, sighed exasperatedly, and grudgingly pulled out some money from her drawstring purse, which she always kept tucked inside her waistband. "Here," she said, stuffing the money into Abida's outstretched hand. "Let this be the last time. Stop making a habit of it."

"I won't ask again, Madam. Thank you." Abida gratefully shoved the money inside her crinkled blouse. After a nervous glance at the cuckoo clock on the wall, she ran to the kitchen and hastily finished the chores. She had promised Imran that she would meet him near Sri pharmacy in the market by 5. She had to. She must. She desperately needed a job, a better job. She was tired of begging for a pittance.

Abida closed the gate of her employer's home and picked up a fast pace towards the market. Although this was her fourth meeting with her benefactor, she was still a little nervous. After the first meeting at the carnival, he had asked her to meet him at a different location every time. She understood—so that people wouldn't notice, they wouldn't talk. She felt his consideration deeply!

When Abida reached the market five minutes past the scheduled time, she saw the kind man patiently waiting for her, pushing his dark hair away from his moist face. He smiled at her, and that smile spoke nothing of disappointment. Heart pulsing, she wondered if he really had a job for her.

"Abida Behn!" Imran addressed her respectfully, delighted to see the woman who was like a sister. "When would you be ready to begin?"

Abida stared at him, afraid to hope. "Do I really have a job, Bhaiya?" she stammered, affectionately looking up at the man who held the status of a brother.

"Yes, it was a little difficult, but the company owes me a favor. So I managed to get a job for you as an assistant at a warehouse. It's Eastern Exports on Park Road. You'll have long hours, but you're not afraid of hard work. Are you, Behn?" asked the kind man, tilting his head to one side. His glance fell momentarily on Kumar who was waiting outside the tea stall.

"Thank you." Abida's eyes filled with gratitude. So many grateful expressions were bursting to be released all at once, but her extraordinary delight smothered her words. He was indeed very trustworthy. "I can't believe it. Such an unexpected stroke of fortune! Bhaiya, I can't imagine getting a job like this without your help."

It was a sticky day in March. Imran took a handkerchief from his shirt pocket and pressed his sweaty forehead, quickly glancing at the tea stall. "How are Saira and Kabir?" he asked kindly.

"Saira is at home studying. Tomorrow is her math exam. She wants to do well in her state exams." Abida wiped her steamy face with her dirty sleeve. When her hijab slipped from her head and got into a tussle with the unexpected breeze, she nervously ran her fingers through her knotted hair, which was unattractively pulled into a bun.

"Well, remember I said that I may be able to get her a job for summer? I have one."

"You do?" blurted Abida, not as thrilled as she should sound.

"What happened?" he asked, immediately noticing her tepid reception of his announcement.

"Bhaiya," she continued nervously, "I don't want to sound ungrateful. But how could I be happy about that? How many young girls work for a living? My child's fate! My family's cursed fate!" sighed Abida, several baffling emotions crisscrossing through her turbulent mind.

Imran's shrewd glance studied Abida's worried expression cradling her troubled eyes, which were waiting to spill a drop of tear at any moment. After reaching quite a milestone with that hunt, he could not let the fifteen-year-old slip through his fingers. His master would be highly disappointed. "What's the matter?" he asked, trying to conceal his impatience.

"Nothing. It's just that my family is destined to..." she suffocated her tears. Here was a man who had been so kind to her and to her children. She should be grateful, enormously grateful. "When will she start?"

"Probably next week, at the Women's Institute. She'll start working by doing simple office tasks. You know, filing and so on. Then she'll be trained at the Call Center." Imran knew the effect of *Call Center*—the instant, gratifying meal ticket of the twenty-first-century middle class, especially the sort that generally hovered just below middle class.

"Call Center? I thought those jobs were for adults, college graduates?" asked Abida, who could not even dream of reaching the middle-class status while slogging below poverty line.

"Yes, usually, but there are several levels of jobs in the area. Don't worry."

"Anyway, I thought she was going to work with me. I remember you telling me..."

"That's what I thought," he cut in. "But do you want your daughter to work all day with her delicate hands, doing manual labor, stitching and embroidering, which will take her nowhere? I thought you wanted more for her."

"But where is the Women's Institute?"

"About an hour from Seloor, near Tirupur, and it's just a bus ride away. It will take a lot of time and money to build a permanent facility closer to Seloor."

"It must be all right then. Will she start soon?"

"Yes, next week, as soon as her exams are over. But, you see, they have boarding facilities. She has to stay there for a week of training to be employed at the Call Center. They'll take good care of her. Don't worry."

"A week away without supervision? She is only fifteen."

"Look," he sighed, his head down, "if you don't want this opportunity for your daughter, you can let it go. After all, you don't know me well. I understand."

"No. No. Please, it's not that. I want what's best for Saira. After all you've done for me like a kind brother, how can I doubt you?" asked Abida, smothering her doubts.

"Good. I wouldn't want to do anything that might hurt you or your children. In fact, the training she receives at Women's Institute will help her do some useful chores next summer at Eastern Exports. I can talk to the manager about Saira. Sayeed Bhai will be happy to help her get settled in a good job." Imran fell silent for a few minutes, secretly glancing at Kumar who was still standing behind a crowded bench outside the tea stall.

"What do you want me to do to prepare Saira?" asked Abida, gathering sufficient courage.

"The Women's Institute will send a bus next week on Monday. Have her ready at the bus stand near the market outside Modern Cafe before five in the morning. Oh, I almost forgot," paused Imran, reaching into his shirt pocket. "Here is a small deposit, or advance, or whatever you might want to call it. Use this money to get a couple of good saris before you start your new job tomorrow. Go to the warehouse and see Sayeed Bhai promptly at 9. And don't use all of the money to buy knickknacks for Saira and Kabir."

"But how can I ever repay?" she asked, touched by her benefactor's generosity.

"Oh, Abida Behn! You call me Bhaiya. If I'm like your brother, can't I do this small favor for my behn? You are, after all, like a sister to me. Now, I will miss seeing you, but I'm going to be stationed at Madurai for a while. I'm glad we had a chance to meet. Inshallah, Abida Behn!" He smiled and walked towards the pharmacy, noticing Kumar's entrance into the tea stall.

Abida smiled gratefully, letting her benefactor's parting benediction sink into her ears like a song from heaven. "Inshallah!" she thanked her adopted brother, shoving the unexpected windfall inside her tattered cloth bag with her trembling hands.

Abida ran from one stall to another in the market. She saw a new dress for Saira. The last time her daughter had something new was for Ramadan when her father was alive. And what about that short pants for Kabir? And he wanted a new pencil box. His old one was dented and rusted. And what else could she buy?

Abida finally got into the crowded bus. She hugged the packages to her chest and tried to imagine the delighted smiles of her children when they opened the presents. One of the parcels slipped from her hands as the bus pulled roughly at the bus stop. A few passengers soon got out, and Abida occupied the now empty seat, depositing the parcels on her lap. Three more stops to her home. She looked at the rapidly disappearing lower-class neighborhoods, making room for high-rise apartments. One day, her children might live in one of those nice apartments—away from the slum, not smelling the sewer, not breathing in the feces from the ditch by the rickety window, not smelling the questionable smoke coming from the group of rickshaw drivers at the corner of her narrow alley. When the bus stopped at the end of the main road, Abida got down carefully with her parcels and began the steep walk towards her slum. She had no choice but to walk. The lanes were so narrow that no bus was able to enter the streets of her neighborhood.

Kumar paid for the omelet and looked impatiently at the entrance of the café. His contact was late. While he was wondering if he should ask for another cup of coffee, a scruffy, muscular man arrived and sat on the bench facing him.

"You're late. I've been waiting for more than an hour," hissed Kumar, cautiously looking around the café.

"I'm sorry. My lorry has been unruly lately. I came as soon as I could. You've an assignment for me?"

"Yes. This is a delicate matter, and I don't want you to go wild about it. You need to pay attention, think, be a little smart. Can you?"

"Don't I always follow instructions?" asked the lorry driver, quite affronted.

"She is fifteen, just out of school. You'll pick her up at the bus stand by the market square. She'll be waiting near Modern Café. She and her mother will be expecting a private bus. You're supposed to take her to the Women's Institute."

"What? Which one?"

"You're not paying attention. I said *supposed to.* You'll start with a dozen passengers. You'll make one stop on the way somewhere by Seloor Junction where you'll lose about eight passengers. At the next stop, all will get down because your engine will have trouble. She'll be flustered and ask you questions. That's when you carefully do your usual."

"Oh!" the man exclaimed greedily.

"I said CAREFULLY. DO NOT go crazy like you did with the girl from Salem. When we acquire and develop candidates for projects, we'd like to keep them intact. Do you understand?"

"What happens while I'm carefully going about it?" the man asked, annoyed by the lecture, shifting his glance from Kumar's gleaming bald head to the entrance of the cafe.

"I'll intervene and rescue her from you. You must remember to spot me in the vicinity before you begin the drama. If I'm delayed for some reason, or if I can't make it there, you do nothing. Do you hear me? If I'm not there, just drop her off near her home. We'll set up another episode later."

"When would this happen?"

"Monday. Come to the bus stand before five. Lotus Auto Shop will have a small bus ready for you. Well, do you want this job?"

"Yes."

"Come with me. I'll show you what she looks like."

The lorry driver followed Kumar to the municipal school on the other side of the avenue and stood outside a corner store that was notorious for selling popular children's snacks—oily savories prepared under unhygienic conditions and watery soda spiked for the wrong reason or the right money.

"Stand behind me," whispered Kumar, quickly moving behind a pillar.

"How do you know that she'll come out right now?"

"She is finishing tenth standard and she is picking up forms for Plus-Two."

"Plus-Two? Oh, you mean the last two years of high school? She's not going to get to *Plus-Two*, is she?"

"No need to discuss that. Be quiet. Here she comes."

When Saira walked through the rusty metal gates with a couple of girls, her exquisite features and dainty figure stood out like an odd lotus in a filthy pond.

"Stop your roving eyes. I didn't bring you here to look at the entire parade. You see the girl in the green dress? Keep your focus on that one," whispered Kumar. "She's a sight to sore eyes! How could she look so beautiful, like a fresh blossom, while she's waddling in poverty?" he asked, his predatory instinct ruffled by Saira's angelic appearance.

The lorry driver looked long at his target, taking in the way she walked, observing her rapt conversation with her friends.

"Did you take a good look?" asked Kumar. "She'll be at the bus stand with her mother on Monday. And you know the rest."

"Yes, I know," replied the driver, eager for the next stage of human indignity. "But what if the mother insists on going with her daughter in the bus?"

"She won't. Her work will come in the way. If..." drawled Kumar, thinking of an alternative, "if she insists on dropping her daughter off at her destination, let her get in. Go for a couple of miles and drop them off near the station saying that you have trouble with the bus. We'll choose another time for your assignment."

- 14 -

Seloor Bus Stand • March 2009

Saira sat on the bench outside Modern Cafe near the market square, and her mother sat next to her, cradling Kabir's sleepy head on her lap.

"Did you pack your new dress, Saira?" asked Abida, surveying the small threadbare suitcase bought at the secondhand store in the shady corners of the market.

A couple of lorry drivers stared at the mother and daughter. When another man whistled loudly before following the other two into the café, Abida pulled her daughter close to her.

"You'll be careful, Saira," whispered Abida, running her trembling hand along her daughter's luxurious hair. "If at any time you're scared and if you miss Kabir and me, write to us. Did I give you a few stamps? Yes, I did. You can go to the public phone, Saira, and leave a message for me at Eastern Exports. My manager is a nice man. He'll convey the message to me."

"Yes, Ammi. I'll be careful. Don't worry." Saira assured her mother softly, as though afraid of breaking the early-morning silence.

A thin woman, with oily hair and a blotchy complexion, stood a few feet from the bench with a duffle bag and quietly absorbed every word exchanged between the mother and daughter.

"I don't like this, Saira. I don't like this at all. I don't want you to go away. I should take care of you. I can. See, now I have a new job, a nice job. Why do you have to go away for training? Why did I agree to this? There's no need for you to work now. You'll get a job after you finish Plus-Two or, with Allah's blessings, after you finish college."

"But you told Imran Sahib that you'll send me for training at the Women's Institute," Saira reminded her mother, a strange determination invading her adolescent mind. "Ammi, I don't want you to change your mind now. Don't you want to break this poverty? I don't want you to search for change to buy Kabir a snack. I want you to smile, be happy, and buy a new sari instead of waiting for used saris from rich men's wives. I want us to get out of the slum. I want to be somebody, Ammi. I'll go to college. Don't worry about that." Saira took her mother's hand in a tight grip. "And this is my new beginning, our new beginning."

Abida wiped her tears as a small bus crawled slowly to a stop in front of Modern Cafe.

"Anybody for the Women's Institute?" the driver shouted through the open window.

"That's for me, Ammi." Saira picked up the suitcase.

When Abida got up, Kabir rubbed his eyes and looked at his mother and sister in the lingering darkness.

"I'll see you soon, Kabir." Saira held the small frame of her brother in a tight embrace. "Take care of Ammi."

Kabir began to cry noisily, unwilling to let his sister leave. Saira extricated her hand gently and pushed back her silent tears. She could not afford to cry now.

"May Allah protect you, my little girl," smiled the mother, walking behind her daughter.

And the little girl got into the bus without looking at her mother even once. She could not look at her mother's empty eyes and distorted smile. But when the bus rolled away from the market, Saira's eyes painfully and involuntarily went to her mother and brother, still standing by the bench. She swallowed her tears again as the passengers stared at her lonely departure.

The thin woman, who had been eavesdropping until that moment, walked far away from the bench, picked up her cell phone from the duffle bag, and called a number which reached Naim's Tailoring. When a man called her back, she carefully repeated what she had overheard.

The small bus snaked through small alleys, avoiding wheezing auto-rickshaws and homeless men and women sleeping on the sidewalk. Saira looked at the passengers in the mini bus—most of them sleepy. A couple of men stared at her with lusty eyes and the women eyed her with sympathetic glances. An elderly woman, who was sitting in the third row, moved a little to make room for her.

Saira thanked her and sat on the edge of the seat, balancing the suitcase by her feet.

"It's no good looking as pretty as you look, child," said the woman, smiling kindly at Saira. "It's not your fault, you know, but you shouldn't be traveling all alone at a time like this. There are hawks everywhere."

Saira understood the message and smiled. "I'm going to the Women's Institute. My mother said it was safe to take this bus. I thought it was directly going there?"

"Women's Institute? I don't know. It's probably going there eventually. But I'm going to get down at the railway station."

The bus turned into the main road and clattered towards the junction. A few passengers, with an assortment of small boxes and bags, got out at the already crowded station. The elderly woman got up to leave, and when Saira moved away to make room for her to get out, she noticed that only about four men remained in the vehicle. The bus started to move fast and turned into a small lane, about a couple of kilometers from the junction, and stalled abruptly with wheezing noises.

"What happened?" shouted one of the passengers.

"I don't know," the driver shouted back. "Get down. I can't go on. I need to wait for help."

Two of the men promptly got down and the other two soon followed them. Saira looked at her suitcase and at the silent alley outside. Trying not to look flustered, she boldly looked at the driver, who was steadily staring at her by now. In the next minute, his hand imperceptibly shut the door.

"I need to...how far is the Women's Institute?" asked Saira, trying to steady her voice. "If you tell me where it is, I think I can take another bus. Where is it?"

Instead of answering, he strangely leered at her. He was massively built, with unkempt hair and slimy, unshaved face. When he took a few steps towards her, she noticed his towering height. With each step, his breathing grew heavier, and he smiled baring tobacco-stained teeth. When he stood in front of her, a nauseating odor of sweat and tobacco emanated from his body.

Saira looked through the window with a thudding heart, desperately hoping for any sign of activity. She saw nothing, nobody. The lane appeared to be a dead end, and not even a cyclist came through. Should she run for the door? But how? The driver was standing right between her and the door, and the window was too narrow for her to escape. Anyway, he was so close to her. He seemed to be distracted for just a minute when the sound of a motor crawled somewhere in the lane. He looked outside and took another step towards her when the sound subsided.

"Please move, so I can get down?" begged Saira, looking at the man's shoeless feet, avoiding his beady eyes.

Instead of moving to the side, he reached his hand towards her and grabbed her long tunic with one hand while his other hand got hold of her ankle-length skirt. Her hijab helplessly slid from her head as he tried to pull her braid.

She struggled with all her strength, pushed his chest away from her, and began to scream. He dropped her skirt on the floor and smothered her scream with his filthy, sweaty hand, pushing her on the floor of the bus. Then, he dropped his trousers with lightning speed and fell on her squirming body. When she tried to push him away, he began to strike her violently on her cheek. Breathing heavily, he mounted on her. She bit his hand, struggled to free herself, and quickly gathered a spellbinding scream from the hollows of her soul. The door burst open, and she saw a mere shadow of a bald and bulky man looming over the driver's prostrate form. When the driver struck her again, she fell unconscious, bleeding along the side of her face.

19 Temple Street, Seloor

When Saira woke up in a dark, dingy room, there was no bus, no railway junction, and no driver. She was on a cot, wearing a light robe that did not belong to her, and a strange large woman was sitting on a stool, a couple of feet away from the cot. When Saira tried to speak, her tongue seemed to be glued to her mouth, and all she could manage was a muffled whisper. When she tried to speak again, her swollen jaw and her distended cheek throbbed in pain.

The large woman smiled kindly and asked, "How are you feeling? You had a scary experience, you poor thing."

Saira began to cry as the recollection trickled into her muddled mind. She peered at the dark room and wondered where she was. Was she in a hospital?

"Don't worry," the woman smiled again. "I'm Maria. I'm a nurse."

Saira looked at the woman in a starched cotton sari, her hair pulled back into a neat bun, and took her trembling hands to her throbbing forehead.

"Do you have a headache?" asked Maria, checking Saira's pulse.

Saira's eyes went to the door as it creaked open.

A bald, bulky man stepped into the room and looked tentatively at Saira. "How is she?" he asked the nurse, his eyes resting on the cot.

"She is awake," whispered Maria, anxiously looking at the door.

Saira desperately tried to get up from the bed, screaming despite the pulsating pain. "Where is my suitcase? I want to go home. I must go home. Where is my dress?" she screamed, as the nurse held her hands to restrain her on the cot.

"Listen. Calm down," commanded the nurse, efficiently pushing Saira back on the cot. "You've been saved by this nice man, and this is how you behave? Do you know what could have happened to you? Do you want to know where that horrible driver was going to take you permanently?"

Saira took a deep breath, and her breathing was painful. Her chest hurt and her back felt like a slab of stone when she tried to move. She remembered the driver's weight on her, pushing her down, hitting her mercilessly, and…

"It's all right," whispered the bald man, a gentle smile touching his lips. He was by now standing next to the cot. "I can understand your fear, but you're safe now. There's no need to be frightened anymore."

And an old thin man, with a silver beard and a white tagiyah covering his head, was standing next to the bald man. "Poor child. How sad!" whispered the old man, and walked out of the room.

Saira looked at the bald man's seraphic smile and felt her fear easing a bit. She remembered this man entering that cursed bus when the driver was on her, and she faintly remembered how he shouted at the driver while pulling him away from her. She directly looked again at the man's face, his forehead covered in a bandage, his right cheek bruised to a blue tinge.

"Look how that monster hurt Kumar Bhai when he tried to save you!" exclaimed Maria, gently scolding Saira for her hysterical behavior.

"Hush, Maria," Kumar scolded the nurse. "She is just a child. Can you blame her for not trusting us, especially after what she has been through? Let her rest. We can take her to her home when she feels a little better, when she can get up," he suggested, looking compassionately at Saira. "I need to take care of some business. I'll be back soon. I hope you wake up feeling better."

"Close your eyes and rest, child," continued Maria, taking Saira's quivering hand in hers. "You'll feel much better when you've rested. Kumar Bhai will return soon, and you can thank him properly for saving you from a horrible fate when he comes back. What's your name, dear?"

"Saira," the girl replied, feeling drowsy and a little parched. She gladly took a few more sips of the lemon juice Maria thoughtfully gave her, although it tasted a little odd.

"The doctor prescribed a medicine to ease your pain. But since you couldn't open your mouth to swallow the medicine, he asked me to crush it and add it to this juice. That's why it might taste a little strange," explained Maria, when the girl suspiciously stared at the drink.

Saira quickly drifted into a dream. She embraced Kabir, who didn't want her to leave. She looked at the new dress her mother proudly brought home from the market. She lovingly took her mother's hand that was smoothing her hair down her back, and...she stopped dreaming.

"Wait just outside the room. Make sure you can hear our conversation. And you remember when to come in?" Usman asked Kumar.

"Yes, Sahib. I do," replied Kumar, pausing at the door.

When Usman knocked, Maria opened the door rather tentatively at first and then respectfully moved away from the entrance.

"How is she?" asked Usman, staring at the pillow, at the attractive face of the fifteen-year-old girl, her long hair, currently draping the pillow, tangled into knots.

"Better, Sahib," replied Maria.

Saira opened her eyes and stared first at Maria and then at Usman.

"Saira, this is the kind gentleman who owns this place. His name is Usman Sahib. You are here in safety because of his generosity!" Maria spoke gently, carefully observing Saira's gathering nerves.

"Are you feeling better, child?" Usman asked Saira, quickly taking in her fluttering lashes, quivering lips, and furtive glance.

"Yes, thank you," managed Saira. She looked down at her robe and began to twist the fringe with her trembling fingers. "I've been here for more than a week, I think. When can I go home?"

"Kumar is still trying to find your mother."

Saira stared, frowning in confusion.

"He has looked everywhere—in your neighborhood, in the warehouse where she is supposed to be working, and in the market. From the information you gave us, he even looked for her at her previous employer's home, the lawyer's house where she was a maid." Usman measured his words slowly, carefully. "We don't know where she is."

"But where is my ammi? Why isn't she waiting for me at home?" asked Saira, unable to grasp Usman's information.

"My men have been waiting for your ammi near your home in the mornings, in the afternoons, and even at night. Even your neighbors don't know where she is. They haven't seen her since the day you got into that bus. What should we do? We even talked to Sayeed, the manager at Eastern Exports. He hasn't seen her in a while."

"But I wrote to my mother, just as she asked me to do. She wouldn't ignore me. She wouldn't," cried Saira. "And Kumar Bhai said he posted it."

The door creaked open and Kumar walked in with an envelope in his hand.

"Yes, Kumar?" asked Usman.

"There's a letter, Sahib, for you." Kumar paused near the cot. He turned to Maria, who was hovering near the door, and said, "You're needed in the manager's office."

Maria quietly left the room.

"A letter for me?" asked Usman. "Can't you give it to me later? I was just trying to comfort this child here."

"I apologize for interrupting, but the sender's name is Abida. Isn't that Saira's mother's name? I thought you might want to see it right away."

Usman took the envelope and read the letter quietly, glancing at Saira every now and then.

"Sahib, what does my ammi say?" Saira asked anxiously. "Is she coming to get me? She got my letter?"

"No, Saira, she's not coming," Usman replied softly.

"Why isn't she coming?" asked Saira, still confused.

"Saira, you might be only fifteen, but you seem to be a mature young lady, and I want to be honest with you. Your ammi...your ammi..." Usman stalled.

Saira looked at him expectantly, breathlessly.

"I'll tell you, my child. Your trust and innocence have already been sullied by a heartless predator," continued Usman, carefully launching the idea of mistrust that sometimes hangs doubtfully on the brink of trust. "And I'm not going to insult your intelligence." Usman took a deep breath, stroking his silver beard, as though searching for appropriate words. "Your ammi doesn't want you anymore. She... I feel bad to say this, but she willingly left you to your fate when you got into that bus."

"But she didn't want me to get into the bus. She didn't even want me to go to the Women's Institute. She wanted to take care of me," cried Saira, covering her face with her hands. "I know my ammi. She has protected me and Kabir by working so hard."

"Kabir is not your brother."

"What?" shouted Saira, unable to believe her host's words.

Usman's glance wavered between Saira and Kumar.

"Usman Sahib is right, Saira," began Kumar, trying to get her to see how her father had been betrayed. "Your abba is not Kabir's abba. Your ammi is...his ammi."

"That's not true. That's a lie. That can't be true. She's a good woman. Ammi wouldn't..." Saira stumbled miserably.

"Saira," continued Usman, patiently looking at the young girl on the cot, at her bruised face, "as unpleasant as it is, that's what your ammi has written. She sent this letter to her manager. Here, why don't you read it?"

Saira grabbed the letter and began to read.

Mr. Sayeed
Manager, Eastern Exports

Sayeed Sahib:

I know this is an unexpected letter, but I need to write to you. I will not continue my work at Eastern Exports. I'm tired of living an unhappy, impoverished life, and I'm weary of going to bed with lies and disappointments. I'm going away with Kabir's abba who is willing to take care of us—away from Seloor, away from prying eyes, and away where nobody knows us. He is waiting to take me to a distant land where Islamic rules would not suffocate me, stifle his progress, and smother my son to ruin. He is willing to take care of our son, but only if I leave my daughter behind. Saira is fifteen, almost a grown-up. She needs to learn that life is unpleasant. And the sooner she comes to terms with it, the better. She will never become a gentleman's dutiful wife and live in a wealthy house. So let her fate take her wherever it may want to lead. And it is her duty to face her destiny, just like I have faced mine, waddling in the slum for years.

Sincerely,
Abida

Usman expected the girl to break down. Kumar expected a little hysteria. But Saira, instead of resorting to tears or hysteria, simply turned her face away from them.

"You said she sent this letter to her employer. How did it reach here?" asked Saira, the note quivering in her unsteady hands. There was a strange determination in her voice—not laced in anger or disappointment, but just tinged with a slowly rising, impassive note.

"The owner of Eastern Exports knows me very well," replied Usman, waiting to make eye contact with Saira. "He is, in fact, one of the greatest benefactors; he supports our worthy organization. I speak to him periodically about the victims who arrive here, and he wondered if you were Abida's daughter, based on the information I gave him earlier."

Saira returned the letter to Usman and directly looked at him, her eyes filled with a new light. And that look was like tonic to the old man. He knew from experience that the vacant, impassive aura was a stepping stone to his success.

"Why don't you rest a bit? We'll talk later and see how we can bring happiness back into your life. You deserve to be happy, child." Usman walked away with Kumar.

As Usman shut the door, he saw Saira burying her face in the pillow and sobbing miserably.

"Yes, I expected her to jump from feeling nothing to feeling everything." Usman nodded his head approvingly, after successfully triggering Saira's tears of frustration and abandonment. "Ask Maria to stay close to Saira's room, Kumar. I'll let her cry alone. She might cry all night. Those are tears of anger and grief. As they flow freely, her rage will develop nicely, and that's where I want her soon. But after tomorrow, her tears will be dry, and she'll forget the taste of tears. And soon, very soon, she'll forget the taste of fear."

Usman knocked on the door and walked into Saira's room. She was sitting on a metal chair by the window, staring at the green paddy fields. When she turned to the door and stared at him, he was surprised to see a change in the beautiful face.

"Saira, you must be feeling better. I see you've left the cot." Usman smiled at the unsmiling face. "Do you want to go to your neighborhood to see if you can find an answer to your misery?" he asked, deliberately choosing his words. "We can help you get there, if you feel strong enough to move."

"No, I don't want to talk about my mother."

"I understand," smiled Usman, realizing from experience how hatred floats uncertainly on the verge of affection. "But you know, talking releases one from pain. Look at me, child." His mesmerizing voice seeped into the room and slowly trickled into her ears. "Turn your frustration and anger to do something good, something useful to benefit others."

"That man, that man who has led my ammi...my ammi away from me, the monster who cheated my family, must hate my abba for being Muslim. Who is he?" asked Saira, still staring at the fields, an incredible sense of pity for her dead father occupying her chaotic mind.

"We can try to find out, but I believe you're right about his hatred. Kumar is investigating with the help of some other people. Even before this letter arrived, my men heard some rumor going around your neighborhood. At first I thought it was just rumor, you know, because your ammi has been alone, without a man's protection, since your abba's death. And your neighborhood has some anti-Islamic thugs, and I heard that they've been saying things about your ammi. But this letter unfortunately confirms the rumor. Can you believe, Saira, what shameful things some people would do because of hatred? You know your family has suffered because of anti-Islamic and fanatic attitude? That man," paused Usman, looking angrily at nothing in particular, "that man who fathered your brother is an enemy of Allah," he finished, leading the naive mind to rebellion, hoping to lead her gullible mind to destruction.

"I DO want to talk about my mother. I hate her. I hate everything about her." Saira's mind—already a victim of hunger, poverty, violated trust, and shattered dreams—effortlessly drifted from trust to disbelief, from warm affection to spiteful hatred.

Usman looked at the beautiful face that turned towards him. Saira's mercurial jump from affection to hatred was typical of her age. Fifteen. But the face, at that moment, did not belong to a fifteen-year-old. It was a cold, harsh face, hungry to appease gushing anger. And the face abruptly turned to the window again.

"We'll talk soon, Saira. But please eat well and rest. As sad as you might be about your ammi's betrayal, think about how you're spared from her disgrace and embarrassment."

Saira turned her face towards Usman again—taking in his fleshless cheeks, silver beard, wiry figure—and began to listen to his voice with significant interest.

"You know, my child, I think, no, I believe Allah sent you to me," continued Usman. "I have great plans to uphold Islam and the revered name of Allah. But you're too tired and wounded right now to listen to my proposals in detail. But I think you'll be one of my helpers. And dear child, you'll be one of Allah's chosen messengers." Usman's voice methodically began to build a weapon within the child's turbulent mind. "You're a ray of light in this hour of darkness. Child, you've gone through a lot. I'll speak with you soon." He got up, confident from her entranced expression that he would soon be her unsung hero.

"Please don't go," begged Saira, looking into her mentor's glowing eyes. "I want to know what I can do. I want to know what I can do to serve Allah."

Usman looked into the child's eyes. He noticed something stoic about her. He even saw a slight trace of a smile. "Soon, child. I believe in your strength. I think I might even depend on it. You should rest now. I'm not leaving you for long," he smiled, patting her hand. "You're a shining star." And with that capital praise, he vacated the room.

Abida waited on the uneven stoop of her tenement and stared warily at the narrow lane while the afternoon sun cast long shadows on the dusty road. The postman came and went, but no letter came from Saira. More than a week after her departure, why didn't her daughter write to her?

"Abida Behn, you look so tired today." Sayeed looked deeply into her disturbed eyes when she returned to work on Monday. "Are you ill?"

Abida, who was sliding her lunchbox under her sewing machine, straightened up respectfully. "No, Sahib. It's just that I'm missing my daughter," sighed Abida, plagued by anxious thoughts of her child.

"How is she?"

"Saira has gone away for training." Abida's tired eyes quickly traveled to the bolts of fabric on the shelves. There was a lot of work to be done, and she was a little behind.

"Training! Good. Where?" he asked, retrieving an envelope from his shirt pocket.

"At the Women's Institute," Abida smiled a little proudly, adjusting the hijab snugly on her head. "She has always been an intelligent girl, and I hope she does well."

"Women's Institute? Where is it? I don't think I've heard of it."

"Oh, I thought it was a well-known place. They train young women to learn useful skills. Imran Bhai said..."

"You should tell me more about it another time. But here, before I forget, this letter came on Saturday. I didn't get a chance to give this to you earlier because you had this Saturday off." Sayeed handed the letter to Abida and returned to his office.

Abida was more than curious. A letter? She opened it eagerly. Perhaps Saira wrote to her at this address? But why? She began to read, her pulse racing like a bullet train.

Dear Ammi,

I meant what I told you about breaking from poverty, just before I got on the bus. I'm going to do something with my life, but not at the Women's Institute. Allah did not give me this beautiful face just to work endlessly with my hands. I'm destined for a greater purpose, and I cannot reveal my benefactor's name now. He has offered me a place in his home, a place in his heart. He is only twenty years older than me. And it doesn't worry me that he is married and has children. He loves me, and I don't really care what the society calls me. I'll probably be known as a despicable mistress, but a wealthy mistress, I shall be. I refuse to walk down the slum that earthed me all the days of my miserable life. I will see no more tears, hunger, and I will have a decent, large meal every day, and I'll not eat one more bite out of charity. Do not bother to find me. You'll never be able to find me. I've decided to stay far away from you, unknown to you and Kabir, so that your society will not make you feel ashamed. Although I've stopped caring about our useless society and honor and all the nonsense that would never end poverty, I know you care about them.

Affectionately, for the last time,
Saira.

A week after receiving her daughter's most unexpected letter, Abida went to her manager's office.

"Come in, Abida Behn. Won't you sit down?" asked Sayeed, anticipating this meeting.

Abida squirmed nervously on the edge of an upholstered chair. But she had no relative to turn to, and she wanted to unload her burden to someone. Who better than her kind manager? "Sahib, did you manage to discover anything about the Women's Institute? She might have done something very impulsive, Sahib. My daughter is fifteen!"

"I'm sorry. I've no useful information to give you. There is a Women's Institute in Tirupur, but nobody there has heard of your daughter. Apparently, she never went there."

"No, she did not. She did not go there at all. She must have... Sahib, will you please find me another job?" asked Abida, her tears breaking loose by now.

"Another job? But are you unhappy here?" asked Sayeed, carefully observing her trembling lips and hands.

"No, I'm grateful for this job. But I'm not able to show my face in my neighborhood. When I go home, I...I'm so scared to come out. And my poor son, Kabir is also suffering. No child is allowed to play with him since his sister ran away. Sahib...my daughter ran away." Abida covered her face with both her hands and cried miserably, as though wishing to drown her shame. "Sahib, my daughter is not the kind of girl to abandon honor, modesty, and all that is decent to eat well and wear rich clothes, under the illegitimate protection of an unknown man, a predator. The man who lured my daughter to disgrace and ruin must be a predator."

"Dear Allah!" exclaimed Sayeed, his innocent smile disappearing from his handsome face to express his deep concern. "I'm so sorry to hear that. But are you sure?"

"Yes. I received a letter from her, the one you handed to me. And the neighbors have concluded that she did run away, although I never spoke about it. Sahib, I can't raise my son in my neighborhood anymore."

Sayeed could not inform Abida that Usman's men were busy spreading the news of Saira's pursuit of a disgraceful but better life at the cost of her mother's bleeding heart. The master's immediate concern was the removal of Abida from her neighborhood and from Seloor, and Sayeed knew that Usman always got what he wanted.

"I'll die of shame if I'm forced to remain here, and Kabir will become an outcast." Abida studied the post mark on the envelope. "Saira has posted the letter from Medur. Do you think she could still be there? No, I don't think so. She would be anywhere but there. That monster who tempted her to follow him wouldn't keep her there. What should I do?" cried Abida.

"You're right. Saira wouldn't be at Medur. That postmark doesn't mean anything."

"And as you know, Imran Bhai is out of town. I can't even consult him until he returns. And he works here and there, so I wouldn't know where to look for him."

"Yes, he is never in one place. And I doubt if he can do anything now." Sayeed thought about Imran's hasty trip to Madurai, where Usman ordered him to stay until Abida was removed from Seloor. "Oh, Abida Behn, I'll look for a job for you this instant. Be patient for a few days," advised Sayeed, who had already lined up a job for her about six hours away from Seloor.

- 15 -

Chennai • December 24, 2009

Theo Edwin parked the car outside Kanika Beauty Salon around ten in the morning.

"Thanks, Uncle Theo," smiled Tina, getting out of the car. She carefully avoided stepping on wet trash on the pavement and crinkled her nose at the nasty odor coming from the open sewer.

"You're not working after twelve, are you, Theo?" Rita asked her husband, restraining her shoulder-length hair with a barrette. "Once you go into your office, you forget everybody. I can't believe you want to work on Christmas Eve."

"Just an hour, Rita. I promise. We'll eat lunch at Cascade. I'll make reservations right away. Is 12:30 okay?" asked Theo, looking at his wife and his niece.

"That's fine." Rita opened the door to the salon and happily accepted the cheerful greeting.

While the aunt went into one of the private parlors, Tina followed a pleasant, tall, slim woman towards another room.

"I'm Jasmine," the slim woman introduced herself with a slight lisp. "And you're Tina?" she continued, glancing at the appointment card.

"Yes." Tina took a quick glance at the luxurious room, trying to erase the ugly sight on the pavement from her memory.

"I'll be back in a few minutes. Will you change into this?" asked

Jasmine, handing her client a robe. She tiptoed out of the room as though afraid of disturbing the serenity in the salon.

Once the door was shut, Tina took in the room leisurely. Soft sitar music was spilling from the walls, and a couple of generous vases were crowded with fragrant, vibrant flowers. When she changed into the robe and sat on the soft mattress with scented sheets, a subtle whiff of sandalwood and rose enveloped her. And thoughts of the dirty outside no longer lingered.

"Herbal massage?" asked Jasmine, walking back into the room.

"Yes, please."

"Are you a tourist?" Jasmine started to massage Tina's back.

"No. I'm a student." Tina closed her eyes blissfully. Jasmine's fingers were efficiently smoothing away the tension on her back.

"A student? Which college?" asked Jasmine, moving her fingers to Tina's left shoulder.

"I'm not from here. I'm from the States," sighed Tina, hoping to curtail further questions.

"Oh, I should've guessed that from your accent." Jasmine transferred the pressure to the right shoulder. "How long are you planning to be here?"

"I'm returning day after tomorrow."

"Leaving already? Did you get to see any places at all while you were here?" asked Jasmine, pouring some more warm scented oil on Tina's back.

"Yes, in the weekends."

Many more questions followed, and Tina stopped closing her eyes.

"I hope you visit us…if you make another trip? Are you planning to visit again?" asked Jasmine, wiping Tina's neck and shoulders with a warm washcloth.

"No. I won't be able to come back. I might be back for a vacation in the future. I don't know."

"If you come back, you must visit us." Jasmine smiled warmly as Tina sat on the bed. "I see you have an appointment for a manicure? You have beautiful, shapely fingers. I'll tell the manicurist to get ready for you. You know, I think you're the only appointment she has today? Have a safe trip," smiled Jasmine, shutting the door after stepping out of the room.

"Did you have a nice massage, Miss Matthew?" asked the manager, offering Tina a glass of mineral water. "Our masseuse had an accident and we had to call a substitute."

"Oh yes, she was great," smiled Tina, diplomatically, although her ears were still buzzing from Jasmine's droning questionnaire.

Edwin arrived promptly at noon to pick up his wife and niece. As the car pulled out, a young man with singularly boyish features, standing in front of Stanley Coffee Store across the street, picked up his cell phone.

"Hello, how was it?" he asked.

"She is leaving day after tomorrow," replied Jasmine.

"Good. I hope you're not still in the salon?"

"Of course, not. I'm walking to the bus stop."

"I see," said the man, looking to his left. He saw Jasmine's willowy figure moving towards the crowded bus stop. "You might have to work here for a week or so until the masseuse gets better."

"That's fine. They think I'm a good substitute. How bad was the masseuse's accident?"

"Not bad. She was hit by a motorcycle on her way home from the salon yesterday. Just a gentle push. More shock than injury." He disconnected and called his headquarters behind Eastern Exports near Seloor.

"Yusuf! How is it going?" asked Usman.

"Going well, Sahib," replied Yusuf. "The date of departure remains the same."

Tina, sitting between Rita and Theo Edwin at St. Antony's Church, looked at the decorations with childish delight. A choral group was singing discordantly to celebrate the birth of Jesus. As the congregation was dispersing slowly, she leisurely observed the women in silk saris and the little girls tripping on long, sequined skirts. So much laughter, so much noise, an uproarious gala around Christmas—Tina was happy to be part of it.

"Tina, this is one Christmas Theo and I will not forget. You've made it extra special for us. Let's go to the Church Hall. The children will be gathering there soon." Rita led her husband and niece to the high-ceilinged rectangular hall that was rapidly filling with people of all ages.

"Tina, Rita is in charge of this year's committee. She has been very busy since the beginning of October." Edwin, looking quite distinguished in a pressed shirt, proudly glanced at his wife.

"But I had plenty of help. And this is what Christmas is all about. Isn't it?" asked Rita, quickly glancing at a pile of saris and other dress materials. "We got plenty of donations this year."

Tina's eyes rested on a different group of people. The children, not dressed in sequined skirts or fancy pants and shirts, smiled bashfully at her, at her brown eyes, staring at her creamy complexion in the tanned congregation.

"Is it too hot for you, Tina?" asked Rita, catching her niece's forlorn expression.

"No, Aunt Rita. It's just that…I frequently feel like I'm traveling between two worlds while I'm in India—a lush land of plenty and a dry land of hollow smiles. It's so painful to watch," whispered Tina, staring at the noisy, impoverished children.

"I know. Do you want to distribute sweets and toys to this group of girls?" Rita took her niece to a loaded table.

Tina smiled warmly at the child in front of the line. A group of girls of various sizes fell into a single file, shyly at first, and more boldly as time went by.

"Theo, I'm going to ask Tina to light a candle for her safe trip back home. Wait for us here," instructed Rita, dragging her niece back to the church.

A young man with boyish features, dressed in his best suit, was standing by one of the great pillars on the steps outside. His eyes, while carefully planted on the congregation, discreetly noticed Tina walking back into the church. He picked up his cell phone, still keeping his eyes on the entrance.

"Yusuf?" asked a voice.

"Yes," whispered the young man. He pocketed the phone at the end of the conversation and waited patiently for Tina to exit the building. She was taking a long time, but he continued his vigil. She came out, finally, with her uncle and aunt walking on either side of her. And Yusuf followed the group while avoiding eye contact with any individual. Rita got into the air-conditioned car, and Tina got in beside her.

"Are you looking forward to your Christmas Eve dinner, Tina?" Edwin asked, sitting next to the driver.

"Yes, Uncle Theo. It's such a new experience. I've so much to tell when I return to Pittsburgh." Tina's eyes were on the receding structure. "How old is this church?"

"I'm not sure. I remember coming here with my grandfather." Edwin, looking unusually impressive, his graying goatee meticulously trimmed for the holiday, tried to estimate the age.

"Then it must be ancient," laughed Rita, never missing an opportunity to tease her husband.

The guests arrived soon to celebrate the holiday. Birdie and Regi, Edwin's aunt and uncle, came first, followed by Dr. Augustine and Dr. Shaker.

"Dr. Augustine, you look better." Tina happily invited the elderly psychologist. She was particularly happy to see him because he reminded her of her advisor, Dr. Katz—the same laughing features, heavy spectacles, and Einstein-ish hair. The hair, unfortunately, had taken some beating due to chemotherapy.

"Well, your uncle and aunt were kind enough to invite me for old time's sake," smiled Dr. Augustine, warmly taking Tina's hand. "I do feel better, thanks to the chemo,' I think. And I'm still sorry that I abandoned you when you came here to work with me. But I'm glad Dr. Shaker took my seat."

"Please don't worry about it. Everything worked out," Tina returned his smile, looking at Shaker, who was chatting with Rita Edwin.

Uncle Regi, stylishly leaning on a fancy walking stick, with a well-polished pipe hanging from his lips, looked like a character from Colonial India. He was perpetually polishing something—first his thick-rimmed spectacles sliding down his nose, then his gleaming bald head desperately clinging to a few strands of white hair, then his silver mustache trimmed to perfection.

"Come here, little girl. How are you?" Uncle Regi invited Tina to sit by him at the table.

It was a long time since anybody had called her a little girl, but Tina did not mind. Uncle Regi was an interesting character to study. She sat next to him and accepted the glass of mulled wine Edwin offered her.

Birdie sat on the other side of Tina and asked, "How have you been, my dear?" And Birdie was another character to study. Her gnarled hands, wrinkled cheeks, and sparse hair pulled back into a silver bun declared her declining years. But her piercing bright eyes and shrewd expression challenged her age.

Christmas dinner was so different from what Tina was used to back home. The long dining table displayed a large tureen of curried chicken, an enormous oval bowl filled with saffron-scented basmati rice, a tray of spicy mackerel fried to perfection, an elegant bowl of creamy eggplant and potatoes, and slim okra, shallow-fried with onions and tomatoes. A ginger-plum cake, studded with walnuts and dried fruits, was sitting on a decorative platter on an end table, along with a variety of cookies. On another small table was a great bowl of fruit salad.

"So, Beena, Regi and I missed you when we were having dinner with Theo and Rita last month. How did you like Pennoor and its suburbs?"

asked Aunt Birdie.

"It was interesting. I liked it," responded Tina, reminding the old woman that she was Tina.

Yes, it was interesting. Tina's eyes went from the elegantly tailored curtains to wall hangings to the oversized collector's vases on the floor. As her eyes returned to the table, for a strange, forlorn moment, shadows of the lonely building at 19 Temple Street began to creep into the luxurious atmosphere and left Tina with a lingering pain. Then...the homeless shelter, signs of poverty, the nauseating smell, roach-infested bathroom, and dirty sheets and pillows invaded her memory. And there she was, beyond everything, the mysterious visitor who had knocked on Tina's door.

"Serena spent some time in Pennoor, Regi," Aunt Birdie told her husband and turned to Tina again. "Regi and I were supposed to go there in October. But we had to cancel our trip."

"We had to cancel because of the bombing incident in that area," offered Regi.

"That was not it, not at that time, Regi," corrected his wife. "You're thinking about the postal strike."

Regi looked at his wife in pity at first, polished his spectacles next, and cleared his throat. "Birdie, what are you talking about? The postal strike did not start in October. Anyway, how could it have anything to do with the derailment? The bombing tragedy was all over the news. Wasn't it?" asked Regi, looking at his audience for support.

"Yes," confirmed Shaker, glancing at Tina.

"Yes, Aunt Birdie," joined Rita, agreeing with Shaker. "Remember, Sylvia lost her neighbor in that explosion?" When Birdie offered a deaf ear, Rita shared a smile with Tina. "In fact, my brother was so worried about Tina's internship here right after that incident," she continued, turning towards her niece. "Peter wanted you to cancel it. Remember, Tina?"

"I know." Tina characteristically rolled her eyes. "He's still a little upset that I came here. And he was very angry that I didn't pack up and leave after the explosion near Breams Road in Chennai last month. But there's always some kind of a disaster going on somewhere in the world. When do we stop living because we're afraid of something exploding somewhere?"

"True. But, Tina, I guess it is a parent's job to worry. I can only imagine, you know, not having children of my own."

Tina smiled understandingly. "But, Aunt Rita, I didn't know your friend's neighbor died in that explosion."

"I heard from Sylvia last week, Tina," said Rita. "She left Seloor for a while to forget her misery. That's why she wasn't there last month when you were visiting that area."

"Rita, how is Sylvia getting along?" asked Regi. "I'm sorry she lost her neighbor. It's bad enough as it is. But when it happens to someone you know well... I can't even imagine what your friend must be going through," He took Tina's hand paternally and continued, "Your father is right. That's no matter for a young lady to decide. You ought to stay out of trouble."

"That's a lot of humbug!" Birdie declared, glaring at her husband. "And how is Serena supposed to do her job? Do you expect her to take a chaperone with her wherever she goes?"

Rita pretended to wipe her mouth with a napkin to hide her smile. Tina, wondering when she had turned into Serena and Beena, looked helplessly at her aunt.

"Well, Tina certainly had a guardian angel in the same train when she was stranded in Seloor." Dr. Augustine smiled at Shaker.

"Yes, she did," agreed Rita. "And we will always be thankful for that, Dr. Shaker."

Shaker smiled awkwardly and began to say something, but he was interrupted.

"See, Birdie, see what I mean?" asked Uncle Regi, trying to prove his point.

"I'll go see about dessert," mumbled Rita, rising from the chair, as Birdie and Regi got into an argument.

Edwin ushered his guests out of the dining room, and Tina followed her aunt.

"Are they always at each other's throat, Aunt Rita?" asked Tina, helping the servant arrange the desserts on different trays.

"Oh, that's Birdie and Regi for you. They're never happy unless they're worrying each other. Over sixty years of marriage, mind you, and they're truly inseparable."

When Tina returned to the balcony with her aunt, Aunt Birdie was talking with Shaker. At Birdie's invitation, Tina sat between them, breathing in the salt-coated breeze from the ocean. *There could not be a more perfect place*, she thought, looking at the silvery water in the distance, as the swaying branches of the willowy palm trees played hide-and-seek with the foaming waves. Tina looked up again at the sprinkled stars and the tall street lamps dazzling in twinkling Christmas lights along the beach.

"Isn't this a very different experience for you, Tina, after the snowy, cold Christmases in Pittsburgh?" asked Dr. Augustine. "But I'm sure the winter there has its own charms."

"Yes, of course," agreed Tina. "But I'm certainly having the time of my life here."

"Rita told me you're leaving day after tomorrow. Is your internship over? Are you going to visit us again, Mina?" asked Aunt Birdie.

"Yes, it's over," smiled Tina, not bothering to tell Birdie that she was not Mina. "I hope I return to do work some other time. But I'll certainly come back for a vacation. Do you have family in Pennoor? You said you were planning to visit there?" asked Tina.

"Yes, a distant relation. Actually, Regi and I volunteer at a church in Seloor. It's a small town, an hour or so from Pennoor."

A heavy hand pulled Tina's heartstrings. Seloor! Of course, she had heard of it, and she had spent a night there, precisely at 19 Temple Street. "I've actually seen the town," said Tina.

The Edwins followed Dr. Augustine out of the balcony as he was ready to leave. Uncle Regi soon fell asleep on the easy chair, and Aunt

Birdie began to crochet.

"Tina, you like it here, I think?" asked Shaker, sitting on one of the cane chairs next to Tina. His sharp eyes, as always, relaxed in his smile. "I always catch you looking at the waves."

"I could stand here and watch the sunrise and sunset all day, every day, all my life."

"Then why don't you?" he asked, staring at the ocean, the salty breeze playing hide-and-seek with his hair.

"What?"

"Why don't you stay here and look at the waves?" he asked again, smiling at her.

"How could I?" stammered Tina, still trying to understand his impossible suggestion. "I don't live here. I must go back, go back to my home, my work."

"Must you, really?"

"But this is ridiculous."

When the Edwins returned to the balcony, a servant announced that there was a phone call.

"I'll get it, Theo," offered his wife, stepping into the drawing room.

Aunt Birdie swirled the sherry with her gnarled hand and smiled amicably at the group.

"It's Sharif," said Rita, looking out through the balcony door.

Edwin got up instantly. "Dr. Shaker, please excuse me. Something critical, I'm sure. Otherwise, Sharif wouldn't bother us at this late hour."

"Really, Theo?" asked his wife. "Sharif lives for work. When has he paid attention to time?"

"Is Mr. Sharif as intimidating as he seems, Shaker?" asked Tina. "I've met him only a couple of times, but you know him better."

"I don't know him very well. And yes, he is intimidating. That's his trademark. But your uncle thinks he's a wonderful man. The problem is Sharif has dedicated his life and his career to counter-terrorism efforts to a point of obsession. But there's no better officer, I'm sure. So you're all packed?" asked Shaker.

"No. I'm leaving day after tomorrow, but I haven't packed one bit," replied Tina, bursting to ask him how he could make a ridiculously impossible suggestion. Perhaps, she thought, he had forgotten about it already.

But he had not. "So you're not going to stand here and enjoy the beautiful sunrise and sunset every day?"

"Oh, stop. We can't always do what we crave to do. You're not a child, and I don't need to tell you that," snapped Tina, as though impatient at a tiresome adolescent.

"Yes, we can. When you want something, if your heart is set on it absolutely, you can always do what you crave to do. But it's getting late." He got up abruptly. "I think I better leave before your aunt offers her spare room to me. Goodnight."

Tina stared at him, wondering if he was going to wish her a good trip, but he did not. After looking at her face at length, he walked out of the balcony.

Uncle Regi got up to leave when Edwin returned to the balcony.

"Good bye, Mina, have a safe trip home." Aunt Birdie took Tina's hands into hers at the gate, kissed her fondly on the cheek, and smiled warmly as she got into the car.

"Aunt Rita, how do you know Sylvia?" asked Tina, returning to the balcony with her aunt and uncle.

"She is a distant relation of mine, but we are more friends than relatives. Aunt Birdie also knows her quite well. Sylvia's mother was one of her good friends. I don't have a chance to visit Seloor often, but Sylvia comes to Chennai occasionally. It's a terrible loss...losing a friend in an explosion. She was really attached to her. And I don't know how Sylvia will ever recover from such a shock."

"Where will this violence and terrorism lead all of us?" asked Edwin, shutting the door for the night. "But let's forget Sylvia and her neighbor and the explosion for a while, Tina. Have another sherry with me while watching the waves."

Tina gladly took the comfortable chair and let her tired eyes rest on the dancing waves. Then *the end of all means is the beginning* slowly, imperceptibly crawled into her mind and began to play with her peace of mind.

December 26, 2009

Usman's phone rang while he was drinking his morning tea in his room at The Jannah behind Eastern Exports. Abdullah, who had joined Usman for a very early breakfast, was equally eager to receive this phone call.

"Sahib, it's over. She is gone," informed Yusuf. "I was at Anna International Airport until the plane was ready to take off, and I made sure Tina Matthew boarded the plane."

"Good. See you soon." Usman sighed in relief, his deep breath relaxing his steely expression just a bit.

"Well, I guess this is good news?" asked Abdullah, noticing his friend's unkempt silver beard and the repeatedly used tagiyah covering his head.

"Yes. This means that there is one less hurdle. I'm running out of men to do this job, Abdul. There are more entities to watch and few eyes to watch them. Aren't you going to eat your omelet?" asked Usman, staring at his guest's untouched breakfast.

"I will. Usman Bhai, this is why it's important to choose and train missionaries at regular intervals. We can't afford to lose men, the ones who will be needed for long-term assignments."

"I know, Abdul. We're trying. A few trainees are getting ready."

"And Maya is shaping up nicely. Don't you think, Usman Bhai?"

"Very well. Still needs some work, but it's just a matter of time. Kumar is working on her, with Manohar's help."

"I'm not comfortable with those two. I know we had this discussion already. Not that they're not efficient. I'd rather count on loyalty sprouting from religion, our holy cause, than having to pay a price for getting a job done."

"I agree. But even Yusuf, who is our breed," Usman smiled indulgently, "is *employed* by us. And so is your Sayeed. They all have to eat, Abdul."

Abdullah did not respond. His bulky frame made the chair creak miserably as he shifted his weight.

"Don't worry, Abdul. I could replace both Kumar and Manohar, but you know why I trained them in the first place."

"I know. I know. To mislead the authorities, if it comes to that. Right? Those two make unexpected employees for our purpose. I forget that sometimes. That's a very intelligent decision!" exclaimed Abdullah, admiring Usman's precise planning and foresight.

"Abdul, I'll keep Kumar and Manohar only as long as they're useful. I won't feel a shred of hesitation to get rid of them. And if I have to resort to that end, you'll be witness to that. Satisfied?"

"I've no doubt you'll do the right thing. Again, I'm glad Tina is out of here. What a relief! And you don't think there is anything to worry about, what's his name, Dr. Shaker?"

"Absolutely nothing. He's not going to be in the country for a long time. Otherwise, I would've taken care of him a while ago. So, don't worry."

"I hope Tina doesn't return. What if she does?" asked Abdullah, digging into his omelet.

"What if she does?" Usman asked in turn. "As long as she stays out of Seloor, her visit wouldn't worry me. Anyway, we've shifted our headquarters from 19 Temple Street. Although Tina spent most of her time in Chennai, away from Seloor, I asked Yusuf never to let Tina out of his sight because she had seen Maya only a few weeks ago. But I wouldn't worry about it anymore. And remember, Abdul, Tina was in Pennoor to work for a week at *The Express* with Mark Stevens. That's not his permanent office. Stevens is moving to his office in Chennai soon. So another visit by Tina to India wouldn't worry me at all. Stop worrying."

- 16 -

Pittsburgh • December 27, 2009

Gia and Peter Matthew received their daughter outside Customs and Immigration at Pittsburgh International Airport on a blustery afternoon.

"I can't tell you how glad I'm to see you, my dear," said the father, gushing in delight at the sight of his daughter.

"Home hasn't been the same without you, Tina," said the mother, almost tripping on a lanky man in a black hooded shirt, who was obstructing the way as Peter steered the luggage cart out of the sliding door.

The lanky man's eyes, concealed behind tinted glasses, carefully followed Tina until her parents embraced her before walking with her to their car. He picked up his phone and dialed a number while still following Tina with his eyes.

"She just arrived, Yusuf. Anything else?" he asked, stroking his trimmed goatee.

"Thanks for making a special trip from Toronto just for this, my friend," replied Yusuf. "I'll tell Usman Sahib. And I'll call you if there's anything else."

The man pocketed the phone, adjusted his glasses, and walked back to the terminal to catch his flight to Toronto.

Pittsburgh • December 28, 2009

Tina took the last sip of her wine, glancing at her advisor's frizzy, gray hair and winning smile. She declined his offer of another glass of wine and reached for the water. She had a long drive home.

"Thanks for having dinner with me, Tina. I can't believe it's been two months since you left for India. Did you have a nice Christmas?" asked Dr. Katz

"Yes, Alan, the best." Tina let her mind wander to Chennai, to St. Antony's Church, to an exotic Christmas dinner with her aunt and uncle, and somehow in the middle of it all, Shaker's parting comment began to play hide-and-seek with her jet-lagged mind. *When you want something, if your heart is set on it absolutely, you can always do what you crave to do.* Well, Shaker's comment should fade away, along with other distressing details, now that she was home.

"And you didn't have to do this today after arriving just yesterday. I'm not such a demanding advisor. Am I?" Dr. Katz's voice revived his student from her daydreaming.

Tina looked at the frosty window and the sea of white covering the landscape. Her heart filled with a new joy at the sight of snow-covered treetops and the sooty smell of crackling logs in the fireplace. "Well, I was eager to tell you everything—all that I couldn't tell you by email." Her hazel brown eyes anxiously studied the flickering flames while her nervous fingers played with the fringe of her long brown hair. There was so much she had to unload from her mind, and her mind was often floating in the middle when she was struggling to begin. Only then she realized that she had not discussed her strange encounter with that strange woman at the strange shelter with Dr. Katz. "But, Alan, I've to tell you something. You wouldn't believe it!" continued Tina, narrating the episode that was still painfully raw.

"That must have scared you! But you said the young lady was safely taken to her family. I'm glad to hear that. But what a night it must have been for you! First, stranded in a small train station, then this incident…" Dr. Katz's concern slowly transformed to a smile. "Does your father know about this?"

"Yes," laughed Tina, finding relief in her laughter when the night at the shelter still haunted her thoughts. "I diluted the incident considerably. Otherwise, he wouldn't let me travel again."

"Tina, I felt miserable when I read your description of the scene of the disaster near Seloor. That must have been a terrible visit for you."

"It was. The explosion occurred exactly in an extension called Kuyil. It means nightingale in Tamil. I met a few men and women—with homes lost, lives taken away—and I listened to their woes when they spoke with Mark Stevens. Mark took me there, you know. He is the reporter I wrote to you about. He was so much help in many ways. If it was terrible for me to visit the scene of the explosion, I can't imagine the agony suffered by the families who lost their loved ones. You know, Mark lost a friend in that tragedy. How horrible is that? In fact, my aunt's friend lost her neighbor."

"Oh, I'm so sorry to hear that!"

"Then I visited the place again with Dr. Shaker. The clinic where the trauma unit is coming up is somewhere in that area."

"Augustine and I had a long talk last week about Dr. Shaker. He's doing very good work, pivotal work, I must add, if he has picked up from where Augustine left off. So...you found a very young, good-looking mentor, I hear."

"Well, it was nice of Dr. Shaker to help me out at such short notice, Alan. So what have you been doing while I was gone? Are you all set to go to Florida?" Tina was eager to change the subject. Somehow it came upon her, at that very moment, that she had left a piece of her heart behind...somewhere along the waves overlooking her aunt's balcony. And she was very nervous about mending that piece. She didn't know how.

"You'll make a detailed report for me soon, I'm sure?" Dr. Katz smiled, helping Tina with her coat.

"Of course. We'll get a paper out of this."

"That's always a good incentive." Dr. Katz opened the door for Tina.

"Until next week, then, when we get back to the grind. Happy New Year to you and your family!"

"Happy New Year, Alan. Please say hello to your wife."

When Tina parked her car on her parents' driveway, she was surprised that she still had not shrugged off the disturbing declaration from her vulnerable mind. Perhaps *the end of all means was the beginning*. She was resolved to let it follow her as long as her research continued.

Ashville, Pennsylvania • January 6, 2010

Tina's nostalgic glance fell on the vending machine that had fed her gallons of cappuccino during her last few years in the university. She picked up a cup of the fragrant brew and knocked on her advisor's door.

"Come in," invited Dr. Katz, staring at the snow banks along the perimeters of the campus. "How are you, Tina? Shrugged off your jet lag, I hope?"

"Yes, Alan. I'm ready to resume the semester and finish my thesis," sighed Tina, taking the usual chair. Then the memory of her conversation with Dr. Katz, almost three months ago, occupied her thoughts. It felt more like three years—her father's paranoia, her mother's confidence, her trip to Chennai, Pennoor, and her accidental visit to Seloor. Annoyed by the clinging, haunting memory of the hostel, she let her glance fall on Dr. Katz's favorite quotation captured in an elegant frame: *The salvation of mankind lies only in making everything the concern of all—Solzhenitsyn.*

"So what's your perspective on the blast of October 15th?" asked Dr. Katz, sitting back comfortably on his chair. "Not what you would publish in your thesis, but your thoughts that you want to share with me."

"Alan, it happened in a small extension, as you already know. I think, from what I read and heard, the explosion was purposely meant to be a small-scale catastrophe. I know the degree of any disaster, small or large, is significant, but what I mean is that the group responsible for the explosion could have easily targeted a wider volume of victims, especially in a big city. My uncle feels that it was a testing strategy for a more widely planned disaster in the future. Dr. Shaker agrees with him."

"Why? On what basis?"

"Dr. Shaker's theory is based on nothing but his theory and his years of analyzing profiles of various disasters and the perpetrators, just as you and I might go about this. But my uncle, well, his assessment is naturally based on years of experience in dealing with counter-terrorism. I couldn't invade his confidence, and he wouldn't dream about stepping out of certain boundaries."

"Of course, but what do YOU think?"

"The last time a bombing disaster occurred in that area was in 1998, which was triggered by Al Umma. I don't know if you remember from our earlier discussions, but this incident happened as a result of gang fights between fundamental Muslims and Hindus. And the series of explosions were masterminded by Basha and his radical associates, mainly to create more rifts and animosities between the two communities; the Hindus and the Muslims. What is ironical is, Umma, in Al Umma, means community of believers. What is their belief? Revenge? Bloodshed? Terrorism? I believe a hundred years of research will not get me an answer. According to the news article I read, the clusters of fights started because a Hindu traffic policeman was killed by an Islamic radical."

"It generally starts like that, and then the situation becomes a blazing fire."

"Well, the recent explosion near Seloor is nowhere near the previous disaster site, but the occurrence in the same state, not very far from that neighborhood, raises many speculations."

"But don't we read about religious, political upheavals in those areas now and then?"

"Upheavals, yes—a few incidents of unrest, political disasters, and other anti-religious fights and what not—but not a strategically planned bombing that kills several human beings and one that creates havoc in a village. Alan, the anonymous call the police received still drives me crazy. The caller bragged about the disaster, how cleverly his organization planned this massacre. And his statement, *the end of all means is the beginning*, is so elusive. Still...it makes sense to me. And sometimes I don't want it to make sense. Do you understand my frustration?"

"Of course. That statement is still stubbornly hovering over your head, I see. The source of the call wouldn't be traced, in spite of growing technology!"

"Yes, the call was made from a public phone booth. You know, one of the witnesses of the disaster was riding his bicycle along the railway tracks. He remembered seeing a woman, somewhat young, sitting under the overpass a few minutes before the explosion happened. He was injured during the blast, but he escaped death because he was quite a distance from the railway tracks. He went to the police, but..." stalled Tina, her enthusiasm to relate all diffused by her sinking courage. "But the cyclist's body was found in one of the rooms in another prison in a town called Medur, I think, where he was sheltered by the police. He was shot."

"Because he could identify the woman, if she was indeed the suicide bomber?"

"Probably. What other reason could there be? Not that the cyclist's memory would help the matter. That young lady obviously died in the blaze." Tina got up abruptly and went to the wide window. "Alan, I fell in love with that small town. Seloor seems idyllic, so innocent—tall coconut trees, streams weaving in and out of dense groves, endless paddy fields—a perfect spot to spend a quiet week. Now the innocence is ravaged by naked violence. *The end of all means is the beginning*... Really, the audacity of it all." Tina began to study her hands, strangely trembling in that quiet, secure room, in a secure corner of the world, surrounded by books, coffee, and the smell of Dr. Katz's peppermint pipe tobacco.

"Tina," whispered Dr. Katz, immediately reading something unfamiliar in his student's familiar face. "I think you want to tell me something. Why don't you spill it before something in that corner of your mind explodes to pieces?"

Tina returned to the chair, startled by her advisor's shrewd observation. "What are you? A mind reader?" asked Tina, taking the liberty to scold her advisor, who was more a wise friend than just a professor. "Alan, I was so eager to come back from India and see my parents, my home, the department, you, but...I feel incomplete. I get this overwhelming sensation that I've forgotten something. I can't get rid of this empty feeling that is eating me. I don't know how long I can go on like this."

"Then don't go on like this. Tina, I don't have to tell you, but you've got to separate your research from your life. You can't let it dictate terms. If it does, drop your doctorate program, find a different major, and explore a different career." Dr. Katz took a long look at his student. "I know you're strong. What's eating you?"

"Don't worry. I won't let my research or the nature of it pull me down. It's that hostel in Seloor and the insane woman who knocked on my door. Whether I become a psychologist or decide to pursue investment banking, that hostel and that woman will haunt me until the day I die. I have this nagging, guilty feeling that I should've done something about it."

"You told me that the men in her family followed her and took her to safety. If they had not, then your restlessness would make sense. Tina, is that what's been bothering you? You handled the situation very well. Stop worrying about it. Now, the hostel is a different matter altogether. What would you like to do to feel at ease about it?"

"That hostel is harboring a few homeless women and children now. I want to go there once a year and help. You know, help with my hands, work there. But, Alan, I wish I had stayed a little longer and continued to work with Dr. Shaker. That's another thing that's nagging me. We had long conversations like you and I have. He's very insightful, and he taught me a lot. He must have acquired a hell of a lot from Dr. Augustine," smiled Tina, strangely embarrassed about discussing Neil Shaker. "I'm quite sure he wanted me to stay a little longer and work with him on some of the profiles he was trying to understand. I should've listened to my instinct and stayed there for a few more weeks."

Dr. Katz took a deep breath and reached for his coffee cup. "Follow me, Tina," he said, rising from his chair.

"Where are we going?" she asked, considerably puzzled.

He did not respond but continued to walk towards the end of the corridor and turned left into a conference room. "Tina, sit down and quietly watch this DVD for five minutes," he said, turning on the giant screen. "Then I'll ask you what I've been waiting to ask you since you returned from India."

She sat down, very much curious. He sat next to her and played the DVD. A series of bombings thundered in the screen. Mutilated, charred body parts gaped in the rubble. Smoke and hungry flames leaped from the ground and disappeared in the cloudy sky. A sequence of settings, from skyscrapers to tiny villages, appeared and disappeared. Men ran, children screamed, and women wailed while beating their hands on their breasts. A man held a body in his arms and shouted angrily at heaven. Then, as though crouching away from the string of nightmarish scenes, the screen went blank.

"Where did this happen, Alan?" asked Tina, trying to catch her breath. She still wondered why her professor brought her there and threw the disaster at her like that.

"Any place. Any time. I've sequentially gathered all the videos of suicide bombings and other explosions. Do I sound crazy, after all the years you've known me?" he asked, pathetically staring at her frightened expression. "I watch this disgrace, the greatest disgrace to humanity, every week, Tina. Do you know why?"

She shook her head, worried about her advisor's grave expression.

"This is what motivates me to do what I'm afraid to do, day in and day out, without running away from it. When I became a faculty member almost forty years ago, I was here for a job, Tina. But this job has changed me, has made me what I am today. Every time I watch these videos, this collapse of mankind, a part of me cries silently, and I never stop wondering why there is such a long wait for peace. But I'm glad I think about peace while I cringe at the videos, glad to be here for students like you, glad that I can give a pep talk to nudge you on. Now, at this point, let me ask you a question. Take as much time as you need and answer me. It doesn't have to be today, or tomorrow, or a month from now."

"What is it?" asked Tina, who had never seen her advisor at such a steep edge of passion until that moment.

"Do you want to complete your thesis for the sake of completing it, perhaps to get a job? Or are you here for more than that? When you have an answer to my question, you'll know how to address your quest; whether you should go back to India and work with Dr. Shaker."

Tina looked at her advisor's familiar face, searching for something she still did not quite grasp. What kind of question was that? And what kind of answer did she have? "I know why I'm here, Alan," she replied, staring at the blank screen. She didn't have to go over what she saw a few minutes ago. She would never forget those few minutes. Never. "I know why I came here. I wanted to find the key that might unlock the secrets to the bond between psychology and terrorism. I wanted to accomplish my five-little-pages-a-day in the process of writing my thesis. But my search has taken me to more than five-little-pages-a-day. This is not a sudden insight. It's been coming on so slowly. I'm glad I'm not here just for the sake of thesis. To hell with it." Tina smiled, feeling relieved at unloading a heavy burden from her restless mind. "The secret is holding on to that moral courage that is sometimes elusive, as you once told me. I don't need a month or a couple of years to answer you. Here is my answer which I've known for a while. I'm here in search of peace. Does it make sense?"

"Yes. You know very well that peace can exist only where truth is valued and..."

"Or peace cannot exist where there is violence intertwined with lies," Tina finished her advisor's thought, rising from the chair. She began to walk towards the exit, and her advisor followed her. "I'm going back to Chennai to work on an extended internship with Dr. Shaker."

"Good. Good. But not until February, my dear. Don't forget that I've an obligation as your advisor. We need to review your collection of five-little-pages-a-day. And I'd like to find a good place to hide once your father finds out that you're resuming your internship in India," he said, smiling with her.

- 17 -

The Jannah • January 2010

When Yusuf came to the kitchen at The Jannah to get a cup of tea, Jamil walked in. Although similar in age, Jamil stopped politely to make room for his contemporary who was the apple of the master's eye.

"Ah, Jamil, just the man I was looking for. How are you doing?" asked Yusuf, appraising the employee who had arrived from the northern borders at the end of an extensive training. Although young, Jamil's tall figure and stoic posture commanded respect like a veteran in the field. His unusually light brown eyes and an extraordinarily fair skin were accentuated by a shock of dark hair combed away from his forehead. "Usman Sahib wants me to talk to you about a candidate and her mission. He wants you to assist me when I travel with her to ensure that everything is going well. Do you have a few minutes now?"

"Yes, Yusuf." Jamil's brown eyes twinkled. The master was already beginning to rely on him, and he was very pleased. "Usman Sahib told me that you would be speaking with me soon."

"She is a unique missionary. We're getting her ready for a mission. She is mostly in seclusion. I'm going to take you to her, and I want you to observe her closely and trace any difficulty that might arise later. Follow me."

Jamil followed his colleague to a secluded room opposite to the master's suite on the second floor of The Jannah, the new headquarters behind Eastern Exports.

A dim light fought for life in the dingy room. A creaky metal cot, with smudged sheets and a damp pillow, fought for breath in one corner. A frail naked body of a young woman fought for dignity on the cot. Kumar, standing by the shabby cot, held his handkerchief under his nose to quell the overwhelming stench of sweat and urine. Usman opened the window slightly to let in some fresh air.

"Maya, will you do it?" Usman asked softly, leaning towards the fragile face on the cot.

"How can I?" she whispered, gasping for air.

"But you must, Maya. You have nobody. Remember?" Usman asked slowly, softly, without raising his voice.

"I have somebody," she cried. "I have…" she cried again, unable to speak.

"Are you going to be trouble again, Maya?" asked Usman, his sharp eyes jumping to her bruises, one by one. "Remember what happens when you disobey me."

Manohar, standing on the other side of the cot, looked at a thickset woman in a cotton sari. Maria understood Manohar's signal and filled a syringe before walking to the patient.

Maya cried silently when her eyes landed on the syringe. Her mind meandered through unknown avenues, dark alleys, and bottomless pits whenever the venomous fluid rushed through her veins. But she had no fire left in her to protest, and she let the sharp needle sink into her bony arm, pumping more poison while the men surrounding her poured evil suggestions into her ears.

"Say 'I have nobody,' Maya. Say it," prompted Kumar, leaning towards Maya's face.

She vaguely remembered her life, troubled and fragmented, tripping and falling into Usman's waiting arms. She didn't respond.

"Listen Maya," continued Usman. "Remember that your father abandoned you. See how he punished you because he hated your mother? Did he ever love you? No. Was he ever kind to you, even when you were a child? No. He took your salary and drank it all away or gambled it in filthy dens. He sold you. He didn't care about your fate for a moment. He left you in the hands of pimps and other predators when he sent you to that interview. He knew you were gullible and helpless. And where is the man who wanted to marry you? He never came to help you, never came to get you. And your neighbor, the only person who cared about you, is dead. Say 'I have nobody,' Maya."

"I have nobody," whispered Maya. Yes, he had abandoned her. Deserted love. Deserted life.

"Say it again. Come, say it again."

She said, "I have nobody" again and again.

"Good. You tried to run away like a traitor. You almost betrayed me. See what happens to a betrayer? Be a good girl and listen to me. You'll get all that you lost when you reach your heaven. And you'll reach your heaven if you listen to every word I tell you now. Say 'nobody loves me,' Maya," suggested Usman, gently taking her hand in his. When she didn't reply, he pressed her hand and prompted his instructions again.

"Nobody loves me," repeated Maya, again and again.

"Say 'my society is my enemy,' Maya. See how your society has made you an orphan. It's wicked. You should kill your society and destroy the world. You will. Won't you? Come on, say it," Usman's voice dribbled softly, gently.

"I'll kill my society. I'll destroy the world." Maya's emaciated body began to tremble.

"I've nothing to live for," interrupted Kumar, shaking her limp body. "Say it."

"I've nothing to live for," repeated Maya, shivering despite the warm temperature in the room. "I've nothing to live for."

"I'm all you have, Maya," Usman whispered softly, intoxicatingly, gently pulling the sheet to reveal her bare body. He opened a tube of ointment and methodically applied the balm on her gaping wounds. He covered her body with the sheet again and rested his hand on her shoulder. "I'm all you have, Maya. Your father sold you. Your fiancé abandoned you. Your society discarded you. You've nothing to live for. Will you do anything I ask you to do? Will you promise me to do anything I ask you to do?"

"Yes." Maya's breathing became strenuous while the drug raced through her veins. "I promise. I promise to do anything you ask me," assured Maya, again and again, and drifted into a dream-filled sleep. As she started to run, Gods, demons, men, and women began to chase her, pushing her towards the bottom of a bottomless ocean. There was no way out. Her father sold her. Her love abandoned her. Her society discarded her. Yes, she would destroy the world.

"Yusuf, I'm glad you brought Jamil with you," smiled Usman, walking towards the two young men who were watching the scene of human indignity from the corner of the room. "All's going well. Finalize the plans for Maya's mission. March or April should be fine. Make sure Jamil is aware of every detail about the mission and about Maya."

"Yes, Sahib, I'll finalize the plans and make sure Jamil knows all the details," replied Yusuf, walking with his colleague towards the kitchen. "Jamil, before you interact with Maya while you assist me in the mission, I want to make sure you know her past. If I may remind you, your memory of every detail is crucial because our missions can collapse if we lose concentration. And..." he stalled, his boyish features turning serious as he hunted for the right words, just like his master often did. "Jamil, you're the counselor, whose encouraging pep talk to the missionary is essential at the point the mission is to be executed. Keeping the missionary dangling on your hook, while you are supervising the assignment, is the only way to complete the task. Occasionally, even the most well-organized missions get aborted because the powerful chain between the missionary and the counselor is severed. You know what I mean?"

"Yes, Yusuf," agreed Jamil, a little in awe of his contemporary. "I've seen Maya before, but I haven't had a chance to observe her because, as you said, she is often kept secluded. But I'm waiting to know more about her."

"Come, let's get a cup of tea and we'll discuss the first major assignment in which you're going to assist me." Yusuf picked up two cups of scalding tea from the counter. "She is a native of Seloor, as you know. Last year in August..." Yusuf began to discuss the paddy-field-incident with his colleague.

Maya • Seloor • August 1, 2009

The dusty Town bus stopped a few hundred feet from the bus stop after considerable groaning. Maya anxiously glanced at her watch—ten minutes past ten.

"All passengers, get down here," shouted the conductor.

"But I need to get to First Cross Street. What happened?" asked Maya, trying to compete with chaotic questions from other passengers.

"The bus can't go farther than here. I know it's late in the night, but the driver says it's engine trouble," replied the conductor, and quickly stepped out of the bus to avoid more questions.

"Do you think there'll be another bus coming this way?" Maya ran after the conductor.

"No. I don't think so," he replied, turning impatiently to the next worried passenger.

Maya walked nervously from the bus stop to look for a taxi or an auto-rickshaw. She saw nothing. She then tried to estimate the distance from the bus stop to her house. It could not be more than three to five kilometers. So she began to walk.

"We're returning from a wedding. Isn't this awful?" asked a middle-aged woman, walking briskly with a large group of men and women.

"Yes, it is." Maya was thankful for the conversation. She was a little afraid to walk alone at night.

"Where are you coming from so late in the night? Aren't you young to be walking alone?" asked the woman, studying Maya's features. She saw a pair of large limpid eyes and a slightly chubby nose looking incongruous on a gaunt face. Her high cheekbones, instead of adding grace, made her thin face appear thinner.

"I work in one of the Call Centers near Town Hall. I'm used to working late." Maya's annoyance at the stranger's direct question would make no difference. Most of the villagers were quite blunt, but they were also unworldly and kind.

"Call Center? My sister's son has a job like that in Trichy. You talk to a lot of foreigners. Don't you?"

"Not just that," smiled Maya.

The group stopped by the paddy fields where the main road forked to three different paths. The road on the left went to High Street and the right formed Market Street. The middle ran into a small stretch of an aged bridge.

"We're going towards Anna Nagar. Where's your home?" asked the woman, standing at the tip of High Street. "We'll be glad to make sure you reach home safely."

"Thank you, but I just have to cross the bridge to get to my house on First Cross Street," said Maya, looking at the crowded neighborhood on the other side of the uneven dirt road. "It's not far. It's a short cut, actually, but thank you so much."

Maya quickly moved towards the bridge after the woman walked away with her group. The generous moonlight made up for the flickering dim lights on one side of the road, and Maya walked carefully and gingerly on the uneven dirt road. A gentle breeze touched her temples and relieved a bit of the August mugginess. She reached the end of the bridge quickly and turned right to cut across a small field and stopped abruptly after a few steps. The way was blocked, and she saw repair signs in the faint light. Now she had to maneuver her way along the long, winding trail towards her home.

Maya retraced her path on the bridge and went to the road on the right. She was used to coming home late, but she had never walked this long stretch alone so late in the night. And she felt a little scared. She pulled her purse close to her breast and began to walk fast on Market Street. A man pedaled on his bicycle in the opposite direction. A car whizzed by her, followed by a lorry, and then there was absolute silence. She walked past the Clock Tower and looked at her watch in the flickering light near the tea stall. It was after eleven. She wondered if she should call for help, but there didn't seem to be anybody inside the tea stall. She walked on while glancing at Sri pharmacy, which was enveloped in darkness.

'A few more minutes, a few more minutes,' Maya uttered under her breath, trying to overcome her steadily rising anxiety. She was out of the market square now. She soon reached a lonely sea of paddy fields—lonely, except for a huge solitary building somewhere in the middle of it. She had seen it often from the main road and had wondered what it was. Now that she was the only soul by the fields, she could hear every minuscule sound, whether she wanted to or not, and the medley of sounds increased her anxiety. A stray dog was chasing a bony cat on the other side of the road. Something crawled by her feet and she hoped it was not a snake. She heard the swaying branches of the tall palm trees rustling in the gentle breeze. Then, she thought she heard a faint rhythm of music. As she walked on, the sound of music gradually grew, and with that her fear thickened. Why was she hearing music in the middle of nowhere? Was there a cyclist on the road with a radio? She looked back, but there was no one. After walking for a few more minutes, she stared at a dilapidated building—a temple-like structure behind a thin cluster of trees. The edifice exacerbated her existing fear in the stillness of the night, and she began to walk faster. Her glance then fell on an enclosure, a cluster of makeshift sheds on the edge of the field. One of the sheds was dimly lit and appeared less rundown than the others. And a small window let out a faint light and music. Maya smiled despite her precarious nerves as relief shot from her tense body. Somebody was playing the radio and this was the sound that had reached her ears a while ago. She had been afraid for no reason. While she sighed in relief, the music stopped abruptly, and she heard faint, indistinct voices. She was about to walk past the enclosure when she heard a man's voice, and she froze in fear.

"No, don't, please don't," he cried.

Maya, involuntarily bound to the spot, waited for more.

"No..." screamed the man's voice again, and stopped immediately when she heard a gunshot piercing the silence, gradually echoing through the paddy fields. She began to tremble, unable to gather her crumbling nerves. When she tried to move away, her eyes fell on the window again, and she saw a faint movement. She thought she saw a pair of eyes looking at her, and she ran for her life. As she moved away, the music began again. She was sure that whoever was staring through the window was coming after her. She looked back one more time on the verge of fainting, but nobody followed her. But those eyes seemed to trail after her. That face—she hadn't seen much of that face, except that a thin line of hair peeped above the windowsill. But it was a glimpse, a brief image caught during a couple of seconds, and nothing more. The vision was already a blur.

As she was nearing the outskirts of her neighborhood, a cyclist went past her, but quite a few men who worked in the mills returned home on their bicycles. As though from nowhere, a cluster of small houses sprouted on narrow lanes, with hardly enough space for two cars to drive by simultaneously. Maya quickly turned left towards First Cross Street and ran to the third house on the right when it began to rain. She covered her head with her scarf and opened the small gate just barely hanging on its hinge. It creaked painfully, and Maya carefully closed it, as though afraid of disturbing the neighborhood. And the neighborhood was peacefully sleeping. She got the key out of her purse with a shaky hand and nervously unlocked the front door. As she stepped inside and pushed the door to shut it, she saw a cyclist going past her house. Maya secured the latch and walked to her room with sweaty palms and dry throat. She stopped briefly by her father's room, but he didn't stir.

She changed into her nightgown and went to the kitchen to get a glass of water. When she stood by the window and took a deep breath, she saw the cyclist again, going past the backyard. Why was he circling the block in the middle of the night? Was he lost? She took another glass of water and went to her room.

The young cyclist pulled out his cell phone from his shirt pocket after parking his cycle at the end of First Cross Street.

"Well?" asked an authoritative male voice.

"I know where she lives. What else would you like me to do, Sahib?" asked the cyclist.

"Destroy the sheds, Yusuf. Aren't they in poor condition? Make it look like an accident caused by the laborers. There's a lot of construction going on there right now. Gather everything you can find about her, her job, her family, and see me tomorrow morning at 11."

"Anything else, Sahib?"

"The young woman might try to file a report at the police station. Ask our man to take down the statement personally. See you tomorrow."

The cyclist made a mental list of his assignments and rode on.

Inspector Ravi opened his eyes reluctantly and looked at his wife through bleary eyes.

"You have a call," she said, holding the phone.

"What time is it?" asked Ravi, trying to sit up on his bed. "Who's calling at this early hour?"

"How should I know?" snapped his wife, walking away from him. "I'll get your coffee."

"Yes, who is it?" Ravi answered the call, looking wearily at the clock.

When Yusuf began to speak, the inspector attentively sat up straight. He grabbed his notepad from the bedside table and began to take down the instructions carefully.

"I'll personally take down the statement if the young woman comes today. You can count on it. I'll instruct the constables to see me first before they do anything," promised Ravi.

Yusuf disconnected the call.

Maya woke up reluctantly, not willing to face a new day when a terrible mystery gaped at her. She opened the front door and picked up the milk packets from the cloth bag hanging by the gate. She went to the kitchen and boiled the milk while spooning coffee grounds into the coffee filter, all the time thinking about the previous night—her lonely walk along the paddy fields, the small shed, and the gunshot puncturing the stillness of the night. Who would believe her if she repeated what she saw and what she heard? She made a cup of coffee for her father and went to the drawing room. And the routine sight welcomed her—her father's rotund form was sinking into the creaky chair, the regional newspaper in his hand, his heavy spectacles sliding on his nose.

"Appa, I need to talk to you," began Maya, handing her father the steaming cup of coffee.

"Not now. I've to go to Medur on urgent business." He did not remove his glance from the newspaper.

"But it's important," insisted Maya.

"Don't bother me, girl. I won't have breakfast. I'm taking the early bus," he barked, quickly walking to the bathroom.

When her father was out of the house, Maya promptly went to her neighbor's home. A middle-aged woman in a plaid housecoat opened the door and stared at Maya with her very round eyes, made rounder by chubby cheeks and a sturdy figure. Her frizzy hair, casually gathered in a ponytail, completed the ensemble.

"Maya!" the neighbor said happily, a little surprised by the early-morning visit.

"Aunt Sylvie, I need to talk to you," whispered Maya, walking into the house and shutting the door.

Sylvia took her neighbor to the sofa. "Maya, what happened?"

"Last night, while I was returning from work, the bus didn't make it to First Cross Street. Auntie Sylvie, the short cut through the bridge was blocked, you know, so I had to take the long way by the market square."

"Alone? What time was it?"

"After 10:00. Almost 11:00."

"Oh my God, and you were alone. I wish I could do something about that. Why didn't you call me? But what happened?"

"You know the lonely stretch of paddy fields? There was a small, enclosed space like a shed, not very far from the market. I saw, no, I heard a man getting shot. I hope he didn't..."

"What? You think someone was shot? Are you sure?" Sylvia asked doubtfully. "Did you tell your appa about this?"

"When have I been able to tell my appa anything?" Maya asked pathetically, her limpid eyes swimming in anxiety. "No, I didn't tell him. I wanted to, but he was so impatient to get out of the house. Anyway, he left home early this morning after having a cup of coffee."

"Have you eaten breakfast?" asked Sylvia, pushing her towards the kitchen. "Have some oatmeal with me."

Sylvia turned off the stove where she was simmering oats in a small stockpot. She ladled the porridge into two bowls and took them to the dining table. "Can you get me a couple of spoons, dear?" asked Sylvia, slicing bananas into the bowls.

"Should I tell the police?" asked Maya. "Aunt Sylvie, isn't that the right thing to do?"

"You know, we don't want trouble because we didn't report right away. Okay, finish your breakfast and go get ready. We'll go to the police station near Town Hall. I'll be ready in fifteen minutes."

Sylvia read the report Maya had just completed in the dusty office of the police station. Sitting nervously on the edge of a wooden chair next to Sylvia, Maya glanced at Inspector Ravi. He was broodingly stroking his mustache that seemed to occupy a good portion of his puffy cheeks. Her glance shifted to the photograph of Mahatma Gandhi, hanging slightly askew on the wall behind the inspector's desk, and fell on the inscription: *Truth alone triumphs.*

Inspector Ravi took the report in his hand and asked, "Why were you walking alone that late in the night?"

"My job is such that I can't help it," replied Maya, a little indignant about the way he was staring at her, measuring her. "I've written all the necessary information, and I've already told you about my job."

"Don't you have a brother, father, or someone dependable who can walk with you from the bus stop?" he asked, not taking his eyes off Maya's large eyes on her thin face.

"I'm an only child, and my father...my father goes to sleep by nine." Maya exchanged a quick glance with Sylvia. "Anyway, the bus usually comes to the main road, and my house is only about five minutes from there. Last night, the bus couldn't get to my usual stop."

"Do you have a cell phone?"

"Yes, given by my company."

"Did you try calling someone when you were stranded away from the usual bus stop?"

"We don't have a landline phone at home, and there was nobody I could call that late in the night."

"She should have called me," interjected Sylvia. "I worry about her."

Inspector Ravi smiled seraphically and asked, "Why did you stop by that shed, or building, or whatever it is?"

"I didn't mean to. I had to walk by the fields to get to my house. I looked at the window only because someone had just screamed..."

"At the small house?" he asked, as though speaking to a child.

"Yes. It was not a house; it was just a shed."

"Was there any number or landmark to identify that shed?"

"I didn't notice anything, except that the big building in the middle of the fields was not very far from the shed."

"Just one small shed?" asked Inspector Ravi, looking at the report, as though unable to believe the description.

"Not really. Looked like there were two or three small sheds with construction equipments, but some light and sound were coming from only one part of the sheds, which is where I saw... I mean I heard..."

"Was this shed close to any road in particular?"

"I don't know. I don't think so. I must have walked for about fifteen minutes from the market, when I heard..."

"And what *exactly* did that person say while screaming?"

"It happened so fast, and I was very scared. I think the man said, 'Please don't,' and then I heard a gunshot. When I looked at the window in fear, I saw someone staring at me. Then I walked away very fast."

"Would you remember the face that stared at you?" asked Inspector Ravi, very slowly, almost unnervingly. "Would you be able to identify that face?"

"I... I don't think so. I saw only those eyes."

Sylvia took Maya's unsteady hand comfortingly.

"Do you think it was a man or a woman?" he continued.

"I think it was a man..."

"Why?"

"I thought at the time I saw facial hair."

"But you're not sure?"

"No."

"And nobody followed you?" he asked. "That's quite strange."

"Why is it strange?" asked Maya.

Sylvia winced and touched Maya's hand quickly, silently begging her to avoid impertinent questions.

"Well, I think it's strange that the killer, if there was a killer, did not come after you when he realized that there was a witness," the officer answered in a cool voice, absentmindedly combing his wide mustache with his stubby fingers. He stressed *if there was a killer* a good deal. "We'll look into this. Thank you for reporting the incident at the paddy fields."

He got up and walked to the door to open it. Maya followed Sylvia quietly out of his office.

Ravi dialed a very private number, which reached Naim's Tailoring near Town Hall. In a few minutes, Ravi's call was returned from another line.

"Well? What happened?" asked Yusuf.

"She was here, and I personally accepted the statement." Ravi told Yusuf everything, confident that he had bagged a significant payment for this transaction.

Sylvia got hold of an auto-rickshaw outside Town Hall.

"You can get down at Lawrence Road bus stand and take the bus to work, Maya. You'll be late to work, obviously." Sylvia tried to talk above the clattering auto-rickshaw and the milieu of honking vehicles.

"That's fine. Remember, I called my supervisor from your house to let him know that I would be late."

"But why are you working today? Don't you have the day off, especially since you worked last night?"

"I'm doing overtime."

"Again? You've to watch your health, dear."

"Aunt Sylvie, I've been thinking about the police report. The whole time we were there, it somehow seemed so incredible. The incident didn't even affect the police as I thought it might."

"I know. Probably because violence has become a very common occurrence, and it does seem incredible that the man didn't follow you when he knew you heard the gunshot."

"I'm glad he didn't follow me, but I wonder why he didn't."

"Maya," whispered Sylvia, her round eyes staring nervously. "Those eyes you saw, staring at you, could have belonged to a woman. Don't you think?"

"Yes, it's possible. But I think I saw hair on that face. I wish I had seen the face a little better. I wish…"

"No, I'm glad you didn't. Then you probably wouldn't be here, speaking with me," said Sylvia, tightly holding her friend's hand.

The rickshaw stopped jerkily near the bus stand and Maya got out quickly.

"I thought you were going home?" asked Maya, when Sylvia followed her.

"No. Now that I'm here, I might as well finish a couple of errands."

- 18 -

19 Temple Street • August 9, 2009 • 10:30 a.m.

Yusuf, who had been following Maya discreetly after the-incident-at-the-paddy-fields on the night of August 1st, parked his bicycle in front of 19 Temple Street. He walked up the stairs with easy familiarity and entered a room after politely knocking on the door, where his master was sitting behind a desk.

"Have a seat, Yusuf," Usman said to his favorite assistant, while referring to a printed sheet in his bony hand.

Yusuf sat down on the edge of a chair like an obedient schoolboy, with very fair skin and straight, short, combed hair. His slim frame, adding to the school-boyish appearance, defied his twenty-five years.

"Sahib, I've some more information about Maya. Rajan, Maya's father, is in deep debt," began Yusuf. Usman's expression did not change. "You already know that Rajan works at Eastern Exports. He owes Abdullah Sahib a lot of money."

Usman's expression relaxed. "Does he?" he asked, getting up from his chair, stroking his gray beard. "And you said a lot of money."

"Yes. In fact, Rajan has been going to Medur frequently, working on an errand to pay off a part of his debt."

Usman smiled a very satisfied smile. He knew Abdullah's errands—absolutely dishonorable. And those errands were worth considerable wages. "That's very good news, and Maya has no siblings." Usman walked to the window and stared at the area in the distance where a cluster of sheds had stood humbly until the previous week. "And she has no mother."

"And Rajan has no family in the area."

"What exactly does he do for a living?"

"He manages some of the accounts at Abdullah Sahib's warehouse, especially the items allotted for export to the gulf. He reports to Sayeed."

"I see. What's Rajan's situation in town? Does he have a house?"

"Yes, the one in First Cross Street. The house was left to him and his daughter by his wife, who died when Maya was a child. Sahib, I heard that Rajan is a poor excuse for a father, and he is not really attached to his daughter. He brags at work that he uses all of his daughter's salary and has no qualms about it."

"Good! Good!" Usman smiled again. He liked the way things were shaping. "Does Maya earn a good salary?"

"She works at the Call Center near Town Hall. I'd say she makes a decent salary."

"The man has one child who is self-sufficient, has a home, and a decent income. Then why the hell is he in so much debt?"

"He gambles, and he likes to drink. In fact, his neighborhood knows about his addiction to alcohol."

"Really? What about friends? Who will miss Maya?"

"A couple of friends have married and gone away and others work in neighboring towns now. None close by. But she is very attached to her neighbor. Her name is Sylvia Joseph. She was at the police station with Maya while she was there to file a report. Sylvia, I believe, was very close to Maya's mother."

"What about a man? Is there a man?"

"Not quite sure about it. I need a little more time to gather details. I think people might have seen Maya with a young man outside the Call Center and sometimes in the restaurants near her office. I've asked Sayeed to explore from the warehouse. I can report in a couple of days with more information."

"That'll be fine. Keep working on it and," paused Usman, fondly looking at his favorite disciple, "you've done very well, Yusuf."

Seloor Town • August 9, 2009 • 5:30 p.m.

Maya tidied her cubicle, a nagging frustration stubbornly clinging to her. She felt she did the right thing by going to the police, but the inspector's lackluster response still made her uneasy. She picked up her purse and walked out of the air-conditioned building. As soon as she stepped on the pavement, the sticky warmth of the exterior greedily clung to her skin while the exhaust fumes, slamming brakes, and the assortment of people scurrying through the streets welcomed her to another ordinary evening. In the middle of everyday chaos, she did not notice a bald man who was unobtrusively watching her from a small corner store, with a bottle of soda in his hand. He took his handkerchief from his shirt pocket and wiped his sweaty face. After depositing the empty bottle on the counter, he began to follow Maya. He paused near Sunshine Beauty Parlor when she stopped on the pavement to answer her cell phone.

"Hello, Maya, Mark here."

"Yes, Mark," she greeted wearily. She knew who it was. He didn't have to announce. "What is it?"

"Are you still angry?"

Maya began to cross the road and turned towards the crowded bus stop.

"The least you can do is give me a chance to explain. Please?" he begged.

"Okay, explain."

The bald man averted his face as Maya walked by his side and continued to follow her after a couple of minutes.

"Not on the phone...when I can't look at your face. Can't we meet somewhere?" asked Mark.

"Okay. Where? When?" she asked, entering Cross Town Road.

"Where are you right now?"

"Just a few minutes from my office, by Cross Town Road."

"I'll meet you at Woodlands in five minutes?"

"All right." Maya shoved the phone into her purse and began to walk towards the restaurant at the intersection of Cross Town and JP Road, and the bald man, after exchanging information on his cell phone, followed her at a reasonable interval.

While Maya thought that finding an empty table in the crowded restaurant would be impossible, a young man in a crisp white shirt came forward to meet her.

"Miss Rajan?" he asked politely.

"Yes," replied Maya, wondering how he knew her name.

"Mr. Stevens called a couple of minutes ago. I saved a quiet table upstairs, if you'll follow me?"

Maya followed him, impressed about the quiet table at a moment's notice. *One of the perks of Mark's job as a journalist*, she thought, while sitting on a plush chair in a very private section. The angular booth was located in the corner of the room, cut off from most of the other dining tables, with a view of Cross Town Road. The dining area was quiet and offered privacy as the walls between booths rose to about six feet in height. A small, neatly dressed gentleman sat down in the booth behind Maya while she absentmindedly looked at the slowly moving vehicles on the busy road.

Mark arrived soon, sat opposite to Maya, dropped his briefcase by his chair, and said, "I'm so glad to see you."

Maya avoided his eyes, anxiously begging for attention through his spectacles.

"What will you have?" he asked, trying to catch her eye.

"Just a cup of tea, Mark."

"Come on, I'm sure you're hungry. Have dinner with me. Please?"

Maya looked at him at length, at his dismal expression, at his carelessly combed hair, and involuntarily smiled. "Why don't you order the usual?"

"We'll have two veggie burgers, spicy fries, carrot-cucumber salad, and please bring two glasses of mango juice," Mark listed their choices and turned to Maya. "You're not expected at home, are you? Your appa..."

Maya continued to avoid his eyes. "No. Appa is out of town."

"How can I speak with you if you refuse to look at me?" asked Mark, frustrated. "I know I lost my temper last week, but, Maya, you're so stubborn. You know I love you. I'll do anything for you."

Maya picked up the glass of water. "I can't elope, Mark. You know that already. I love you so much…it hurts, but I'm waiting for my appa to accept you. He'll come around. Believe me. It's just that I'm trying to appeal to his better side."

"Maya, 'My daughter will not marry a Christian,' were his exact words. What makes you think that he'll agree soon?" asked Mark. "And does he have a better side? I'm sorry, but we've been through this before. Do you love him?"

"No." She realized then, more suddenly than shockingly, that she never developed any affection for the man who had been her only parent all her life.

"Does he love you?"

"No," sighed Maya.

"Do you respect that man? I'm sorry to ask this question, but do you?"

Maya didn't respond right away. "No. I don't," she whispered a little shamefacedly.

"I know what he has put you through and what you've suffered. Then why can't we marry on our own?" he asked, desperately trying to understand her hesitation. "Aunt Sylvie is on our side."

"My appa hates you, especially because you are Aunt Sylvie's nephew. The fact that she is on our side upsets him more. You know, he told me that he's in a lot of debt. He is," she paused, ashamed to continue, "probably worried about losing my salary if I got married."

"But he can have all of your salary. I don't want any of it, if that's what's worrying him. Maya, I can convince him that we can live with what I make."

Maya looked at him gratefully, unable to swallow her meal. "I wonder why you still love me."

"What is love, Maya? Tell me. What is love? Love endures in spite of ups and downs and every damn thing in the way. I love you, no matter what's ahead of us," Mark said sincerely, taking her hand and holding it tightly. "It's just that it hurts me so much when I'm away from you, wondering if I'll see you tomorrow. Can I come and talk to your father one more time?"

"No, no. Don't do that. I'll talk to him again. Do you think I have a moment's peace when I worry about not being with you, Mark? I'll find a way to convince him. And thank you for being so patient."

"There's no need to thank me, Maya. All I want in my life is you. That's it. You."

She looked at him, her wild hair restrained in a loose braid. She wanted to burst into tears. And there was a flood building in her. But only a tiny tear broke loose and trickled down her cheek—despite her restraint, despite her newly developed, impassive attitude. She quickly brushed it off and whispered, "Mark, you have what you want, and you'll always have that. I love you."

"Then why didn't you call me last week after our argument? I left a message on your phone. I know you were angry, but..."

"Oh, I've to tell you something. I worked the evening shift on August 1st, and while I was returning home late..." Maya narrated everything that happened from the moment the bus stalled to the morning when she was at the police station to file a report.

"What? Why didn't you call me earlier about this?"

"I'm sorry, but what could you have done?"

"And why didn't you call me from the bus stand so that I could have taken you home? Why did you walk alone?"

"Mark, I would have stood at the bus stand, all alone, for at least forty-five minutes, if I had to wait for you to pick me up. Don't you think that's as bad as walking alone? Anyway, I was ashamed to call you after our argument, after the way I walked out..."

"Ashamed? Your safety is more important than anything else. Don't ever forget that, Maya."

"I'll remember that the next time I find myself alone somewhere, deserted and dark. All right?" asked Maya, smiling gingerly. "Come on, Mark, everybody is entitled to a little ego."

"And why didn't Aunt Sylvie tell me anything about this?"

"Because I told her not to bother you with that while we were both angry."

"Maya!" Mark sighed exasperatedly. "Now, what's all this about shooting and police report? Goodness, why did you have to walk alone?"

"But guess what happened two days ago? The police came to Aunt Sylvie's house and told her that there was no such shed anymore in that stretch of the paddy fields. The only small shed that was there got destroyed during the last week in July when the workers were repairing the roads."

"Why did the police go to Aunt Sylvie? Why didn't they come to you? You're the one who filed the report."

"Aunt Sylvie had asked me to write down her address as well in the report, you know, in case the police required more information. I was at work, so they went to her house. Anyway, how can my statement or the report make any sense when the shed doesn't exist?"

"Then what you saw and what you heard?"

"I saw nothing and I heard nothing, I suppose. You know, the police asked Aunt Sylvie if I was in the habit of drinking and if I used drugs?"

"What? Then what do they think really happened?"

"That's what Aunt Sylvie asked them. Why would I make up such a thing? The inspector thinks that I imagined something out of fear after listening to the radio from a passing car or a cycle."

"So the report is closed? The police will not pursue?"

"No, they won't, I'm sure. And what's there to pursue, from their standpoint? I feel like an idiot. Aunt Sylvie believes that the incident-at-the-paddy fields happened," hesitated Maya. "Do you believe me, Mark?"

"Of course, I believe you. And I know you're not an alcoholic or a drug addict!" He laughed with her. "Come on, I'll take you home."

"Are you sure? What if my appa has returned?"

"Don't worry, I'll ask the taxi driver to drop you off at the corner of First Cross Street, and then I'll see Aunt Sylvie before going home."

While Mark and Maya walked towards a taxi, the small man, sitting quietly behind their booth, slipped away silently to the exit. He soon met the bald man, who had been following Maya from her office to the restaurant, inside a cramped café across the street.

"I've a lot to report, Kumar," the small man whispered. He had diligently noted down every word exchanged between Mark Stevens and Maya, and he was ready to regurgitate the information.

Kumar smiled satisfactorily at the end of the narrative and went straight to 19 Temple Street to make an instant report to Usman.

- 19 -

19 Temple Street, Seloor • August 10, 2009

While Usman closed the file on his desk, someone knocked on his door.

"Come in," invited Usman, pushing the file into the cabinet. He pulled out another document, most recently completed, and went to the door.

"Abdullah, it's been a long time," greeted Usman, affectionately embracing his portly friend. "Please sit down."

"I've been busy. So have you," smiled Abdullah, sitting on a chair opposite to the desk.

Usman offered him a cigar. "I guess it's too late to stop this nasty habit?"

"I guess." The guest accepted the imported cigar. "What can I do for you? You wanted to discuss certain details about Rajan, one of my employees?" Abdullah asked respectfully, observing his friend's dark circles around his hawk eyes, his beard appearing whiter against the tanned wrinkles on his face. He knew Usman had an important assignment in mind. Otherwise, he wouldn't have summoned him here for a private conversation. A messenger with specific instructions would have been sufficient.

Usman quickly narrated the incident-at-the-paddy fields. "I was interrogating the clerk at the shed, you know in front of the ruined building we use for observation, a mere front. He was part of our mission in Salem, and our men misjudged him. That idiot, Salim was there with me. The clerk was being difficult. So I asked Salim to take care of him, not that instant, but eventually. Salim misread my instructions and pulled the trigger on him."

Abdullah winced.

"I know. I wish he had used a knife, at least. Can you imagine the impact of a gunshot in the silence of the night? I was standing by the window, making sure nobody passed the shed, and there she was. I'm sure she heard the gunshot when she was staring at the window."

"Do you think she can recognize you?"

"I don't know. I don't think so. Only the last slat on the window was open, and she couldn't have noticed my face clearly enough to identify me."

"And her identity is confirmed?" asked Abdullah, not at all doubtful of getting a positive response.

"Yes, she is Rajan's daughter, the man who takes care of some of your unmentionable business details."

"He is one of the *few* who might take care of the unmentionable details. Rajan is useful, but he's not important or valuable."

"What particular incentive do you give him, I mean other than money?"

"He needs a job, and I offer him several assignments," paused Abdullah, "he's in considerable debt. Drinking and gambling!" he said, confirming what Usman already knew.

"And a useless man altogether. Lets his daughter walk late in the night without protection, leaving her a prey for vultures."

Like us, thought Abdullah, smiling. "Yes, he's a useless man. So she saw and she heard. Is that all?" asked Abdullah, trying to understand the fuss. "Can't you get rid of her as you get rid of others? An accident at the bus stand or something? I know Rajan won't miss her. The only thing he'll miss is the money she brings home every month. He's a rotten man, but you know that by now."

"I could get rid of her in a simple accident. It's not what she heard, but what she saw. I can't have her killed in a normal accident. In case she has opened her mouth about what she saw, it would impede our missions, and I can't risk that."

"So what do you propose?"

"I want to buy us some time, enough to see if any news of what she saw has seeped into the community. And our assignments are not cheap. Why not use her in a mission?" asked Usman, his eyes scanning the document in front of him.

"Sure, why not? Might as well make her useful while getting rid of her. And while waiting to use her in a mission after a lapse of time, we'll know if she has said anything that might compromise our situation."

"Exactly. Here is every detail about her, from her date of birth to her current rendezvous with a young man, who is a reporter."

"Anybody who'll miss her?"

"Only the ones you already know about—the reporter who wants to marry her and the neighbor who adores her; Sylvia Joseph. I hear that she has been like a mother to Maya."

"Oh! So there'll be a buzz if Maya disappears—missing notices and all that nonsense."

"Yes, unfortunately. So I've decided to fake her death during another mission near the junction. A train derailment due to an explosion. What do you think?"

"Which one?"

"The one scheduled for October. We can make her write a note to her neighbor of her arrival by the train. Nothing could be more natural. But she won't arrive in the train, alive, because of the terrible disaster. She'll be right here, at 19 Temple Street," smiled Usman. "Anyway, once the letter arrives, her neighbor will be convinced that Maya died in the explosion, and so will others who might be interested in Maya's affairs."

"And no trace of a body in the explosion. No loose ends." Abdullah noticed his friend's deadly smile. *There is something else*, he thought. "What can I do?"

"Maya's father doesn't want his daughter to marry this reporter, Mark Stevens. Is it because Rajan is a devout Hindu and this young man is a Christian?"

"No. Rajan is agnostic, from what I know."

"That makes sense. Otherwise, he wouldn't be working for you, knowing your strong beliefs in Islam, especially realizing the nature of your commands. But what doesn't make sense to me is why Rajan is opposed to Mark. Is he waiting for a richer alliance for his daughter?"

"With his debts? When he can't offer a decent dowry?"

"Rajan must really hate Mark because he is Sylvia Joseph's nephew, and Mark is very close to his aunt. Abdullah, I want Rajan to sell his house to you. The incentive will be his release from most of his debts."

"That'll work, particularly when Rajan is convinced that there'll be some cash left over."

"Persuade Rajan to move to Salem to work in the warehouse near the station. Doesn't your cousin own that business there? Then Maya has to follow her father. But I'm worried about Mark. My man told me that he is persistent about marrying Maya. We need to remove him from town until she is brought here."

"When you say *remove him*...where?"

"Our informant at *The Express* told me that Mark is going away on a long-term assignment. If that assignment is rescheduled for some reason, then we must find a way to keep him away."

"Is he reliable, our man at *The Express*?"

"He is. He does some freelancing, but doesn't have much influence beyond this district. But we must accept whatever little help is available. Mark's absence should be a perfect time to stage Rajan's new job and his daughter's. I'm sure he'll be kept away until the derailment."

"Would Maya agree to move with her father when she has to leave this neighbor who has been like a mother to her, especially when Mark is waiting to offer her love and marriage?" asked Abdullah.

"Yes. I can give you two reasons."

Abdullah looked at his senior in awe and respect. When Usman planned something, he considered every important and every insignificant detail. Nothing, not one strand of hair, was left unnoticed.

"What reasons?" asked Abdullah.

"Maya will be under the impression that marrying Mark is absolutely out of the question," smiled Usman.

"But Maya has a job, a decent job that pays well. She can certainly live on that, independent of her father's help. Don't you think?"

"That's where the second reason will become useful." Usman snuffed his beedi in the ashtray. "A few intimidating debt collectors at the doorstep will change Maya's mind. You see, Abdul, it's so important to study human nature. From what I've known of Maya, she is very loyal. I've not come across a young woman who cares about what happens to her father, despite not having any affection for the man. I was very happy to learn several details exchanged between Maya and Mark recently at a restaurant. My men have been very busy. So you see, if the sale of the house and moving to a better job can release her father from a jail sentence, especially since her happiness with Mark is blasted, why wouldn't she consent?"

"Oh! I see. If Maya does not bend to the second reason, do we have a backup?"

"Absolutely, we have one. She will lose her job. I can make that happen in a day."

"Of course, Usman Bhai, you can make anything happen in a day!" Abdullah exclaimed proudly. "You can even make sure that Maya doesn't get another job easily."

"You know me well, Abdul. I try." Usman took a stab at modesty.

"There's one thing that worries me." Abdullah's concern creased his spacious forehead. "Rajan, as we know, is a useful employee. But there's something lacking in his understanding and in his nature that always makes me keep him at a distance. I don't have any faith in his loyalty, if he has any, and I would worry about buying his silence once his daughter is pulled to our side."

"I've been thinking about that, Abdul. Would you agree that Rajan's life should end with an overdose, perhaps a questionable glass of homemade concoction from the small toddy shop at the outskirts of Seloor? We both know he's glad to have a cheap drink. I also know that he takes some prescription drugs for his blood pressure. Occasionally, wrong medicines go with the right labels. Don't they? I'll think of the best way to get rid of him. The point is, I don't think he should linger once he signs off the deed to his house."

"Now what would you like me to do, Usman Bhai? Anything specific?"

"I'd like you to talk to Rajan, discover why there is no affection between him and his daughter. And I know you can twist his arm to sell his house to you and encourage him to move."

"And I can see why a different job in a different town is necessary. Perhaps it's the best way to tie all loose ends, specifically to shut the neighbor's mouths."

"Especially since Maya works, there must be quite a few people who might wonder about her whereabouts when she disappears. A job interview in Salem, her return from Salem to her neighbor's house, a train accident—they will fall neatly in place. And it doesn't hurt to cash that property. Rajan's house must be worth something. And start the process immediately, if you can?"

"I'll make it my priority. Once Rajan dies, I hope Maya doesn't back off from the interview, especially influenced by her neighbor. If she does, we can easily set up another scenario. Just a matter of time. Don't you think?" asked Abdullah. "And what about Salim? His impulsive action, killing that vendor in the shed like that, can really hurt our cause."

"Yes, but Salim is very devoted. A little impulsive, as you said, but he is nineteen. If we weigh his impulsiveness and his fierce loyalty, which will stand up to any test, then we have to forgive his first-time impulsive action. His father dedicated his life to our cause, as you know." Usman's gratitude for his friend, who gave his life during an assignment abroad, made him speechless for a few moments. "I've sent Salim to the northern border to get some serious training. Our men there will train him well. When he returns, I'll leave him with Yusuf or Sayeed for some reinforcement. That'll be all for now, Abdul. It's very good of you to come."

"Inshallah." Abdullah hoped for God's will.

"Inshallah," smiled Usman, embracing his dear friend before walking him to the door.

Seloor • October 6, 2009

Maya sat on the edge of the compound wall that separated her house from her neighbor's. The tripping breeze from the hills descended gently and made the thin branches of the neem tree quiver helplessly.

"Isn't this the wall where my mother whispered secrets with you a long time ago while she was missing the man she loved?" asked Maya, listlessly staring at the cascading hills. "Everything happened a long time ago—distant dreams, distant hopes—except my present mess. Why is my appa forcing me to move, Aunt Sylvie?"

"You know he has lost everything, Maya. He must not have anticipated debt collectors on the doorstep. But I wish he had not forced you to resign from your current job. I can wish and wish all I want. What's the point?" asked Sylvia, frustrated at her helplessness. "Are you sure you don't want me to go with you to Salem for your interview?"

"No, don't worry. I'm going to stay with my friend, and I'll be returning in a few days, unless something comes up. Otherwise, I would've taken you with me."

"I'm glad your amma isn't alive to see all this. You know how much it pains me? Debt collectors! It's as though your amma has died all over again. Your appa's mismanagement..."

"Let's not talk about him, Aunt Sylvie. I don't want to think about him tonight." Maya still held Sylvia's hand, reluctant to let it go. "Leaving you is like leaving a part me here."

Sylvia did not look up. She couldn't. Pushing her curly hair away from her moist face, she let her heavy tears fall leisurely on the clayey flowerbed. Maya took the fringe of her sari and wiped her friend's chubby cheeks.

"I'll miss you, Aunt Sylvie. I'll miss you terribly." Maya hugged the only soul who held any charm in her childhood and youth and walked quickly to her backyard. She stepped on the stone patio and looked at the mossy corner, where a rusty pipe trickled water into a dented metal pail. She remembered how her mother used to sit on the washing stone, letting the water overflow while vacantly looking at the distant hills. Her backyard looked the same in the last twenty odd years, as though frozen in time. She wondered if anything ever changed in that small town where traditions thrived effortlessly. But she was pleased to look at the neat garden, her garden—with a couple of coconut trees, a few jasmine and hibiscus bushes, and a sprinkle of basil and balsam plants. A small vegetable patch reminded her of her endless toil and endless joy—planting, weeding, and harvesting—her frequent diversion from the stifling indoors. She longingly looked at the blue hills in the distance, blue hills standing majestically against the humble, green paddy fields, and methodically picked up a mug of water from the pail and rinsed her hands and feet. A cool breeze nipped her earlobe, and she pulled the sari tightly around her shoulders before entering the kitchen.

When Maya opened the shutters and looked into the small drawing room, a tall, thin, elderly gentleman, with silver hair and startlingly white beard, was standing by the front door. Her father was standing in front of him, with his back towards Maya.

"I'll see you next week, Rajan," the elderly man said to her father, adjusting the white cloth cap on his head. "Take a tablet before dinner. Take another a little after dinner. That should ease your chest pain a little. If you find this helpful, I'll bring you some more."

Maya's eyes caught the gentleman's. She had never seen a set of eyes like those—steely, powerful eyes—and she was inevitably drawn to them. He stared at her for a few seconds and walked out of the room. Rajan closed the door and returned to his favorite chair.

"Appa, who is that man?" Maya asked her father, the image of those eyes still vivid in her mind.

"A friend," he said, reaching for the water pitcher on the side table. He swallowed a tablet and took a long look at his daughter, wheezing instead of breathing. The easy chair moaned in agony as he settled his rotund body on it. "He's the one who has been kind enough to arrange for a job for you in Salem. Do a good job at the interview."

"But I was happy with my job here. If you hadn't forced me to resign..."

"Stop complaining. A young unmarried woman to live alone? You need to go where I go. So where have you been, girl? How long must a man wait for his supper?"

"I already started supper. I was just talking to Aunt Sylvie for a few minutes."

"Oh, that woman? What evil thoughts has she been feeding you this time? Just because she was your mother's best friend, she takes undue advantage of our family's time. *Aunt Sylvia this and Aunt Sylvia that* all the time!" he barked, bitterly stressing the *aunt*.

"What's wrong with her? I love her. She is like an aunt to me. That's why she is my Aunt Sylvia. When I see her, I feel like I'm seeing my mother."

"Oh, enough of that nonsense," he shouted, his existing annoyance accelerating at his daughter's indignant tone. "Get busy cooking. Get out."

Reluctant to argue with her father, Maya returned to the kitchen. She seasoned the cooked lentils, staring at the faded, off-white walls and the small window with narrow spindles. The blue paint on the spindles had begun to look a shadowy gray. The house needed a coat of paint, among other things—a mother, some laughter, and a little happiness. She reached for the canister of rice from the bottom shelf and rinsed it carefully to wash away the dirt. *There was more dirt than rice*, thought Maya, cursing the adulterated provisions from the ration shop.

Rajan sat at the table and began to eat slowly.

"Shall I scramble some eggs?" asked Maya, hoping her father wasn't upset. They had not been able to afford meat, but her father insisted on having at least eggs.

"No," he grunted, without glancing at her. "I'm not feeling well." He got up abruptly, reached for some water, and swallowed the other tablet from his pocket.

Maya picked up his unfinished plate. "Not feeling well?" she asked, worried about how rapidly he was turning pale. "Do you want to see the doctor?"

"No. I'll just sleep this off." Taking a deep breath, he walked to his room, one hand resting on his distended belly.

Maya warmed the leftover milk to turn it into yogurt—the last monotonous event of every tedious day—and switched off the dim light before walking to her room. She slid on her cot, not at all sure about how she would face her future. She smoothed the hand-loom bed sheet which had sheathed her bed since she was ten and glanced listlessly at the familiar things in her room—the aged mirror on the wall, the dented metal wardrobe, and the wooden desk that desperately needed a coat of varnish. Her restless mind willingly stumbled on the past, afraid of stepping into the future. And it hurt to plunge into what seemed to be a long-winded future with not even a glimpse at a short-lived hope. Then, thoughts of Mark stubbornly crept into her weary mind. Where was he? How was he? All alone, staring at the gathering stars on the black carpet, she said her prayers, and she wished for the first time that the night would never end.

But the night ended most unusually and welcomed a day Maya could not face.

"Maya," began Sylvia, warily looking at the thickening crowd on First Cross Street. "I didn't know your father was so ill."

"I should've called the doctor last night, Aunt Sylvie." Maya took her hands to her face, shaking her head. "He didn't look all right. He just took some medicine and went to bed. I thought he would be fine this morning."

"It's not your fault, Maya. The doctor said that your father died of a heart attack. You couldn't have prevented it. Wasn't he already taking medicines? What more could we do?"

It was almost sundown and the funeral procession started from Rajan's veranda.

"Come with me." Sylvia took Maya to the backyard.

"My life has never been such a mess as it is now, Aunt Sylvie. My father made me quit my job here. My interview in Salem is not until next week. The house is sold. Jobless, homeless, what am I supposed to do? If only..."

"My dear," interrupted Sylvia, pulling Maya closer to her. "You may be jobless temporarily. But you'll never be homeless, as long as I'm here. And I'll always be here for you."

"Thanks, Aunt Sylvie," whispered Maya, staring at the rushing clouds. "I'm glad I don't have to go to my father's cremation."

"You're spared. That's one tradition we should be thankful for."

But Maya was not really sure whether she should be glad or sad. "I feel awful, Aunt Sylvie. I don't feel any attachment for him, and he was my parent! But seeing his body leave this home, where he had been miserable and had made me miserable..." Maya began to ache for something unknown, something nameless, and it pulled her tears. She sat on the washing stone and opened her heart for a man she never really knew or loved.

Salem • October 12, 2009

Maya got off the train at Salem junction and looked warily at the crowd of faces. She felt a little lonely while standing on the platform, gaping at the stream of luggage wagons and screaming children. She wondered if she should have brought Sylvia with her. Reminded of her neighbor's instructions, she promptly went to the phone booth.

"I reached Salem, Aunt Sylvie." Maya shouted above the cluster of noises in the crowded junction.

"We need to get you a cell phone, my dear," responded Sylvia. "Good luck. Be safe and send me an e-mail from one of the internet cafes, if you cannot get me on the phone."

Maya walked out of the station, uneasily staring at the market-day crowd. Quickly stepping into a waiting auto-rickshaw, she asked the driver to take her to Jairam Complex. She nervously let her eyes travel from the crammed bus stops to the dusty stalls skirting the main road. She wanted a job badly, but not there, when she had to be uprooted from her dear Aunt Sylvie. Determined not to be distracted from her interview, she silently rehearsed appropriate canned answers for monotonously canned questions. She stepped out of the vehicle, anxiously glancing at the assortment of motorcycles and cars parked along the side of the building. Once again wishing the interview were in her hometown, Maya took the elevator to the third floor and quickly stared at her reflection in the glass panel. She smoothed her braid with nervous fingers and wondered if her large eyes echoed her anxiety. Wiping the bead of perspiration above her quivering lips, she knocked gently on the door of Room 312.

A young, lanky woman opened the door promptly and smiled. "Yes? May I help you?" she asked, with a slight lisp.

Maya wondered at the missing cubicles and the general hubbub of an office. Except for a couple of men walking back and forth from a filing cabinet to their desks, the office was rather quiet. "I'm Maya Rajan. I'm here for an interview," hesitated Maya. Was she at the wrong place?

"Yes, come in. I'm Jasmine. Please wait here," smiled the woman, taking Maya to a comfortable chair. "The employees are at a quarterly conference today. Let me see if the manager is ready."

Maya sat down on the edge of the chair, wiping her sweaty palm on her sari. Was she the only candidate there? Was it because her father had specially arranged for this interview through a close contact? She was rather relieved that she didn't have to wade through a stream of prospective employees.

Jasmine knocked on a door at the end of the hallway and entered politely.

"Yes, Jasmine?" asked Sayeed, who had made a special visit to Salem after relinquishing his managerial duties at Eastern Exports for the day.

"Maya is here," replied Jasmine, smoothing her combed hair, hoping she fulfilled the role of a well-groomed, professional assistant.

"Send her in. Call Temple Street right away. Get the van ready." Sayeed went to the door to receive the candidate.

Maya walked in and accepted the manager's most decorous welcome with considerable relief. She thought he looked so young but so gentlemanly.

"Did you have a pleasant trip?" inquired Sayeed, taking Maya to a chair opposite to the desk. He asked a few questions about her previous job, dropping the most winning smile.

She answered hesitantly at first and eased considerably as his smiles grew wider.

"May I get you anything to drink?" asked Sayeed.

"Thanks. Just some water, please." Maya tried to unglue her nervous tongue that refused to relax. She could not find a nameplate on the desk. She had thought the manager was a woman, from what her father had told her.

"Of course." Sayeed poured ice water into a shiny glass from an elegant pitcher and offered it to her. "I'm sorry to hear about your father."

"Thank you." Maya took a few sips of the water, wondering how charming and thoughtful he was. This was not at all what she had anticipated. He had no airs, no frills—just a warm and down-to-earth demeanor. She took a deep breath as a wave of weariness swept over her, and she closed her eyes for a minute. When she opened them, the gentleman smiled from the other side of the desk, the smile enhancing his handsome features. She saw his striped, pressed shirt, neat tie, elegant watch, and felt that they all suddenly converged and distorted into something unrecognizable. Perhaps she was really tired! She took another generous sip of the water and placed the glass on the desk with a thud. Her body began to feel so heavy, and she was unable to sit straight on the chair. "I think I'm not feeling well," she stammered, closing her eyes, and then she stopped seeing and feeling anything.

- 20 -

Seloor • October 13, 2009

Sylvia went to the verandah to receive the postman at the sharp clanging of a bicycle bell and was rather surprised to see a taxi pulling outside her house. When she walked curiously to the gate, her nephew got out of the taxi.

"Mark, what are you doing here?" asked Sylvia, delighted and surprised.

Mark wrapped his arms around his aunt.

"Come in first. I didn't expect you back so soon." Sylvia took her nephew to the drawing room. After talking about yesterday's rain and today's clouds, she asked Mark about his long assignment, his unanticipated return, and waited for him to ask about Maya.

He did. "Auntie, I feel terrible about leaving the way I did, but Maya's father was...I was so angry. How much could I tolerate? Well, I'm back. How is she? Shall we go see her?" he asked, letting his glance slide to Maya's garden.

"I've so much to tell you." Sylvia tried to unload her weary mind while refilling her nephew's coffee cup. She longingly looked at Maya's garden through the window which was not Maya's anymore. "Oh, where shall I begin? Remember, a week after the-incident-at-the-paddy fields? Well, how can you forget that? After you stormed out of my house and stormed out of the country because Maya's father wouldn't let her marry you..."

"I was upset because Maya would not come out of Rajan's hold and marry me."

"Well, Rajan was on the point of being arrested. The neighbors still don't know the details, but Maya, of course, explained to me."

"Arrested? Why?" asked Mark, incredulous and shocked. "I know he had many faults, but..."

"You know Rajan had debts. He had embezzled funds at work and his employer called the police. Anyway, Rajan had been looking for an opportunity to find a means to pay off his debts. So he sold his house, found a better job in Salem, and you know the rest."

"Aunt Sylvie, why did Rajan force her to resign her job here?" scowled Mark, looking uncharacteristically stern. "If he must sell the house, let him. But why make Maya move?"

"But where would she stay, Mark, once the house is occupied by the new owners?" asked his aunt, staring at his familiar spectacles and untrimmed shock of hair. "Even if Rajan had not died, he would be working in Salem now, and she would be following him. Maya is welcome to stay with me all my life, but do you think that would be feasible in this community? Rajan wouldn't have let her stay with me, or by herself, for that matter. Anyway, she resigned before her father died. Otherwise, there wouldn't have been a need to resign at all. But I've encouraged her to look for a job closer to Seloor. She wants to. You know, the company in Salem which has invited her for an interview has a branch in Seloor. It's quite possible for her to get transferred here, or she might even start the job here. She'll find out soon."

"I can't accept her father's drastic decision. This man sells his house, finds a new job for his daughter and himself. It's as though Maya's presence here is completely wiped out."

"Are you telling me that we're living in an innocent world where such decisions don't exist? Are you so naive, Mark? My only frustration is that I could do nothing. I've encouraged Maya to look for another job here, if transferring to Seloor is difficult for some reason, and she has promised she will." Sylvia's round eyes rested on her nephew's sad face.

"And why didn't you inform me anything about what's been going on? I know Maya is silly and independent, but I thought I could always count on your common sense."

"Don't scold me, Mark. Maya told me in the strictest terms that I was to say nothing. How long will you be in Pennoor?"

"I'm returning to Chennai on the 18th. But I'll visit Pennoor in November, for a week or two." Mark's glance followed his aunt's and fell on the garden that was once Maya's. "Is she calling you everyday to let you know she is doing fine?"

"Well, she had to return her cell phone to her company when she resigned because the phone belonged to the firm, but she called from the public phone when she reached Salem. We'll shop for a cell phone for her as soon as she returns." Sylvia looked at her nephew's concerned expression with a pang of guilt. "When are you and Maya going to start talking to each other, Mark? Do you want me to let her know that you've returned from your trip?"

"No, let her get through the interview peacefully," smiled Mark. "I'll make it up to her for leaving her angrily when she returns."

"And why don't you stay in Seloor with me? You can take a taxi or bus to Pennoor and back everyday."

"No, Aunt Sylvie. There are so many meetings and other nonsense to take care of. I'll visit you in the weekends."

Seloor • October 14, 2009

While waiting for Maya to return to Seloor, Sylvia was glad to go to her church. There was so much to do, and the Church Restoration Committee was a little behind. Another meeting within two weeks, but Sylvia welcomed the distraction as the busy hours took her mind away from her worries. When she came out of the laborious meeting, the October skies appeared gray and weepy, setting the stage for a storm.

Sylvia looked at the thickening dark clouds, thankful for the small umbrella squished inside her big purse. Her eyes rested on the tall, old church—her church—sometimes, her everything, especially after she was widowed.

A tightfisted breeze from the surrounding trees relieved some of the mugginess while Sylvia patiently waited for an auto-rickshaw outside Holy Cross Church. When she wondered if she should take the bus that was crawling to a stop outside the vast iron gates, she saw a group of men and women running towards the bus. A cyclist, who was waiting by the gate, moved quickly to avoid one of the children running headlong to the bus and fell down in the process of dodging the missile. Sylvia looked at him anxiously, wondering if he got hurt, and ran to him to offer a hand. But he got up in the next minute, brushing off the dirt from his clothes. She thought she recognized him. Had she seen him in her neighborhood? But it was a small town and she remembered many faces without names.

In a few seconds, more raindrops followed. No wonder it had been so humid. Sylvia quickly stepped into an auto-rickshaw and asked the driver to go to First Cross Street. As the noisy vehicle turned towards the main road, Sylvia looked at the ancient structure of the church, built in the late 1800s.

When the rickshaw carrying Sylvia disappeared, the cyclist near the gate picked up his cell phone.

"Yusuf?" asked a voice. "Was the e-mail sent to Sylvia Joseph?"

"Yes, Sahib, yesterday. She is in town. I've made sure of that. She was at Holy Cross Church until a few minutes ago. In fact, I'm still at the church."

"If she is not in the habit of checking her e-mail, find a way to inform her that Maya is returning on October 15th. She must get this information."

"Yes, Sahib. I understand." Yusuf placed his phone inside his pocket and pedaled out of the church grounds.

Sylvia paid the rickshaw driver and rushed to the veranda. By then the gentle rain had turned nasty, and the downpour beat on her face with a vengeance. When she quickly unlocked the front door and promptly switched on the ceiling fan, the loosely left papers and magazines on the center table helplessly fluttered in the breeze. Her eyes fell on the dusty coffee table. She was getting too old to catch up with the quickly gathering dust. She began to straighten the mess when she noticed the stack of unopened letters from the day before. The last two days had been so hectic. She sat on the sofa and began to open the mail. One was from her cousin, another was a letter from the Restoration Committee Chair, the third was from Life Insurance Company, and what was the last one? A new bill from the T. N. Cable Company. She could not believe that the fee for broadband services was raised again. Reminded of her request to Maya, she started the computer, hoping for an e-mail from her young friend. She was not disappointed, and she instantly picked up the phone.

"Mark, I got an e-mail from Maya. She is coming home on the 15th," said Sylvia, raising her voice to speak above the rain beating on the window pane.

"How did her interview go? Is she all right?"

"Her interview went well, she says. But the best part is I'll see her tomorrow!" Sylvia squinted her eyes to get a better look at the small print. "The train arrives here in the afternoon. Here, I'll read it to you.

Dear Aunt Sylvie,

How are you doing? I've been fine. My interview went very well. I already miss you so much, Aunt Sylvie. The manager of this Call Center seems very nice. He assured me that it is quite possible for me to transfer to Seloor branch after about six months, or even sooner if things work out. I start my work on November 1st. I thought I'd spend a few days with you, pack my things, and return to Salem by October 25th. I checked a few apartments in the area. I'll talk about everything in detail when I see you. I tried calling you this morning. You were not home, I think. I'm coming home on October 15th. I'll be arriving by the Bhavani Express that reaches the junction at 3:00 or 3:10. I'm not sure. I can't wait to see you.

Affectionately,
Maya.

Do you want me to forward this mail to you, Mark?"

"No, don't do that. Send her a reply, but don't mention anything about me. Maya wouldn't know I'm back from my trip. I think it'll be a good surprise. I'll come home. We'll go to the station together after lunch?"

"Mark, you're sure you want to go with me to the station? Then you're not angry anymore?" asked Sylvia, relief filling her affectionate heart.

"No, I'm not angry. I'm frustrated at her decision, for not marrying me before I went on my assignment, but I can never stop loving Maya. And, Aunt Sylvie, I want her to know that."

"You tell her that tomorrow, Mark. That'll mean a lot to her."

"Yes. That means a lot to me, too. See you tomorrow."

October 15, 2009

Sylvia was sitting next to Mark in an old taxi on the way to Seloor station. Yesterday's rain had eased a bit, leaving a cool air trailing behind it. Sylvia opened the window to breathe in the fresh air, but the agreeable sensation started to disintegrate as a medley of smells, from exhaust fumes to stale coffee, seeped in through the window.

"Auntie, look at the traffic behind us," sighed Mark. "Do you think there is an accident?"

A black Chevrolet, a sore leftover from the seventies, was following the taxi closely, but Sylvia did not notice it particularly. Besides, her mind was preoccupied by how she would greet Maya, and Maya must have a lot to tell.

The driver of the Chevrolet quickly glanced at a cyclist who was riding along the avenue while carefully keeping an eye on the taxi. His earphones, attached to the cell phone in his shirt pocket, fed him information from the Chevrolet.

"Yusuf," said the voice through the earphones, "we're going to turn left at SI Church. You're following the taxi till you come to GH Bus Stop?"

"Yes, Kumar. And the news should come around that time."

"That's what we've heard." Kumar switched off his phone and turned towards Manohar, who was driving the car. "Exactly where is the disaster supposed to strike?"

"About fifteen minutes before the train reaches the junction, I think near Kuyil Extension." Manohar turned left at SI Church.

"And Yusuf made the arrangements?"

"Yes, of course, with Sayeed's help," smiled Manohar. "I told you already. He is in a different league altogether."

"He is shaping into Usman's right hand," sighed Kumar.

"Right, left, and everything. They're one of a kind. Let's not forget that. And I'm not just talking about religious affiliation here. What time is it?"

"2:55. Must have happened by now."

Manohar parked the car about a kilometer from SI Church. "Let's wait here for our signal." He pulled out a couple of cigarettes from his pocket and offered one to Kumar.

"It's already 3:10," Mark sighed impatiently, checking the time on his watch again. "We're going to be late."

"Don't worry, Mark," comforted his aunt. "I asked Maya to wait for me at the station when I replied to her mail. She was supposed to call me this morning. I don't know why she didn't. Anyway, she won't be worried if we are delayed. She'll probably guess that the traffic is heavy on our way there."

"Can you please turn on the radio?" asked Mark, tapping on the driver's shoulder, when the taxi came to a complete halt a couple of kilometers from Kuyil Extension. "May be there is an accident."

The driver fiddled with the channels for a few seconds when the news came from *All India Radio...*

> *This is a special news bulletin. There has been a terrible accident in Seloor district. The Bhavani Express, scheduled to reach Seloor junction at 3:05 p.m, derailed due to a bomb blast near Kuyil Extension. The explosion occurred approximately at 2:55 this afternoon, a few kilometers from the junction. Minutes before the terrible blast occurred, the district Police Inspector received an anonymous phone call...*

- 21 -

ATS Bus Stand, Chennai • January 2010

Jamil stood by a crowded tea stall at ATS Bus Stand in Chennai and looked tentatively at the gathering passengers. His peripheral vision expertly kept in touch with a young boy of about thirteen, with searching eyes and a thin face, who was sitting on a concrete bench with a stack of newspaper on his lap. It was the typical end-of-the-day crowd, but Jamil's trained eyes ignored the routine and measured the grounds for the booking clerk. He impatiently glanced at his watch again and checked for new messages in his phone before taking a few paces away from the tea stall to avoid suspicion. When he was on the verge of giving up, his restless eyes fell on a puny man—with a sparse mustache and an almost shaved head—wearing a bold batik-print shirt that somehow looked insipid on his thin frame. Jamil wearily looked at the man while exchanging a swift glance with the boy sitting on the edge of the bench.

"I'm sorry for the delay," whispered the clerk, wiping his greasy face with his sleeve, "I almost didn't come at all."

"What do you mean?" hissed Jamil, his light brown eyes turning a nasty tint at his impatience and anger. "Timing has to be precise. Don't you know that? Now we've to wait for another opportunity."

"I was afraid that I was being followed. Yusuf Bhai told me to meet you here, but I didn't anticipate trouble. I was afraid to call in case my number is..."

Jamil rolled his expressive brown eyes in exasperation and asked, "Have you been doing something you shouldn't be?"

The clerk squirmed in shame, nervously looking up at Jamil's towering frame. Taking quick, deep breaths, he spluttered, "My son lost his job. My daughter's marriage is approaching soon. I...I meant to return the money, I promise. I didn't think it would be traced." The clerk unwillingly explained his shameful indiscretion in the recent financial fraud at work.

"I wonder what Yusuf Bhai would say, and Usman Sahib would... Allah save you from his wrath," Jamil's voice trailed menacingly. "You shouldn't have come. You could have compromised the entire organization, you idiot."

The clerk's terrified eyes expressed fear at the thought of Yusuf, and his fear knew no boundaries as his thoughts extended to Usman. Then his nervous glance quickly flew to his tiny office at the other end of the terminus and returned to Jamil's tall figure. Desperate to make amends, he whispered, "My office is empty. I'm the only one during this shift. I've left the materials in the dark green box by the telephone stand."

Jamil's taut expression relaxed a bit. "Why didn't you say so before? I expected the other clerk to be there with you in the office."

"Yes, usually, but he's not there now. He is not well, I heard. This was unexpected, naturally. If I had known I was going to be at my desk alone, I would have requested you to come to the office directly." The small man took a deep breath. "The other clerk and I both take turns for tea around this time and for supper break a little later. But tonight I'm the only one there," smiled the clerk, as though hopeful of placating his superior. "Shall we move on?" he asked, looking in the direction of his office.

"This is your tea break? Go get a cup of tea. Not from this stall," Jamil added hurriedly. "Go to the cafe on the other side and get a cup. Don't look at me even once and walk to your building. I'll follow you soon." When the contact disappeared in the crowd, Jamil quickly picked up his phone. "Yusuf, I'm glad you answered promptly."

"What's the matter, Jamil?" asked Yusuf, worried at the concern in his colleague's voice.

Jamil quickly explained the clerk's embezzlement at his work.

"I'll inform Usman Sahib. That should be taken care of right away," agreed Yusuf. "Thanks for alerting us instantly. Jamil, good luck with your mission tonight. Keep the damage on the low side. Remember, this is just a practice for the big mission. Usman Sahib is counting on your efficient supervision of Maya when she is sent on the crucial task."

"Of course, thanks for choosing me for the assignment," replied Jamil, grateful for the organization's confidence in his skills. "But what do we do about the clerk?" hesitated Jamil.

"I'm sure Usman Sahib will send someone right away to take care of that. Don't worry. Finish your mission and return to The Jannah. Inshallah."

"Inshallah!" Jamil repeated 'If God wills' and moved over to the concrete bench, with his eyes anywhere but at the boy. "Ready, Salman?" he asked his young colleague, who was sitting on the edge of the bench with an eager, ardent expression.

"Yes, Jamil Bhai. I'm ready," replied Salman, a passionate light illuminating his innocent eyes. Jamil understood the effect of the beacon that never failed to enthrall their master.

"Follow me with your eyes," whispered Jamil. "Then follow me to the clerk's office. Don't look at the customers' faces if they buy a copy of the paper. Make sure nobody notices you as you enter the building. All right?" asked Jamil, and walked towards the other end of the bus stand in the next ten minutes and stepped into the tiny booking office. There was hardly enough room for two people to sit in the narrow booth. The clerk stood up respectfully and glanced at the green box by the telephone stand. Jamil's glance briefly rested on the box and traveled swiftly to the clerk's sticky face. He crinkled his nose at the odor of stale sweat emanating from the clerk, blending with the already overpowering stench of tobacco.

"You may leave now." Jamil, staring at the clutter in the stuffy room, did not look at the clerk or at the door as the man quietly vacated the room.

Salman, in the meanwhile, walked slowly towards the booking office, avoiding eye contact with anybody in the busy terminus. Once outside the building, he began his sales pitch, and a couple of men and women traded their spare change for a newspaper. Satisfied that he had done his bit and making sure that the puny man had vacated the office, Salman discreetly entered the building to join his senior associate when he was absolutely certain that he was not observed. Jamil was waiting for him.

After assisting his senior colleague, Salman quietly exited the office through the back door. Between 8:15 and 9:30, several buses crisscrossed paths in the busy, large terminus. But only one express, empty and parked near the office from which Jamil had walked out an hour earlier, suffered slight damage as a portion of the small building exploded with a frightening noise. While passengers getting in and out of other buses gaped at the smoke and leaping flames in fear, a young woman screamed in terror at the sight of the booking clerk whose body was tossed on the sidewalk a kilometer from the bus stand. She continued to scream hysterically as her fearful eyes took stock of the gash on his bloody neck, the batik-print shirt clinging to his sweat-soaked body, the flies on his sparse mustache, and his shaved head cradled by the wet trash on the floor.

- 22 -

Chennai • February 2010

Mark picked up Tina around six outside British Council Library and cautiously merged into the evening traffic.

"Sorry about the congestion, Tina," apologized Mark. "Rush Hour."

"Oh, Mark, as far as I can remember, isn't it always rush hour here?" laughed Tina, habitually combing her brown hair with her manicured fingers.

"I suppose," Mark laughed with her. "This traffic is something to talk about. I'm glad to see you again, Tina. How did you convince your father to comply, and so soon?"

"Well, that was not easy. My unfinished thesis was a big help to start with, and then Dr. Katz nudged me to continue work here. Then...Shaker was very welcoming, and let's say I know my way around my father. So how is work?" asked Tina, wonderingly gaping at the colorful fabrics and dresses displayed at the wide windows of different boutiques. And they were crowded, as always.

"Work is going well. Quite settled in my new office."

"Actually, I'd like to take a glance at your new beachfront office some time."

"Why don't I show it to you right now?" Mark expertly weaved the car through the multi-lane traffic that was meant to be a three-lane main road. "I was thinking of going to my office after dinner to pick up something, after dropping you at home. But if you want to see my office, let's go right now."

"How do these people manage to go home on a daily basis without accidents?" asked Tina, wincing nervously when an auto-rickshaw got in front of their car and swerved to the other lane.

"Thanks to slow-moving traffic, I'm sure," replied Mark, quickly changing two lanes. He turned right on Isabella Avenue and made another right towards Beach Road.

Tina followed Mark to the fourth floor and looked at the expansive shore from the window. "This is not work, Mark. You guys really know how to live, or work, in this case. Don't you?" asked Tina, admiring the rows of scattered catamaran dancing on the waves. And it was a perfect hour to watch the sinking sun as it slowly and stunningly spread the skies with shades of amber. "How lucky you are to sit in an office that has a beautiful view of the ocean!"

"But, Tina, we do work here," chuckled Mark. "I reserved a table for us at Cascade. Is that all right? Or would you like to go somewhere else?"

"Wherever you wish to go is fine, Mark. Did you say Cascade? Sounds familiar. I think I had lunch with my aunt and uncle at that restaurant the last time I was here. I loved the food. A bit of fusion cooking, I think."

"That's why I like it. Your uncle and aunt live in this area?"

"Yes, they do. I don't think it's far from here. They have a condo' with an excellent view of the ocean. Mark, they wanted to meet you. Aunt Rita is thinking of having a party at home."

"I'd love to meet them. Now let me take you to my new office. It's not cluttered like my old one." He unlocked the door of the third room down the corridor. "Please come in."

"Mark, you're incurable," said Tina, looking at the mess. Notepads and bits and pieces of paper occupied every flat surface in the room. A four-drawer filing cabinet was still bulging with files and documents.

"Oh, I know, but neatness is overrated, Tina."

Despite the mess, the room looked cheerful, cozy. While he was busy looking for the document, her eyes began to wander again from one corner of the room to the other when she noticed a small photograph precariously placed behind a stack of notepads and envelopes. The picture was encased in an antique-looking metal frame. *There is more frame than picture*, thought Tina. Actually, it was the beautiful frame that had initially drawn her attention. She looked at it again, and the face within the frame captured her eyes. When she moved closer to the desk and stared at the face, her throat went dry and her hands became moist.

"Would you mind waiting here, Tina?" asked Mark, leading her to a chair. "I'll be back in a couple of minutes."

"Oh, take your time, Mark." Tina smiled nervously and sat on a chair. She wanted a little more time to study the photo.

Was it her imagination? Tina looked at the photo again. There was no doubt in her mind. It was the same face she had seen a while ago at 19 Temple Street. Was that girl related to Mark? Was she his sister, cousin, or did she mean a lot more to him in a different way? If she did, did he know that she was insane...trying to run away from something, someone, helpless?

It can't be the same person, thought Tina, trying to explain her confusion logically. She had seen that young woman for a few minutes, a very few minutes, under distress and extraordinary circumstances. Then she had briefly seen a photo that the bald man showed on the highway for a second. How could she remember that face so well? Not possible. While Tina looked at the photo again, the door opened.

"Thanks for waiting, Tina." Mark was standing by the door.

"No problem at all. Mark, who is that girl in the photo?" Tina asked casually, trying her best to sound apathetic.

"That's the girl I was going to marry."

I was going to marry? She was dying to know more.

"Shall we go?" asked Mark, leading Tina out of the room. "The restaurant is only about five minutes from here. I hope I didn't make you wait too long for dinner."

"Not at all," Tina replied absentmindedly. It was an important visit for her, and she had meant to consult Mark on a variety of articles, but her attention was unfortunately snared by the face in the photograph. Who was she? Why did that face follow her and drive her crazy?

Mark soon parked the car outside Alsa Arcade that was home to a couple of salons, a mobile telephone store, upscale bars, and a cluster of trendy boutiques. When he opened the front door to Cascade, the most recent fusion melody of A.R. Rahman burst from the interior. Tina saw the piling crowd; a very young and noisy clientele.

"I've reserved a table overlooking the ocean. I knew you'd like that," smiled Mark, leading her to one of the tables in the back.

"Thanks." Tina sat down, facing the window. But her mind refused to be lured by the foaming waves. It stubbornly made a quick journey to Mark's office, to his desk, to that inevitable photograph.

"Tina, you don't like the bajjis?" asked Mark, offering her the plate of vegetables, dipped in a spicy batter and fried to perfection.

"Oh, it's great, Mark. I came here for lunch last time. Sitting here in the evening, after sunset, is a whole new experience!" exclaimed Tina, pretending to be exhilarated by the ambiance. She tried to be engrossed in Mark's account of his recent articles while her mind furtively traveled to the photograph. *And his account is specifically why I'm having dinner with him*, she thought, annoyed by her distraction. He talked animatedly, intelligently. The minutes crawled leisurely, laboriously.

When Tina followed Mark to his car, she was frantically looking for an opportunity to ask him about that photograph. "Thanks, Mark, for a nice dinner," she began. "I appreciate your time, entertaining me while you should be home with your family," continued Tina, slowly groping for an entrance into his personal life. She had to know about the girl in the photograph.

"You're welcome. I had a very nice evening. Anyway, I've nothing to go home to."

"You mean you don't have a wife and children to run to?" asked Tina, trying to force some humor into her question.

"No, I don't, but you know that, Tina. I'd like to have a wife to run to," he whispered, "but the girl I wanted to marry is no more."

The girl I wanted to marry is no more?

"I went to the station to receive her when she was returning from a short trip, but the train derailed before it arrived, and..."

"Oh my God, I'm so sorry," murmured Tina, sincerely regretting her curiosity. But if she was dead, what was she doing in that shelter? Then, the girl in the photo in Mark's office was not the same girl she saw in the musty shelter in the middle of paddy fields. Tina felt a strange sense of relief.

"You look like you saw a ghost. I still haven't come to terms with it, although it's been a few months since she died. I simply cannot accept the fact that she is dead."

"I'm sorry I brought this up, Mark," mumbled Tina. *Although it's been a few months...* Yes, yes, that meant the girl in the photograph was not the distressed young woman she saw earlier. But what about the striking resemblance? "Mark, I don't remember seeing that photo in your office in Pennoor when I came to India last year. And I was in and out of your office a few times. You didn't have it on the shelf then?"

"No. Remember, I had a temporary office at that time? It was a cramped room, and I had cleared a lot of stuff from there. I wanted to wait till I settled into my own office before I brought out extra things. And her photo, since it's so precious to me, was resting safely in a box."

"I see," swallowed Tina, not at all seeing anything. "Good God, it's so terrible."

"I checked and double-checked the list of passengers. Maya was definitely traveling in the train, and the explosion took her away. October 15th will be an unforgettable, venomous date in my life." He looked meditatively at Tina's face. "I'm sorry for rambling on like this and making you sad."

She died in October of last year. So she was that 'someone very dear' he had lost in that explosion. "I remember you had said earlier, when I first met you, that you lost someone in that explosion, but I didn't realize it was the girl you were going to marry. I'm so sorry," apologized Tina, surprised at the way the conversation was turning. "And don't think twice about discussing it. I'm glad to be here to listen to you."

"Thanks. All that has remained of her is her photo and her memory." Mark turned the car towards the gated community. "Did you say your aunt's home is in Villa Circle?"

"Yes. # 45." But if his fiancée died in October of 2009, what was she doing in the hostel in November, looking the way she did, knocking on a stranger's door to escape? Tina was frustrated, but she felt that she was getting close to something.

Mark parked the car in front of the Edwins' driveway. "This is another photo of my Maya," he said, retrieving a small photograph from his wallet. He turned on the light over the dashboard, adjusting his spectacles.

Tina looked at it. It was the same face she had seen in Mark's office, taken at a different time. Was it the same face she had seen a while ago in a vast, lonely building in the middle of a sea of paddy fields?

"She is beautiful," whispered Tina, recovering her composure. She had to retain him there for some more time. "You know, Mark, Shaker is coming here for a drink. We were just going to sit for a while in the bar at the condo' and, he wanted to see you again. Why don't you join us?" she asked, trying not to sound desperate.

"I'll be glad to. Let me first drop you off at the entrance."

Tina went in through the swivel door into the pleasantly air-conditioned foyer. She opened the glass door to the lounge and saw Shaker patiently sitting at one of the corner tables.

"You took a while," smiled Shaker, pulling out a chair for her.

"Shaker," Tina began softly. "I've asked Mark to join us for a drink. I hope it's okay?"

"Of course."

"And," she whispered, hurriedly looking at the door. Mark was not there yet. "That girl I saw in the hostel last year... I saw her picture in

Mark's office."

"In Mark's office?" asked Shaker, incredulously staring at her with his sharp eyes.

"Yes. And what's more, Mark was going to marry her. And he told me she died a few months ago, in an explosion, you know the one near Seloor junction last October, when the train she took..."

Shaker held her hand gently. Mark was at the door.

"But I've to ask him. I've to tell him that I saw her."

"Then go ahead," Shaker mumbled, smiling at Mark who joined them at that instant.

Tina was not sure how to go ahead, but tell him, she must.

When the waiter left with their order, Shaker asked, "How was dinner?"

"It was great, Shaker. And I had a chance to see Mark's new beachfront office. It's beautiful, and it's very nice of Mark to entertain me in the evening," smiled Tina, groping again for another opening about the photograph.

"So your evenings are your own, Mark, because you're a bachelor like me." Shaker paused while the waiter set the tray on the table.

"Yes," agreed Mark, taking a sip of his brandy.

"Well, you're still young, but I'm not," laughed Shaker. His eyes momentarily exchanged something with Tina's. She thought it was an encouraging signal.

"Mark, I've to tell you something," began Tina.

"Why? Are you going to tell me that you, unlike Shaker, think that I'm a lot older?" asked Mark, laughing, but stopped suddenly at her serious expression. "What is it, Tina? Is something wrong?"

"Mark, it's about the photograph in your office. When I saw that and...and you won't believe this," lingered Tina, looking at Shaker for further encouragement. "I... I saw her a few months ago," she whispered, her anxious memory stealthily crawling to 19 Temple Street.

Mark looked alternately at Shaker and Tina. "You saw her? But you couldn't have. Tina, I told you that she is no more," Mark's incredulous expression shoved Tina's memory farther into the grimy corridor of the shelter. "You came to Pennoor and Seloor in November of last year, didn't you? She died in October, and I explained to you how she was taken away. She was one of the victims of that terrible explosion in October."

"I shouldn't have started like this. Maybe it was someone who looked just like her," blabbered Tina.

"Tina, why don't you describe the whole incident to Mark? I mean the night at the shelter?" Shaker asked helpfully.

And Tina recited her brief meeting with the fugitive.

"She looked like the girl in the photograph which you saw in my office?" asked Mark, still bewildered. "Did she tell you her name?"

"No. There was no time for all that," replied Tina. "But she left a crumpled piece of paper, you know, before the men took her away."

"A piece of paper? Do you have it?" asked Mark, shaking his head. "How could you? That's most unreasonable."

"That's not at all unreasonable, Mark. It's in my room. It was an incredible incident, meeting her like that, and that paper never left my backpack. I'll be glad to show it to you." Tina rushed out of the lounge.

"Are you all right, Mark?" asked Shaker, noticing the pain in the young man's eyes. "There's no better way to tell you something like this."

"No. I understand. It's just that it's so unexpected, so sudden." Mark buried his face in his hands, on the verge of angry tears. "I don't know what to say, what to think. It's unbelievable. This means she is alive. She is alive, if Tina really saw her."

Tina returned and placed a distressed piece of paper on the table, and Mark impatiently reached for it.

"Mark, why did she leave this paper with Tina? Does it mean anything to you?" whispered Shaker, eager to break the silence.

"Did I tell you her name is Maya?" asked Mark, pointing at the name of the program on the crushed paper; *Mayayoga*. "That's perhaps why she left it, hoping someone, somehow, would do something about it."

"But what are the chances?" wondered Shaker, glancing again at the paper.

"And my Maya was kept in that shelter, and those rotten men told you that she was insane?" asked Mark, a strong tinge of red settling in his eyes. "I've to tell Aunt Sylvie. Good God, she won't believe it."

"Your aunt?" asked Tina, trying to see the point. "Shouldn't Maya's family be informed first?"

"She has no parents, no family. Well, her father was alive till last year, but he was not much of a parent. My aunt, Sylvia Joseph, is Maya's neighbor in Seloor," Mark began to explain. "My aunt literally raised Maya. She was like a mother to her."

"Sylvia Joseph? Where does she live in Seloor?" asked Tina, swiftly checking the information she already had in her small notebook.

"Where does she live? First Cross Street. Why?" asked Mark, wondering at Tina's sudden interest in his aunt.

"Your aunt is a good friend of my aunt, Rita Edwin. And she had written down your aunt's name and address for me, in case I needed someone while I was traveling there last time. In fact, I was thinking of contacting her when I was stranded at Seloor station during my previous visit, but I didn't because she was away from town at that time. And my aunt told me that her friend, Sylvia lost her neighbor in that explosion."

"You know, Aunt Sylvie left Seloor to forget her pain of losing Maya. Who would have thought? And now...I should let my aunt know. But if the girl you saw at the shelter is my Maya, shouldn't I go to the police right now?"

"Not right now, Mark. Remember, under what circumstances Tina saw her?" asked Shaker. "If Maya is branded as mentally retarded, then she must be kept captive for some horrible reason. We don't know what it is. There is such a long way to trace back, a lot farther back before Tina met her on that night."

"Then what the heck should I do now?" asked Mark, considerably frustrated.

"We should consult my uncle, Theo Edwin," suggested Tina. "He has connections with the police. He'll be able to help you, Mark. Can your aunt come to Chennai, or can we go to Seloor to see her?"

"I'll ask her to come here. Anyway, consult your uncle. Would he be available tomorrow?" asked Mark.

"No, he has gone away with my aunt for a couple of days. Mark..." hesitated Tina. "Are you going to tell your aunt about Maya, I mean that I saw her?"

"No. I'm going to just tell her that a couple of my friends wish to see her. I'll make up some excuse. You know, I want to see that shelter in Seloor. Did you say it's in Temple Street, Tina?" asked Mark. "Not that I expect Maya to be there, but I can never rest until I've seen it with my own eyes. I'll make a quick visit to Seloor and bring Aunt Sylvie to Chennai."

- 23 -

Seloor

Mark got out of the taxi by the front door of the lonely building in the middle of green paddy fields and looked at the number plate nailed on the lintel: 19 Temple Street. A couple of colorful signs with "Office spaces available" stood by the front door. He was surprised to find a uniformed doorman opening the door, letting out a faint odor of fresh paint and mortar. A few construction workers were busy working on final details. Mark thought, a little disappointedly, that the place did not resemble Tina's description—her little memory of her earlier visit was already fading.

"Yes?" asked the doorman, a little curtly.

Mark's spectacled eyes quickly scanned the wall where a list of various businesses was printed on a rectangular board. He chose the third name to help him open a conversation. "I came to see the manager of Lakshmi Arts," smiled Mark.

"What time is your appointment?"

"10:30, I think," Mark smiled again and checked his pockets thoroughly. "I feel bad, but I seem to have lost the card where I had written down the time. Can the secretary or someone in the office verify my appointment?"

"Wait here, please. Sir, what's your name?"

"My name is Joseph and I need to place a bulk order," replied Mark, as the doorman picked up the phone to make inquiries.

"Go to the second floor. Lakshmi Arts is the first room on the right. The owner will see you."

Mark knocked on the door and entered. He was rather surprised to see a very clean, spacious, well-equipped office, with a couple of computers, contemporary furniture, and impressive modern art pieces on the wall. A middle-aged woman, dressed in a bright two-piece salwar pantsuit, was sitting behind a vast desk. She rose from her chair politely at Mark's entrance.

"How may I help you?" asked the woman, wiping her glasses with her handkerchief.

Strangely, she reminded him of his dear Aunt Sylvia, with curly hair and plump cheeks.

"I'm so sorry for barging in like this. I thought I had made an appointment, and I can't seem to find the note where..." went on Mark, trying to assess the woman's reaction to his presence in the room. Was she the formidable warden Tina had described? But that woman didn't appear formidable at all.

"No need for an appointment." The woman smiled graciously. "We require advanced notice only for bigger projects which need extensive work. We're happy to offer an open-door policy."

"I'm glad. I need to order a couple of sets of business cards and advertisement materials." Mark quickly tried to gather excuses for his visit.

"Oh? Please have a seat. Did you say that this is for your business? What kind?" asked the woman, walking to the shelf near the window. She pulled out a couple of bulky catalogues and returned to the desk.

"I'm going to begin a tutorial institute with a couple of friends of mine. There is such a need right now." Mark guiltily looked at the woman's eager expression.

"I'm glad you found us. We are new here." The woman brought the catalogues to Mark and opened the first set of prints. "We just downloaded these new designs. Where is your institute? Or isn't it open yet?"

"Not yet. We're trying to finalize the location. In fact, I didn't know that there is space in this building that is still available for rent," Mark paused, smoothing his ruffled wavy hair, as though trying to make a decision. "I should check this out."

"You should, and do that quickly. All the office spaces are going fast."

"Actually, I'm surprised this building is no longer what it used to be. I didn't know that this facility went up for sale."

"Have you been here before?" asked the woman, looking intently at his face.

Mark tried to trace something in that expression that should not be there, but he noticed nothing. It was just a harmless, curious countenance.

"Yes, I've been here before. It used to be a temporary homeless shelter when I came here to do some work. Whatever happened to that organization?" asked Mark, looking intensely at the designs in the book.

"They closed. And Sri Bala Real Estate bought the property," the woman responded without hesitation. "What do you think of design # 49? It's simple and catchy. Do you like it?" she asked, trying to turn the customer's mind back to business.

"Yes, I like it. I feel bad for those children and adults who needed a home." Mark promptly reverted to the problem that was occupying his mind. "I wonder where they are now."

"The homeless residents were sent to other shelters. I heard this facility ran out of money. They had no choice but to close." The woman looked at Mark a little impatiently. "Do you want to see the designs in the other catalogue now? Or can I show you some more on the computer?"

"Let us look at the catalogue first. I wonder who owned this place when it was operating as a shelter?" asked Mark, closing the first catalogue and opening the second book of designs.

"I don't know for sure, but the rumor is that Abdullah donated this facility for charity. He is a great benefactor, as you know. Owns many businesses in the community," sighed the woman, by now tired of discussing issues which had absolutely nothing to do with her business.

Abdullah? He must explore that. Mark flipped through the designs, desperately searching for any clues which could lead him to an unopened door where he might stumble on something, anything that would take him to his dear Maya.

"I like this design," Mark said to the woman, pointing at a silly caricature. "And I also like that design in the other book. Number 49, I think? May I take copies of these two to my colleagues before I make a final decision?"

"Sure!" smiled the woman, finally glad to have his undivided attention. "How many prints would you require?"

"Oh, at least about two thousand!" Mark chose the figure generously, again looking at her content expression with a slight feeling of guilt.

"Here is my card. This has the contact information you'll need. And you said you'll require some posters?"

"Yes, of course. But I'll finalize all that when I return. You know, I wonder if I could look at the office space that's available, since I'm already here. Then I can discuss that also with my partner."

"Sure. There are two rooms available. There is one on this floor, the third on the left side. The rent on that one runs higher because it has a set of staircase that exits directly to the grounds outside. The other room is downstairs."

"Thank you," smiled Mark, eager to get out.

"Sir, may I have your card?"

Mark stared at her for a few seconds. "I'm so sorry. I can't imagine how I left home without it. My cell phone is not in order, and I don't know which number to give you. Why don't I give you a call tomorrow morning? And thanks again for your time."

Mark quickly walked out of Lakshmi Arts to avoid further questions and stepped into the room across the hallway. There it was, the staircase that warranted extra rent. He walked over to the dusty, wide window and stared at the green paddy fields. He took the small notepad that contained all his notes from his conversation with Tina and Shaker and flipped through the pages to find Tina's account of 19 Temple Street.

Her description of the foyer no longer existed. The group of construction workers could definitely testify to the changes. And the interior was no longer derelict and stinking because of the new coat of paint and various improvements, obviously added by Sri Bala Real Estate.

Then, Mark's glance went to Tina's description of the room where she had spent the night—a room with a staircase in the back; of course, the only one upstairs that had an exit to the grounds. Wasn't that what the fugitive had told Tina when she was frantically trying to escape? Mark wiped his sweaty forehead with a trembling hand. Was this the room where Tina had stayed that night, the room into which Maya desperately tried to enter? Mark shoved the small notepad into his pocket and went to the door that was supposed to open to a staircase. He tried the handle, but the door was locked.

He walked out of the room quietly and decided to explore the office building before returning to his aunt's home. He noticed nothing unique or different. He saw an insurance office, a couple of business consultants, and a tailor's shop. He went downstairs and saw a well-furnished auditor's office through the wide glass window and a couple of office clerks chatting over a cup of tea. Then he went to the grounds. It was an extensive land, but it would soon disappear. Sri Bala Real Estate would take care of that. He stopped by a doorway and looked up at the second floor—the room upstairs, the only room upstairs that opened to a door that directly led to the grounds. And Maya was that close to escaping... if the foul group of men had not caught up with her, if the door had not been locked, and if...there were too many *ifs*, Mark thought bitterly. And he was sure it was Maya. The fugitive had to be Maya. She had to be alive. Mark got into the taxi, the familiar agony sitting heavily on his heart.

- 24 -

Krishna Mansions, Chennai • February 2010

Shaker picked up Tina from her uncle's circular driveway in a taxi that belonged to another era. It was a muggy morning, with the promise of getting muggier. Tina opened the window to breathe in the salt-coated breeze, generously mixed with everything floating in the air.

"Tina, were you able to tell Mr. Edwin about Maya?" began Shaker.

"Yes. He is actually quite eager to meet Mrs. Joseph and Mark, especially because of the nature of Maya's death. You know," she paused, nervously observing the receding beach. She repeatedly combed her brown-black hair with her nervous fingers as the bright sun danced with her beautiful eyes. "It's all happening so fast. Only a few days ago, Mark picked me up for dinner, and I was stunned to see her photograph on his desk. Actually, I'm still stunned. It's the weirdest thing that has happened to me. Well, not as weird as opening the door at that shelter to look at an insane fugitive."

"But aren't you glad you saw that photo? It's probably impossible to trace her whereabouts, but there must be a reason why you saw Maya for a few minutes at the shelter. If you hadn't, seeing that photo at Mark's office would mean nothing."

The taxi entered the compounds of Mark's new apartment complex in Egmore where cultivated neighborhoods hid behind tall trees and secure fences from the cluttered and dusty metropolis. Mark introduced his aunt to the visitors before leading the group into his apartment.

Tina's eyes flew from one item to the next in the drawing room—muslin curtains, a built-in cabinet that was bursting with knickknacks, a beige paisley sofa, and a couple of arm chairs. The glass-topped coffee table was home to *Readers Digest*, *The Express*, and a few paperbacks. Her eyes soon shifted to Sylvia Joseph, who was sitting next to her nephew on the sofa with a broad smile on her face. Her chubby cheeks, youthful smile, and big round eyes were mocking at her fifty odd years. Everything about her seemed to be smiling as a gentle breeze from the ceiling fan made the edges of Sylvia's scarf flutter like a butterfly. And her effervescent smile fluttered blithely, unaware of the impending news.

"May I get some tea?" asked Sylvia, quickly rising from the sofa.

"Tea is Aunt Sylvie's cure-all. I'll go help her." Mark followed his aunt to the kitchen.

While Shaker went to the window to answer his cell phone, Tina's eyes roamed to the pictures on the walls and to the built-in cabinet. The second shelf displayed a photo gallery. There was a picture of a much younger Sylvia in a bright sari, with a veil on her head, standing next to her handsome groom. Next to it was a photo of another middle-aged couple with Mark—probably his parents. Tina saw a more recent picture of Sylvia and Mark beaming in front of a waterfall. Somewhere in the corner of the second shelf was another photo of Sylvia and a young woman. Tina went closer to the cabinet to get a better view when a huge knot settled in her throat, and she gingerly walked back to the armchair.

"Is that Maya?" asked Shaker, sitting on the other armchair.

"Yes," whispered Tina, staring at her hands on her lap. "But, Shaker, the woman I saw was much thinner. I wonder how she is, where she is right now. This is so bizarre, sitting here in this room, waiting to talk about a woman who is dead and is not dead. I've no idea where to begin, how to begin."

"You'll begin and end well," assured Shaker. His smile, while gently and effortlessly reassuring her, relaxed his sharp features. He brushed his wavy hair back from his forehead and whispered, "Mrs. Joseph will be happy that you came to see her and that you came to talk about Maya. Don't worry."

Sylvia walked into the room with a steaming teapot on a tray. When Shaker got up quickly to help her set the tray on the center table, Mark followed with another tray holding tea biscuits and samosas.

"Miss Matthew," began Sylvia.

"Oh, please call me Tina," smiled Tina, tentatively taking a sip of the spicy tea. "You've gone to so much trouble. Just tea would have been more than enough."

"It's no trouble at all. I hope you like samosas?" asked Sylvia, offering her guests a plate of savory pastries filled with potatoes and peas. "Tina, I'm sorry I wasn't there to help you when you were stranded in Seloor last year. It must've been an unnerving experience, lost among strangers in a small station like that. How did you manage?"

"But Dr. Shaker was there to help me," replied Tina, still wondering how to tell Mark's aunt about her dead neighbor who might be alive. "I don't know what I would've done otherwise."

Sylvia smiled, looking alternately at her nephew and at her visitors. "Mark said that you wanted to see me about something?"

"Yes, it's about my earlier visit to Seloor last year. When I saw..." Tina nervously looked at everything in the room and continued at Shaker's encouraging smile. "Mrs. Joseph, I was visiting Mark's office day before yesterday. And..." Tina slowly but gladly began to unload her weighing mind.

"Are you telling me that you saw Maya?" asked Sylvia, shaking her head incredulously.

"Yes." Tina desperately began to hunt for words. "This may not make sense, but I did see her."

"No, no, it cannot be Maya you saw at the shelter, Tina." Sylvia, reluctant to hear more, began to cry. "Mark, how could that be Maya? Didn't we lose her in that explosion? Tina probably saw someone who looked like Maya."

"Here, Auntie. That woman left this with Tina," said Mark, pulling the paper from his pocket.

Sylvia looked at the front and the back of the crumpled paper and then covered her face with her hands and let her tears flow silently. Mark pulled his aunt closer to him.

"I'm so sorry. But doesn't this somewhat prove that it was Maya?" asked Tina. "I know it seems silly, but it's remotely possible?"

"Tina," Sylvia continued, "you said a group of people took that young lady away. Did you notice anybody you might recognize? If Maya did not die in that explosion, she is alive somewhere. But where do we start looking?"

"I saw that man again, Mrs. Joseph, you know the man who told me that she was mentally disabled."

"Do you think you would recognize him now?" Sylvia asked eagerly.

"I'll never forget that face. You see, after he spoke with me in the hostel, I saw him again on the road, just after a couple of hours. There was a bald man with him. I'm sure I can recognize him if I see him again."

"How did she end up in a place like that?" asked Shaker. "Mrs. Joseph, can you tell us about Maya and her father, particularly the time before the explosion?"

"So much happened, especially before the explosion. Rajan, that is Maya's father, was in a financial mess. He was forced to sell his house," began Sylvia, "and he died a week or so before that tragic derailment. The doctor thought he died of a heart attack, Dr. Shaker. Rajan was in poor health. He was an alcoholic and had a reckless eating habit. And he had a reckless spending habit as well. That's what forced him to sell the house."

"I wanted to make her happy, and I never had a chance," interrupted Mark, walking to the window. "That bastard ruined her life. Motherless, fatherless, in spite of having a father, Maya was so unhappy."

"What do you mean? Why was Maya fatherless, in spite of having a father?" asked Shaker.

Sylvia, glancing at the set of photographs on the shelf, began to explain. "Tara, Maya's mother, was my best friend since our childhood.

She married Rajan, a man her father chose for her, and moved next door to me. It was a miserable match, but it was too late to mend. Rajan knew that Tara was in love with another man and that she couldn't marry the man she loved. What was worse...Maya knew. Rajan," paused Sylvia, swallowing another bout of tears. "He made his daughter miserable for her mother's mistakes."

"Perhaps he wanted his daughter to suffer like her mother did. That's probably why he wouldn't let his daughter marry me, marry for love," Mark screamed, returning to the couch. "I hate him for what he did to Maya, what he did to us."

"When Tara died, I hoped Rajan would develop some affection for his daughter, especially since he was the only parent," continued Sylvia. "Maya was only about five at the time. But my hope died with Tara. His habits, instead of improving, steadily got worse. His drinking and gambling got him into so much debt, including financial fraud at work. That's why he had to sell the house to his employer."

"We know what happened in Maya's past. What do we do about her present? How long must I wait before I go to the police?" asked Mark, looking seriously at his aunt.

"Police!" shuddered Sylvia, covering her face. "Not again. But I know we must."

"What is it, Mrs. Joseph?" asked Tina, exchanging a painful glance with Shaker and Mark. "What do you mean *not again*?"

"Did you know that Maya used to work in one of the Call Centers at Seloor? One day last August, due to her cursed job, she was returning home very late at night, and..." explained Sylvia, relating all the events connected to the paddy-field-incident.

"What happened then?" asked Tina, unable to believe Sylvia's narrative of the woman who had been chasing her thoughts since the previous year.

"Nothing, other than a series of episodes from Rajan's frequent absence from home to the debt collectors at his house." Sylvia stopped suddenly, directly looking at her guests. "Maya was like a daughter to me.

And she was so young, not yet twenty-five."

"Mrs. Joseph, wasn't there a relative who could help Maya, someone she could go to about her father?" asked Tina, frustrated. "I know you were there, but..."

"No. Rajan antagonized every relative from both sides of the family. Tara was an only child. And Rajan's only sibling died a few years ago. I was there, as you said, but there was nothing I could do." Sylvia began to cry like a child. "And that's what frustrates me more than anything else."

"You did everything you could, Aunt Sylvie." Mark took his aunt's hand in his. "It's my fault for leaving her like that," he said, angrily staring at nothing in particular.

"You've been listening to me patiently. This is quite an obligation." Sylvia apologized to her guests, not really sure about how to handle Mark's anger. "I'm sorry."

"Not at all. I'll never be in peace if Maya is not rescued," smiled Tina, rising from the couch and extending her hand to Sylvia. "I'll see you at my aunt's house day after tomorrow?"

- 25 -

Breams Road, Chennai • February 2010

The neon lights outside Amir's Sweets at the corner of Breams Road flickered doubtfully on a dusky February evening. The wide avenue could boast of many amenities—broad sidewalks, clean road, closed sewer, and graffiti-less concrete walls. Amir opened the front door to let in some fresh air and gaped confusedly at the unexpected appearance of Yusuf. His mind swiftly tripped to the day when Zakir had been dropped off in front of the store, minutes before the notorious suicide mission in November.

"Yusuf bhai, how are you? It's so good to see you," Amir, hiding his annoyance at the surprise visit, infused a significant dose of enthusiasm in his voice and greeted the visitor as his brother, although Yusuf was young enough to be his son. He adjusted the white tagiyah covering his bald head and wiped his sweaty face with his crinkled sleeve. His glance quickly assessed the young man, with brown eyes and a handsome smile, standing by Yusuf.

"Amir bhai, have you met Jamil?" asked Yusuf, following the owner into the store.

While a couple of underlings were busy sweeping the floor, clearing the gluey mess of sugar syrup and sticky grease, Amir silently took his guests to a dark anteroom and switched on a dim light. Yusuf occupied the only chair in the room and asked Jamil to sit by him on a dusty stool.

Amir promptly shut the door and waited to hear the reason for Yusuf's sudden visit.

"Jamil did admirable work during the ATS Bus Stand project, Amir bhai. You were away when he was here earlier to take care of the preliminary details, and we couldn't count on your assistance," continued Yusuf, reminding his host of the minor incident at the largest bus terminus in the city.

"My daughter was having a baby at that time, but Usman Sahib knows about that. He understands that I had to go away."

"Of course," smiled Yusuf, brushing a speck of dust from his sleeve. His lazy glance went from one end of the claustrophobic room to the other, taking in the rolled-up tin foil, sacks of sugar, and dusty containers of vegetable shortening. "The mother and the baby?"

"Doing very well," smiled Amir, baring tobacco-stained teeth. His shirt pocket bulged with a dozen cigarettes, snugly hiding like sneaky culprits.

"We're getting ready for an important mission near Kalpadi. I will be there, of course. Jamil will appear as the missionary's husband. I want you to accompany us as her father. She is kept in seclusion at The Jannah, you know, our new headquarters in Seloor. Well, what do you think?"

Amir knew all about the incident-at-the-paddy fields and about the young missionary. He had personally transferred phone messages and other vital information to assist during the hunt. But this development? An important mission in Kalpadi? He had been a small piece in the large puzzle so far. Short errands. Quick phone calls. He had been happy to play ancillary roles from the secure environment of his shop or from the comfort of his home, which was compactly situated on the second floor of his store. He was beginning to feel his age and was looking forward to retiring soon. Now this vital role in an important assignment?

"Usman Sahib thinks you would be a wonderful player in this mission," drawled Yusuf's voice, when Amir kept staring at his visitors instead of responding gratefully. "He trusts, and I agree with him, that you will handle the situation calmly and practically. Are you interested?"

Was Amir interested? He was not used to weighing options when the grand master organized a plan. Why would it matter whether he was interested or not? "Yes, of course. It is indeed a great honor, and it is my privilege to serve. I am very grateful for our master's faith in me, and yours, too, Yusuf bhai." Amir looked at his watch. Three minutes to closing time. "Please wait here, bhai. I'll let the servants go."

When Amir returned to the shop to ensure their privacy, Yusuf went to the exterior wall of the stifling room and stood on his tiptoes to reach up to the small window facing the main road. He saw the servants walking out of the store, curiously glancing back at the entrance. He then heard the loud drawing of bolts and waited patiently for Amir to return.

"We can talk now," continued Amir, sitting on a barrel of flour.

"Your wife?" asked Yusuf, doubtfully glancing at the closed door.

"Not in town. It is safe to talk now."

"Well, as I said earlier, the mission is scheduled to happen in Kalpadi," began Yusuf. "We have a few weeks, but we need you to come to Seloor a week before and prepare for the event. Who takes care of your business whenever you're away?"

Amir's hesitation was transparent through his flitting glance that began to study the disheveled pantry. "My cousin takes care of the store, bhai. My son, who used to help here, is usually busy managing the store in Nadar Colony." Amir uncomfortably shifted on the stool, and Yusuf knew the reason. Amir's son, who was not quite efficient in executing Usmanic principles, was a sore subject.

"Well, I'm glad you are eager to take this assignment. It takes about five hours to reach Kalpadi from Seloor. The main difficulty is keeping the missionary focused on the job. I'll take care of that, especially with Jamil's help. If you can do the needful," paused Yusuf, transferring his glance to the small window, where the slats of broken glass let in filtered moonlight. He walked to the window and looked out again, as though suspicious of a stealthy activity. "And your excuse for leaving your home and business for a week would be?" he asked, returning to his chair.

"Meeting a couple of vendors near Seloor. My family is used to these routine meetings. When should I reach Seloor, bhai?"

"Not until March," responded Yusuf, rising from his chair. "Be prepared to leave at a moment's notice, Amir bhai. Expect a call from Naim's Tailoring."

"Yes, of course." Naim's Tailoring was the most commonly used central circuit, and every devotee of Usman was familiar with the establishment. Amir walked his guests to the front door where a green van was parked right outside the entrance to the store.

Yusuf brought his hands together to take his leave, and Jamil imitated him. The guests were gone in the next minute.

- 26 -

Mason Colony, Chennai • February 2010

Sylvia tentatively looked at the beautiful, cultivated neighborhood and the bougainvillea-covered gate at Edwin's house. Her nervous glance soon glided to the golden waves dancing leisurely in the sunlight. She wiped her moist face with her handkerchief as the salty air added to the stubbornly lingering humidity.

"Sorry, Mrs. Joseph, Rita is not here to greet you. She's not coming home until next week," smiled Edwin, leading her and Mark to the drawing room where Tina and Shaker were waiting. His warm and friendly greeting swallowed some of Sylvia's anxiety.

While everybody awkwardly looked at everybody else, Edwin took Sylvia to a comfortable chair. A servant brought a tray with cold lemonade and biscuits.

"Now, Mrs. Joseph, tell me everything I need to know about Maya," began Edwin, without messing about, as soon as the servant vacated the room. "I had a long talk with Tina, but I'm waiting to know more."

Sylvia let her round eyes travel to the people assembled in the room and began to tell everything she could, with intermittent help from Mark.

"You know, I've been thinking about the explosion that had been Maya's end. I don't know if you remember, but the disaster was tied to Lashkar."

"Lashkar?" asked Sylvia, confused. "But how?"

"Lashkar-e-Taiba? But isn't their primary goal Kashmir Jihad?" asked Shaker, trying to make a connection. "Would they waste their time organizing an attack in an insignificant town in South India?"

Edwin did not reply for a few moments.

"I'm sorry. If it means a breach…" Shaker said hurriedly.

"No, it's not that." Edwin looked at his attentive audience, absentmindedly stroking his salt-and-pepper goatee. "I'm not telling you something that you haven't seen in the newspaper or heard in the news. And Mark knows enough about terrorist activities, perhaps more than I do."

"Go on, Mr. Edwin," encouraged Mark, sitting up straight in his chair. "I've been working on terrorism and counter-terrorism during my career as a reporter, but I wouldn't say I know enough. I don't think anybody does."

"True," agreed Edwin, "surely, there is always something sprouting up which frustrates the officials. It certainly frustrates me like hell. Remember the attack near Delhi? They were testing at random locations, small unusual targets, as Dr. Shaker said. Our sources discovered, only recently, that the railway station at Seloor might be one of the testing regions."

Sylvia covered her mouth with her hand to stifle a cry.

"This is just a thought, Mrs. Joseph. A train disaster was organized by the terrorists. What I'm trying to understand is the coincidence behind Maya's journey in that train on that particular day." Edwin looked at his audience for a response.

"I wondered about that," responded Shaker. "Was it a coincidence, after all?"

"What do you mean?" asked Sylvia, her expression steeped in anxiety.

"Mrs. Joseph, if Maya was not inside that train, according to the e-mail she sent you," continued Shaker, "somebody wanted you to think, no, believe that she was definitely coming by that train. What if she did not send that e-mail?"

"Maya's death was staged, you mean?" asked Mark.

"Yes," agreed Shaker. "The fact that her name was included in the list of passengers is evidence enough."

"Do they ask for proof of identification when you travel by train here?" asked Tina. "When I was traveling from Chennai, the last time I was going to Pennoor, the ticket collector looked at me and checked the ticket. He did not ask for any identification."

"It's not difficult for someone to travel under another name. Happens very often," confirmed Mark.

"Which means some other woman could have easily used Maya's name when the ticket collector checked her ticket, and she could have got off the train in the next station before the train reached Seloor," finished Shaker.

"Exactly. But why?" asked Mark.

"But Maya went to Salem for an interview, and if the terrorist's attack was organized by Islamic fanatics..." lingered Sylvia's voice.

"Mrs. Joseph, that has nothing to do with the situation," explained Edwin. "They could have used false names. And these radical groups will use anybody, Islamic or otherwise. This is where mercenaries are very useful."

"And if they wanted my aunt to believe that Maya was traveling in the train that day, what are they doing with her now? Why was she involved in...whatever it is?" asked Mark, thoroughly frustrated.

"Maya's journey in the train on the day of the explosion is anything but a coincidence," repeated Edwin. "I'm convinced, after listening to all of your accounts, that whoever is behind Maya's misery planned that explosion and the derailment of the train very cleverly. Maya's e-mail to Mrs. Joseph, before the calamity, and her convenient death prove that Maya is being held for a very foul purpose."

"Mr. Edwin," quivered Sylvia's voice. "That's what I can't understand. What foul purpose? Please explain to me why someone would go through such lengths to hurt Maya."

"I wish I knew, Mrs. Joseph," replied Edwin, looking closely at

Shaker, Mark, and Tina before continuing. "Usually, young women are abducted for prostitution. Sex trade has become a monumental crisis. Sex trafficking is, by far, the most lucrative organization here and in other countries, and that is the number one reason why innocent women are exploited."

"Do you think that's what happened to Maya?" asked Sylvia, after a few moments of hesitation.

"Probably, but something doesn't click in the sale of Rajan's house, the explosion, Maya's letter, and everything else. This shows meticulous, extensive planning. If Maya was sighted by someone for prostitution, where is the necessity for such lengthy preparation?" asked Edwin, looking for a response from the rest of the group.

"I agree. What worries me is…" hesitated Shaker. "I think an e-mail was sent to Mrs. Joseph to prevent her from going to the police."

"Why?" asked Sylvia, bewildered by the entire development.

"Probably because Maya might be exposed in public for some reason," continued Shaker, exchanging a very meaningful glance with Edwin, "and the group that is responsible for her disappearance does not want anybody looking for Maya or identifying her."

"But I don't understand," cried Sylvia, frustrated and angry.

"Let me try to explain," intervened Edwin. "Mrs. Joseph, if Maya had not sent that e-mail about her arrival in that train and if she had not died in that explosion, which the passenger list confirmed, you would be expecting to hear from her or waiting to see her. Won't you? If not, you would be concerned and perhaps make a report about a missing person. And if she had continued to be in the missing list, there would have been posters, flyers, etc, with her photograph and a good description of her. Am I making sense?" asked Edwin. "Now, let's think about this. Maya contacted you, and she died. Now do you see what Dr. Shaker is suggesting? Her appearance and description are not publicized. When she is brought into public, if she comes out, she will not be noticed by anybody particularly looking for her. Do you see our point?"

"Yes," whispered Sylvia. "But would a terrorist organization kill hundreds of innocent people just to stage Maya's death?"

"These explosions are scheduled methodically, well in advance, and whoever is behind Maya's disappearance probably took advantage of the coincidence, or planned such a coincidence. That's all," explained Edwin.

"What makes you think that?" asked Mark, hoping he understood the glance exchanged between Edwin and Shaker earlier. "Shaker, do you think Maya would be exposed in public that could endanger her life?"

"Probably," replied Shaker, avoiding Mrs. Joseph's eyes.

"Tina, I thank God for that chance meeting, when you saw Maya briefly after we thought she was dead. And it must be Maya's extreme good fortune that you saw her photograph on Mark's desk. We wouldn't be looking for her now, otherwise. If there is any chance to save Maya," cried Sylvia, unable to continue.

"We'll try every method to find her, Mrs. Joseph," Edwin earnestly assured Sylvia. "I'll treat this as my personal mission. Maya's father, from your account, has to be somehow involved in this affair. I wonder if I could see that building, that shelter. Where is it exactly?" asked Edwin.

"Temple Street. But it's now nothing like what Tina saw," replied Mark. "I was there only a couple of days ago. It is an office complex with many modern amenities." Mark described the current condition of 19 Temple Street and his conversation with the woman at Lakshmi Arts. "What should I do now?"

"Mr. Stevens, you do nothing now. All right?" asked Edwin, compelling Mark to listen to him with his authoritative voice.

"All right, then. What are you going to do, Mr. Edwin?" asked Mark.

"I can't do anything now on my own without consulting the right authorities. I shouldn't. However, once I begin certain procedures, I don't think Mrs. Joseph should live in Seloor alone," continued Edwin. "Whoever has Maya now knows you by sight. They know where you live, and they know your routine. Before I do anything at all, I've to make sure you're safe."

"Where shall I send my aunt?" asked Mark.

"You're not going to send her anywhere, Mr. Stevens," responded

Edwin, again taking charge of the situation. "You're going to be with her."

"Mr. Edwin," exclaimed Mark. "Are you suggesting that I should hide? I would like nothing better than going with my aunt somewhere, but your suggestion is ridiculous."

"Why?" asked Edwin, as though confronting an adolescent. "Do you want me to list the problems we could anticipate if you went around town like a determined sleuth? Mr. Stevens, you have to listen to my suggestion very carefully if you want me to go anywhere from here regarding Maya. I'm not issuing commands on a whim. I'm speaking carefully from experience."

"But what about my job? What would I tell my employer?"

"Tina told me last night that Varma is your boss. Do you report to him?" asked Edwin, referring to his notes.

"Yes, but why?" asked Mark, still unwilling to bend.

"Then that makes my job easy. No other media specialist knows more about terrorism than Varma. He is an authority on every explosion that has occurred since 1987. That was his first project, I remember, when the militant activity around Kashmir was at its peak."

Sylvia's round-eyed apprehension was obvious when she squirmed at Edwin's last sentence.

"Mrs. Joseph," continued Edwin, eager to alleviate her anxiety, "All I'm saying is that the series of developments involving Maya makes me wonder about terrorist activities in the future. And as frightening as it may be, we cannot rule out the possibility."

"Of course, Mr. Edwin." Sylvia smiled nervously. "All I want is my Maya. I'm prepared to hear anything, do anything."

"Good. I'm glad you understand. Now, Mrs. Joseph, can you tell me anything more about where Maya's father worked?"

"Rajan worked for a company that manufactured various goods, mainly garments, for foreign vendors. I think he managed accounts there. It's called Eastern Exports. It's on Park Road, just outside Seloor. This is the only job which he did not quit quickly, Mr. Edwin. I think he has stayed with this company for a few years. Only after selling his house, he decided to move to Salem for a new job."

"But he didn't start his work in Salem?"

"No. He died of a heart attack a week before he was supposed to move."

"We'll continue to talk, Mrs. Joseph. Right now I've to make arrangements to take you and your nephew to a safe place," paused Edwin, picking up his cell phone from his pocket. "Please excuse me."

"Mark," began Shaker, when the young man got up from the sofa and turned towards the balcony. "Mr. Edwin is thinking of your safety, and he is worried about you because you were close to Maya. If that group realizes that the officials are on its track, you might be their target. Now be mature about it and listen to Mr. Edwin."

"Oh, I can be mature about it, Shaker. But how can I sit somewhere within four walls, impassive and unaffected, while people are looking for my Maya? Try to place yourself in my situation."

"I understand. Mark, someone who has a special place in your heart is alive, hopefully, and it must be hell not knowing where she is or if she is safe. How can I not understand what you're going through? How can anybody not feel for what you feel right now?"

"You understand?" Mark did not let Shaker finish. He began to wipe his spectacles with unnecessary force, as though wishing to remove piles of dirt. "Then what about you and Tina? You two were in the hostel when Maya was there that night. Well, you did not stay there the whole night. But Tina did, and what's more to the point, she saw Maya. Doesn't that place Tina in danger? Tina can identify Maya. So can you, if it comes to that. Then why isn't Mr. Edwin taking you and Tina to a place of safety?"

"I can answer your question," said Edwin, returning to the drawing room. "Tina is staying with me and my wife. I can guarantee that she'll be safe. Because of the nature of my work, my house is guarded, and we'll keep Dr. Shaker safe. Again, my decisions are made from years of experience, and I don't work alone. I have a lot of professional help."

"Mr. Edwin, I…" Sylvia looked at her host, unable to continue.

"What is it, Mrs. Joseph? Is something the matter?" Edwin asked kindly, sensing Sylvia's hesitation.

"It's just that...you see, Tina called you day before yesterday. We're here today, and already plans are being made for my stay somewhere, Mark's absence from work, and so much more." Sylvia fell silent for a moment or two. "I'm still trying to understand how things can move so fast."

"Do you have doubts about how genuine the help is or how efficient our men are?" asked Edwin, not upset but a little confused.

"No, no, of course not, Mr. Edwin. You are no stranger to us. We trust you. You are Rita's husband, and she is my friend. Besides, you are Tina's uncle," paused Sylvia, searching for the right words.

"The fact that I'm Tina's uncle or Rita's husband should not sway you and Mark towards a good opinion of me. You hardly see Rita, and you barely know Tina. Mrs. Joseph," hesitated Edwin. "I'm asking you and Mark to trust me because I sincerely feel that I'm in the right position to help. And I want to help, not because Tina saw Maya under very extraordinary circumstances, but because Maya deserves to be rescued. It's her fundamental right to be brought to safety. Human rights abuse should be everybody's concern, Mrs. Joseph. It is my duty to help."

"Thank you, Mr. Edwin. I know it may sound silly, but I needed to hear that from you. You do understand. Don't you?" asked Sylvia, "So much has happened since day before yesterday, and I don't want to hang on to the idea of seeing Maya again if the chances are slim."

"I understand perfectly, and you must understand that I don't want to make vacant promises. A person in Maya's situation...I must warn you that it's rare to see a victim again, but I must also add that it's not utterly impossible. It can go either way, but we must try. Mrs. Joseph, do you remember the company where Maya went for an interview?" asked Edwin.

"It was one of the Call Centers in Salem. Rajan had told her that he had arranged for this job for Maya. She thought that the interview was just a formality."

"I shouldn't have left Maya alone," began Mark, continuing his fateful regrets, and the rest helplessly stared at each other.

- 27 -

The Jannah, Seloor • March 2010

Yusuf parked his bicycle just outside Eastern Exports and shouted, "Open the gate."

When the stocky guard obeyed his command, he walked in with a soft whistle on his lips.

"Salaam-Alaykum, Yusuf Sahib," the guard saluted respectfully and took the cycle to a rectangular building nestled discreetly behind a curtain of trees in the backyard of 248 Park Road.

Yusuf walked up the stone-paved steps to the wide veranda and accepted the greetings of another guard at the double doors. On his way to Usman's private room upstairs, he surveyed the development of the most recent projects—a twenty-something man going over every detail of a minister's impending arrival from New Delhi to Chennai, a middle-aged woman's repetitious memorization of her forthcoming interview at the American Embassy in New Delhi, and other strategic recruits of the master's grand missions. His shrewd glance quickly moved to a group of craftsmen who were skillfully measuring a hollow bronze chain while a couple of men were working on thin wires to be threaded inside the long chain. Nodding gracefully at the respectful glances from the men and women, Yusuf walked to his master's room.

"Yusuf, how have you been?" asked the master, smiling affectionately at his favorite prodigy. "Have a seat."

"Busy, Sahib, but I'm doing well." Yusuf sat on the edge of one of the chairs, his curious eyes briefly resting on the master's white tagiyah on his head, the gray beard, and the steely eyes. The man who had been like a father to him was getting older, had somehow changed through the years, yet not changed. Strange.

"I know. I've kept you busy." Usman observed the mature expression on the young man's handsome face.

"No, Sahib, not at all. I'm happy to serve our cause, and you know that."

"Of course. Son, I thank Allah for sending you to me. It was a great day when we met. How long ago was it? Twelve years?" asked Usman, directing the young man's mind to his moldy past.

"I think it is," acknowledged the disciple, recalling his youth with a slight ache, desperately trying to scrub away the memories. He did not like the way his decayed past crawled into his carefree present, repeatedly gnawing at his peace of mind.

"Yusuf, I know it's painful for you to remember your past..." lingered Usman, relying on suggestive flashbacks to reassert his organization's importance and to remind the disciple about his master's significant role in his life. "But I like to recollect the bitter days once in a while. My youth was sorrowful, too. I had to extricate myself from a rotten, stinking hole. But I force myself to remember the hurtful past because I believe it's a marvelous way to thank Allah for sending us his blessings. You see, Yusuf, you're a blessing to me."

"Shukriya, Sahib. All praises go to Allah!" Yusuf thanked his master and respectfully inclined his head.

Usman smiled like a saint at the young man's grateful and pious recitation. The ever-rising maturity on his disciple's angelic face continued to amaze him. "I'm so proud of you, Yusuf. Now I'm going to leave Salman in your hands. I would like you to take him under your wings and slowly, carefully groom him. I've prepared him. He's come a long way since Manohar reeled him in from Inspector Ravi. As you know, he is learning a few skills. And I'll continue to work on him. I want him to be another Yusuf, if that's possible," smiled Usman, inserting a trace of paternal pride in that smile.

"Yes, he has come a long way from the day he was brought to us."

"Of course. You supervised the last and the most important segment of that recruitment, I know. I wouldn't have trusted that idiot, Manohar, if I didn't have the comfort of your support there!" exclaimed Usman, pumping up the young man's ego.

And the pep talk was always useful. Yusuf visibly swelled in pride.

"Thank you, Sahib. I'm always glad to offer my services to you. Jamil told me that Salman performed exactly as he was told at ATS Bus Stand. What do you specifically want me to do with the boy?" asked Yusuf.

"Let him be your shadow for a while. Start with small assignments, only those where you can always keep an eye on him. Give him confidence. Most importantly, Yusuf, show him how this idol-worshipping society hates Islam, and report to me regarding his progress. He is very mature and knows the ills that have dictated his life. He's here to seek salvation—salvation from poverty, from abuse, and most importantly, from the villainous law," paused Usman, his mind rapidly assessing ways to strengthen Salman's already brewing hatred with more potent examples. He knew that Salman was not just an angry, bitter child of thirteen, and he remembered how the young boy was treated at the police station. Inspector Ravi did not just take a piece of Salman's skin off his jaws when he questioned him inside the dark cell. He stripped the boy's dignity and left his soul vulnerably bare. That was the ultimate wound.

"Sahib, thank you for leaving Salman's future in my hands. I'll be glad and honored to train him." Yusuf meant what he said. He knew that only the most valuable and vital recruits came into his hands. The more dispensable candidates went through Manohar's hands or Kumar's training before disappearing permanently.

"Thank you for standing by me, Yusuf. I know I can always count on you." Usman smiled in relief, fully aware of his primary strength; psychology. And he knew how to use it to feed terrorism and to cultivate violence. "I want you to meet Salman again and assess his improvement. Come, I'll take you to him," invited Usman, leading the young man out of the room. "And I also want you to see how much Saira has improved. She is not yet sixteen, but she is a priceless girl who is dedicated to our cause. Eventually, she'll assist you. I'm glad Sayeed did a lot to get her to us."

"Sayeed is meticulous!" Yusuf generously praised Abdullah's principal assistant.

The master and his disciple walked into a spacious room downstairs, facing the backyard. It contained small coir mats scattered on the floor, a few copies of *The Koran* neatly placed by the mats, and a few children deeply involved in their lessons. Yusuf spotted Salman in the right most corner of the room. He was sitting in front of a girl of about fifteen or sixteen, a very good-looking girl, who was teaching him at the moment.

Salman looked up at Usman and smiled. His eyes did not hold the once vacant expression anymore. Rather, there was a light—bashful but full of mellow fire—filling the big, round eyes. He ran to his master, but Yusuf's eyes were no longer on Salman. They wandered to the girl's dark, expansive eyes. What did that expression mean? *Those eyes could speak volumes*, he thought. Something about her was wrong, very wrong, and Yusuf nervously averted his glance.

"Salman, Yusuf Bhai is going to be your instructor." Usman, while reintroducing Yusuf to Salman as an affectionate elder brother, looked down at the boy's thin frame, although not so miserably meager as it used to be.

"Salaam Alaykum." Salman inclined his head, bringing his small hands together.

Yusuf repeated the respectful greeting.

"Come here, my child," Usman spoke to the good-looking girl, who got up obediently and stood next to Salman. "Yusuf, Saira has been doing very well," continued the master, taking her hand in a fatherly manner.

"Salaam Alaykum," Saira looked up at the visitor, and Yusuf knew what was wrong about her. Everything. He stared at her cheap cotton skirt, wrinkled long tunic, and the hijab covering her head. But her face… that face belonged to an expensive portrait in a museum. Something that was ethereal about her expression took his breath away. *Was Saira going to be the weapon itself? Or would she merely assist in a mission?* He hoped, for some strange reason he desperately hoped that his master had the second choice in mind. He wanted to ask his leader what he intended to do with Saira, but he could not. It was not his place to question his master. Then he remembered, with a touch of relief, Usman's recent statement: *Eventually, she'll assist you.*

"Saira, I see you're spending a lot of your time tutoring children. Didn't I tell you, my child, that Allah sent you to me for a purpose? Look at you, a young woman who has been deceived and abandoned by her mother and her MAN! And you've turned your strength to serve Allah! How fortunate that you were sent to me!" exclaimed Usman, spreading his hands and looking up reverently at the imaginary sky. Usman knew that his success was cemented on how successfully he was able to influence the lives he touched.

"Thank you, Sahib. I'm glad to be useful," smiled Saira, mature beyond her years. She colored quickly at the recollection of her *mother and her MAN.*

Salman returned to his mat, and Saira followed him. Yusuf walked out of the room after his leader.

"I'll walk you to the gate," suggested Usman, leading his disciple to the stone-paved steps. "Now, Yusuf, you must rest a bit. You look a little tired. Sure you're all right?"

"I am, Sahib. Thank you. I just wanted to inform you that I've been periodically checking on past incidents to ensure there are no loose ends. And I'm taking care of normal assignments at the regular pace. Nothing to worry."

"Past assignments? That reminds me of something, Yusuf. Remember, that young reporter, Mark Stevens? He was supposed to return to his Chennai office. Did he?"

"Yes, Sahib. He returned a long time ago. I made sure of that."

"Good, Yusuf. May Allah protect you! And may all praises go to Allah!" Usman embraced his devoted assistant and walked back towards Jannah.

- 28 -

North Stanes Road, Chennai • March 2010

Theo Edwin was sitting behind his desk while waiting for a cue from Officer Sharif. He looked at Varma, a stalwart personality in the field of journalism, who was nervously sitting beside Sharif. Dr. Neil Shaker, seated to the left of Edwin, appeared restless. *And the cue was not going to come*, thought Edwin, glancing at his friend's sour expression.

Sharif meditatively looked at Dr. Shaker, who appeared older than his thirty-five years, probably due to his perpetual, preoccupied expression. His glance reluctantly shifted to Varma, to his rather tall frame and neatly combed gray hair which gave him an extra ounce of distinction. He hated any interference from civilians and did not like newspapers, but he needed Dr. Shaker's professional assistance and Varma's cooperation as a leading journalist. His glance finally and gratefully settled on Theo Edwin, his faithful friend and colleague.

"Thank you, gentlemen, for taking the time to come here, when you're very busy," began Edwin, hoping to ease the tension in his expansive office.

"Any developments that might lead to Maya?" asked Shaker, looking alternately at Edwin and at Sharif.

"My man found nothing. NOTHING. We hoped his visit to Eastern Exports would be fruitful," hissed Sharif, sounding angry, but not appearing angry.

"Some of us don't know the details behind your man's visit. Can you repeat what you said just now, and a little slowly please?" asked Shaker, studying Sharif's stone face. He could not tell if the officer meant anything he said because Sharif's face did not reflect his sentiments. How did he manage to do that? Was that the secret of his power? His sparse mustache, thinning hair, spectacled, pockmarked face, and unimpressive attire presented an ordinary man whom nobody would notice. Yet everybody paid attention to him. And although Sharif was not hefty or tall, there was no doubt that he was a very powerful man.

"Let me please explain, Dr. Shaker," jumped in Edwin, noticing Sharif's narrowing eyes. "One of Sharif's men went to Eastern Exports in the border of Seloor. According to the information provided by Mrs. Joseph, that was the company where Maya's father, Rajan, was working. Since Rajan owed his employer money, we thought it was best to start the investigations at the place of his work where he was drawing a salary. Other than the fact that Eastern Exports is owned by Abdullah—who has been under scrutiny now and then—Sharif's man did not get anything else out of his visit."

"Why is Abdullah under scrutiny?" asked Shaker.

"He has been in trouble, more than once," Sharif explained in his monotonous tone. "Tax evasion, for one. Substandard working conditions at the warehouse, hiring minors, and there is a rumor that some of his employees are forced to serve as indentured laborers."

"Indentured labor? No, I can't believe it." Shaker turned to Edwin. "And Mark heard a rumor that Abdullah was a benefactor, who donated that facility which operated as a shelter on Temple Street."

"Why is it hard to believe, Dr. Shaker? Don't you read about blatant human rights abuse? Abdullah, a benefactor?" Sharif rolled his eyes. "I would like to see that."

Theo Edwin exchanged a knowing glance with Varma, who had been quietly listening to the conversation.

"Dr. Shaker," interrupted Varma, clearing his throat. "My reporters have gathered some information on Abdullah since we came to know about Eastern Exports, Abdullah's business, from Mrs. Joseph. Abdullah is definitely a questionable character. The authorities can get him on misdemeanor charges, just to question him for now, in the hope of exploring further."

"Doesn't he have a trusty assistant, Theo?" asked Sharif. "His name did come up during our last meeting."

"His name is Sayeed. I believe he is related to Abdullah in some way. They've been together for a long time. He manages Eastern Exports and handles other businesses as well," responded Edwin. "But that's all we know now."

"May I see the girl's picture again, Theo?" asked Sharif, reaching for Maya's photo.

The enlarged copy of the photograph soon changed hands, and all eyes, in turn, despondently stared at the thin face of a young woman, at her high cheekbones, at her large eyes.

"Theo, your niece saw this woman briefly at a hostel or whatever that place was at that time, and then she thinks she saw her photo again in Mark Stevens' office. How can we be sure that it's the same woman?" asked Sharif, turning Maya's photo this way and that.

"Sharif, unless Tina was sure of what she saw, she wouldn't even imagine talking to Stevens about it. She is sensible and dependable. Why this doubt?" asked Edwin, trying to look for something definable in Sharif's normally indefinable disposition.

"It's not that I doubt Tina's words. If Maya is a victim of sex trafficking, she could be anywhere—from the slums of Chennai to a desert hole in the Middle East. Where do we begin our search? It's just that... Listen," sighed Sharif, looking at the group. "I'm sorry to be a pain in the ass, but quite a few women, young and old, are absconding at an alarming rate. There isn't enough law-enforcement assistance to keep tabs on red-light dungeons and drug-infested corners. Let's get this straight. Why are we—and let's have a very good reason—searching for this young woman who might be dead?"

"Mr. Sharif, do you think it's a waste of your time to launch this search?" asked Shaker.

"No. That's not what I mean," came Sharif's monotone voice. "If I felt that way, I wouldn't have placed Mark Stevens and his aunt in a safe place at the expense of tax payers."

"Then what do you want to know?" asked Shaker, a little impatiently.

"Answer my question." Sharif looked at the group. "WHY ARE WE SEARCHING FOR MAYA WHO IS SUPPOSED TO BE DEAD?"

"May I?" asked Shaker, quickly looking at Edwin and Varma. "One, Maya knocked on the door of a stranger while desperately trying to escape. Why was there a need to escape? Why was she kept there as a prisoner? From Tina's description of her, Maya had visible bruises indicating that she was hurt. Insane or sane, here is evidence that a human being was being treated inhumanely."

"But they could be self-inflicted wounds, as one of the men explained to you and Tina when those men stopped to talk to you at the railway crossing," argued Sharif, not particularly looking at anyone. "But we don't know that for a fact. Go on."

"Two, Maya was labeled insane. This was in November when there was no evidence of insanity when she disappeared in October. Three, Maya was supposed to have died in October during a devastating explosion. Why was she knocking on the door where Tina was staying, a month after her tragic death?"

"Thank you for your reasons, Dr. Shaker. I asked for one, and you've given me three. I'm glad because I wanted to hear the reasons one more time. I know. I'm a crazy man. What can I say?" Sharif asked in the most unaffected manner in response to Shaker's incredulous expression. "And your explanation has put things in perspective for all of us to see clearly, that is, assuming the woman Tina saw was Maya. I hope, sincerely, she has not been abducted for sex trade." Sharif began to flip the pages of the report absentmindedly. "I feel for this missing woman, just as I feel for others who are missing. And if I can find the men responsible for her abduction, if that's what happened, I'll be glad to wring their necks with my bare hands and bring her back to safety. Believe me, I've done it before."

Edwin, who knew Sharif very well, nodded his head.

"But I want to be honest with you," continued Sharif. "The primary reason for my presence here, frantically thinking of ways to look for this woman, is because of the way she was supposed to have died: the explosion in the train in which she was traveling. I want to find the man who was behind that explosion, and my instinct tells me that he or his group is brewing something else."

Nobody spoke a word, but everybody's eyes were on Sharif.

"And I believe he's brewing something else," repeated Sharif, staring at the thick file on his lap, "because of the course of events described in this report about Maya. Do we need any other information before I interrogate Abdullah? I need to issue an order to detain him and his faithful assistant, Sayeed."

"Does Abdullah have any other business?" asked Shaker.

"Well, a few here and there," responded Sharif. "A scrap metal business, a grocery corner, and a small automobile garage—all located in Seloor, close to Park Road. Why?"

"I'm just wondering if there is a home or office which is unknown to you yet that needs to be explored?" asked Shaker, doubtfully looking at the group.

Sharif picked up his buzzing cell phone. "Excuse me. I've an urgent phone call." He quickly stepped out of the office.

"Is it really that easy to get Abdullah on a slight misdemeanor charge?" asked Shaker, for the sake of breaking the unnerving silence in the room.

"It's easy," assured Edwin. "He can't be kept inside for a long time, but we can certainly buy some time by keeping him restrained for a short while."

"And Sharif can easily take care of that. Can't he?" asked Varma, tentatively staring at the closed door. "You know, as a reporter hunting for clues, I've carefully followed the tracks of Islamic militants. I tell you, I've been scared at times. But I wouldn't want to do what Sharif is doing, especially when…"

"Especially when Sharif is a Muslim?" Edwin finished Varma's point. "Muslim, or Hindu, or Christian, Sharif was born without fear. And look at us, Varma. Your Hindu faith, my Christian faith, and Sharif's Islamic faith must all converge harmoniously for one universal cause: humanity and its welfare. And excuse me for sounding corny."

"Corny? Not at all," Varma smiled at Edwin's embarrassed expression hiding behind his goatee. "Despite the fear of bombings and the terror caused by radicals, we must find a way to live."

"Yes, we must. How long have you known him, Mr. Edwin?" asked Shaker.

"I've known Sharif for more than thirty years." Edwin warily glanced at the door and whispered, "He saved my life once. He won't admit it, but he did."

"Sharif is all right," said Varma. "It's just that his manners are strange."

Edwin laughed. "Sharif can be very severe. And he doesn't care about his audience. In fact, his impassive and unbiased treatment of certain high-ranked officials, just as he might impartially treat certain low-ranked clerks, has resulted in his stagnant, although important position in the government. His bedside manners do need repair, I know. But he has seen the worst in his career. Gentlemen, believe it or not, he has a heart of gold."

"Sorry for the interruption, but you'll be glad to know about the call I just got," smiled Sharif, walking back into the room. His usually unsmiling, pockmarked face creased awkwardly as the sudden smile broke the routine. "It's from my man who has been observing Abdullah's warehouse. Apparently, there's a building located behind Eastern Exports. It's not easily visible from the avenue. And what makes it interesting is that nobody is exactly aware of what's going on in that building. My men are checking it out as discreetly as they can. They've asked for reinforcement."

"Do you think it's worthwhile?" asked Edwin. "Who is in charge of investigations right now?"

"You can bet it's worth the search. Raj, my deputy, is in charge right now."

"I'm sorry, but I must leave. You'll keep me posted?" asked Varma, getting up.

"Absolutely. Have a good trip to New Delhi." Sharif saw Varma out of the room.

"Have a seat, Sharif. Your expression scares me, even though I've known you for a heck of a time. What's wrong?" Edwin whispered, anxiously looking at the closed door where Sharif was still standing.

"Theo, that building behind Eastern Exports is worrying my deputy." Sharif whispered back.

"What is he worried about? Aren't we sending some reinforcement?"

"That's not his worry. The building seems to be filled with people. He noticed children, some very young, and naturally he is wondering what's going on there. It's not a school, or a hospital, and it's not listed under anything legitimate. Listen to this. There is a direct access from that building to a side street that leads to Park Road, but that's blocked. So the only access now is through the gates of Eastern Exports."

"I see. So that building is behind Abdullah's warehouse. That could not be Abdullah's home?" asked Edwin. "Your man would have checked that out"

"Of course, he did. Abdullah is single. Well, he was married twice, but he has outlived both his wives. And he lives on Medur Road. Has quite a mansion, I heard."

"No children?"

"No."

"But, then what's going on in that building, Mr. Sharif?" asked Shaker. "Somebody ought to know. There must be provisions delivered, or how about the milkman or the postman? How can there be no activity in and out of that house?"

"Nothing is clear. There is no visible nameplate, address. Nothing. But my men have observed a pattern. A large woman has been seen a few times in the back of the house. She meets a few men whenever she is outside, and then she takes them inside. We've to wait and see what's going on."

"You'll call me for an update, Mr. Sharif?" asked Shaker, not missing the elusive expression in the pockmarked face. He had no idea how to read the man's expression.

"Of course, Dr. Shaker. I hope you're not tired of seeing us on a regular basis for an update?"

"Certainly not. I'm glad to be of any assistance. But I just wanted to know if so much fuss is necessary regarding my whereabouts?" asked Shaker, trying to imitate Sharif's poker expression.

"Are you bothered by my men shadowing you, Dr. Shaker?" asked Sharif, directly coming to the point.

"Not really, but those men's time could be used better elsewhere. I…"

"What's with men and the invincible guard that they yearn to cling to, Theo?" asked Sharif, looking round-eyed. "Do you understand Dr. Shaker's doubts?"

"Yes, I do. And don't bully everybody, Sharif. Leave the poor man alone." Edwin got up politely as Shaker rose to go.

"Dr. Shaker, I'm sorry if I ignored your question just now," apologized Sharif. "You see, your familiarity with Maya, as remote as it might be, places you in a vulnerable position. If that's not enough, the unknown enemy's men saw you with Tina at 19 Temple Street and elsewhere afterwards. And Maya spoke to Tina, remember? So, yes, a bit of fuss regarding your safety and welfare is necessary."

"Then let the shadow follow me as long as you please." Shaker smiled unexpectedly, his sharp features softening, and walked out of Edwin's office.

"Mark Stevens is another young man who thinks he doesn't need protection. Stupidity, actually. I'm going to lose my patience with him one of these days," confessed Sharif.

"I wouldn't worry about that," comforted Edwin.

"Oh, I'm not worried about Stevens. I just hope I didn't scare his poor aunt."

"No, don't worry. Mrs. Joseph seems to be sensible. She's come through this mess so far with such understanding. She's probably glad someone is reminding her nephew that there's no room for his ego while we're hunting for the love of his life. Young Mr. Stevens has to get out of the Romeo-Juliet mindset, and a little scare is good for him. Now get out and get some rest," ordered Edwin, mindful of his friend's deep-set, sleepless eyes.

- 29 -

Nadar Colony, Chennai • March 2010

Officer Sharif got out of his car and looked at the cluster of very middle-class apartments in a very middle-class neighborhood. While a couple of his men discreetly checked various corners of the building, Sharif casually went into the convenience store that occupied the ground floor of the first set of apartment complex. His eyes rested on everything from cheap oily snacks to greasy hair oil. He pretended to be interested in a couple of sleazy magazines showing buxom models and seminude actresses. When one of his men signaled to him that all was clear, he bought a packet of Gold Flakes and lit a cigarette while standing under the awnings of the store. He looked to his left and right, pulled at his cigarette a few more times, and took the stairs slowly to apartment 25-C. Mark opened the door and offered a lackluster greeting.

"How are you Mrs. Joseph?" asked Sharif, looking at Sylvia who was serenely crocheting on the sofa. "No, no, please sit down," he said, when he saw her getting up.

A couple of men followed Sharif with a carton full of groceries. They walked straight into the small kitchen and started to load the refrigerator and the pantry. Sharif politely declined Sylvia's offer of coffee or tea, feeling sorry for the worried expression occupying her chubby face. He followed Mark with his eyes as he walked back and forth from the sofa to the window like a caged animal. Sharif's assistants marched out of the apartment and gently shut the door.

"Mark, you're driving me crazy. Please settle down for half hour. Half hour is all I'm asking." Sylvia begged her nephew, worried and embarrassed about his obvious lack of etiquette. "I wish he could work on something quietly."

"Mr. Stevens, how would you like to do some research for me?" asked Sharif, opening the thick file he had brought along with him. "Varma says that you're an expert on Lashkar..."

"So it's confirmed?" Mark asked wide-eyed. "I knew Le-T must be behind the explosion."

"Slow down, Mr. Stevens. Nothing is confirmed yet. We're working on it."

Mark's face fell, visibly retreating to its former grief. "What kind of research do you have in mind? May I return to *The Express* then, if you want me to go back to work?"

"Return to *The Express*? No." Sharif paused, taking in the despair and disappointment slowly stealing into Mark's face.

"Then how do you expect me to work for you, assist you?" asked Mark, his indignant tone callously piercing the tense atmosphere.

Sylvia threw desperate, warning glances towards her nephew, but Mark thoroughly ignored her.

"Here is a stack of information gathered by my...well let's say by various individuals in my organization," continued Sharif, not at all ruffled by Mark's attitude. "They're chronologically categorized. I'd like to have your opinion on each one in detail." Sharif paused abruptly, deliberately searching for the right words. "Theo Edwin and I would appreciate your help."

"Am I allowed to use my laptop now?" asked Mark, his tone still unbendingly severe. His marked lack of good manners brought a reddish hue to his aunt's cheeks, and she determinedly looked anywhere but at Sharif's face.

"Yes. Your laptop is safe and clean now. But you may only go on the link that my organization has set up. That firewall is imperative for your safety. All right?" asked Sharif, looking alternately at Mark and Sylvia. He pulled out a computer case from his bag and placed it on the center table. "That's the only way to prevent infiltration."

Mark returned to the table.

"Have a seat. Mr. Stevens, I know it must be maddening sitting here, unable to even step out of the apartment. But this secrecy is necessary. And there is nothing lacking in the apartment. Is there?" asked Sharif, turning towards Sylvia.

"We can't ask for anything, Mr. Sharif. We're very comfortable, and thank you," responded Sylvia, hoping to make up for her nephew's tepid and unenthusiastic reception. "Don't you agree, Mark?"

"I'm glad about this arrangement for my aunt's sake, Mr. Sharif. But I could be of some use if I'm let outside, but nobody seems to agree with me. And it's useless to expect you to understand." Mark continued to ignore his aunt's pleading expression. He looked quite young, with a tuft of his casually combed hair reaching down to his spectacles and his juvenile behavior matching his appearance.

The visitor said nothing for a while as the moments trickled through an awkward silence. "Do you want us to keep looking for Maya?" Sharif barked, standing up and facing Mark. "I don't have the time or the intention to understand your stubborn and adolescent pouting over this very serious business. All right, you love Maya. That doesn't give you the right to run loose around Chennai or Seloor and the neighboring districts like a damned movie actor looking for his lost love." Sharif remembered Edwin's analogy regarding Mark's fervor to be let loose. "You're not really Romeo looking for his Juliet. If you care about Maya, shut up, stay patiently here with your aunt, and comfort her for a change. Leave the dangerous job of searching for Maya to us, to the professionals. Risk is part of my job. It is also my job to protect you, no matter how foolish you are. The next time I come here—and I'll come here to ensure your aunt's safety and to dig into any updates you're expected to work on using the files I'm leaving with you—you'll behave sensibly and you'll behave like an adult. Do you understand?"

Mark gaped at Sharif's livid expression but said nothing.

"Have a good day, Mrs. Joseph." Sharif smiled kindly at Sylvia who was sitting through his severe lecture to Mark with an embarrassed and harassed expression.

"Thanks again for everything." Sylvia got up to see him off.

Sharif walked out without a glance at Mark. When Sylvia returned to the drawing room, her nephew was still sitting on the chair, staring at his laptop. Without a word, she sat on the sofa and picked up her knitting needles.

"Aunt Sylvie, I don't like the way that Sharif bullies people. He treats me like an idiot. Look at me, chained to this apartment, when I could be doing something useful out there. How can I relax and act normally?" asked Mark. "You understand my problem. Don't you?"

"What problem, Mark? What's there to understand? You're constantly complaining about Mr. Sharif. You want to go? Then go. Just don't come and see me anymore. All I care about right now is Maya, and I hope she's not already dead or forced to sell her body. Think about that when you think of your problem. I'll suffer through anything if it means there is a chance Maya might be rescued. Mr. Sharif has been very decent and considerate. The least you can do is watch your manners and *pretend* to be polite."

Mark said nothing at the end of his aunt's slapping words, but he looked up at her pathetic face—the once smiling face which had permanently lost its smile. Her usually bright eyes had become a victim of furtive glances, longingly staring at nothing in particular. Her vacant expression and tremulous lips had forever ravaged her cheerful personality.

"Aunt Sylvie, I'm so sorry," apologized Mark, quickly sitting next to Sylvia and gently taking her hand. "I've been behaving like a selfish bastard. Will you please slap me next time I behave so ungratefully?"

"I came close to doing so, Mark," whispered Sylvia, trying to gather her vanishing courage. She covered her face and released her tears, which were reluctant to be seen by Sharif.

Mark pulled her close to him. "I'll never embarrass you. Aunt Sylvie,

I promise."

"I know, my dear. But you've been under such stress. Don't worry." Sylvia quickly wiped her eyes. "Now go start the kettle. Let's have some tea."

- 30 -

North Stanes Road, Chennai • March 2010

Edwin patiently waited for Sharif to look up while he had his nose buried in a file, his thinning hair making a road map on his gleaming bald head.

"That document is not going to reveal anything more than we already know, Sharif," sighed Edwin, as exasperated as his colleague was. "I'm sure we'll get more news in a few days."

"ATS bus stand is vast, the biggest in Chennai, Theo," said Sharif, finally looking at his friend. "Whoever organized the blast knew the extent of the damage."

"Aren't you glad there wasn't much damage? I know what you mean. It was purposely planned to be a minor disaster, you think?"

"Yes. And the booking clerk's body was found around the same time, not very far from his office in the bus stand. Do you see any connection at all? Was he somehow involved in the incident? What surprises me is that he wasn't intentionally left inside the booth when the blast occurred. Why?" asked Sharif. When his friend did not respond, he continued, "I think I know why. Because the blast was meant to be no more than a fizzle. And the clerk wouldn't have perished if he had been sitting at his desk. Somebody wanted that clerk dead. And the same somebody wanted to create a little scare with that blast." When his friend had no response, he continued, "Do you think that I'm letting my imagination run wild?"

"No. We must keep guessing. Otherwise we can't stay in this game." Edwin sighed exasperatedly, which was familiar to his colleague. "And this damned dramatic scare, as you describe it, is distracting us from our current purpose."

"I know." Sharif stopped abruptly, scowling, when there was a knock on the door. "Come in," he said, and both men were eager to see Dr. Shaker.

"Any news?" asked Shaker, hopefully looking at Edwin and Sharif.

"We still have no concrete answers to that mysterious building behind Eastern Exports," replied Sharif. "But my man continuously noticed a pattern, as I said earlier. There is a large woman who takes the men inside and the men leave in about a couple of hours."

"Sharif, is that building a brothel? Is that why they are so secretive?" asked Edwin. "Good God, you said there are children inside that building."

"That idea crossed my mind, but I'm not sure. It's quite likely, but I'm not convinced."

"Why?"

"I don't know. Something doesn't fit. My men also observed a very slim young man, who looks almost like a high school student. He visits the building every day on a bicycle. One of my men overheard the guard at the gates of Eastern Exports greeting him as 'Yusuf Sahib,' but he could not discover anything more about him."

"Yusuf!" Edwin repeated meditatively. "Does the name mean anything to you, Sharif?"

"No, Theo," responded Sharif, not really keen on 'Yusuf' at the moment.

"How big is that elusive building?" asked Edwin, concerned and confused about the latest developments.

"It's not a small establishment, I heard, although it appears ramshackle. It has two floors, and it's considerably big. A long time ago, the entire property—the warehouse and this building behind it—was owned by Balu Gounder, who ran a couple of mills in the area. About fifteen years ago, Abdullah's father bought that property and turned it into his lucrative export company. Ever since he died, Abdullah has been running the business. Here, my deputy has emailed a map of the area to me. Look," said Sharif, turning on his cell phone. "The warehouse looks rather clear, but the building behind it looks fuzzy. The grove between the warehouse and the building seems to be thick and doesn't let in much sunlight."

"Do you think the answer is in that building, in that house?" asked Shaker, walking to the window.

"Here is a picture my deputy has sent me." Sharif answered the text message and clicked on the image. "Let me send a message to Tina. I would like her to tell me if she recognizes anybody," he paused, sending a quick message. "Dr. Shaker, would you say you recognize this person?"

Shaker walked away from the window and took Sharif's phone anxiously. He tilted the phone this way and that. "No, I'm not sure," he said disappointedly. "Perhaps I've seen the bald man," blurted Shaker, not sure of what to think. "But that would be a fantastic coincidence."

"You don't have to be sure, Dr. Shaker. A doubt is not a bad thing, and life sometimes is a fantastic coincidence." Sharif's phone beeped. "It's Tina," said Sharif, checking the message in the email. "She doesn't recognize the bald man. Too bad, his face is shadowed. Theo, your niece wants to know what we are going to do next. She says the suspense is killing her."

"The suspense is killing me, too! What should we do now?" asked Edwin.

"What should we do?" asked Sharif. "We'll fly quietly this afternoon. I'll inform Varma."

"It would be no use if I asked you to take me with you?" Shaker asked Sharif.

"You're right, Dr. Shaker. We can't take you with us. This is a highly classified business and most probably quite dangerous. So, be safe here and," he paused, twinkling, "keep an eye on Tina."

Highly classified business. Yet, Sharif conveniently depended on analysts to understand the psychological insights of terrorism, thought Shaker, bitterly glancing at the officer. Then, without offering a response, he left Sharif's office.

- 31-

The Jannah, Seloor

Edwin and Sharif arrived at Pennoor International Airport by four in the afternoon. Their men, scattered near the carport in nondescript garments, picked up the pair very quietly in a dented, ancient, blue Fiat. The driver looked much like a scruffy street vendor and his other colleagues cleverly blended with the workers hovering around the airport.

"How far is Park Road from here?" asked Sharif, looking suspiciously at the pile of vehicles ahead of their car.

"Sir, we should be there in about half hour," answered the driver, turning the car through very heavy city traffic.

"It's so congested here," sighed Sharif, wiping his pockmarked face with a crumpled handkerchief.

The driver drove silently past the busy junction, went around CSI Hospital and CSI Church, and drove carefully past Holy Rosary Higher Secondary School as several uniform-clad children walked out of the school perimeters. He finally maneuvered the car expertly near Medur Extension, perpendicular to Park Road, and parked the car near the intersection of Pearl Street and Park Road. Sharif looked at his watch. It was just after 5:00.

"Sir," said the driver, looking alternately at both gentlemen. "Your vests are right under your feet."

Adjusting the vest snugly over his chest, Edwin looked outside the window. It was a small, quiet street, with hardly any activity. Slowly, during the next fifteen minutes, a few other sundry vehicles drove past the blue Fiat. Sharif recognized most of the passengers, but neither he nor the other passengers waved in recognition. A couple of jeeps slid quietly behind the blue car, and a few other vehicles noiselessly scattered along Park Road.

"Is there enough reinforcement behind the warehouse?" asked Edwin. "I know Abdullah is out of the way. I hope his assistant doesn't interfere."

"He won't. A group of our men have been sitting around Sayeed, poring over his files. He cannot even breathe without permission from this group. And don't worry about reinforcement. Every corner is plugged," responded Sharif, looking at the map of the area again.

Even as Sharif was speaking, a few vehicles went imperceptibly behind The Jannah and stopped on the marshy land.

"We wait here for our signal?" asked Edwin, looking anxiously through the window. He was sitting behind the driver, closer to the small lane.

"Yes. We go in at 5:30," whispered Sharif, lighting a cigarette. He opened the window slightly to blow out the smoke.

"Sir, don't do that. It's bullet proof!" the driver whispered cautiously.

"This piece of trash?" asked Sharif, staring at his friend's salt-and-pepper goatee, which was losing quite a bit of pepper.

"Sir, it's part of the set up!" the driver exclaimed defensively.

"It's part of your excellent training, Sharif!" Edwin laughed, rather relieved to be able to laugh off a tense waiting period.

Sharif looked at his watch. Fifteen more minutes left. He adjusted his vest and touched the smooth gun that was resting in its sheath.

"Sharif," continued Edwin, doubtfully surveying the small shops and cars down the street. "I've no doubt about the reinforcement, but I want to thank you for giving all you can to… I don't even know what we're going after."

"No need to thank me, Theo. Do we ever know for sure what we're going after? My instinct tells me that somehow I'll find the key to the explosion that killed hundreds last October. I hope it's not a wild goose chase. And if it is, it wouldn't be the first, and it wouldn't be the last. That's a curse that goes with our territory. And if I can rescue a life in the process, just one, it'll be worth the risks."

"Maya?" asked Edwin, almost afraid to mention her name.

"Perhaps," smiled his friend.

"You know, Sharif, when this madness is somehow over, you have to come home and have a meal with us. You haven't come in a long time."

"Thank you. I will. How is Rita doing?"

"Very well. She is busy with Tina right now, but she's very happy."

"And Tina?"

"Fine. She's working only with Dr. Shaker. She's mostly on house arrest, though," laughed Edwin, recollecting his niece's persistent objections.

"Good. Dr. Shaker is an intelligent man, but he seems a little careless to me."

"Every man seems careless in your hawk eyes, Sharif!"

A loud siren pierced the air, followed by a storm of fire engines and ambulances. Both men abruptly stopped talking, as though aware of the hour closing in on them.

"That's our cue. Let's go." Sharif tapped on the driver's shoulder.

Eastern Exports was an unappealing, gray building that stood tall, surrounded by a concrete wall. Almost all the windows were hiding behind dusty blinds or aged curtains. When the blue Fiat carrying Edwin and Sharif neared the warehouse, dozens of employees were being ushered out of the building while the emergency crew from the Fire Service was scuttling noisily.

"Sharif, it looks like a haunted place to me," said Edwin, looking up at the dreary building. "This is a clever arrangement!" he continued, glancing at the firemen.

"Of course, Theo. How else can we make sure that the warehouse is empty? That's the only way we can move on to the house behind the building." Sharif's attention went to the men and women who were carefully quarantined to one side of the compound before being taken away in groups from the broad avenue. "All the employees would be urged to go home as the emergency crew would require the rest of the evening to ensure the safety of the warehouse. No late-shift work would continue this evening. Now let's get down, if you're ready?"

"This way," said an officer, respectfully leading Edwin and Sharif to the backyard. A couple of Sharif's men followed them.

"Please tell me Sayeed is out of the warehouse?" asked Sharif.

"Yes, sir," responded the guide. "He is in one of the vehicles outside the compound. There's nobody inside the warehouse. We've made sure of that."

The men walked through a thick set of trees in a small grove, eerily shadowed by amber shades of dusk. The Jannah, a tile-topped building with low awnings, slowly appeared between the swaying branches.

"But where are the people in that building?" asked Sharif, looking suspiciously around him. "That place is supposed to be swimming with men and women. Didn't they hear the fire alarm? Aren't they curious?" Sharif eagerly looked at a well-built man running from the side of the house. It was his deputy. He went close to him and whispered, "Raj, why aren't those people outside the building? Aren't they curious or concerned?"

"Sir, they might be curious, but the house is situated far enough from the warehouse. They don't have to be really concerned. Some of the people are outside." Raj glanced at the back of the house. "Please follow me carefully."

Slowly, cautiously, and very quietly the men moved to the backyard. The first thing that caught their eyes in the verandah was a group of children huddled together like a pile of blankets. Edwin held Sharif's elbow for a moment when he noticed the hollow expression on the children's faces. Were they afraid, sad, or worried? He could not tell. A couple of Edwin's men approached the children, and then one began to scream, the noise frighteningly and violently piercing the dense grove.

Several noises followed the child's agony. A large woman, her hair pulled back into a tight bun, screamed frantically as she was taken to a corner by one of the officers. A man ran out of the house with a gun in his hand, shouting obscenities. Another followed, dragging a young girl with him, her long skirt sweeping the floor. Someone fired a gun, and soon a succession of firearms thundered through the house and shattered the quivering branches in the woods.

"Take the children to safety. Take them to the vehicles in the back." Raj shouted to the men who were waiting beyond the thick fence facing the backyard.

When Edwin and Sharif ran indoors, another group of children, mostly teenagers, ran recklessly into various rooms branching from the hallway. A few of them were holding assorted knives and other weapons in their hands.

"Get them. Don't let them get out of the building," Edwin screamed at a couple of his men and ran upstairs after Sharif. Raj and two other officers quickly followed them.

On the landing were two rooms—one facing the front of the house, the other facing the back. A very young man, with the face of a child, was sitting on the floor against the wall, laughing like a mad man.

"You'll never get to the root of us, you bastards, you enemies of Allah," the young man screamed and began to foam at his mouth, before the men could run to him.

"Leave him alone. He is gone," whispered Sharif, walking into the room on the right with his deputy.

In the middle of the room was a cot with rumpled sheets, and on the cot was a woman. She was sitting upright, with her back propped up against the headboard. Sharif took a good look at her. She was young and cruelly emaciated, and she was staring listlessly at the wall. She turned her head at the sound of the opened door and looked at Sharif, but she didn't appear to see anything, anybody. Her attention returned to the wall again. When Sharif gasped audibly, she quickly turned and looked at him, as though searching for something in his face. And he could not help staring at her face, her hollow eyes—languid, lifeless eyes. As the color slowly drained from her bony cheeks, her chapped lips began to tremble, and her wide, vacant eyes rapidly filled with fear.

"Maya, it's all right. We're here to help you," whispered Sharif, swallowing several times to unhinge his tongue that seemed to be glued to his throat.

She began to scream. Sharif was not prepared for such a nerve-wrecking scream. He couldn't have been prepared for this relentless crying born out of naked, deadly fear.

"Maya, we've come to help you," repeated Sharif, running to the cot and holding her shuddering body in his arms. He gestured to Raj, who instantly lifted her onto his shoulder. As she lost consciousness, a long rope-patterned metal chain, with a pendant, slid from her grip and fell on the floor. Sharif quickly picked it up and pocketed it. "Let's get her out of here," he whispered, urging his deputy out of the musty, filthy room.

Edwin and the two officers, in the meantime, crept into the room on the left. An elderly man, with a white beard, a tagiyah covering his head, was sitting behind a vast desk, holding a gun in his right hand—the gun aimed exactly at his temple. The taller of the two officers shot the man precisely on his right shoulder, and the gun slid from the elderly man's hand.

"Dushman," screamed the old man, calling Edwin his enemy. With an unadulterated, violent rage, he tried to pick up the fallen gun with his left hand.

The other officer jumped on the elderly man and floored him mercilessly, while the tall officer pulled a handcuff to tie his hands behind his back.

The elderly man slithered on the floor like a wounded snake, staining the distressed mosaic floor with his bleeding shoulder. He shook his head while spitting on the officer's face and continued to shout obscenities while crying out 'Allah' several times.

"Shut him up," whispered Edwin. "We need to get him out of here in one piece. For heaven's sake, shut him up."

At Edwin's command, the tall officer hit the elderly man behind his neck, and the slithering body went limp as it lost consciousness.

- 32 -

City Jail, Chennai • April 2010

Dr. Neil Shaker looked steadily at the elderly man tied to a chair in the middle of the room while a dim ray of light from the corridor spread a dull hue inside the bleak, windowless cell. Shaker's eyes slid from the tight-fitting tagiyah on the prisoner's head to his wrinkled, scrawny, scorched face where a pair of steely eyes menacingly glared in rage.

Unable to withstand the criminal's unwavering and compelling glare, Shaker's eyes crawled to the man's bony chest and dropped to his lanky arms. Then his glance went to the floor where a heavy hook kept the prisoner's chair shackled to the floor. Although confined to the metal chair, despite his incredibly gaunt frame, the prisoner emanated untamed energy of a wild animal. Sitting a few feet away from the imprisoned man, Shaker listened to his own thudding heartbeat, in perfect discord with the steadily beating rain on the roof.

"How many missions did you organize?" asked Shaker.

The prisoner didn't respond and continued to stare at the door. Soon, his enraged glance rested on Tina, at her bent head, her brown eyes studying the notepad on her lap.

"How many missions, Usman?" insisted Shaker. His uncertain mind wondered why he accepted the assignment. Questioning the old man was exhausting, and he wasn't quite sure how he was going to get a glimpse of his radical mind.

"About forty, sixty. I don't know exactly," replied Usman, turning his gaze on Shaker. "Does it matter?"

"Does it matter?" asked Shaker, a strange fury brewing in the back of his mind. "They matter. All those lives..."

The prisoner shrugged his shoulders and quickly averted his eyes.

"All those lives have caused no remorse in your mind?" Shaker took a deep breath, trying to douse his own fury. He had a disturbing feeling that he was going about the questions the wrong way. When he exchanged a quick glance with Tina, he noticed her tightly clasped hands trembling a little.

"I FEEL NO REMORSE. Why should I?"

"Why, you ask? Don't you ever wonder how many died during your missions?"

"No. It's not my concern. Didn't I tell you already that my mission in life is to execute these missions? That's why Allah sent me to this earth. You took notes last week and the week before. Refer to it," Usman said arrogantly, noticing the notepad on Shaker's lap, "or ask your friend here," he continued, staring at Tina, who was shifting uncomfortably in the chair.

"But your conscience?" asked Shaker, wishing his voice steadied a bit. He felt like a novice, unable to control the discussion.

"I have none."

"Why?"

"I don't need one. Conscience is for cowards. I've a place in heaven. Why would I worry about conscience?"

"YOU have a place in HEAVEN?" asked Shaker, the fury in his mind traveling to his eyes. He was not supposed to lose his composure. He was well aware of that. But his sense of justice swelled in agony. Everything decent in him cried silently. His well-controlled poise, on that day, was a little wobbly.

"What kind of a question is that?" asked the prisoner, indignantly sitting up. "My belief is secure. My faith has never wavered, not once. I'm going to heaven."

"Going to heaven?" Shaker asked softly, slowly, regaining his balance. "And while you're planning a journey to heaven, you create a hell right here on this earth. You've turned naïve human beings into weapons."

"Naïve? I've chosen naïve human beings?" Usman laughed. "All human beings are naïve. It's all in the perspective. Didn't your education teach you that? What in the name of Allah do *you* mean by *naïve* human beings?"

"You brainwashed your missionaries with many lies to create havoc, to turn this world into hell," exclaimed Shaker, trying to control his rising voice.

"Hell? Well, if you want to look at it that way, sure, let it be hell. Those naïve human beings, as you might have it, were sent to me by Allah to do God's work. They were born for a purpose! And the purpose is my mission, my brothers' missions. I told you once. I'm telling you again. Every drop of blood shed during these missions is worth it. Heaven is worth it."

"Lies! Your lies breed more violence while you supposedly do God's work," shouted Shaker, his temper running loose again. "Your life has been a series of lies," he continued, painfully thinking of the radical's violence sustained by his lies. "You have slaughtered many lives through your lies."

"My lies breed my violence? What the hell are you talking about?" asked Usman, puzzled by Shaker's ramblings. "Those who died did a service."

"Terrorism is no service to anybody but the terrorist," shouted Shaker, staring at the criminal, unable to digest his atrocious words. To corroborate his outraged feelings, he took out a couple of photographs from his briefcase and brandished them in front of the prisoner. "Do you remember this? This happened in October when you ordered a massive explosion near Seloor. And this, near Breams Road in Chennai, in December."

Usman decidedly glanced at the door.

"You take innocent lives and train them to take other lives. Look at this now." Shaker stood in front of the prisoner, compelling him to see the pitiful photos. "Take a good look at the charred bodies and bleeding eyes and tell us that these harmless men, women, and innocent children were sent to this earth by Allah with the sole purpose of getting you and your equally muddled associates to heaven. I REPEAT. Terrorism is no service to anybody but the terrorist."

"Terrorism? Islamic terrorism? A scary thought!" Usman laughed obnoxiously. "And the rest of your men and women, following various glorious faiths, are all pacifists? Let's start with the Hindu radicals who created havoc after the Gujarat riots. Do you think I'm not aware of that? And what about the group of Hindu extremists who ransacked the church and hurt the priest in Orissa? And do you think your public has ignored the bombing incidents outside abortion clinics by fundamental Christians?" He glared at Tina with red-shot eyes before returning his glance to Shaker. "Why am I talking to you about Hindu extremists? You are a Hindu, I think! And your friend here is a Christian. And the Hindus and the Christians have always had a steady love affair!"

"I'm not here to defend any group or faith, or speak on behalf of Hindus, or Jewish, or... I don't care what else." Shaker regained his fluctuating self-control, taking a deep breath. "I'm not interested in religion or religious affiliations. Fanatic activity by any group is a crime."

"You may not be interested in religion or religious affiliations, but religion is everything. EVERYTHING," Usman shouted passionately, ready for a verbal attack. "Religion is my heart and soul, and it should be everybody's. And when one is bound by religion, one cannot draw boundaries to the path to heaven."

"Stop hurling religion at everybody like a hunter throws raw meat at a beast. Your religion has nothing to do with the monstrous path you have chosen. You and YOU alone are responsible for your gruesome, barbaric path. How can religion be responsible for a man's crimes?"

"Crimes? What crimes?"

"You cannot justify treating human beings as pawns, as tools, and as your means to reach heaven. Before you enter the path to heaven, what about the hell you have created for hundreds of men and women on this earth? Which religion would endorse your actions?"

"Stop analyzing heaven and hell. See, you live in a chasm between heaven and hell. You are in it, you and your whole lot," hissed Usman, looking directly into Shaker's eyes. "To me, there is nothing between heaven and hell. There is heaven and there is hell, and that's it. And I can turn that HELL into HEAVEN. This is why I cannot leave religion alone. It is what makes me what I am."

"No, it's not religion. It's you. You have made what you are. Understand that first before you preach about your rehearsed beliefs on religion and heaven. Does your heaven have such a hold on you?" asked Shaker, making an effort to tap on an open nerve. "Answer me!" he insisted when the prisoner gave a deaf ear.

"Yes." Usman looked directly at Shaker. "My heaven is an all-consuming, superior, glorious haven into which only a few dignified humans can enter. It is my salvation."

"And you think you've earned the status of a dignified human?" continued Shaker, exchanging a glance with Tina, wondering if she was brave enough to pick up from that point.

"I have no doubt about that." The prisoner, instead of glancing at Shaker or Tina, looked directly at the camera and began to smile.

And that smile, hanging on an unidentifiable tinge of abandonment, anger, and insolence, scared Tina and unnerved Shaker. And his gaze did not falter once. Then, as he threw a piercing glance at Shaker and Tina, a slow whistling sigh burst from his leathery lips and broke into a manic laughter.

Tina cringed at the fanatical amusement and sat up straight in her chair. "You're not going to heaven, any heaven. There's no heaven for you." She shouted to speak above the prisoner's wild cackling noise and threw a quick glance at Shaker. He returned her glance with a perfect understanding of her intention.

Usman's laughter gradually lost its sizzle and began to sink into a soft gurgle. "What did you say?" he asked softly, incredulously, his already enraged eyes filled with repugnance and fury.

"There's no heaven for you." Tina repeated, not letting the prisoner's revulsion and wrath intimidate her.

"How dare you? You rotten liar!"

"There's no heaven for you," Tina repeated again in a flat tone. "All the souls you have tormented will stand bloody and unified on the threshold of heaven and torment you as you beg for mercy. There's no heaven for you."

Usman's shoulders began to quiver in anger, and he let out an angry, outraged cry while shaking the metal chair, as though determined to get it unshackled from the floor.

"And unless you tell us what pushed you in this path where you unflinchingly ruined many lives, you're going to be strapped to that chair. I can guarantee that. The men who are waiting outside to question you will not conduct the interview as politely as Miss Matthew and I have done." Shaker looked at the prisoner quietly for a few seconds. "Tell me. What was your first mission? What prompted you to reach for your heaven, your ultimate goal, while slaughtering innocent children, men, and women?"

"I don't remember," the captive responded, staring at his bony hands.

"What made you execute your first mission?" Shaker insisted, wearily pushing his hair away from his wide forehead.

"I can't tell you. Go to hell, both of you. All of you go to hell." Usman resumed studying the ceiling.

"But," began Shaker, trying to bury his frustration, and paused. When he pressed the bell on the small desk, a couple of guards entered the cell. "We're done," said Shaker, taking a deep breath.

- 33 -

North Stanes Road, Chennai • April 2010

"Dr. Shaker, I'm sorry your last session with Usman did not go well," began Sharif, trying to break the silence. "He's tough. It's extremely difficult to penetrate his mind. I've tried. It drained all my resources and," he continued reluctantly, unwilling to discuss his department's procedures, "and my goal, our goal, is to extract as much information from him as possible."

"I don't think I was prepared. What infuriates me is that he made me feel like a novice. He is not the first prisoner I've interviewed..."

"Of course, not. I wouldn't doubt your capability, Dr. Shaker," assured Sharif.

"There's something about him," hesitated Shaker, groping for the right words. "It's as though…he is not human. I've never come across a radical like him."

"Usman is not human. There cannot be a shred of humane instinct in him. Otherwise he wouldn't be what he has been. Would he?" asked Sharif. "What constantly worries me is that Usman is just a single branch of a very fast-growing poisonous tree. And this tree has planted its snaking roots in several places, especially in the borders of India and Pakistan and various areas which still remain elusive. We must dig into his network of contacts, and we've to keep him talking. Even if he spills bits and pieces, it'll be useful."

"I should've been better prepared. Damn!" Anger, frustration, and a significant degree of embarrassment governed Shaker's thoughts. "Usman dominated the conversation. I don't know how it happened, but it did. He can run a show while buried in a box. I doubt if I'm the right person for this job."

"Dr. Shaker, you are so hard on yourself," whispered Sharif, persuading the analyst to see reason. "You're not here to be judged on your performance, perfect or otherwise. We all understand that you are a normal human being who is entitled to a bad day. I saw the video of your interview with Usman. I don't think you lost your control. In that session, I saw in you a man who cared for the lost lives instead of a perfectly poised psychologist. Who says you can't lose your bearing under stressful circumstances? Don't we all? I've to find out, one way or the other, which Islamic Jihad Militant Organization has been paying him generously to help conduct his missions. Dr. Shaker, I can't think of anybody more suitable to question Usman, assess him, and break the barrier to his secrets. You are our best hope. We simply cannot let him slip through our fingers, not now, not after what we've gone through," begged Sharif. "We need to...you need to keep trying."

"But he is in prison, arrested with clear evidence of several counts of murder. Why or how can he slip out of here?" asked Shaker, quite confused.

"That's not what I meant when I said he might slip through our fingers. In fact, he's here for life. Although several heads would like to see Usman hanged, that's not what we want," Sharif explained hurriedly, looking alternately at Varma and Dr. Shaker. His glance quickly slid to Edwin for suggestions. "I'll be damned if he slips through my fingers. We need to probe Usman's mind, his secrets, every move he made in the last twenty years..."

"Hold on, Sharif," interrupted Edwin. "I've been thinking about this. Dr. Shaker could use some assistance."

"But what kind of assistance do you wish to have, Dr. Shaker?" asked Sharif, afraid of losing the analyst's cooperation.

"I need Tina Matthew's help, I mean on a regular basis."

"Why?" asked Sharif.

"Why? Because she's very efficient," replied Shaker, a little annoyed.

"Tina Matthew?" Varma asked incredulously. "Dr. Shaker, she is hardly experienced. Yes, she is working with you on some cases, but she's very young and she's still a student."

"But Mr. Edwin and Mr. Sharif allowed her to accompany me to the prison a few times while I questioned Usman," protested Shaker. "I'm glad I had her with me. Since she's not experienced, as you just reminded everybody, I did most of the talking. But if she continues to work as my partner, she would certainly have a significant role in this project. She should."

"If she is so efficient, why doesn't she extend her research in her country? Terrorism is not exclusive to India!" exclaimed Sharif, glaring at Shaker.

"You're right. Terrorism is not exclusive to India. Then does it matter where Tina continues her research, as long as she is trying to understand the maddening reasons behind it?" asked Shaker, his sharp expression turning bitter. "Didn't we discuss only yesterday the fear of Al Qaeda cells being established in remote parts of India, Pakistan, and other secular parts of the world? And, Mr. Sharif, didn't you stress yesterday that terrorism is a global concern?"

"What about it, Theo? You are Tina's uncle. Do you approve of her continued involvement in this affair?" asked Sharif.

"Why not?" asked Edwin. "My wife and I might be Tina's hosts, but that's where it ends. We want to protect her, but what she chooses to do professionally is entirely up to her."

"What happened to our generation of uncles who were overprotective and paranoid?" asked Sharif, not at all relishing the prospect of the imminent quandary.

"Tina doesn't need a paranoid uncle as well as a paranoid father. Peter, that is my brother-in-law, can write a book on paranoia. Anyway, Rita and I don't believe in sheltering children. I know we have no children of our own," paused Edwin, looking awkwardly at the group.

"You don't have to be a parent to feel affection oozing from your heart, Theo," smiled Sharif, defending his dearest friend's sentiments. "You and Rita have saved several children from ruin, and that matters as much as raising one of your own, perhaps even more. But letting Tina into the thick of things requires some serious thinking. That's all." Sharif glanced at his watch again. "Then let's get to it. Should I ask her, or would you, Theo, since she is your niece?" asked Sharif, getting up from his chair as Shaker stood up to leave.

"I'll ask her," Shaker said softly. "I'm seeing her today in my office. Now let's make it official. And..."

"Yes, Dr. Shaker?" Sharif smiled, his inherent kindness invading his abrasive demeanor.

"I went to see Maya this morning. I'm worried if she would ever recover. Mr. Sharif, I'm still confused about Usman's decision to abduct Maya for one of his missions. I can't understand his rationale because it doesn't make sense to me."

"Why? Because Maya isn't a child of Islam?" asked Edwin, while Sharif was contemplating a response.

"No, not just that. Why would Usman snatch a woman like Maya, go through several stages of drama, when he could have trained other willing individuals, I mean those who are as fanatic as he is?" Shaker tried to clarify a nagging, elusive doubt. "I don't see the logic here."

"Usman's actions do not denote reasoning because they just don't. I understand a lot now after questioning Abdullah. Maya saw and heard something she shouldn't have seen and heard, which you already know. And that was the cursed beginning. Then things just fell in place. Usman started from the root—Maya's father and his employment at Abdullah's warehouse. Two factors worked to Usman's advantage; Rajan's debt-ridden predicament and his aversion to Mrs. Joseph. Rajan disliked Mark Stevens because he is Mrs. Joseph's nephew. So you see, Rajan's predicament and aversion fueled Usman's purpose, and he is a radical who wouldn't hesitate to use anybody to fulfill his missions." Sharif paused. "But, call it fate, Tina saw Maya, and things just fell out of place."

"I can see that. But I still don't understand something. Why should Abdullah get away when Usman is kept imprisoned under maximum security?" asked Shaker. "You told me earlier that he doesn't pay taxes."

"Who said Abdullah is getting away?" asked Sharif. "Unfortunately, I don't think we can prove that he was directly linked to recruiting missionaries, or that he is an Islamic radical. He is a very clever man who did not get his hands dirty, not dirty enough. And that's how Usman would have wanted it. But we can prove that Abdullah was indirectly involved in Usman's grand missions. Maya is just one example. That bastard, Abdullah, told me that he didn't know that the building behind Eastern Exports was what it was. He thought it was a school! But, Dr. Shaker, we cannot use tax as a bait to get a man like Abdullah. Yes, we used that as an excuse to question him earlier while we had doubts about the building behind his warehouse, and that's how far we can go. But you must understand that half the businessmen in the city don't pay taxes on time, or they fudge their accounts. It's a crime, yet it's not a crime, and I'm ashamed to say this. Abdullah's lawyers would make my organization the laughing stock if I purposely channeled my attention towards his accounts. As you can see, I'm focusing on chasing more horrific crimes." Sharif took a deep breath and muttered, "And, Dr. Shaker, we all hope that Maya recovers."

- 34 -

The Missionaries

A grey jeep stopped in front of an austere set of tall gates sheltering a guarded facility, located a mile away from the railway tracks near the outskirts of Chennai. A couple of guards with machine guns saluted before opening the gates. The old building, constructed in the 1920s, used to be a warehouse that stored locomotive parts until the government transferred ownership to Central Intelligence. Lately, it found multiple uses—from a secure site for interviewing questionable criminals to a halfway house that protected missionary-victims of terrorism. Presently, the facility actively guarded Usman's missionaries who were categorized as criminals, but who were essentially victims of circumstances. Sharif received Edwin right outside the front door.

"How are things?" Edwin asked eagerly, while his driver parked the jeep next to a blue van that had *R and J Construction* painted on the side—one of the three vehicles repossessed from The Jannah, Usman's compound behind Eastern Exports near Seloor. *Rand J construction...a phantom company of a phantom hero*, thought Edwin.

"Where shall I begin, Theo? You won't believe the degree of insanity among some of the inmates. They are not fit to be let loose in public. One of the children, Salman, keeps repeating that he has an appointment with Yusuf."

"Yusuf? But he died. Wasn't it confirmed?""

"Of course, it was confirmed," hissed Sharif, standing on the weathered steps, smoking his favorite cigarette. "Theo, why did he die? I feel he could have opened a door for us."

"You know that his mouth would be clamped. He was supposed to be the most devoted assistant of Usman and a confirmed, dangerous fanatic. Didn't one of the inmates describe him as the next Usman? He would voluntarily die rather than share information with us."

"Which is exactly what he did," sighed Sharif, tossing the cigarette butt on the ground, bitterly chewing his blackened lips from years of smoking. "I can't believe he took his life. We saw his distressed face as he was sinking, right outside Usman's room when we raided his headquarters, but we didn't know who he was at the time. Not that we were there in time to stop him from taking his life. I'm still surprised that he didn't raise his gun at us."

"He was probably too dazed to raise his gun. I can't forget the way he looked at us, like a mad man, before he croaked foaming at his mouth."

"Well, let's forget him, Theo," Sharif sighed bitterly, with one hand on the door. "Are you ready?"

Edwin followed his friend. They checked on the status of all thirteen members—five children under seventeen, five women, and three men. All of them were kept behind bars inside rooms which were partitioned into smaller chambers. Sharif and Edwin stopped in front of a cell from which a bulky, bald man was staring at the door, with beady eyes filled with animosity.

"Does he look familiar?" whispered Sharif. "Remember we saw his photo taken outside the house behind Eastern Exports, and Dr. Shaker thought he recognized him?"

"You're right. Is he…what's his name? Kumar?"

"Yes. He refused to talk at first, but he is coming around. My deputy is taking care of that. And it seems he doesn't need much push."

"A mercenary, naturally, with no ties to Islamic faith. I'm sure Usman knew that."

"Of course, he knew. My worry is that Kumar wouldn't be capable of revealing much to us. Usman wouldn't have shared crucial secrets with him. Still, whatever sordid information he can pass on would be helpful."

"And the villain did lure Maya into Usman's den. That, at least, can be confirmed."

"Yes, he was one of the few who got Maya into Usman's organization. Unfortunately, Manohar, the man who was with Kumar when they both intercepted Dr. Shaker and Tina near the railway gate, died during our raid." Sharif quickly read the list of names.

"Wasn't Manohar the man who explained to Tina that Maya was an insane woman on the loose when she knocked on her door?" asked Edwin, confirming the information in the document.

"Yes. I wish he didn't die. I would've liked to interrogate him, Theo. And one of the children is so sorry that Manohar died during the raid because he was the one who rescued this child from the abusive police. He says all policemen are enemies of Allah because of the way he was treated and because of the way Manohar was killed."

The couple moved on to the section where the children were quarantined.

"What the hell is this?" asked Edwin, staring at a boy who was restrained like a dangerous criminal. "He is just a child!"

"He may be just a child, but he is dangerous. This is Salman. He bit the officer and clawed at him badly. Theo, he took out a chunk of flesh, and the poor guy needs treatment, more than a few stitches. The guards are finding this boy uncontrollable. It requires two, three officers to restrain him. I can't believe he can be so treacherous at his age. He has sworn that he would kill the officers, all of them."

"WHAT?" Edwin asked incredulously, following Sharif along the corridor. "But he is just a child. Is he so deluded that he would try to hurt a police officer, especially when he is a captive in the hands of the law?"

"Salman is about thirteen. He is enraged that Usman was taken prisoner. He worships that old man as though he were God. Theo, he is mourning the absence of his savior. Usman promised these children and those childlike adults—who unconditionally believed in his cause—

heaven, and now they have missed the boat. In a way, Usman was the means to every end in their eyes—heaven, eternal life, ultimate happiness, and the most coveted trophy: salvation. Now, without Usman, where will they go? Remember, these children have no homes to run to. And Salman is persistently asking about Yusuf. It's a good thing he doesn't know that Yusuf is dead. Theo, we have a huge mess here. Look at the condition of these children. Even if we bring the best clinicians from around the country, I don't think these children can be rehabilitated."

"What is it that makes Salman despise police officers, Sharif? Was he in trouble before Usman's men recruited him?"

"Yes, Theo. He keeps yelling that he would like to murder, no, that he is going to murder an inspector near Town Hall in Seloor. Remember the child who was 'rescued' by Manohar? Salman is that child. The counselors are going to take a long time to even talk to this boy. That bastard should go to hell. Usman should go to hell. Look how he has played with these innocent children? That radical was making weapons out of children! See how he has tarnished and corrupted their vulnerable minds? No wonder, they're in such a frightening condition. They were trained under extraordinary circumstances, and the salvation they were promised is gone forever. Now they're convinced that they've nothing to lose."

"I know. Is there anything else Salman says? Any connection we can make?"

"The only other person he talks about is Saira. She is another inmate, who is about fifteen. I think Salman got really attached to her while they were being trained. Remember the girl in the corner room?" Sharif asked, leading his colleague to the office in the front of the building.

"How is that girl dealing with the current situation?"

"Saira is angry. She was asking about the Women's Institute in Tirupur."

"Why? Does she know someone there? Is she looking for someone who might rescue her from the present mess?"

"We don't know yet. Oh, one more thing. Her mother was a seamstress at Eastern Exports. What do you think about that?"

"Really! She was Abdullah's employee? And Sayeed was Abdullah's right hand, and I heard that he was in charge of hiring the workers. Did you say she *was* a seamstress? She must have quit her job at the warehouse. Otherwise, Usman wouldn't have kept Saira in the building behind Eastern Exports where her mother was working."

"Yes. Saira thinks that her mother left Seloor, which is where they used to live. She was extraordinarily angry when she talked about it. We believe, from the girl's choice of words, that the mother left under questionable circumstances. Saira is furious that her mother sold her while throwing Islam to the dust. This girl is very bitter, Theo. She frequently refers to her duty and her commitment to Usman. He promised her heaven through the work of God, promised her salvation if she could serve his cause. And now she feels violated that the man who was like a father to her has been captured. She is under constant scrutiny. She is not uncontrollable like Salman, but her behavior is very erratic and disturbing."

"There is no injustice as a-child-without-a-home. What will these children do now? Anyway, they can't go back to their lives. In most cases, there is no home to start with, no weeping mother, or a father in torment. What's that?" asked Edwin, distracted by the chain Sharif had just pulled out of the drawer. It was a rope-patterned metal chain with a pendant.

"The chain I picked up in Maya's room at the end of our raid. Remember? Looks like a wedding chain."

"Do you think that's what Usman had planned? To make Maya wear this during a mission?"

"Yes. I've heard of this device before. See how hollow the chain is, and it is such an inexpensive metal. This can easily be wired for his purpose. And who would suspect a wedding chain? Usman was going to make Maya wear that during a mission, I'm sure. You know, I want to wring his neck with my own hands, Theo."

"You do? Take a number. I still haven't looked at all the documents we retrieved from Usman's den. Are they sorted out at least to some degree?"

"Some degree, yes, but there is so much paperwork. Here, this is the updated list of inmates." Sharif retrieved a printed sheet from a file and gave it to Edwin.

"Maria?" read Edwin, glancing quickly at Sharif. "Usman, who ran a campaign against non-Islamic individuals, used men and women from all different faiths."

"We both know that extremists like Usman wouldn't hesitate to use anybody as long as the mission is accomplished. Theo, I can't believe this villain ran a one-man organization so efficiently."

"It was not really a one-man organization, Sharif. He had so many levels of assistants, and that's what amazes me. Getting to the bottom of his many-layered establishment will be a wretched ordeal. But we have to get through this." Edwin went through the list of the names of the three men: Imran, Kumar, and Salim. The list of women's names included Maria, Jasmine, Farida, Nutan, and Badrunisa. "Here it is, the list of unfortunate children: Saira, Salman, Amjad, Nasir, and Farah." Edwin threw the sheet on the desk disgustedly and went to the window facing the stark gates. A light breeze seeped in through the screen, mingled with the scents of the herbs sprinkled along the hedges. "When was the last time you went home?"

"Day before yesterday," replied Sharif, smiling sheepishly.

"What's the matter with you?" shouted Edwin. "You need to separate your work from your life. Go home today, for heaven's sake, or come home with me."

"Oh, stop lecturing, Theo. What's there to go home to? My apartment has a bed, a bathroom, and a small kitchen. Look at that room," said Sharif, gesturing towards an anteroom behind his office. "Although this is my temporary office, there is a cot, an attached bathroom. There's no kitchen, of course. But food comes to me when I need it. So what's the big deal?"

Edwin picked up his briefcase. "You're incorrigible. Let's go."

"Where?"

"Aren't we supposed to check on Maya?"

"Sorry, I forgot." Sharif picked up the necessary documents and quickly followed Edwin. "Your niece and Dr. Shaker were here earlier. I think they went to see Maya straight from here."

"Dr. Shaker seems to be doing fine with his sessions at the prison. I haven't seen him in a week, but Tina told me that Usman is getting annoyed."

"That's exactly what I was hoping for. Not that annoyance is sufficient to ruffle a fanatic's mind that has been steadily nurtured during his lifetime." Sharif stopped by the jeep to light another cigarette before stepping inside the vehicle. "I'm glad you and I realize that psychoanalysis is an important tool."

"You and I, of course," sighed his friend, brushing his sparse hair with a pocket comb.

"Some of our nearsighted colleagues don't really understand the effect of psychology, not all of its impact. It is the backbone of Usman's strength, a great resource of any fanatic mindset, and the tool that strengthens him can also weaken him. Usman is not a perfectly wired machine. He is, after all, a man with some weakness. A part of him has to crumble to expose that weakness."

"And that flaw, in turn, would hopefully reveal certain elements necessary to understand the mind of a terrorist. All we can do is keep hoping patiently."

"That's why it's essential to use Shaker's analysis as a bridge between Usman and the counter-terrorism unit, particularly considering Shaker's interest and experience."

"And don't worry about the difficult colleagues, nearsighted or otherwise. Skepticism will always exist, no matter what ideas you throw out there. It's human nature."

When Edwin and Sharif walked into a new apartment complex,

the large foyer was empty and quiet except for a clerk and a couple of servants who were busy cleaning. Sylvia opened the door immediately when Edwin rang the bell.

"How is Maya doing?" asked Sharif.

"She is all right, I think, Mr. Sharif," hesitated Sylvia. "Dr. Shaker and Tina came in the afternoon. He left, but Tina is still here."

"Yes, Tina called me. May we see Maya, if she is not asleep?" asked Edwin."

"Yes, of course." Sylvia took the gentlemen to an airy room where there was a double bed, an armoire, and a small table next to the bed with a vase of red and yellow carnations. A mild scent of rose and magnolia wafted from the balcony. Mark was sitting on the right side of the bed, steadily staring at the patient's face. Tina was sitting on the left, holding Maya's limp hand.

"I've never seen such anguish in anybody's face, Theo," whispered Sharif, staring at the patient's sunken eyes and distressed expression. "What Usman has started is the collapse of mankind. Is she ever going to come out of her misery?"

As though in response to Sharif's query, Maya's face contorted in fear while her body began to twist like a wounded animal's.

"It's all right, Maya. See, they're our friends," Mark took Maya's hand and gently whispered.

"Maya, this my uncle, Theo. Don't you remember?" asked Tina. "He came here to see you before. And that's Mr. Sharif, Uncle Theo's friend, our friend. He has helped us a lot."

"Aunt Sylvie is not dead. She is not dead," cried Maya, not at all heeding Tina's comforting words or Mark's. "Everybody has cheated me, but how can I destroy the world?" Her disturbed, warped mind insisted on carrying her to dingy corners and filthy lairs. Usman's mesmerizing voice continued to whisper in her ears… 'Maya, say you'll destroy your society.' And Maya mechanically repeated, "I'll destroy my society," again and again and again.

"Of course, your Aunt Sylvie is not dead. She's right here, Maya, and she'll be with you always." Tina's helpless glance went to her uncle.

Maya shook her head and buried her face in the pillow.

Sylvia, unable to witness Maya's torment, moved swiftly to the drawing room, and Sharif instantly followed her.

"Mr. Stevens, go see how your aunt is doing, please," Edwin suggested softly. "Tina, she'll come around. It takes time," he continued, placing his hand on his niece's tense shoulder when Mark vacated the bedroom. "Maya is getting better. I heard she is keeping her food down. And her eruptions are fewer and less frequent. Don't you think so?"

"Yes, Uncle," whispered Tina, "but I doubt if she'll…" she halted, staring at Maya's still form. She had fallen asleep.

When the night nurse walked into the bedroom to begin her shift, Tina went to the drawing room with her uncle.

"Mr. Sharif, I've not yet thanked you properly for rescuing Maya and bringing her safely to us." Mark took Sharif's hand, on the verge of manly tears waiting to spill on his troubled face.

"It's my duty, Mr. Stevens. And I had plenty of help, especially Edwin's." Sharif's rare smile softened his usually rigid face. "You have to give Maya some more time," continued Sharif, looking kindly at Sylvia's nervous expression. "She has gone through a tremendously trying time. Maya's doctor tells us that she was methodically made to feel useless and unwanted. And Dr. Shaker confirms that. When her trust is violated, how can she quickly bounce back to normal condition? Mrs. Joseph, you and Mark have to be strong and optimistic if you want to help Maya recover. You need to get out of the apartment occasionally for a change of scene. At least, Mark goes to work. But you need to get out. Otherwise, the monotony will soon get to you."

"Will Maya's life ever get back to normal?" asked Sylvia, not particularly looking at anybody. "Mark and I are here for her, but… Our lives will never be the same again. And I don't think Maya can return to Seloor with me, not any time soon." Sylvia's mind raced to her small house with her neat garden, the backyard that welcomed generous shade from the swaying branches of the mango trees. Then, an assortment of images—Holy Cross church, Father William, Church Restoration Committee, and her choir group—began to clutter her already crowded mind and rapidly swam in her sloshing memory. "But thank you, all of you, for helping us." Sylvia smiled unexpectedly, trying to retreat to her cheerful nature, although her round eyes were devoid of the old sparkle. "And, Mr. Edwin, I promised Rita that I would have tea with her soon. So I'll get out of this apartment for a change."

"Good. My wife is looking forward to that, Mrs. Joseph. Now I'll take Tina home." Edwin rose, and his niece followed him.

- 35 -

City Jail, Chennai • Usman's Heaven

"Shaker, thank you for choosing me as your associate when you could have done better," said Tina, getting out of the jeep on the gritty drive right outside the entrance to East Gate. The jagged fence and the eerie silence continued to accelerate her heartbeat, in spite of her repeated visits.

"No, don't misconstrue the offer as a compliment. Being your mentor, I can make you work hard, which I can't do with someone else." Shaker got out of the jeep and waved at the guards who were discreetly waiting a few feet away.

One of the guards opened the door after a tedious security check.

"Did I ask for your compliments? Please tell me how much you want me to talk when you question Usman today."

"As much as you wish. I've asked the officers to set up our chairs a certain way so that you can constantly see me while facing Usman. You're not nervous today?" asked Shaker.

"Are you kidding me? I'm nervous as hell!" Tina looked behind her anxiously.

'Do you want to change your mind?" asked Shaker, genuinely worried about her uneasy smile. "I'll be glad to do this alone, Tina."

"Are you kidding me?" Tina asked again, gathering her long brown hair into a ponytail. "I'm not going to miss this opportunity. I'll be all right. What about you, Shaker?"

"As unpleasant as it is, I'm always looking forward to questioning Usman. How else can I know his mind? Did I mention that Mr. Sharif will join our session today?"

"He will?" Tina doubtfully paused on the way. "Well, that's his job, I suppose."

"Don't worry. He makes everybody nervous. I believe he can even make Usman nervous. But he is a good man, very efficient."

A couple of guards stood by the door that opened to a dark, maximum-security section. They led the way, their boots ominously clapping on the cold stone floor, and the tall officer opened the door of the last cell that let in just a dull ray of light from the corridor. Tina squinted her eyes to see clearly inside the windowless cell. And Usman was ready, strapped to the prisoner's chair.

Tina glanced at the video camera on the wall. Then, slowly, she shifted her glance to the prisoner in the middle of the room—his eyes glinting on the verge of reddish explosion, his pursed lips twitching in contained rage, and his whole body taut and pulsing with animosity. Usman's presence permeated the air like a gush of exhaust fumes and penetrated into a vulnerable corner of her anxious mind.

"Describe your heaven to me." Shaker began abruptly, looking directly at the prisoner.

Usman's glance shot up, as though caught by surprise, but he bounced back momentarily. "You'll never understand it." He bitterly looked at the ceiling, as though the cold concrete might open wide to show him a glimpse of his heaven.

"Try," Shaker commanded.

"It's not your business." Usman's face was still facing the ceiling.

Shaker looked at Tina, exchanging a very speaking glance.

"It's his business, my business, everybody's business," said Tina. Her voice did not reflect even a shred of her anxiety. Only her right hand, mildly tapping on her notepad, revealed her fear. "When you decided to use a human being to ensure your journey to your heaven, when you focused on destruction and human indignity, everything you've done from then on becomes everybody's business now."

Usman returned her glance, letting his eyes roam over her pale face, her hazel brown eyes, and her pursed lips. "So this woman is going to question me today. What audacity!" he exclaimed, his angry tone piercing the stillness.

"You will address me as Miss Matthew, and you will answer my questions." Tina responded when Shaker was about to reprimand Usman for his impudent outburst. When she looked at her mentor, a faint twitching of his lips told her of his approval. "Describe your heaven."

"Where the righteous go at the time of death." Usman refused to look at her.

Tina thought that it was a good thing, but it was not. "Look at me when you speak to me. The righteous? Do you know what that means?" asked Tina, getting bolder.

"It means the virtuous, the honorable." Usman began to list, looking directly at Tina. "Why? Didn't your university teach you vocabulary?"

"Cut that shit and behave. Otherwise I'll send you to your heaven in the next minute," barked Sharif, barging into the cell. He loudly dragged the third chair next to Usman and sat by him. "Answer Miss Matthew. What makes you righteous? Killing innocent people and turning children into weapons?"

"I...I was sent to earth to do Allah's work. I died every time a human faced death. And that makes me honorable and virtuous." Usman's tone had lost some of its bite.

Sharif quickly glanced at Tina, encouraging her to continue.

She followed his cue and turned to the prisoner. "So you died several deaths for your cause. That makes you a martyr in your own right, but no God, no heaven, and no law would make you righteous."

"I don't need the approval of a half-and-half to believe that a place is assured for me in heaven. Don't you realize I know your biography? You are a half-baked Italian and Indian, probably with no religious convictions." Usman stared at Tina with absolute, undiluted anger.

"You're preaching me about heaven and virtue, you insolent heretic? I should have eliminated you when I had the chance."

Sharif rose and struck Usman violently across his cheek, and the old man began to bleed at his mouth. "You, cutthroat! How dare you speak to Miss Matthew like that? YOU WILL TREAT HER RESPECTFULLY. Otherwise…" Sharif's angry eyes glared at the prisoner.

Tina cringed at the sight of blood. Shaker gasped in shock.

"Otherwise, what?" Usman paused, spitting his blood on the floor, and continued. "You'll mistreat me. So what's new about police brutality?"

"Mistreat you? Police brutality? You have the gall to speak about that! I had a long conversation with Ravi, yesterday, at the police station near Seloor. He told me how he assisted you in a few of your hunts."

"What?" hissed Usman.

"Well, one of his colleagues offered me vivid details about Salman and how Ravi had the poor boy hanging from the ceiling like a slaughtered animal. And do you know who was the anonymous devil who was paying Ravi? You, you rotten scoundrel!"

"Such methods are necessary when one is in pursuit of God's work. My heavenly journey cannot function without essential, sometimes unpleasant assistance." Usman bent his head and wiped his bloody mouth on his shoulder. "Martyrdom takes a lifetime of work. Islam..."

"Your martyrdom can go to hell, and so will you," shouted Sharif, standing menacingly in front of Usman. "*Unpleasant assistance* is what you call your degrading, inhumane treatment of men, women, and innocent children. *In pursuit of God's work?* God? Islam? Do not mention those words ever again. You don't deserve to. You have no right to make your God or your religion your scapegoat, a convenient excuse for your inexcusable, ruthless decisions. Your God had nothing to do with the decisions you made. You made them, endorsed by your malicious superiors and your equally foul associates. Stop foisting the blame on religion. You hear me?"

"Aren't you ashamed to treat *me* like this?" Usman's glance pleadingly rested on Sharif's raging expression on his pockmarked face. "You are a Muslim, but you treat me like an enemy when you should be treating me like your brother."

"You are my enemy. You are the enemy of humanity, and don't rattle on about my religion. No religion should dictate any bad choice one makes. If something good cannot be churned out of it, it is not religion." Sharif's disgusted glance settled on Usman's eyes. "And even if you were my brother, I would send you to hell. I'm going to leave this room for a short while. You will talk to Dr. Shaker and Miss Matthew respectfully. Remember, your foul mouth and your red-hot anger are being videotaped for eternity." Sharif did not wait for a response and walked out immediately.

Usman looked alternately at Tina and Shaker and asked, "Do you think I'm afraid of death?"

"You were certainly not afraid of sending many to death." Shaker responded while looking at Tina.

"Why Maya?" Tina asked without hesitation. "Why did you target her and leave her in this dreadful condition?"

Usman did not answer promptly and appeared to be momentarily stumped. "She was in my path, and she irked me."

"Irked you? You sentenced her life to a living hell because she *irked* you?" Tina asked incredulously.

"Yes. Why? You have a special sympathy for her?" Usman's eyes fell on Tina's face with a nasty impudence, searching for a nerve he could tap on.

Tina glared at the prisoner and said, "Watch your words. What were you planning to do with Maya while you were brainwashing her?"

"What if I don't want to discuss it?" Usman asked.

"You will discuss it. Remember, while Dr. Shaker and I are talking with you, Mr. Sharif and others are questioning your long-term friend, Abdullah, including some of the associates from your establishment."

Usman appeared to be suffering from an internal debate. He looked sourly at the video camera, swallowed a couple of times, and said, "A suicide mission."

Tina gasped in horror but recovered quickly. "When? Where?"

"Next month. At the bus stand near Kalpadi."

"How?" asked Tina, controlling an overwhelming sensation of nausea. Her mind raced through the variety of devices which had been used in the past—from waist belts to wired footwear. When Usman did not answer, she shouted, "HOW?"

"A wedding chain," Usman answered, his eyes on the camera. "A hollow wedding chain...wired," he continued, trying to catch Tina's eyes. "Don't tell me you haven't heard of that one before."

Tina tried to calm her thudding heart, avoiding the prisoner's taunting eyes. She was too young and her newly gathered courage was too fresh for Usman's raw, callous confession. Unable to sustain her fluctuating courage, she tentatively glanced at Shaker. He readily followed her cue.

"I know how Maya came into your path. But why did you decide to go through a new job interview and such nonsense?" asked Shaker, letting Tina collect her calm. He knew from experience that persistent questions regarding missionaries eventually unlocked at least some of the secrets stored in a radical's mind, and he was determined to step deeper into Usman's mind.

"She was to be eliminated. In that case, why not use her death to accomplish a part of my mission?" asked Usman, as though his logic purged his ill intentions. "Maya's father was a drunkard, a useless man. He was in knee-deep debt, and I wanted his house. Anyway, Rajan would have lost his house to the debt collectors. My missions cost money."

"And that's supposed to justify stealing a human being, torturing her to bend to your ways, poisoning her mind, depriving her of her basic human rights, and God knows what else you did."

"Yes, my holy end justifies the means." Usman looked intently at his bound hands.

"Does your heaven have such a hold on you?" asked Shaker, remembering to ask the same question every time he interviewed Usman.

His instinct, guided by his research, assured him that the master key to open Usman's mind was in one word; heaven. "Look at me and answer!" Shaker insisted in a steady tone, projecting a very calm and unaffected demeanor.

"Yes." Usman looked directly at Shaker, as though considerably annoyed. "My heaven has a hold on me. I've been sent to this earth on lease, and my heaven will take me back when the time is right. I've told you before. My heaven is a magnificent haven, and only a few chosen, distinguished human beings can enter."

"And you think you're a distinguished human being?" Shaker asked, hunting for a way to ruffle him.

Usman closed his eyes exasperatedly and opened them with a scathing look. "I've no doubt." His eyes soon were glued to the camera as he indulged in a manic laughter again, just like he did during the previous interview.

Tina flinched and shouted at the prisoner, "There's no heaven for you, and I'm willing to repeat a thousand times. There's no heaven for you."

Usman's laughter stopped abruptly.

"There's no heaven for you." Tina repeated again, looking absolutely calm.

Usman's shoulders began to quiver in anger, and he let out an angry, outraged cry while shaking the metal chair, again determined to get it unshackled from the floor. Tina warily looked at the iron chain, as though worried that it might really come unhinged during one of his attempts. Shaker got up quickly and stood by Tina, instinctively placing a protective hand on her tense shoulder. The door opened to let in the guards, who swiftly ran towards Tina and Shaker.

Sharif followed them in the next minute and asked, "What happened? Is the monster getting restless?"

Tina wiped her trembling, clammy hand with a tissue and spoke softly while standing by Shaker. "I told him that there is no heaven for him, Mr. Sharif."

"You bastards, all of you, will rot in hell. You cannot shake my conviction. Nothing will," Usman shouted, regardless of the guards and the intimidating Sharif.

Sharif asked the guards to leave the cell.

"Let me handle him, please?" Tina held Sharif's sleeve gently and whispered in his ears.

"Go ahead," Sharif whispered back.

"There's no heaven for you because of your ruthless, cruel treatment of hundreds of men, women, and children. Those souls, unified and bloody, will stand on the threshold of heaven and torture you mercilessly, just like you tortured Maya." Tina's mind was nailed to her encounter with a very strange, young woman, a bruised and terrified captive, when she was frantically trying to escape. Her sore mind groped for scorching words to unnerve the prisoner. "You have sinned beyond hopes of receiving pardon."

"You don't understand. None of you will ever understand." Usman's fury had surprisingly deflated, leaving a sickly calmness behind. Only his telltale, glinting eyes spoke of the existing internal struggle. "As long as my actions are dedicated to Allah, no matter what I do, all sins will be forgiven. In fact, I've committed no sin, absolutely no sin. And nobody can haul that conviction away from me. I AM GOING TO HEAVEN."

Sharif led Tina to a chair and sat by her.

Shaker sat again on the other side of Tina and whispered, "May I?" When she sighed, relief filling her hazel eyes, he turned to the prisoner and said, "When you described your heaven to us earlier, you said that it's a place where the righteous go at the time of death. The question is: Describe your heaven."

"My heaven?" asked Usman, raising his eyebrows.

"Yes, your heaven, a place you're determined to enter, your final home that you seem to know well." Shaker looked steadily at the prisoner's glaring eyes. "Can you describe it or not?"

"My heaven is a luxurious haven where there is no poverty, no grief. One can attain immortal life in heaven. It is a glorious place where martyrs and devout people live when they're dead. And I will see my ancestors there and we will all be happy." Usman recited proudly, happily, as though regurgitating a memorized doctrine, visibly in the hold of a tempting paradise.

"How do you know that? Have you been there?" asked Shaker, his chiseled features expressing no emotion.

"No. What kind of a ridiculous question is that?" responded Usman, scowling. "I know because I read…I was taught…" Usman, uncharacteristically baffled, fumbled for the right words.

"Brainwashed, you mean?" asked Shaker, injecting a dash of doubt and sympathy into his question. "I feel sorry for you. There you were, all those years, working meticulously on random hearts and innocent souls, waiting for your heaven. And as my colleague explained earlier, those hearts and souls would be your obstacles in entering your heaven. But you're right about one thing. Your means justify your end. You'll go to hell."

"NO! NO!" Usman, who had meandered through and mastered the art of brainwashing, was on the brink of losing his temper again. He looked up at the ceiling, breathing deeply.

"Perhaps you can remedy some of the damage, may be atone to some degree, by telling us who is relentlessly backing you up?" asked Shaker, effortlessly camouflaging his curiosity behind his professional visage.

"You expect me to sell my brothers' names?" asked Usman, directly looking at Sharif, ignoring Shaker. "An incentive to reduce my punishment?"

"Answer Dr. Shaker," came Sharif's booming voice.

Usman transferred his glance to his bony hands on his lap.

"Who paid for the latest mission near Breams Road, the massacre that staggered a suburb of Chennai?" asked Sharif, steadily keeping his eyes on Usman's face, as though willing to force the prisoner to look at him.

Usman did look up at his adversary, but he spoke nothing.

Shaker, remembering Maya's recent wrenching agony, exchanged a glance with Sharif and asked the prisoner, "Who has been sponsoring your missions?"

Although Usman glared at the analyst, he spoke very calmly, regaining that psychotic glint in his deep-set eyes again. "Answer you? I'll do no such thing because I'm afraid of none."

"Yes, you're afraid," asserted Shaker. "You're afraid to reveal your sponsors' names. And you cannot justify your actions any other way. You're brainwashed that your means justify the end. That makes you a coward, not a martyr."

Usman's face no longer revealed any emotion. He took several deep breaths and alternately looked at the ceiling and his bound hands. He finally looked at his audience. "You can call me anything you want, but my means have no end. They'll never have an end."

"Why?" asked Shaker, disconcerted by Usman's cool, collected tone.

"The end of all means is the beginning."

Shaker exchanged a knowing glance with Tina. Although she was trembling lightly at the moment, he knew she had been waiting to ask the terrorist, who had made that infuriating remark when the fateful explosion occurred near Kuyil Extension—the explosion that was supposed to have killed Maya. So he let her speak.

"What do you mean by that?" Tina asked boldly. All the maddening emotions she had suffered in the past converged and made her heart miserably heavy.

"That means, Miss Matthew, I might go now, not exist anymore, but my mission will never end. So you see, there is really no death for me. My mission is my life, my every breath, my heart and soul. And when I stop existing in your world, my heaven will accept me with open arms. My end will result in a new beginning. My mission will thrive in another hand."

Unable to endure Usman's chillingly calm tone, Tina averted her eyes from his gaunt, cruel face and stared at her folded hands on her lap. "I need a break," she said, rising.

"Of course." Sharif pressed the bell.

"How long am I supposed to wait in this hell hole?" asked Usman, when Sharif looked in his direction.

"Until you go to hell," replied Sharif, opening the door for Tina to exit.

- 36 -

A Breath of Air

"Tina, are you okay?" asked Sharif, ignoring his driver who was waiting politely on the other side of the paved drive.

"I am, Mr. Sharif. Thanks. I needed a breath of air." Tina began to fan her face with a tissue, oppressed by the infuriating heat. "And I'm sorry I decided to leave abruptly."

"No need to be sorry. We all needed a break. It's maddening to deal with that monster." Sharif's smile softened his harsh face as he took her hand gently. "You've done well. I'm very impressed and sincerely thankful. And I'm sure, we'll miss you when you return to Pittsburgh. Won't we, Dr. Shaker?"

Tina was glad to see Shaker's smile, but she could not understand the flickering expression that fleetingly touched his face.

"Well, I must leave. Shall I give you a ride home?" Sharif asked Tina.

"I'll take her home. It's on the way to my apartment," offered Shaker, signaling to his driver.

The tedious drive to her aunt's house was never pleasant in the sultry traffic. It was peculiarly quiet after the emotional interlude inside the confining prison cell, and Tina still had not felt that breath of air. She didn't know how to break the silence when several questions were eager to spill out of her baffled mind. She stole a glance at her mentor, but his eyes were steadily fixed on the slow-moving traffic.

"Tina," Shaker hesitated, as though wondering if he should go on. "Has this been too much for you—the prison, the insane prisoner, the questions and answers, and the whole stinking situation?"

Tina did not expect such a question, but there was no hesitation in her answer. "Yes, but I've no regrets."

"I'm glad to hear it. But you didn't expect your research to take you to a prison cell?"

"I didn't. But if I have to start all over again, I would still do this, and I realize one thing. Thesis looks good on paper, but... I've learned so much in the last few months by coming here, twice, and working with you."

"Again, I'm glad to hear it." Shaker's smile, instead of easing his taut expression, disappeared to make room for a somber something Tina did not understand. "That's exactly what I told Dr. Augustine several years ago."

"Oh? How is he doing?"

"He's retiring, finally. Unfortunately, his poor health will not allow him to work anymore. He has decided to transfer all of his responsibilities into my hands, and I'm flattered."

"Well, I think you're the natural choice. And didn't you want to linger a bit longer here, before returning home?"

"I don't know about the natural choice, but I guess I asked for it when I voluntarily decided to work on the terrorists' profiles under Dr. Augustine a long time ago. And once in, I'm permanently in like a stubborn stain, I guess."

"Would you have...rather chosen a different path?"

"No. I'm glad to do what I'm doing. And an occasional Usman is worth all the bleak, endless research. And when a victim like Maya is rescued, every breathless moment is well spent." Shaker stared at Tina's rapt expression and asked, "Don't tell me you're going to do exactly what I've been doing."

"Of course. Why shouldn't I?"

"I thought you were eager to return home?"

"Do you think Maya will ever recover?"

"What?" asked Shaker, as though irked by the change of subject.

"I sensed no improvement at all when I saw her last time. At times, I hope and pray that Usman would be sentenced to death within a week. You know, I want Maya to know, one day, that I'm no longer nervous about visiting Usman. And it's important to me, somehow, that she knows that. But her condition still frustrates me. And what frustrates me even more is that we haven't made much progress with Usman."

"What kind of progress do you expect, Tina?" asked her mentor. "Sharif's main concern is keeping Usman alive. And you know by now that Usman would rather end his own life in a heartbeat than confess any fact about his organization and his associates. But he's crumbling, perhaps inch by inch, and our goal is to keep him unhinged. We'll question him tomorrow and another day and another day until he comes unhinged further. If we can take him by surprise, even occasionally, then we've done our job."

"I'm glad you think we're making progress, for Maya's sake, and for the sake of all the children who remain imprisoned, almost insane and hopeless."

"And I've been worried about Maya's condition, too. From my observations, I've come across few inmates benefiting from rehabilitation. Not that medical assistance or counseling is deficient. The gradual, methodical art of brainwashing is like injecting poison into timid veins, and the victims who undergo intense brainwashing in the hands of individuals like Usman become abnormal entities. Unfortunately, they don't respond well to treatment. That's why Usman's missionaries face indefinite trauma. Maya is one such regrettable victim. But," he paused, trying to sound positive. "We must give her time. She'll improve, not entirely, but she will. She ought to, with two such dedicated souls in her life."

"Mrs. Joseph and Mark? I agree. And Mark still wants to marry Maya. Do you think that's wise?"

"Wise? Regarding her precarious nerves or his unconditional love?"

"I don't know. Both, I think." responded Tina, a little confused. "I worry about them."

"Nobody said you shouldn't."

"What?" asked Tina, not appreciating his aloof tone. But when she fixed her glance directly at him, the light in his eyes did not at all echo his aloof tone. And she wasn't sure if she wanted to understand the message in his eyes. "I don't need your permission," blurted Tina, looking at the silvery ocean, the bleached shores, the misty horizon, and the canopy of swaying branches skirting the foaming waves. Her aunt's neighborhood was always a welcoming sight to her tired eyes.

"Of course, you don't need my permission. But when has unconditional love been a problem? You think Mark's unrestricted love for Maya is unnecessary or untimely?"

"No. No. Why would I think that? It's rather enchanting that a man's happiness is entirely dependent on one woman's love for him. But can Maya handle marriage?"

"In her case, from a psychological perspective, yes. And if she must marry Mark, one who hopes to stand by her, one who has stood by her through the most trying, frustrating time of her life and his life, yes, it will absolutely work. And Mark knows that it wouldn't be a marriage out of a romance novel. It will take much patience, understanding, and enduring affection. But it can work."

"I'm so glad you think so," smiled Tina, breathing deeply. That breath of air was finally at her reach.

"Did anybody tell you that your smile is like a child's? You have an undiluted smile that delights as it gently seeps into the room."

"Thanks." But thoughts of her impending trip to Pittsburgh crawled into her mind and imperceptibly stole her smile.

"Tina," began Shekar, letting his eyes admiringly roam over her soft blushing cheeks and her twinkling brown eyes, but stopped abruptly to answer his phone. His expression changed drastically by the end of the message. "It's Sharif. He called about Maya," he paused, unable to go on.

"What is it? Shaker, what happened?" asked Tina, alarmed by his distressed expression.

"Maya has been taken to the Emergency Ward at Victoria. Sharif didn't have much time to offer details. He called on his way to the hospital."

"Can we go there? I'd like to see her."

"So would I. Let's go." Shaker tapped on the driver's shoulder and said, "Please go to Victoria Hospital and park near the Emergency entrance."

The driver instantly steered the vehicle through crowded avenues and narrow streets to find the quickest way to the hospital.

"Mrs. Joseph is right. Maya's life will never be the same again," sighed Tina, restlessly letting her eyes move from the slow traffic to the congested shops on both sides of the road. "Their lives will never be the same again."

"I wonder what happened to her. This damned traffic is getting worse by the day," hissed Shaker, impatiently cursing the bumper-to-bumper procession.

So many questions were on the verge of spilling, but not one word was spoken.

The driver parked the vehicle in front of the hospital on the edge of the wide avenue. Sharif received Shaker and Tina at the crowded waiting area. Tina searched for other familiar faces in the sea of people, but her eyes caught none. She impatiently looked at Sharif's elusive expression, wondering why he was still retaining her and Shaker there when they were eager to see the patient.

"Will you please take us to Maya, Mr. Sharif?" asked Tina, slightly annoyed by the delay.

When he turned his face to the entrance of the emergency unit without making a move, Shaker asked, "What happened, Mr. Sharif?"

"Maya was highly hysterical. Mrs. Joseph thought she was having a panic attack. It happened suddenly," replied Sharif, still avoiding their eyes.

While Tina's eyes flitted from Sharif's poker expression to Shaker's worried face, she silently began to rehearse how she would comfort Maya and Sylvia and Mark.

"She took her own life," continued Sharif. "The doctors think it is overdose. Probably her prescription. They'll confirm soon. She left a brief note, no more than a line, that she could not face another day. Edwin is waiting with Mr. Stevens. Follow me."

Tina was not sure how she would follow him when the shock of his words kept her rooted to the floor. Sharif led them to a tiny lobby where Mark was standing by the wide window, staring at the slow traffic on Marshall Avenue. Tina could not find a single word to spill at the moment as she sat on the bench nailed to the floor. Her uncle promptly sat by her and took her hand in his.

"Your aunt has taken Mrs. Joseph home," Sharif informed Tina when her eyes searched for Sylvia.

"Mark," began Shaker, staring at his stiff back.

"Life has cheated me. I hate this rotten world, everything in it. She came back to me and now..." Mark spoke very softly, still staring at the traffic, but his calm frustration unnerved his audience.

"But, Mark," whispered Tina, while Shaker stood there speechless.

"No, don't say anything," snapped Mark, refusing to look at anybody. "Now my Maya will be reduced to part of your research and Shaker's, and she'll be nothing but a chapter in psychology journals. You'll be glad to get another paper out of my misery, my Maya's misery. And I don't want sympathy from you or anybody else."

"You're a selfish bastard, Mr. Stevens." Sharif's voice broke the intensely awkward silence that followed Mark's bitter response. "At least, have the courtesy to look at your friends who have gathered here to comfort you."

"How dare you? Do you know what my pain is? Can you imagine what I've suffered?" asked Mark, finally facing the group. He appeared years older than his age, and he couldn't have sounded more bitter or angry.

"I still say you're a selfish bastard," insisted Sharif.

While Mark looked ready to strike Sharif, the rest exchanged worried glances at an excruciatingly painful time.

"Easy, Mark. Calm down." Shaker guided him to the other end of the lobby.

"Sharif, what the hell is wrong with you?" Edwin, uncharacteristically irate, lowered his voice to a whisper. "Let Mark rave and rant, if that'll help him grieve. You must understand that people don't come in packages of *good* and *bad*. We all know that he is a little childish. Let him be."

"But he's not a child. When will he think about his aunt?" asked Sharif, a bitter anger invading his usually impassive expression. "Maya was like a daughter to her. And what about Maya? She is nothing but a victim of that maniac's wicked schemes. Look how Usman has played with an innocent life. Only God knows what possessed her that prompted her to consume a considerable overdose of her prescription, if that's how she ended her life. Mark and his childishness can go to hell. I've no patience for selfish people, Theo."

A senior staff member entered the lobby and silence resumed.

"Dr. Shaker, will you please take Tina home?" asked Edwin, when Mark began to speak with the staff member. He soon followed the other two out of the lobby.

"Mark's pain must be unbearable," whispered Tina, as Shaker took Edwin's vacated seat. "I can understand. Still, I wish he would let us comfort him."

"I wonder if there is some truth in Sharif's assessment of Mark. But selfish bastard or not, he needs us, his friends, and we'll be there if he wants us."

"My uncle couldn't have said it better. People don't come in packages of *good* and *bad*. Just like life, with its complicated mosaic of good and bad, right and wrong. See how that villain has played with Maya's fate, Shaker, while preaching about his heaven."

"Usman's convictions about heaven can go to hell. Lies. Nothing but lies. Which God endorses violence? Not Usman's. Not mine. Not yours. Blaming God for man's fanatic greed is the ultimate insult to God.

Maya's trauma must have been unbearable. I didn't anticipate this, but one can never be sure about what to expect in such a case." Shaker's frustration took a pause. "So much trauma in so many people's lives—all for Usman and his heaven! That must be another heaven.

"Another heaven? Yes, another heaven."

"Come, I'll take you home."

Tina followed him quietly to the main lobby, still unable to believe that she wouldn't be able to see Maya again. A few men and women were waiting where Sharif had met Tina and Shaker a little earlier. A middle-aged woman was crying, her face buried in the fringe of her sari. A young man had his arms wrapped around her, whispering soothing words in her ears. Tina did not know their pain, but she felt their tears as she stepped out of the air-conditioned lobby. The sticky, thick air was overpowering as she walked to the jeep parked on Marshall Avenue. She looked up at the window where Mark had stood just a while ago, bitterly pouring his grief—his grief over his lost love, an unfinished life, a singularly cruel injustice to humanity.

"Sir, to Mr. Edwin's home?" asked the driver, respectfully opening the door. He awkwardly took a glance at Tina's tear-soaked eyes and at Shaker's grim expression. "Dr. Shaker, what happened?"

Shaker told him, and a new grief touched Tina as though Shaker's explanation made Maya die again.

"I can't believe that after going through what she did, as incredible as it still seems to me, she would throw her life away like that," cried Tina, shaking her head as the memory of the last hour stubbornly crept into her mind. Something snapped in her which she had struggled to hold together since the day a strange woman had knocked on her door crying for help. She buried her face in her hands and sobbed as she had never sobbed before. "She was found alive for nothing? I wake up every morning thinking I'd go to Mark's apartment in the evening to see Maya. Now there's no Maya to see. Mark's not the only one who feels cheated. So do I. So do all of us."

Shaker said nothing but simply gathered her close to him and let her cry.

"She came to me, Shaker. Maya came to me, knocked on my door, and I did nothing. Nothing. This guilt is going to kill me. How can I ever find peace when those few words she exchanged with me haunt me day and night? Mark is probably right. Is Maya going to boil down to a chapter in my thesis?" continued Tina, unable to contain her gushing tears. "How can I let that happen? I was so delighted that she was rescued beyond anybody's hope, and now she is lying there, wasted, cheated. How can I go on?" asked Tina, her agony sitting on her already burdened mind like a tombstone. "I want to take my research and tear it to pieces. To hell with psychology. To hell with research. I'm so sick of it all."

"Do you think that's what Maya would like you to do?" asked Shaker, still holding her sobbing figure tightly in his arms.

Tina could not find a word in response while her misery sat heavily on her chest.

"Think, Tina. What would Maya want you to do? Think about your tears, think about why you returned to India to work with me, think about what prompts your search, and then tell me. What would Maya want you to do?"

"She wouldn't want me to stop," Tina said softly, as though able to grasp Maya's thoughts.

"What do YOU want to do?"

Tina stared at the slowly receding boutiques, congested bus stops, and the winding traffic. "I don't want to stop," she spluttered, almost involuntarily, her turbulent mind swinging from frustration to determination. "I don't want to give up. I believe that my search, which has led me to where I am right now, has a better purpose than tackling words on a stack of paper for approval from my university."

"If you want to continue your research to probe Usman's mind and other radicals' minds in the future, you should be willing to continue regardless of whatever nonsense life throws at you. And Usman's statement, *the end of all means is the beginning*, as evil as it is, cannot be ignored. You should be willing to face the inevitability of that harrowing statement, maddening or not. Can you?" asked Shaker, staring at her reddish eyes.

"I know by now that I can't bury *the end of all means is the beginning*, and I'm not going to try to run away from it. I know I must face it, digest it, and deal with it. But, Shaker, Maya meant a lot to me. She'll always mean a lot to me, and the other missionaries snared by that monster will..." her painful memory of the young children made her stumble on her own words. "Maya is more than an unfortunate victim of violence. It's not that I'm afraid or that I'm losing heart. The point is…it's very hard for me to compartmentalize my work on one side and restrain thoughts of Maya and those children on the other. They were all in the same building when I spent the night at 19 Temple Street, trapped in various stages of brainwashing and stripped of their basic human rights. It's just that while my mind has been passionately searching for the insights of fanatic compulsion, I've not been prepared to face the fanatic's victims, and I feel deficient. I feel I've failed."

"I know how you feel. I've been there. I could still be there, but I believe I've steeled my mind to be objective. I don't doubt your intention or your endurance to continue to work in this field, and crying your heart out for those victims is not a failure. That makes you sympathetic, caring, but never deficient. And you shouldn't feel compelled to compartmentalize your work and emotions, but," he paused, taking her hand in his. "You should be cautious not to let the inevitable sadness dominate your senses. If you let it control you, it'll eat you. Your task is to help those victims through your work, not become a victim yourself. It's very important to remember that." Shaker's brief, tentative smile filled his sharp eyes with a mellow light.

"I cannot do this." Tina pulled her hand away from him, fiercely shaking her head, her mind swinging back to frustration. "I just cannot. I'm done with psychological garbage and violence and human rights."

Shaker stared at her, stunned by the frustrated words jumping out of her like leaping flames.

"I'm absolutely sick of it all. I want to forget I came here and whatever nonsense happened here." She pulled a tuft of tissues from her purse and thoroughly wiped her cheeks. "Maya is the end of my research. Thanks for your help so far. I want to go back to Pittsburgh."

Shaker turned his head to the window and continued to speak without looking at her. "I was hoping we would work together. We work together very well. Don't you think?"

"Perhaps, but I cannot continue. I'm sorry."

The busy traffic gradually thinned to newly paved roads and bleached shores. Tina anxiously looked at the tall palm trees skirting the wide avenue as the salty air seeped into the car in leisurely swirls.

"One day, someday, if you change your mind, let me know, Tina. My offer still stands. It was a pleasure working with you."

The driver pulled the jeep into Villa Circle that was quiet as a graveyard.

- 37-

Ashville, Pennsylvania • October 30, 2010

A crisp fall day. A time of year when nature sliced a generous chunk of coolness and precariously placed it on earth like a thick layer of frosting. Another autumn, another season, and another sigh at an unknown future that held no answers. Not one. Tina reached for the diploma on her desk and glanced at the steady rain dripping down the eaves. Her eyes soon traveled from the gushing downpour and rested on every corner of the tiny room where she had pored over volumes of articles and papers, hoping to understand the psychology behind terrorism. Psychology behind terrorism?

Psychological fraud of terrorism.

The bold letters on the diploma reminded her of her new responsibility, unspoken responsibility, a vision that stubbornly remained a blur. Dr. Tina Matthew. *Doctor.* Strange. Her daily routine of five-little-pages had oddly concluded, six months after she abandoned her research with Dr. Shaker, six months after running away from India. And now? What was she supposed to do? Her intermittent research wouldn't be sufficient to keep her employed or help sustain her financial independence. And the other job offers had fizzled even before snaring her interest. If only…

Startled by the knocking, she turned to the door and was pleased to see Dr. Katz.

"Still packing?" he asked, taking stock of the half-filled cartons of books and papers.

"Almost done, Alan," responded Tina, her memory sliding to hours of conversations with her advisor. "I'll miss this, all this, and you."

"Well, in that case, come to my office for a cup of coffee. Perhaps a last cup together in your advisor's office?"

Tina gladly followed Dr. Katz to the familiar room and was not surprised to see the loaded bookshelves and the dusty desk in the midst of coffee and peppermint pipe tobacco. The welcoming habits—unchanging, unyielding—enveloped her like a warm blanket. She remembered sitting in that room while a furious rain beat on the window panes, more than a year ago, when she was troubled by *the end of all means is the beginning*. That statement did not nag her much like it used to, but she knew she had several milestones to cross before she could feel more at ease.

"I see you haven't packed even a single book, Alan. You keep threatening to retire. Are you going to, or is it just a ploy to extract university funds for your current projects?"

Dr. Katz smiled his sheepish smile which told Tina nothing. "So what have you decided to do?" he asked, pouring the steaming coffee into two tall mugs.

What did she decide to do? "I'm still waiting for my proposal to come through. Do you think it will be approved?" she asked, afraid to hope. And her doubts were justified. The proposal, outlining a very complicated undertaking, surpassed usual boundaries and awkwardly imposed on international regulations.

"What do you think?"

"I'm asking you."

"When you returned from India a few months ago, at first I thought I saw the last of you. But something told me it was not the ending but a new beginning. At least, I hoped it would be."

"I'm still sorry I ran away like that. No part of my experience—the prison, the crazy prisoner, his victims—frightened me to give up. I was disturbed, but the bitterness was like a tonic that pushed me to do something about it." She glanced at the steamy window and wrestled with her memory, a painful memory that took her to Maya's squirming body, her delirious words."But I could not handle Maya's death. The way she suffered after she was rescued kept haunting me. I would have gotten over that slowly if she had recovered bit by bit and had lived, but she ended her life, unable to go on. Her death killed a part of me and nothing could revive that and," she paused, as though embarrassed to go on. "I have apologized to Dr. Shaker more than once for taking off like that, especially after he offered to be my mentor when Dr. Augustine was taken to the hospital. I hope I get a chance to work on a project with him in the future, to let him know that I am truly sorry."

"I'm sure he understands."

"I needed these few months to recover, Alan, to get over the grief of losing Maya, to come to terms with the way fate took a nasty turn in her life."

"Time is the greatest healer, I've heard."

"I'm sure it is. I thought Maya's horrific death concluded my research. I now know I was wrong. My bitterness and agony blinded my focus, my vision. But these few months have somehow made me stronger, have bleached my doubts, and have even confirmed my convictions. I don't have a shred of doubt about where I want to go, what I want to do, and I sincerely hope my proposal is approved."

Dr. Katz looked long at his advisee's nervous expression, her pathetic glance flitting from the moist window to the framed quotation on the wall; *The salvation of mankind lies only in making everything the concern of all—Solzhenitsyn.* Salvation of mankind seemed to be a very ambitious idea in a world steeped in violence. He tried to subdue his frizzy white hair with both his hands and opened an envelope. "Here, I got this letter just this morning," he whispered, pushing a piece of paper across the desk.

Tina took the paper eagerly and read the bold headline embossed in silver; *Office of International Human Rights.* Afraid of facing a painful disappointment, she looked away. Soon, unable to stand the suspense, she returned her glance to the long paragraph. When she finished reading the document, she sighed as a new milestone appeared to be at her grasp—in the distance, yes, but a reachable distance.

"Congratulations, Tina. I admire your vision. How does it feel to lead the Center for Human Rights and Counter-Terrorism? CHRACT will thrive in your hands. Not because it's your brain child, but because of your passion that has helped launch this non-profit undertaking. I cannot think of a better individual to manage this vital project, a crusade against human rights abuse."

"Feels good, Alan," paused Tina, humbled and touched by the most recent development. She took several deep breaths to swallow the overwhelming euphoria, her hazel eyes rapidly getting smudged. "It feels wonderful. Thanks for standing by me, believing in me, particularly when I went through spurts of doubt. I feel honored, and what an incredible honor this is. The project is definitely a tribute to Maya and those children who are suffering from the trauma of that radical's brainwashing. You see," paused Tina, the image of 19 Temple Street restraining her flow of thought. "Maya's suffering and death will always remind me to keep going, never to stop, and that is an abiding promise I have made to her memory."

"And I see from the letter that you've decided to set up CHRACT in Ashville."

"Yes, hoping to persuade you to linger for a while, so I can continue to consult you and visit you for pep talk."

"No need to persuade me. Florida can wait. Warm weather is, after all, a state of mind."

State of mind. Tina's thoughts tentatively went to Shaker.

"You're welcome to consult me as long as you want to, but my consultation would dwindle soon. I am getting old, Tina. It is Dr. Shaker who would continue to offer advice in the long run, which is your wish as well. Have you heard from him recently?" Dr. Katz tried to catch her eye. "By the way, is he just a mentor? Or is he something more, if I am allowed to ask?"

"Of course, you may ask."

"And?"

Tina ran her fingers up and down the coffee mug, searching for a response. "I'm not sure. Well, sometimes I think I am, but I'm not ready to take a step in that direction. Let's say he is a good friend, perhaps a bit more than just a friend, and I'm going to leave it at that for now. I know my path will cross with his, particularly now with the new project. But right now I'm interested in CHRACT and nothing else." Tina was acutely conscious of Shaker's advice; *you shouldn't feel compelled to compartmentalize your work and emotions.* And she must remember not to let the inevitable sadness dominate her senses, as he had cautioned her, so she could help victims of terrorism while not being victimized by its cruelty. Plenty of advice from her mentor. Loads of reassurance from her advisor. She had her whole life to make a difference in a violent world.

"Remember, I told you last year that I would see a different Tina after your internship? You have changed, for the better, but you have changed. Your visits to India and your long-and-short internship have somehow made you stronger, Tina, and I am glad to see that." Dr. Katz studied his advisee's serious expression. "Your rationale for CHRACT is right on target—victims of human trafficking channeled to feed the psychological fraud of terrorism."

"Well, isn't that my research, at least the psychology behind terrorism?" asked Tina, revisiting her conversation with her advisor, in the same room, before traveling to India to pursue her internship with Dr. Augustine. A year ago, she had not anticipated an eventful, precarious voyage which ended with Maya's death. "Now I see, better than I did before, how a radical's mind, infested with lies and violence, effectively conspires to destroy innocent individuals. No matter how we analyze this, it boils down to one thing and one thing only; violence is born of lies. With that, everything decent in mankind is in danger of collapsing." Tina's glance settled on her advisor's frizzy hair. She was rather relieved to see his relaxed features, his serene smile, despite the grim topic. "Human trafficking and terrorism are not new or unknown ills in our society. My hope is to get the world to notice the vulnerability of the victims of human trafficking who are in danger of being consumed by radicals who thrive on terrorism. I'm not naive enough to believe that I can stop them. But..."

"But you and I and the rest must work on it. Otherwise, we are not worthy of being human beings." Dr. Katz's glance flew from his advisee's determined expression to the framed quotation on the wall; *The salvation of mankind lies only in making everything the concern of all—Solzhenitsyn.* "Human rights abuse is every man's concern, or it should be," he paused, his glance switching to the clock. "I should let you get back to your packing. Good luck, my dear. Let the journey you're about to begin be the best of all journeys you make in your life."

"Thank you, Alan." Tina took the elderly professor's hand, feeling the warmth of his friendship and affection seeping into her once timid veins. Her beautiful brown eyes assumed a new light while her lips broke into a contented smile—long overdue, as her concerned father had reminded her only the previous day. "I can never thank you enough for guiding me and bringing me to where I am now."

"I might have guided you, my dear, but you came to me with a clear focus. Now go on and make your vision a reality."

Tina walked out of her advisor's room, eager to begin her new journey.

About the Author

Annu Subramanian is the director of The Writing Center at Brown School in Schenectady, New York. Keeping with her goal to write for a cause, she has written *Another Heaven*, and the proceeds from this novel will be used to benefit organizations dedicated to helping victims of human trafficking. She is using her debut novel, *Waiting for the Perfect Dawn*, to bring awareness about suppression of women and domestic violence. Written in a unique style, this novel allows a three-way conversation between the author, the readers, and the characters.

Subramanian has cofounded Albany Women Connection, a support group in Albany, New York. She was chosen as one of the four national finalists by Norman Mailer Center in 2011 for *So Fair and Very Lovely*, a short story, and she was chosen as an Educator of Excellence in 2011 by New York State English Council (NYSEC).

www.facebook.com/subramanian.annu

www.annusubramanian.com

Talented writers, innovative students, fresh minds at work.

Apprentice House is the country's only campus-based, student-staffed book publishing company. Directed by professors and industry professionals, it is a nonprofit activity of the Communication Department at Loyola University Maryland.

Using state-of-the-art technology and an experiential learning model of education, Apprentice House publishes books in untraditional ways. This dual responsibility as publishers and educators creates an unprecedented collaborative environment among faculty and students, while teaching tomorrow's editors, designers, and marketers.

Outside of class, progress on book projects is carried forth by the AH Book Publishing Club, a co-curricular campus organization supported by Loyola University Maryland's Office of Student Activities.

Eclectic and provocative, Apprentice House titles intend to entertain as well as spark dialogue on a variety of topics. Financial contributions to sustain the press's work are welcomed. Contributions are tax deductible to the fullest extent allowed by the IRS.

To learn more about Apprentice House books or to obtain submission guidelines, please visit www.ApprenticeHouse.com.

Apprentice House
Communication Department
Loyola University Maryland
4501 N. Charles Street
Baltimore, MD 21210
Ph: 410-617-5265 •F ax: 410-617-2198
info@apprenticehouse.com •w ww.apprenticehouse.com

CPSIA information can be obtained at www.ICGtesting.com
Printed in the USA
BVOW082029130513

320605BV00002B/13/P

9 781934 074879